I0628744

TIME TRAVEL FOR LOVE AND PROFIT

JEFF ABUGOV

Time Travel for Love and Profit
by Jeff Abugov

Copyright © 2017 by Jeff Abugov

J-Stroke Productions
January 2017

All rights reserved.

Without limiting the rights under copyright reserved above, no part of this publication may be reproduced, stored in or introduced into a retrieval system, or transmitted, in any form, or by any means (electronic, mechanical, photocopying, recording or otherwise) without the prior written permission of both the copyright owner and the above publisher of this book.

The following is a work of fiction. Names, characters, places, brands, media, and incidents are either the product of the author's imagination or are used fictitiously. The author acknowledges the trademarked status and trademark owners of various products referenced in this work of fiction, which have been used without permission. The publication/use of these trademarks is not authorized, associated with, or sponsored by the trademark owners.

ISBN-13: 978-0-9985784-0-8 (EBOOK)
ISBN-13: 978-0-9985784-1-5 (PAPERBACK)

LIBRARY OF CONGRESS CONTROL NUMBER: 2017902066

Cover design by Dino Buljubasic

Cover images by:
Shaun Jeffers/Shutterstock.com;
Leolintang/123rf.com;
Rrraum/Shutterstock.com

Author Website: www.jeffabugov.com

J-Stroke Productions
Los Angeles, California

PRAISE FOR JEFF ABUGOV

In this time-travel caper, a thief obsessed with making a fortune experiences sublime moments in history and hard truths. ... The twists that follow see Abugov performing a literary M.C. Escher impression, in which motifs and characters interlock in satisfying and often unexpected ways. But the author's sense of humor results in nightmarish time-traveling conditions for his protagonist. ... Fans of time-travel tales will kick themselves if they miss this one. A shimmering sci-fi ode to the '6os and true love.

KIRKUS REVIEWS

Fresh, gripping, and heartbreaking. In Abugov's quest to make every nuance of this fantastical tale "as real as it could be," he sought out experts in science, art, police procedure, and even the paranormal. The result: a magical yet plausible yarn of cunning, deception, romance, and crime that leaps and reverses across nine decades.

DAVE ZOBEL, LECTURER AT CALTECH, USC, MENSA. AUTHOR, *THE SCIENCE OF TV'S THE BIG BANG THEORY* AND *DAVE ZOBEL'S BENT BOOK OF BOATSPEAK*. HOST/WRITER FOR PUBLIC RADIO'S *SAYS YOU!* AND *THE LOH DOWN ON SCIENCE*.

Abugov twists and torques the sturdiest tropes of time travel fiction and romance novels until they snap open to reveal something much bigger than the sum of their parts.

DON FOSTER, EXECUTIVE PRODUCER/WRITER FOR *TWO AND A HALF MEN, THE BIG BANG THEORY, MIKE & MOLLY*

Terrific fun, masterfully plotted time travel twists, and an ending that brings together every theme explored in the novel. Well done!

KLAUS SCHULLER, EXECUTIVE DIRECTOR, *SECOND CITY TORONTO*

An instant time-travel classic.

CHARLES HORN, AUTHOR, *MEAT LOGIC, THE LAUGH OUT LOUD GUIDE*. WRITER, *ROBOT CHICKEN, FUGGET ABOUT IT*.

A twisty, turning, logic puzzle inside a mirror-laden funhouse. This isn't your ordinary time travel story. It's an experience.

CHRISTIANA MILLER, WRITER, *GENERAL HOSPITAL*. AUTHOR, *SOMEBODY TELL AUNT TILLIE SHE'S DEAD* SERIES.

CONTENTS

PROLOGUE

THE DREAM IS ALWAYS the same.

No, wait, that's not entirely accurate. Let me start over.

The end of the dream is always the same—crushingly brutal and tragic—but the beginning is always different, each one magical, wonderful, and perfect.

We're in a rowboat, she and I. I don't know what lake it is because all I see is her. I'm aware of the crystal blue water surrounding us, the green grass and the towering trees on the shore miles away, but they are only a peripheral blur.

I know I'm rowing because I feel it in my muscles, the leaning forward and back, the pull of my arms in and out, my knees bending toward me and away. I feel it while I sleep. Yet all my attention is on her twinkling, green eyes, her shimmering jet-black hair that flies off her shoulders to float in the gentle wind, and her merry, loving smile.

Another dream starts with us in a museum. I pontificate about the meaning of each piece, the symbolism, the history, the anecdotes. In reality, in my non-dream state, I know nothing about art, but in the dream I am an expert, and I'm showing off just to impress her. Matisse this, Renoir that. She knows that I'm showing off for her, and she finds me adorable because of it. My perfect lady loves me.

Sometimes we're at the theatre, other times a carnival, a concert, a state fair, the ballet. We dine at fine restaurants, and we chow down in cheap, roadside diners. Sometimes we just laugh hysterically together. Reality-me doesn't know why we're laughing, but she and dream-me find it the funniest thing in the world.

We have made love many times, and I have no doubt that we will again, but never in the dream. That's not what the dream is about. The dream is pure.

I stand before her on one knee, and I hold a purple velvet box in which rests a sparkling diamond ring. My heart races because I fear her answer. She smiles, a tear falls down her cheek, and she pulls me up to her. "Yes," she says, and we kiss.

We know in our hearts that we were once a single soul in Heaven, one entity separated into man and woman who came to Earth to live our lives together, and we will never be apart. We can't be. We are one.

But it always ends the same.

We're in a park, sitting on a bench, and she's sad. She says that she's grown feelings for someone else. She doesn't know how it happened, she says, she never expected or wanted it to happen. Her affection for me remains true, she says, but she has fallen for this other man completely. She will marry him, and our wedding will never be.

I don't understand at first. No matter how often I have the dream, I'm always hearing it for the first time. It makes no sense. It's not possible. I can't look at her.

I know this man who has taken her from me. I had considered him a friend. I'm filled with rage towards this Judas, this snake. I look back to her, my heart filled with pain and fury, and I see the tears rolling down her cheeks. She's crying because she knows she's hurting me, killing me, and all I want to do is wipe away her tears, hold her in my arms, and make her feel better.

Then I wake up. Sometimes I cry.

My psychologist during my first stint in juvenile detention said that the woman in the dream represents my mother who died when I was very young, and that my tender subconscious absorbed her death as a personal rejection. The shrink during my second stint in little boy prison said that dream-woman represents my father, whom I never knew at all. My San Quentin Prison shrink said that the dream as a whole is my way of re-enacting the pattern of my life as I see it, a pattern in which I always come so very close to love and happiness only to have them randomly yanked out from under me. She said that my subconscious purposely re-creates this pattern time and again, and that therefore only I can change it. Until I do, she went on, I'd continue to be afraid of making close, emotional connections with anyone.

But they all could not have been more wrong because, as you'll see, the meaning of the dream has nothing to do with psychology.

PART 1

FIRST, A LITTLE ABOUT ME

CHAPTER ONE

Turning a profit off of time travel isn't as easy as one may think. You can't just pop into the 1930s, buy some shares in IBM, then pop back home to collect your millions. Well, you can, it's just a lot more complicated than that.

I'm a thief. I'm twenty-eight years old, 5'11", wavy brown hair, fit, attractive according to most women, which is nice, and I'm an exceptionally good thief. In fact, depending on how one gauges such things, one may say that I'm the most ingenious thief the world has ever known, but then I think about those Wall Street guys so such a claim would be untruthful. I'm nowhere in their league. Nobody is.

I don't steal from anyone who can't afford it, and I always try to use my skills to help my fellow man in need. I'm not a thug, and I'm not a goon. I'm not a blackmailer, confidence artist, or bully. I've never beaten up anybody, and I've never killed anyone. But the way I see it, if you can afford to have a thirty-million-dollar painting hanging on your wall, then you can afford to live just as well without a thirty-million-dollar painting hanging on your wall.

A number of years ago, I was walking into a supermarket when a one-legged homeless man crutched himself up to me and asked for money. I could tell by his smell and demeanor that he was a for-real homeless guy who hadn't eaten for quite some time, and not one of the many scammers who give panhandlers-in-need a bad name. I had had a pretty good score a few days prior so I had the scratch to be generous, but I decided to do the starving man one better.

Give a man a fish, feed him for a day, as the saying goes. Teach a man to fish, and you feed him for his life. It was my intention to teach him how to fish.

"Come with me," I told him.

He staggered back a step, as if suddenly worried that I was store security or something, and that he was in some kind of trouble.

"It's okay," I said as I flashed him my world-class, disengaging smile.

I'm not bragging about my world-class, disengaging smile, by the way. It's nothing but a survival skill. I never understood the thugs who talk back to cops with hostility and threats—far better to be friendly, courteous, and whenever possible, white. If the cops don't have anything concrete on you, they'll let you walk and forget all about you. Talking back just confirms their hunch that you did something unlawful—which in my case is usually correct—and they'll just mess with you until they find something.

"It's all right," I smiled again. "I just want to show you something."

I put my hand on the hungry man's back and gently led him inside. He was confused by my friendliness yet malleable, as if no one had ever taken the time to actually *see* him. Let's face it, even when we give the street beggars money, we rarely actually look at them, as if their homelessness might somehow be contagious.

Maybe you won't admit that but I do. See? I'm more honest than you, thief that I am.

"What's your name?" I casually asked as I led him toward the dairy section.

"Rog," he said.

"Hi, Rog. I'm T.J. So how much money have you scraped together so far?"

"I dunno. About three bucks in loose change, I think, and I got a couple of singles, but that ain't enough to get me anything substantial."

"Oh, you'd be surprised, Rog," I said as I grabbed a half-gallon carton of milk from the bin and led him to the health food aisle, which was void of all patrons. I pulled apart the cardboard edge, handed Rog the carton, and said, "Drink."

"Now?" he said. "Here?"

"It's good for you. Calcium. Drink."

And so he did. Man, he guzzled down that milk like a frat boy in a chug contest. When a patron sauntered into the aisle, I quickly yet subtly shook my hand, and Rog immediately got it. He snapped the top of the container closed and looked at the shelves like he was seriously interested. The second and third time a patron rolled in, he needed no help from me at all. Rog was no dummy.

"The granola weeds look delectable," he said with authority.

By the time he finished knocking back that milk, he thought he knew it all.

"That's only part one, Rog," I said with a smile. "Now, we shop."

I pulled open the top of the carton to its full width, and then we stuffed that cardboard box with hot dogs, cheese, peanut butter, oranges, avocados, carrots, cucumbers—anything that wouldn't squash. Once it was so packed you could shake it and not hear a sound, I led Rog to the school supplies section where I picked up a roll of double-sided scotch tape, then resealed the carton leaving no evidence that it had ever been opened at all. I put the tape back on the shelf, and we got in line.

An interesting side note: at no point did Rog ever show any desire to go into the liquor section. Just sayin'. This was a man who was seriously hungry.

There were six people in front of us when we got into the line, and nine behind us by the time we got to the front. The twenty-something cashier picked up the carton and swiped it over the scanner. "This feels heavy," she said with a Ukrainian accent.

"Is it?" I responded quickly for fear that Rog would get flustered. "Do you think there's something wrong with it? Hey Rog, go grab another one," I said to the one-legged man. "I'll hold our place in line, long as it takes. We'll all wait."

The cashier looked at the long queue that had formed behind us, recalculated the weight of the carton with the magic scale that her hand had become, then reconsidered. "No, I'm sure it's okay," she said. "$3.99."

"As long as you're sure," I replied. "Pay the girl, Rog."

He took his crumpled singles and loose change out of his pocket, and paid her. Despite his crutches and the difficulty they bring, I insisted that he be the one to carry the milk carton outside because it was *his,* and it was important for him to feel the pride of his accomplishment. By the time we were back in the parking lot, he was smiling from ear to ear with watery eyes because he knew that he would never have to go hungry again.

"Thank you," he whispered, too overjoyed to speak at full volume.

"There's one more thing, Rog," I told him. "If you ever get caught—which is likely at some point—don't ask for a lawyer. You can't afford a decent one anyway. Just politely ask store security if you can phone your buddy at the LA Times."

"I don't have a buddy at the LA Times."

"They won't know that. And if they happen to call your bluff, you *will* have a buddy at the LA Times. Oh, you'll have lots of buddies on lots of papers, news stations and podcasts."

"I don't understand."

"The press'll *looovvve* this story, Rog," I explained. "Major supermarket franchise incarcerates a starving cripple for stealing *food*? It's straight out of *Les Mis*—story goes national in a heartbeat. They don't want that. You're Teflon, man."

Then he broke down, and he wrapped his free arm around me.

"Thank you, thank you," he wept. "How can I ever repay you?"

He couldn't repay me because he had nothing to give me. But his proud smile and joyful tears were more than payment enough. I told him so, and I walked away.

I never saw Rog again, and he doesn't reappear in this story. But ever since that day, whenever I'm near a supermarket and approached by a legitimately starving person or couple, I walk them inside, teach them the same lesson, and give them the same gift. They always break down at the end with smiles and tears, just like Rog did, and they ask how they can repay me. I always tell them the same thing I told Rog—they can't, and yet they already have.

That's the kind of thief I am.

CHAPTER TWO

M Y ONLY MEMORY OF MY mother is that of a sickly, skeleton-skinny, pasty-white, bald lady in a bed, and I never knew my father at all. I vaguely recall someone, maybe Mom, telling me that he had left her before I was born. I have no idea whether he split because he had knocked her up, or whether he was just a one-night stand who never knew of my existence in the first place, and at the age of four-and-a-half it didn't occur to me to ask.

We were all alone, Mom and I, just the two of us. Whether that was because she was an orphan, like I was soon to become, or because her family had thrown her out once she became a pregnant teenager, again, I have no idea, and again, it had never occurred to me to ask. Truth is, I don't know that she had me as a teen—I have no idea how old she was when I was four-and-a-half.

Our isolation from the world never seemed strange to me. I wasn't in school so I had no friends to tell me how unique our situation was, and I had no cousins, aunts, or uncles to show me what a real family looked like. We didn't even own a TV. As far as I knew, every little boy took care of his bedridden mom.

Despite her illness—again, I don't know what it was—she was always very kind to me. I remember sitting on her bed playing games with her, and how she tried so hard to finish one before fatigue got the best of her.

I remember walking with her through the little grocery store near our apartment building, carrying all the bags myself because she lacked the strength, and hoping to get her home before she fell down, which happened from time to time. I remember how she commended me when I brought meals on a tray to her bedside—just SpaghettiOs or canned tuna fish or something simple enough for a little boy to make. I remember her telling me what a wonderful chef I was, and I remember feeling very proud. I also remember her crying from time to time because everything was backwards, she said, and that she was supposed to be the one taking care of me, not the other way around. I didn't understand what she was talking about because, like I told you, our life together was the only reality I knew.

I remember bringing her lunch one particular day—baked beans from a can—and having a difficult time getting her to wake up. I set the tray down on the little table next to her bed, then I sat and waited. She was still asleep by dinnertime so I took the tray back to the hotplate and heated the beans again—there was never much food in the cupboard so wasting any didn't seem like a good idea. I brought the tray back to her bedside, but she still wouldn't wake. That bowl of beans was then relegated to her next morning's breakfast, then lunch, dinner, breakfast, on and on and so forth. After a few days of this, I had to throw them out because there was a bad smell in the apartment, which little boy me figured had to be the beans.

Then came the banging on the door. It was the building super—I can't remember what he looked like—and he was yelling about the horrible odor that was seeping into the hallway, and the neighbors that were complaining about it. I opened the door for him and told him that my mom was asleep. A full whiff of the stench must have blasted him in the face because he suddenly shouted, "Oh my God!"

The next thing I knew, our little apartment was teeming with strangers. One was examining Mom, who still hadn't woken up despite all the noise, while two others went through the house complaining about the unwashed dishes and general filth, as they called it. I remember being very offended by that because Mom had always said that I was an excellent housekeeper, and I had been very proud that she thought so. Who were these strangers to say she was wrong?

Then one of the strangers took me aside and told me that my mom was dead, and that I'd be going to live with another family.

And that was that.

All three of the institutional shrinks I've had over the years—despite their varying interpretations of my dream-woman—say that I've never truly dealt with this moment in my life, and that I describe the events only in factual terms, never emotional ones. They point out that I never say I loved my mother, or blame her or hate her for leaving me, or struggle through the complex ambivalence of all those feelings at the same time. They say that I show no curiosity about the father I never knew, and that I reveal no sadness over his absence from my life. In essence, they say that I shield myself from the bleak, excruciating pain that I keep buried deep inside me.

To which I say . . . wouldn't you?

* * *

My life of crime began when I was eight. My foster parents at the time—my third in four years—weren't the worst I ever had because they never actually beat us, and that's about the best that I can say about them. They had five of us foster kids and two of their own. Their own kids would eat what they ate—pot roast or spaghetti and meatballs or take-out Chinese—while the rest of us were pretty much relegated to peanut butter and jelly sandwiches, canned tomato soup, and gruel.

Just kidding about the gruel. Orphan humor. Sorry.

In addition to their real kids getting better meals, they were also given fifty cents every day to buy candy at the convenience store next to our elementary school, as were most of my classmates. I'd walk over with my new alleged buds, explaining how I had forgotten my money at home, or that it had fallen out of my pocket on the school bus, or that I was saving up for a VCR, or some stupid thing like that.

What was I going to say? That nobody loved me? Even the easy lie "my parents are too poor to give me fifty cents for candy" was almost as bad. No, I wanted to be accepted. So I lied.

But one day, one magical, wonderful, perfect day, my world got better. We all burst into the candy store like any other afternoon, my classmates grabbing their various treats and charging the front counter like a cackle of cackling hyenas, Old Man Candy Store doing his best to keep up as he banged away on his cash register. As usual, I hung by myself near the back and waited, pretending to browse the Hershey-bar-with-almonds display, and then something incredible occurred to me.

I was all alone. It was just me and the Hershey bars. The hyenas had their backs to me, Old Man Candy Store's focus was on the register, his view of me completely blocked by the hyenas, and there was no one else in the joint. For a very brief window of time, I could do anything I wanted.

And I knew what I wanted.

I wasn't particularly hungry—my nine-billionth peanut butter and jelly lunch had adequately filled me—and I never even particularly cared for almonds.

I just wanted the same thing that everyone else had.

My heart pounded as I slowly stretched my arm toward the display, peering this way and that over and over to make sure no one was watching me, probably the most suspicious-looking boy in the history of crime. I breathed heavily as I took the bar in my hand, studying it as if I was considering an actual purchase. I turned toward the hyenas, staring at their backs and the profile of an oblivious Old Man Candy Store, then I let my hand ease down to my side and lazily dropped the candy into my tattered jacket pocket.

I thought my chest was going to explode. My instincts screamed for me to bolt out of that store at the speed of light, but somehow intellect prevailed. No matter what I was feeling, I knew I had to *look* calm. So despite the booming thunder in my little heart and the battery acid that coursed through my tiny veins, I strolled over to the school supply section, picked up a notebook as if I was going to make a purchase, flipped through it, put it back on the shelf, then breezed my way out the door. I shot a quick glance back to Old Man Candy Store, who remained as unaware of my existence as he had been when I started.

I had done it! And it was so easy! I mean, ridiculously easy! And I knew that I could do it again anytime I needed, anytime I wanted, forever and ever.

That first bite of that Hershey bar remains the most delicious thing I have ever tasted. Not just because it actually *was* delicious—which it was—and not just because of the giant adrenaline rush I had just experienced—which I most assuredly had—but because after four years of living at the mercy of random grownups who didn't give a rat's rear about me, begging for their little handouts, their paltry prizes and bribes, hoping against hope that I didn't somehow upset them so that they'd punish me by withholding my meals, I was at long last self-sufficient. I was my own man. I was proud.

I once heard that the very first time Bob Dylan put his little lips to a harmonica, he was already able to play, and that he instantly felt his calling. That was me with the Hershey bar. And also, I now love almonds.

They taste like freedom.

CHAPTER THREE

Y CAREER IN THIEVERY TOOK a brief hiatus when I was ten. Jack and Jen Carpelli lived in Torrance, and they were by far the best foster parents I ever had. He was an electrician, she a nurse, and they were both fair and decent human beings. They didn't hit us—they never even yelled at us. When they were displeased, they would merely sit us down and talk to us like we were, I don't know, people.

They loved folk music from the 1960s, particularly Bob Dylan, so we came to love folk music from the 1960s, particularly Bob Dylan. I vividly remember the first song I heard of his, *Mr. Tambourine Man*. The music and the melody were like thunderbolts of joy blasting into my heart. I didn't understand the words or their meaning at that young age, but I could absolutely tell that they were meaningful, and I yearned to one day understand them all.

Yet best of all, Jack and Jen had begun legal proceedings to officially adopt me and my foster sister. Yay!

Myra was hands-down my favorite foster sibling. She had dirty blond hair, was a few months younger than me but several inches taller. We'd bicker and squabble and argue and fight like brothers and sisters do, and she always had my back. She also had this annoying knack of knowing whenever I was lying—and I had grown into a damn fine liar by then. I loved her so much.

One day, very early in the adoption proceedings, Myra and I were at Tower Records, and she happened to spot me slipping Bob Dylan's *Blood on the Tracks* CD into my backpack. Jack and Jen's anniversary was coming up, and I thought they'd appreciate it because the original vinyl they owned was by then old and scratchy.

Before I knew what hit me, Myra's oversized hand was clutching and squeezing the back of my little neck. She shoved her free hand into my backpack, pulled out Mr. Dylan, tossed him back in the bin, and dragged me outside.

It was the only time I had ever been spotted, and I felt sloppy.

She reamed me out like nobody's business. "You idiot!" she shouted. "We're almost home, and you're going to blow it for a CD? What is wrong with you? You really think Jack and Jen are going to adopt a stupid, little thief, you stupid, little thief?! Hey, no skin offa' my nose—they're taking me no matter how much you mess up. But you and me, we can be like a real brother and sister and love each other and care for each other, even when we're grownups. And Jack and Jen'll be good to us. They already are. You really wanna risk all that and get sent back to the beaters and the rapers?! For a CD?! Where is your stupid head?!"

No one in my life had ever looked out for my best interests the way she did.

Of course she was right, I just hadn't thought it through. I always knew there was a risk of getting caught, but with my other foster parents it would mean a beating or withholding of meals—although meal withholding had ceased to be an issue because I always had a large stash of candy hidden under my bed. With Jack and Jen, I figured I'd be grounded, lose TV privileges, maybe even get stuck with extra chores. It never occurred to me that they wouldn't adopt me anymore.

To be honest, I couldn't really imagine that happening, not with Jack and Jen. They were good, forgiving Christians. But as Myra made me see, it simply wasn't worth the risk. So I vowed that I would never steal again, never ever, forever.

Roughly eight months later, the adoption papers all but approved, Myra and I counting down the days till we felt safe enough to call the Carpellis "Mom" and "Dad," Jen found out that Jack was banging one of his clients. She threw him out of the house, filed for divorce, and Myra and I were split up and thrown back into the system.

And that was that.

* * *

MY SKILLS AS A thief grew as I grew. Gone were the days of candy bars and CDs—it was all about cash and jewelry. I had taught myself how to case a joint, track the comings and goings of the residents, and navigate all the intricacies of the various locks and alarm systems. By thirteen, the year of a Jewish boy's Bar Mitzvah, I had my very own fence.

I was a man.

Wendy Washington was a very large black woman who owned a pawnshop in Watts. She was in her fifties when we first met, close to six feet tall and almost as wide. She was the toughest person I had ever met, yet also the warmest and kindest.

Let me give you an idea of how nice a lady Wendy actually was. When I was fourteen, I was placed in a foster home in Tarzana, which was a two-hour bus ride to Watts—that's two hours one way. Wendy would actually drive up to Tarzana to meet me—roughly thirty minutes no-traffic for her—then take me to Baskin Robbins for a milkshake, where we'd exchange loot for cash and then chat well into the evening. I mean, fences don't typically take their robbers out for milkshakes.

True, I figured out years later that she had been ripping me off, but I was making a crazy amount of money for a kid my age so, in retrospect, it was a good deal for both of us. By the time I knew enough about jewelry to confront her, she merely laughed and patted me on the back.

"Well, it's about goddamn time, Teej. I was starting to worry about you."

"I can't believe you've been doing this to me all these years."

"Tough love, sweet thing. If I ain't the one to help you get your head on straight, who will be? Now, tell me what you think this stuff is worth, and we'll negotiate from there."

In the world of crime, that's pretty darn honest.

The truth is, Wendy was the closest thing to a mother I ever had. Not to cast any blame on my real mom who did her absolute best for me, but her best was pretty limited. As for Jen, well, I had a great year with her, but she did throw Myra and me away. I understand why she did—I would most likely have done the same thing in her place—but the bottom line was that Jack cheated, and Myra and I were punished for it. Doesn't exactly win Jen "Mother of the Year."

But Wendy was always there for me no matter what. When I got busted, she was my phone call. She'd get me my lawyer, front the attorney fees, and she was always willing to chat on the phone when I needed advice. The nights I felt it unsafe to return to my foster home, she'd let me crash on the couch in her apartment above the pawnshop. If I was particularly freaked out, she'd stay up with me all night, regaling me with stories of her childhood in the Deep South, and how she came to Los Angeles to be a movie star.

"And I don't gotta tell you how that all worked out, sweet thing," she'd laughingly add without a single trace of bitterness in her voice.

She was my Fagin, and I was her Artful Dodger—that is, referring to the movie, not so much the book. Fagin was a prick in the book.

And for the record, yes, I got busted twice as a kid, but only because I had worked with partners, and *they* messed up. I don't blame myself too much for the first time because I didn't know any better. I guess I figured I had just teamed up with the wrong guy. But that simplistic approach to life went out the window after my second bust. Ninety days in juvenile detention gives a kid a lot of time to think, and so I made the decision to never team up again. The only good partner is no partner at all.

After my release, I was shuffled off to my eighth foster family. Rowland Kowalski was a former professional wrestler and a giant brute of a man. His wife Lana was wearing sunglasses when I met her, even though we were indoors and it was night—it didn't take a rocket scientist to figure out why. They had no kids of their own, but the other three foster kids were all bruised and terrified of him.

"So I hear you like to steal," was the first thing he said to me as he led me to my new room. "Well, not on my watch. You get me? *My* kids don't steal. Because if they do, they know what's coming next, and it's coming from *me*. You get me?"

"Yes sir," I said—he seemed to be the type who'd like to be called "sir."

"Dinner's in ten minutes," he said as he headed back out. "And *my* kids are never late, and they got the black eyes to prove it. You get me?"

Despite the fact that what he said was utterly self-contradictory, I nodded that I understood, and widened my eyes to show the fear he clearly wanted to see.

But Rowland never laid a hand on me. That's because in the middle of the night I packed up my stuff, left the house, and walked out of the system for good.

Free at last, free at last, thank God Almighty, I was free at last!

Wendy let me crash on her couch for a couple of weeks until I could find my own place. She co-signed my lease, set me up with a nice fake ID, and fronted me the money for my first month's rent and security deposit. She knew my skills as a thief so she had no doubt that I was good for it.

I was fifteen.

CHAPTER FOUR

I SPENT THE NEXT NINE years living large, and having the time of my life. I had a nice little one-bedroom in North Hollywood, and I always had money for booze, weed, and women. I only worked when I had to, always alone, and never in the same neighborhood without at least a six-month spread in between. I even started giving Wendy cash to pay me as an employee of her pawnshop so if anyone asked where I was getting all my money, I had the tax returns to show for it. I opened a bank account, got a driver's license under my real name, and bought myself a sleek, black, six-year-old Camaro.

Life was good.

Shortly after my twenty-fourth birthday, Wendy called me into her shop. She was moving boxes when I got there, sweating and grunting from the effort, sounds I had never heard from her before. It occurred to me that she was in her sixties by then, and it didn't seem right that a woman of her age should need to perform such physical labor. When she put down the box, rubbed her lower back and stretched it out, I knew I had to step in. "Let me get those for you."

"I can move my own boxes," she indignantly snapped, too proud to acknowledge her years.

"I can move them, too," I replied pleasantly. "What I can't do is make tea."

"How can you not make tea? You just boil the water and plop in the bag."

"I don't understand what you just said. Why don't you make us some tea, and I'll move the boxes."

She laughed. "You're a sweet thing, sweet thing. All right."

A little bit later, the boxes stored and the tea steeped, we got down to business. She told me that a "colleague" of hers was putting together a big heist, and that she had recommended me for it because, she said, I was the best B & E guy she had ever seen—that means breaking and entering. Of course, she added, she would take ten percent of my twenty percent cut as her "manager" fee.

"I don't know, Wendy," I told her. "I mean, thanks for recommending me, but I don't like working with partners."

"Hear the job first," she told me, and so I did.

Apparently, some big shot movie studio president had just bought an original Jackson Pollock from some New York art dealer, the painting eloquently titled *Number 4, 1951*.

"Don't those things usually get actual names?" I asked her.

"I guess this guy gives them numbers."

"He sounds lazy."

"Do you want to hear the job or not?"

She went on to explain that the studio president's Bel Air mansion had a pretty awesome alarm system that had yet to be upgraded to the state-of-the-art security that typically protects such treasures, and that there was a very small window of time before the new Fort-Knox-like system was to be implemented—which is why her colleague was willing to take a chance on a stranger and not wait for his regular guy, who still had a few months until his parole hearing.

Now, I knew nothing about art, but all good thieves know the equation: an artist you've heard of plus the word "original" equals millions.

"That's amazing," I sighed. "But still, the only times I ever got caught was when I teamed up."

"You were a gifted kid working with amateurs," she said. "These guys are pros. One of them is even connected"—that means they're friends with members of the Mafia. "It's time to step up your game, sweet thing."

It was hard to say no to all that money. It was hard to say no to never needing to steal again. It was hard to say no to being connected to a connected guy, which I have to admit sounded pretty cool. It was so hard to say no, in fact, that I didn't.

"Okay, I'm in," I told her. "But on one condition. No guns."

In the eyes of the law, a firearm at the scene of a crime turns a burglary charge into an armed robbery charge, and that could add an extra five-to-ten years to a sentence. Now, I had no intention of getting caught, but one must always think ahead to minimize the downside. It's just good business.

Also, guns scare me.

"Agreed," Wendy told me. "No guns. I'll make sure of it."

"Okay," I said. She gave me the information I needed, and I went to work.

My task was to case the joint in advance, find the way in, the way out, and a bunch of alternate escape routes just in case. It was something I had been doing for years by that point so it was quite comfortable for me.

I was to have no contact with Wendy's colleague who put the heist together and ran it from afar, but I met my new partners Angelo and Tony a few days later at the Hermosa Bar and Grill on Melrose. Those weren't their real names, they told me, and they didn't want to know mine. They would simply call me "the kid."

They were big guys, obviously muscle, and very intimidating. Angelo, the connected one, was in his fifties, tall, quite obese, with a shaved head and a skull-and-crossbones tattoo on the back of his neck. Tony was in his thirties, slightly taller than Angelo, and buff. I'm talking ten-hours-a-day-at-the-gym, steroid buff. He wore a plain white T-shirt that was purposely a few sizes too small in order to show off his enormous, rock-hard pecs and his anaconda-sized arms. Neither of them ever smiled. I flashed them my own world-class, disengaging smile a couple of times, told them some of my best jokes . . . nothing.

Still, I felt cool being on the team.

We sat at a booth in the back and ordered a couple of beers. I quickly realized that they had zero experience at actual burglary so even though I was low-man-on-the-totem-pole, I was also kind of the brains of the operation—a position of superiority that I knew to keep to myself. Once they agreed to leave their guns at home, I felt comfortable enough to tell them the simplistically brilliant plot that I had hatched, said with all modesty.

"Surveillance cameras are all over the place, so we wear ski masks, black clothes, black gloves, and black wool caps so there's nothing to identify us if we're caught on tape." Then I turned to Angelo, "You'd better wear a turtle neck so your tat doesn't give you away. In fact, we should go uniform. We all wear turtle necks."

"Done," Angelo said stoically, maintaining his role as heist leader.

"Now, here's the thing about alarm systems. An alarm gets tripped, and it sets off a signal in the main office. No one in the main office is particularly concerned because they assume it's a false alarm because ninety-nine per cent of the time it is—they're not supposed to make this assumption, but they do. It's human nature.

"Eventually, some representative phones the house. If no one answers, they wait a minute or two, then they phone again. Some companies even phone a third time before actually sending someone out.

"Bear in mind, the security guys they send out aren't actual cops so they have to drive within the speed limit—and once they finally get to the scene, they're not permitted to go inside the house. All they can legally do is walk around the perimeter, peek through the windows, see if they see anything suspicious. If they don't, that's that. If they do, they radio the cops who whiz over at the speed of light, and then, unfortunately, that too is that.

"Typically you have about thirty to forty minutes from the first *whoop-whoop* of the alarm till the cops arrive. Our movie guy has a better-than-most system so I calculate it at fifteen to twenty, so let's say ten to be safe. Normally that's nothing, and far too risky to pull any job. But on this one, we're only taking one thing, and we already know where it is. A big rock through the sliding glass door in the back—we're in, we're out, and we're gone."

There was a long pause as they sized me up. Then, for the first time, they burst out laughing. I couldn't tell if they were laughing with me or at me, but it reminded me of the scene in *The Godfather* when everyone laughs at Al Pacino for saying that he'll kill the police captain and the heroin dealer.

"That's it?" Angelo chortled. "That's your master plan? We just walk in and take it? Just like that?"

"This kid's got balls," Tony guffawed. "Big brass watermelons. Salute, kid."

"It'll work," I insisted.

"What if one of the neighbors hears the glass breaking when the alarm goes off, and puts two and two together?" Angelo asked.

"They'll wonder what the sound is for a couple of minutes at least, then they'll figure the alarm company will take care of it. Even if they do call the cops, we'll be long gone before they do. We won't be wasting time picking locks, rifling through drawers, stuffing stuff in bags, searching around for added treasures. We grab one little painting off one little wall, and we know exactly where to find it." Then I felt a sudden pang in my stomach. "I mean, we do know exactly where to find it, right?"

"Main foyer," Tony said. "Ten steps from the front door. Guaranteed."

"Then this is the safest way to go."

"You'd better be right, kid," Angelo said with ice in his eyes. "You'd better be right."

CHAPTER FIVE

THE HEIST WAS SET FOR a week from Saturday, during which time, according to Angelo and Tony's source—presumably the mystery man in charge—the studio president and his family would be in New Orleans for Super Bowl weekend.

It was a brisk LA night, which was good—black turtlenecks in ninety-degree heat can get quite uncomfortable. We pulled up to the mansion at precisely 10:15, a time I chose because it was late enough for no one to be paying attention to a neighbor's home, but not so late that Tony's unmarked Subaru sedan parked in front would raise any eyebrows. Angelo and I put on our ski masks—Tony was already wearing his curly wig and fake handlebar mustache—then we got out of the car and walked quickly along the dog-walk to the back of the house. I smashed the big red brick that I had brought with me through the sliding glass door to the family room, and we stepped inside.

Whoop! Whoop! Whoop!

The countdown begins.

The Pollock was right where Tony had said it would be, ten steps from the front door, a thirty-million-dollar finger-painting hanging on a wall. I mean, seriously, it was a mess—no wonder the guy never bothered to give it a name. The only way I can think to describe it is . . . if vomit exploded. Had I not been in thief head zone, I probably would have laughed at the insanity of it all, but time was of the essence. All we had to do was take the crazy thing off the wall, carry it out the front door where Tony waited, drive off before the security company made the first phone call, then spend the rest of our lives on a beautiful beach somewhere.

But no one had ever mentioned that the painting was bolted or crazy-glued or something to the wall. Intel-screw-up-number-one. If we had known, we would have brought the necessary tools to yank the thing off, but ole Jackson was stuck on good. Try as hard and long as we did, Angelo and I could simply not pry it loose.

Then the phone rang, right on schedule.

We had seven of our ten minutes left, and that painting wouldn't budge. My heart raced, but my head stayed cool. I knew from experience that once a job veers off course, it only gets worse. One is much smarter while planning a job than doing it because there isn't a ton of adrenaline coursing through your veins, so it had always been my policy to bolt at the first sign of trouble and live to steal another day.

"Forget it," I calmly shouted over the *whoops* of the alarm and the *brrrings* of the telephone. "We should go."

"I got thirty million dollars between my fingers!" Angelo snapped back. "We ain't going nowhere without it!"

There was a darkness in his eyes that I hadn't seen before, an evil that went far beyond the intimidating quality I had felt at the Hermosa, made even more sinister by his black clothes and ski mask. What could I do? He'd track me down and kill me if I ran out on him. I could see it in the fat thug's eyes.

"We don't need the frame!" I shouted the moment it occurred to me. "Let's just peel out the painting!"

He nodded, and we both proceeded to try to remove the canvas from the frame, but it too seemed glued or something. When Angelo accidentally tore a small piece of the corner, he elbowed me in the head.

"Dumb idea!" he shouted as I fell to the ground, my vision hazy, my nose filling with blood. "We can't tear it!"

He reached up to the top of the frame in a useless attempt to use leverage to pry the thing loose. His turtleneck rolled up from his waist to reveal the top of his butt crack, and that was when I saw the Glock tucked behind the back of his pants.

"Jesus Christ!" I exclaimed. "You said no guns!"

"And you said you weren't a pussy! Now go find me a hammer or something! We'll just knock through the drywall and take the whole wall with us!"

"Where am I going to find a hammer?"

"I don't know! Just get one!"

This is nuts, I thought as I raced to the kitchen in search of a toolbox, sweat pouring from my pores, blood dripping inside my mask, when I discovered intel-screw-up-number-two. For right there, hiding under the kitchen table, was a very frightened teenage boy with a cell phone in his hand.

"Please don't hurt me," he quivered. I could barely hear him over the blaring *whoops* of the alarm, but I could see the terror in his eyes and in his tears.

"Give me the phone," I whispered loudly. "And don't make a sound."

I grabbed the phone from his hand—he had already called 911.

Jesus!

I raced back to the living room to try to convince Angelo that we had to run, but I had no idea what to say. I couldn't tell him about the boy— the fat brute would most likely take the kid hostage, or worse. Then the banging started.

Angelo, tired of waiting for me to find a hammer, had grabbed one of the movie guy's Golden Globe Awards off the mantel and was using it to pound holes through the drywall, all around the Pollock frame.

"We've taken too long!" I pleaded. "We gotta go! Now!"

"I told you! We're not going nowhere! Now grab the other trophy and help!"

Then Tony burst in from the family room. "What the hell is taking so long?!"

"What are you doing here?" I shouted at him. "You're supposed to be waiting in the car with the engine running!"

Then we heard the sirens. The goddamn sirens.

"We've got to run!" I shouted. "But I know a way out!"

"Do I look like I can run?" said the fat man. He moved from the painting to the front window, removing his Glock from the back of his pants along the way. The sirens were growing louder and louder, their volume now rivaling that of the whooping alarm. Tony removed a pistol of his own, took position on the other side of the window, and the two thugs prepared for the shootout to come.

"You gotta be kidding me!" I shouted.

Angelo turned to Tony and bravely offered, "You can run. You should run."

"I ain't leaving you out here alone, Fat Man," the buff thug said amicably as if they were Butch and Sundance.

Idiots! I thought. Did they really think they could shoot their way out of this? Criminals are so stupid!

"I-I can't do this," I told them. "I'm sorry." Then I sprinted off to the kitchen, not sure if I had asked for permission or forgiveness.

"Go!" Angelo shouted after me. "Run and hide, little girl!"

I had no intention of hiding, of course, but kitchens have back doors, and I had scoped out plenty of alternate escape routes. I raced into the room where the boy was still crouched under the table. "Come with me," I panted as I held out my hand for him to take. "It's too dangerous for you to be here with those guys."

But the boy was as afraid of me as I was of Angelo and Tony—I was, after all, dressed in black and wearing a blood-soaked ski mask. He crept further back under the table and against the wall, bending his knees into a fetal position.

"Fine," I told him. "Do what you want. I tried."

I raced out the back door just as the shooting started. You could barely hear the sirens and alarms over the deafening blasts of gunfire, and the boy was quickly at my heels. We sprinted across his family's sprawling backyard, leapt over the bushes that separated the estate from its neighbor, sprinted across that sprawling backyard, along their dog-walk then out onto the street, when a giant burst of whiteness obliterated all sight.

I couldn't hear the police rifles being cocked over the gunshots and sirens and *whoop-whoop-whoops*, but I knew they were there. I dropped to my knees and put my hands on my head before the cops even screamed that I should, and the terrified teenage boy followed my lead.

Goddamn partners.

* * *

THEY THREW EVERYTHING AT ME. Armed robbery, possession of a weapon, possession of a weapon for unlawful purposes, destruction of property, eluding police, endangering the welfare of a minor, and even kidnapping because I had taken the boy with me. The holes in the drywall around the Pollock made clear what we were there to steal, and it was appraised at thirty-seven point two million dollars.

I was so screwed.

Personally, I don't think the cost of what you're stealing should have any bearing on the length of a sentence. Why is robbing an expensive painting from a rich guy worse than robbing a cheap painting from a broke guy? It seems to me that the law gives more protection to the wealthy than to the poor. Of course, I was in no position to argue politics.

On my side was the fact that it was considered my first offense because juvenile records are sealed. I had a steady job and a small-business-owner boss who told them that I was a good kid with a rough past who had simply made a mistake. The teenage boy told them that I had only *suggested* he come with me, that I had left the house without him, and that I may have saved his life. And the A.D.A. believed that neither gun was mine because I had clearly taken off as soon as the shooting started, and because both Angelo and Tony had records of gun violence.

I also cooperated fully, fudging only certain little facts. I obviously left out my vast knowledge of security systems, but I did tell them that we had planned to be in and out of the house quickly. I also kept Wendy out of it, and said that I had met Angelo and Tony by happenstance, purposely mentioning the Hermosa in the hopes that my partners would do the same and our stories would match. There was some risk that Angelo or Tony might tell a different tale, but the likelihood was that they wouldn't say anything at all. For connected guys, keeping quiet is a badge of honor.

In retrospect, I was glad the guys had only given me pseudonyms. Referring to them by their real names could have been construed as ratting, and that could have proven fatal for me. That is, of course, if they were even still alive. I didn't know.

In the end, my high-priced attorney—thanks again, Wendy—got the state to drop all charges except attempted robbery—"attempted" because we never actually got the painting off the wall. I was offered a plea of twelve years, eligible for parole in four. My alternative was to go to court, in which case I would be charged with the whole kit 'n' caboodle, and I'd be looking at twenty years or more.

Given that the only thing for which I wasn't blatantly guilty was the kidnapping, I didn't see much point in fighting.

I was off to big boy prison.

CHAPTER SIX

W E SIT ON A BEACH, she and I. It's night, and it may be a little cold but for the fire we had built that dances and flickers before us. Beyond the fire is a great sea, its dazzling blue waves gently massaging the edge of the sandy shore with soft, tender hushes. The sky above is black as black can be, and its myriad of infinite stars shimmer and sparkle and bedazzle us. We are all alone, not a person or building in sight, no sign of a world of men except for the empty stone caves that had been abandoned by their inhabitants decades or centuries or millennia ago.

My arm is around her waist, and her head rests upon my shoulder. We don't need to speak—the depth of our eternal love is such that words are no longer necessary. Yet we speak nonetheless, and we laugh, and we love.

We know in our hearts that we were once a single soul in Heaven, one entity separated into man and woman who came to Earth to live our lives together, and we will never be apart. We can't be. We are one.

We're in a park, sitting on a bench, and she's sad. She says that she's grown feelings for someone else. She doesn't know how it happened, she says, she never expected or wanted it to happen. Her affection for me remains true, she says, but she has fallen for this other man completely. She will marry him, and our wedding will never be.

I don't understand what she is saying. It makes no sense. It's not possible.

I can't look at her.

I know this man who has taken her from me. I had considered him a friend. I'm filled with rage towards this Judas, this snake. I look back to her, my heart filled with pain and fury, and I see the tears rolling down her cheeks. She's crying because she knows she's hurting me, killing me, and all I want to do is wipe away her tears, hold her in my arms, and make her feel better.

I wake up. I want to cry but I don't dare. I'm in my cell in San Quentin Prison—cracked stone walls, metal bars, and howling animals—and I know that such an unmanly display is but an invitation to a gang-bang, with me as the bangee.

* * *

MAXIMUM-SECURITY PRISONS ARE as brutal as the most brutal prison movies show them to be. Guards can be savage, and inmates often worse. Daily life is based on racism, tribalism, warfare, and détente, and those unaffiliated live in greater risk and constant fear. I obviously lacked the complexion to have been taken in by the Mexicans or the Brothers, and I wanted nothing to do with the Aryan Nation because those guys are dicks.

I actually came to be appreciative of my time in juvie. During my first stint at age fourteen, I allowed my fear to show and I received a pretty severe beating from the other kids because of it. By my second stint, I had the thousand-mile stare down pat, and I was very grateful to possess that skill in this new dungeon of horrors.

Angelo and Tony—a.k.a. Fat Phil and Marco—pled to twenty years, eligible for parole in God-knows-when. Had they been found guilty at trial, they would have received life because of the shootout, which the law calls attempted murder.

I was worried they would blame me for our plan going so off course, but once they calmed down they realized that the bad intel had come from their end. They even conceded that they should have listened to me when I insisted we bail. They also respected me for never having told the cops about Wendy, a friend of theirs too.

"He's all right, that kid," Fat Phil would say about me. "He's okay."

Being connected to connected guys made me sort of connected myself. I even befriended a few of the younger made guys—meaning actual members of the Mafia—who encouraged me to join in their little handball matches in the yard. I had never played before and I was surprised—shocked, really—at how easily the sport came to me. Before long, I could have won every single game had I so chosen, but that would have been stupid. I needed these guys to want to keep me around so I allowed myself to win only often enough to make their victories over me feel meaningful.

Of course, that didn't mean my new Mafia pals would come to my defense if need be, but it didn't mean they wouldn't. Nobody, including me, knew. It was like having a very crappy health insurance policy. You just don't know what's covered.

So I knew how to act, walk, talk, and stare. I may or may not have had real live mobsters to provide me muscle if I needed it. I even lucked out with my cellie, Juan Gomez, a small, skinny grifter from San Diego who was as non-violent as I was. All in all, it could have been a lot worse.

It was still awful, though. The terror that consumed me became almost normal, and that scared me even more. The sounds of those automatic cell doors clanging shut every night sent a ghostly shiver crawling up my spine. I was safe from the savages, but only because I was caged like an animal.

I wanted out, and as soon as possible. I was eligible for parole in four years, and I had no intention of being one of those inmates who gets chronically rejected. I learned all the things that a parole board wants from a candidate, and I set out to have every single one of them shining brightly throughout my file.

I started with the prison chaplain because he seemed the most accessible. I admitted to him that I had never been much of a believer, adding that I just needed someone wise that I could trust and with whom I could speak freely. I did it this way because the system *loovvves* to see growth, and I felt he would become a stronger advocate if he believed it was he who had brought me to Christ. It worked.

I attended regular weekly sessions with the prison psychiatrist. I spoke honestly about my mom, the father I never knew, dream-woman, the crushing blow regarding Jack and Jen, my sadness over losing my almost-sister Myra—and I gradually let the kind lady doctor fix me. Advocate Number Two.

I even volunteered for the prison plays so I could win over some of the guards. My claim to fame was playing Rizzo in *Grease*, the most butch of the female roles.

I set out to get my GED. Personally, I never saw the need for school, and I certainly didn't see how a diploma would matter once I was released. I was a good thief, a great thief. My only mistake had been teaming up, which I would never do again. Still, I busted my hump to get the best grades I could just to show that I did.

Then something weird happened. Something no one could have predicted. If someone had told me it would happen, I would have laughed in his face.

Math was fun! Algebra was a blast! Geometry a delight! They were riddles and puzzles. They were board games and video games I could play in my head. And physics was the most captivating of all.

I know. It's crazy, right? I wish I could explain it, but somehow some warped part of my brain just connected. Maybe it's simply a factor of how boring prison life is—when it's not utterly terrifying—but I'd lie in my cell each night working out equations that weren't even assigned as homework, just for the kick of it.

On one of those nights, I came across "$e^{i\pi} + 1 = 0$." It's called Euler's Equation, and many in the know have dubbed it "the most beautiful of all equations." It's been compared to a Shakespearean sonnet. The concept it represents, the intertwining of five seemingly unrelated quantities into one interlocking whole, struck me as more dazzling than a billion twinkling stars on the blackest of nights. It combines the five most important numbers—the dream team of numbers, some call it—into one simple, elegant equation: zero, the additive identity; one, the multiplicative identity; pi, the—

No, wait. I don't want to turn my story into a physics manual. You don't need to understand the equation for my tale to make sense. All you need to know is that it blew me away. It was another thunderbolt to my heart. Like the first time I stole, or the first time I heard Bob Dylan sing, my soul had been lifted.

Sure, I took some ribbing for it from my Mafia buddies, but it was all in good fun. They may have even thought that my new ambition to "go geek" was kind of cool. They never said that, but I think they did. Maybe they didn't.

By the time of my parole hearing, I had received my high school equivalency with a three-point-eight GPA. Advanced placement classes weren't offered in San Quentin so four was the highest score one could achieve, making three-point-eight a damn fine number. I had recommendation letters from my teachers, the chaplain, the shrink, even a few guards. I barely had to lie.

Criminals, as you may know, are the best liars in the world—therefore, employees of the Department of Corrections, by necessity, possess the best BS detectors of anyone. So when I told my parole panel of my desire to go to college so I could one day become a proud, productive member of the scientific community, my passion could not be ignored, and my authenticity could not be denied.

In fact, if purposely omitting certain pertinent facts isn't considered a lie, then I didn't lie at all.

CHAPTER SEVEN

I HAD NEVER MET A parole officer before, but I had never heard anything but bad things about them. It was a good lesson in not generalizing because mine wasn't so terrible. Yes, he made it clear that he would send me back to jail on a dime if I messed up, but I believed him when he said that he didn't want to have to do that.

Seymour Lancing was a skinny little man with a big bald head. I figured him to be in his mid-to-late forties. There was always a can of Dr. Pepper on his desk, as well as a pack of Camel filters with which he fumbled incessantly, clearly ruing the day it was made illegal to smoke inside government buildings.

He told me about the high recidivism rate among us cons, and how it used to tear him up when he had to send one of us back. But after a time, he said, he came to accept it as the norm, a routine part of his job, and that the ones who were able to stay straight were the remarkable exceptions. His face lit up with pride when he spoke about the parolees that he had successfully helped re-enter society. He compared himself to a doctor and all of us parolees to cancer patients, and he had learned not to put the blame on himself when the cancer won. "But boy oh boy," he beamed. "When I help the cancer go away, it is a tremendous feeling that I cannot describe."

I didn't know why he was telling me this. My best guess was that it was his usual "get-to-know-me-I'm-a-nice-guy" opening spiel, but still, like I said, I believed him.

"And you have great potential to make it, T.J.," he said, one hand skimming my file, the other fondling the Camels. "I mean, you went in bad, no doubt about it. But you really seem to have turned yourself around. Your recommendation letters are off the charts, and your GED transcripts are terrific. I hope it wasn't all an act."

Most of it was an act—you know that—but the best part of it wasn't an act at all, and you know that, too. "Not an act, sir," I said. "None of it. I want to be good."

What was I going to say? Convicts have virtually no rights, and this man could send me back to San Quentin for no good reason at all. He had absolute power over my freedom, and I needed him on my side in case one of my future heists went awry—I had to come up with my tuition money somehow. Sure, if I got caught red-handed, that would be that. But if the events surrounding my arrest were somewhat circumstantial, a good word from Seymour could make all the difference. That said, of course, I had no intention of ever getting caught again.

We spoke about my plans to go to college and get my BS in physics, my February release making it too late to apply for the 2017 Fall Semester, and how I would use my time to crush my SATs to get accepted somewhere the following school year. I told him that my former boss, Wendy, would sponsor my education, leaving out the part that she would do so with money that I would steal and give to her.

He seemed pleased that I had worked it all out. He said that if I applied myself to the job he got me, stayed clean, was accepted into a good school, and had the means to cover my expenses, he would allow me to concentrate on my studies full time. It was actually quite nice of him because he had the power to insist that I keep a job while in college, or to prevent me from going to college at all before completing my full sentence eight years later. He was proud of me in advance, anticipating that I was to be one of his cancer patients that he could cure.

I was disappointed to learn that he wouldn't let me return to my old job at Wendy's pawnshop—the one where I'd give her part of my heist money that she'd then give back to me in the form of an official paycheck with taxes removed. Part of the condition of parole is that one is not allowed to consort with known felons. Technically, Wendy wasn't a felon because she had never been convicted of anything, but she had been arrested and charged a bunch of times. Still, Seymour wasn't sure she'd be a good influence on me, and he didn't want me to spend too much time with her.

I knew better than to argue. "Too much time" is a rather ambiguous term, and one that I knew I could work around. If I had made hanging with Wendy an issue, Seymour could have decided to not let me see her at all, and then, when I did anyway, he could cite it as a parole violation and send me back inside.

So when he told me, smiling and glowing over the great triumph he had achieved on my behalf, that he had found me a job that was "right up my alley," I smiled back excitedly. When he told me that he had secured me gainful employment on the overnight janitorial staff at the California Institute of Technology, I *forced* myself to smile back excitedly.

I mean . . . really? How excited would you be to learn that you'd be spending your nights mopping and picking up people's garbage? And not to offend anyone but even if you *are* a janitor, how excited are you to show up for work every day?

"Starting Monday," Seymour boasted. "You're going to Caltech!"

Well technically, sure, but not really.

Yet that, dear friends, is where our story truly begins.

CHAPTER EIGHT

THE CALIFORNIA INSTITUTE OF TECHNOLOGY campus in Pasadena was the most beautiful thing I had ever seen. The ensemble of majestic architecture resonated with the brilliance of those who taught and studied within her walls. Clean, crackless walkways connected one glorious structure to the next, artful fountains sprayed water into manmade ponds like a hypnotic ballet, and they were all surrounded by the greenest, most exquisitely groomed grass that could be. It was hard to believe that this belonged to the same dismal, dreary county in which I had been born and raised.

My janitorial duties themselves were mind-numbingly boring and gross, but I could deal with that. What was truly frustrating was walking into the classrooms and seeing all those mystifying equations on the chalkboards. Remember, I am not a genius, I am not Matt Damon in *Good Will Hunting*. At twenty-eight years old, I was the equivalent of a very smart high school kid. It was February, six months into the school year, so even the equations on the freshman chalkboards were way over my head. I even bought some first semester freshman textbooks to try to catch up, but it was useless on my own. I had too many questions with no one to answer them. I was like a first-grader who had just learned to read, and was suddenly trying to tackle *Ulysses*.

Night after night, I would stare at the chalkboards and try to comprehend the incomprehensible, and it was tortuous. Why couldn't Seymour have assigned me to a loading dock like any other parolee? Why did the system have to flaunt before my eyes the one thing I wanted most, then force me to mop up after those who had it? Once again, I was the kid without the candy bar—only one can't rob an education.

And for the record, I had no illusions about ever being admitted to Caltech. Sure, I had every intention of applying—Caltech and MIT were my dream schools—but I was trying to remain realistic. This was a place for geniuses, and I was only smart. Beyond that, my criminal record alone would almost guarantee me a rejection. But somewhere in this great country there had to be some lesser-known institution that would admit me based on good grades and a solid SAT score.

Life on the home front was also pretty dismal at first. During my first month out, I had to live in a halfway house, and the managers there were real sticklers. If I missed curfew by two minutes on a Saturday night, I'd get a call from Seymour who'd talk my ear off about following the rules. When I'd get home from my shift in the wee hours of the morning and make myself something to eat, I'd get complaints about the noise I made washing my dishes, and I'd get a call from Seymour saying how I must respect my neighbors. If I didn't wash the dishes—call from Seymour about self-respect and hygiene.

But once I was allowed to get my own place, things began to fall in line. It was a bit of a dump, one commensurate with my janitor's wages, leaving me my heist money to do with as I pleased. Two-thirds was always socked away for tuition, the other third for fun. I got my Camaro out of storage, found this nice little online escort service, stopped kicking myself for the equations I couldn't solve, and buckled down on my SAT practice tests. All in all, things could have been a lot worse.

It even turned out that having a night job made for a pretty good alibi. Two random nights a week, I would bust my hump through the first half of my shift, drive off to pull a job—never in Pasadena—then whip on back to Caltech, bust my hump through the second half, and punch out precisely at 5:00 a.m. like always. If I was ever suspected of anything, I was at Caltech all night. Duh. How else did all those classrooms, offices, and labs get cleaned?

Of course, I never needed the alibi, but better safe than sorry.

"You'd better slow down with all these jobs, sweet thing," Wendy would constantly warn me. "You don't know when you're being watched."

She hadn't aged well in the four years I had been away. She moved slower, and she grunted at the smallest of physical efforts. When I changed the subject and tactfully asked if she had ever thought about retiring, she laughed at me.

"Of course I done thought about it. You think I enjoy lugging all this junk hither and yon? You think I like living every moment one rat away from incarceration? But how would I support myself? Social security? Hell, I'm already taking that, and it ain't near enough for a lady of my fine refinement." Then she paused, and sighed. "Had that Pollock job gone the other way, that could've been my ticket. Just wasn't in the cards, same way all my other cards ain't never been in the cards."

"I bet you could get a good price if you sold the shop."

"Damn, this hole ain't worth nothing. The real money comes from the fencing, but I need the shop as a base. No, I made my choices in life, and I got stuck with them . . . which brings us back to you, sweet thing, because you are making some truly bad choices these days. Don't you go making the mistakes I made. You're robbing too much, too often, and you're taking too many chances."

I tried to explain that I didn't have any other options. I didn't want to have to pull jobs once I started college because I wanted to devote all my time to studying, which meant that I had eighteen months to come up with four years of tuition—yes, I saw the irony that in order to go straight I needed to steal more than ever before.

"Now hold your horses," Wendy interrupted. "I ain't saying not to pull *any* jobs, just take it slow. Settle down. Find a girlfriend."

"What do I need a girlfriend for?" I pleasantly replied. "I have prostitutes for sex, and a parole officer to point out every little thing I do wrong. I'm covered."

"You're bad," she laughed.

* * *

I took my SATs in the early spring, and I knew that I did horribly. I wanted to shoot myself in the head for all the time I had wasted. Who was I kidding with this college nonsense? I'm a thief, and I'll never be anything more.

I would find out weeks later that I got a combined 1430—specifically, 740 math, 690 reading and writing—which is a pretty darn terrific score.

Funny how the mind works.

* * *

IT WAS AROUND THAT time that I first met Professor Aldous Szabo, the most amazing man I have ever known. I had been mysteriously reassigned to the Sloan Annex, and I entered the Professor's massive laboratory with mop and rolling pail that same night, a little after two. Strange giant machines I couldn't understand were roaring and humming—some of them shiny and futuristically high tech, others so grimy they seemed to be to a hundred years old. An elderly man in a rumpled brown suit and bow tie was perched over his desk, banging away on a laptop, pausing only occasionally to scribble fresh equations on a scrap piece of paper.

"Oh, I'm sorry," I said to him. "I'll come back."

"No need, m'boy, no need," he said pleasantly with a slight trace of a woodsy accent. "Just go ahead, don't mind me. This place would never be cleaned at all if one had to work around my schedule."

I figured him to be in his late seventies or early eighties. He was short and pudgy, with John Lennon glasses, a happy round face, and a twinkle in his eye that told you he knew stuff that you didn't.

"Okee-doke," I said, and quietly got to work.

"You're the criminal, aren't you?"

"Excuse me?"

"The convict. The parolee. The burglar. The B & E man. I'm sorry, I don't know the politically correct term, but you're he, are you not?"

It seemed that my reputation had preceded me, and I didn't like it one bit. With my fine SAT scores in tow, Caltech didn't seem as much of a long shot as I had first suspected, so my sordid past wasn't something I wanted bandied about. I sighed and figured I'd make the best of it. What else could I do?

"Yep. That's me," I told him.

"Did you like it?"

"Prison?"

"Thievery."

"It paid the bills. I'd rather do what you do."

"Very good," he smiled. "Very nice." Then he returned to his scribbling, and that was the extent of our first encounter.

Over the days and weeks that followed, he would continue to engage me in conversation while I cleaned up after him, sometimes in his lab, sometimes his office. At first it was only trivial small talk, but it quickly escalated to detailed questions about my life in crime, like I was his own personal Tarantino movie.

I didn't mind. As you must have gleaned by now, I can weave a pretty decent tale when I so choose, and having a man like Aldous Szabo in my corner sure wouldn't hurt my college applications come January. The delight the old man took in my unsavory adventures surprised me, and I began to realize that maybe my ugly past wouldn't be such a hindrance after all. As much as I longed to be a part of the science geek world, it seemed that the science geeks fantasized about the romance of my criminal past. I was cool to them.

The Professor seemed particularly intrigued by the so-called "honor among thieves" on which literature loves to dwell, and I felt compelled to set him straight. Crooks won't rat out other crooks, true, I told him, but it's not because of any moral code. It's simply because ratting gets one killed. Crooks will steal from each other, beat up each other, murder each other, but they'll never take any grievance to the law—unless they're looking at a very long prison sentence of their own, in which case some do buckle under, but they typically end up paying the piper as a result.

One night, I arrived at his lab only to find a small Post-it stuck to his laptop screen. "T.J. Meet me on the roof."

It was odd, but I saw no reason not to comply. In a sense, Professor Szabo was my boss, and my boss was ordering me to take a break. Why wouldn't I comply?

I arrived on the rooftop to find him seated on an old, rust-worn lawn chair, gazing out over the campus, a crystal glass of booze in one hand, a fine Cuban cigar in the other. There were three other rust-worn lawn chairs, all empty, surrounding a rickety old card table upon which stood a bottle of Pappy Van Winkle, one of the rarest, most expensive Kentucky bourbons in the land. They sold for over a thousand dollars a bottle, a hundred bucks a glass in bars. Next to the table, on the ground, was a medium-sized plastic cooler in which were a few plastic bottles of water, a little wooden box of additional Cubans, and several more crystal glasses.

"You wanted to see me, Professor?"

He turned to me and smiled delightedly. "M'boy, m'boy! Come. Sit. Take a drink with me." He pulled another crystal glass from the crate, filled it halfway with the Pappy, then replenished his own. He offered me one of the cigars, but I declined—I never understood the appeal.

It did occur to me that he could be some kind of sick, old pervert trying to come on to me, but that didn't ring true. Besides, what was the worst that could happen? He was, like, eighty. I could take him.

I was also dying to know what a hundred-dollar shot of booze tasted like.

I took my seat next to him, thanked him for the drink, and then he raised his glass to the air. "To a life of crime," he proclaimed.

It was an odd toast for an eightyish-year-old physicist, and I felt uncomfortable repeating it given my new ambition, so I clinked his glass and replied, "Skol."

"I like to come up here after my work and sit, take a drink, and soak it all in," he said dreamily. "This truly is a magical place." He breathed a deep breath, as if inhaling the entire campus into his nostrils. "Now, tell me more of your adventures."

That's all it was. I told him stories, and he asked me questions. After my second drink, I politely told him that I needed to get back to my janitorial duties.

"Of course, m'boy, of course," he replied pleasantly. "But meet me back here on Thursday, around this time. We can talk easier up here without the distractions of my work. That is, of course, if you'd like to."

I couldn't understand why he was befriending me like this—and it would be some time before I did—but I certainly wasn't about to complain. Two nights a week through the end of that semester and all through the summer, I would bring my brown-bag lunch up to the rooftop, allowing the good Professor to provide the ridiculously expensive beverage and some astonishing conversation.

He was a kind man. When I told him how I had discovered my passion for science while in prison, he couldn't have been more encouraging. When I described my method of helping the starving homeless, he chortled with delight. When I mentioned my SAT scores, he beamed with a personal pride as if I were his own son or grandson. Even before I asked, he offered to write me a recommendation letter that I could attach to my college apps.

And man oh man, could he knock them back. He seemed to have three or four drinks to every one of mine. And the more he drank, the more the conversation shifted from me to him, an outcome with which I was perfectly fine because he was such a fascinating ole coot. Originally from rural Pennsylvania, he had spent most of his life at Caltech, receiving his Bachelor's degree and PhD in the 1950s. He began teaching in the early 60s and received his first research grant from LBJ himself. He was responsible for more patents than he could remember— some for government work, some for private industry, and some that he personally sponsored in order to keep the patents under his own name, hence his ability to drink from a thousand-dollar bottle of hooch whenever he pleased.

His discoveries had been responsible for matters so complex I could barely follow along as he described them, some classified ones that he wasn't permitted to describe at all, and some so mundane it was hard to believe there was a time when they didn't exist. The push-through tab on soda cans, that was him.

And on one particularly drunken evening, he confessed that he had been illegally siphoning money from all his grants all those years in order to fund his secret pet project.

Time travel.

It was why he had befriended me, he explained, why he had had me reassigned to his building so we could just "happen" to meet. He had been sizing me up all along. For decades, he had been desperate to speak to someone about his project, but he felt that only a crook could be trusted to keep silent about another's crime. The people in his circles would have turned him over to the authorities in an instant had he told them of his lawlessness, and they would have laughed him out of the business had he told them what he was trying to accomplish.

I, of course, immediately shifted into thief head. "How did anyone not notice all those missing millions?"

"Because I always succeeded for them, and often beyond their wildest expectations. I made corporations billions of dollars in profits, and I helped our nation win the space race. So enamored were they with my successes that they barely checked the accounting. The few times I was questioned, I simply told them that I'm not good with money. Oops.

"You know that story about Einstein failing elementary school arithmetic? Not true, but the bumbling genius stereotype it created sure helped the likes of me."

"But if you ever tell the world of your discovery, they'll know what you did."

"Given such a contribution to humanity, I'll be easily forgiven. I'll be honored. And I'll go down in history as quirky."

He was the greatest thief I had ever met. I was in awe.

"Does it work?" I asked him. "Time travel, I mean."

"Not yet, but I'm honing in on it," he said with a proud smile. "Then again, I've been telling myself that since the Carter administration," he slurred with a frown.

I couldn't tell if the liquor was inspiring him to tell tall tales, as it so often does, or if the liquor was giving him the courage to be honest about secrets his sober mind knew never to reveal, as it so often does. I didn't care. The conversations were so riveting that it didn't matter whether they were the truth or simply a great yarn.

Many nights he would prattle on about the benefits his invention would bring to mankind. "We could know who killed Kennedy. We could observe the birth and death of Jesus and put to rest the questions of religion one way or another."

"We could see the Big Bang," I added, just trying to participate.

"Actually, we couldn't see that one, m'boy, for we'd have nowhere to land. There were no planets yet. But we could confirm what rendered the dinosaurs extinct. The accepted theory is asteroids, but it remains a theory nonetheless.

"And asteroids, oh my goodness. The single greatest threat to us all. Imagine an asteroid of, say, five hundred kilometers in diameter, careening down into the ocean. Imagine shockwaves at hypersonic speeds, debris blasting up into low orbit, only to return back down to obliterate everything it touches. Firestorms envelop the world to extinguish all life in its path. Tsunamis a mile high. Giant earthquakes across the globe. Volcanic eruptions for a thousand years . . . but the thousand years isn't important because the planet's surface had been rendered uninhabitable on that very first day. From what we can tell, this has occurred at least six times since the Earth was formed. And do you know what we can do to prevent it?"

"What?"

"Nothing," he answered as he refilled our glasses, for which I was grateful under the circumstances. "Our only hope would be to divert the asteroid before it got here, but even our most powerful telescopes are unable to detect one coming at us until it's too late."

"Jeez," was all I could think to say.

"Jeez indeed. But what if one could travel back in time to warn past governments to take the necessary actions to save the world? What if one already has? What if I have, or will? Wouldn't that be nice?"

Other nights, he would describe the problems and setbacks of his project, often in theoretical equations that soared miles above my head. I would just listen and try my best not to zone out—hey, if Stephen Hawking was telling you the meaning of life, would you tell him to shut up just because you didn't get the math?

Other times, he laid it out in simple sci-fi terms that would delight any Star Trek nerd.

"Is it possible to change time?" he'd ask. "To alter history? If one could go back to a bygone era, would our mere presence disrupt our future? Or would we merely be fulfilling the destiny that time had prescribed to us from the start? In other words, were we *meant* to be back there? Are we back there now?

"If one went back to try to kill Hitler, using the most common hence boring example, could he succeed? Many attempts were made on Hitler's life, and they all failed. Did time travelers make any of those attempts? Did I? Did you? Maybe Hitler could not be killed because he wasn't killed, and the time-traveller assassin would have to go back to fail over and over because he already had, hence he always must. Or maybe it *is* possible to kill Hitler, and it wouldn't make a difference."

"How could it not make a difference?" I asked.

"Maybe the conditions in Germany at the time were such that they would naturally cause a Hitler-like figure to emerge. The country was broken, the people starving, angry, humiliated. Maybe such conditions were like a vacuum that had to be filled, and a different charismatic demagogue would have risen to accomplish the same destructive chaos. And the only difference today would be that instead of using the sound 'Hitler' to describe the embodiment of all that is evil, the word 'Goering' or 'Goebbels' would be the one plastered across social media."

He took a brief pause to let this sink in, savored a small sip of his Pappy, then returned to the blowing of my mind. "Now let's take it a step further. What if it was another evil man that was initially responsible for World War II and a time traveller killed *him*, and Hitler was the one to emerge in his stead?

"Or what if one killed Hitler and his replacement was even worse? Perhaps he was smarter. Perhaps, under his leadership, Germany managed to discover the atomic bomb just as the United States did, leading not to the nuclear destruction of two Japanese cities, but of all the cities in the world. What if Hitler, evil as he was, was the better choice?

"But here's the kicker. Even if one could substantially alter history, kill Hitler, and spare the world all the misery he caused, you wouldn't even know."

That's where he lost me. "Why wouldn't I know?"

"Well, first of all, you probably would never have been born. More than a hundred million people died as a result of World War II. A hundred million people now alive in this new, non-Hitler reality, choosing new husbands and wives, or remaining with the spouses that they had previously widowed. A hundred million people marrying and having children with those who otherwise would have married and had children with someone else. Hundreds of millions of children would be born who otherwise would have never been, and hundreds of millions of others, alive in our current reality, would never come to exist at all.

"But let's say, despite all probabilities, all four of your grandparents did meet in this new reality, did marry, and copulated at the precise moment necessary for their genes to combine in just such a way to produce your mother and father—the statistical probability of your birth continues to dwindle. Your parents would have grown up in a completely different world with different people, different history, different wars and scandals, different experiences. They would essentially be different beings. Yes, they would be genetically the same, but we are as much the sum of our experiences as the makeup of our DNA. The likelihood of your parents even meeting would be remote at best, let alone liking each other given their new personalities, let alone copulating at that one, precise moment to produce you.

"And even with all that, even if you were somehow miraculously born, and even if you yourself were the one who killed Hitler, you still would not know."

"Wait. If I'm the one who did it, how could I not know that I did it?"

"Because you would have been born into a world that had never heard of Adolf Hitler. There would have been no World War II, no atomic bomb. Whatever devastations would have happened in its stead —because we humans do have a propensity for devastation—nobody knows, but that new reality would be the history you'd have studied in school, and the outcomes of that history would be the current events of your life."

"Then how could I go back to kill Hitler in the first place?"

"Oh, that paradox is the biggest trope of them all—debated to death and by far the most boring. For the sake of discussion, let's just say that either the paradox is proof that one *cannot* alter the past . . . or it's not a paradox at all, merely an equation that has yet to be solved."

"So what you're saying is that maybe we can't change the past and maybe we can, and even if we can, it may not make a difference, and even if it does make a difference, we wouldn't know about it anyway."

"Now you see why it's kicking my ass?"

* * *

I WAS WALKING UP the stairwell to the roof one early Autumn night, one horrible and fantastic early Autumn night, my brown-bag lunch of tuna fish sandwich and Fritos in hand, when I heard voices. The Professor was in conversation with someone. I didn't know if it was appropriate for me to barge in on him so I pushed the door open just a crack, and I couldn't believe what I saw.

He was sitting slumped back on one of the lawn chairs, naked as the day he was born, except for a shiny dark Apple Watch strapped to his wrist. He was sweating and breathing hard as if he had just run the LA Marathon. Of course I was concerned, but what I noticed next simply floored me.

Standing next to the Professor, comforting him and urging him to take a sip from the plastic bottle of water, was the Professor.

Let me say that again, in case you missed it.

Standing beside Professor Aldous Szabo was Professor Aldous Szabo.

CHAPTER NINE

I HAVE SEEN IDENTICAL TWINS before, but they're never *that* identical.

The Professor who was standing was fully clothed, and he seemed quite worried about his naked counterpart. "Drink this," he said as he poured drops of water into the naked man's mouth. "It'll make you feel better."

"Thank you," said the naked Professor after a few sips. "I'm all right. But I must warn you, that first step is a doozy."

"I can see that. Should we get you to the hospital?"

"No, no, it's starting to ease up. Sit. Please."

The clothed Professor took his seat. They both sat quietly for a moment, then a smile grew on the naked Professor's face. "We did it," he said proudly. "Einstein, Galileo, Newton, and us. Can you believe that?"

"It's hard to believe."

"Pour the Pappy."

"Are you sure you're up for it?"

"We must celebrate this moment, my friend."

The clothed Professor did as he was told, then they raised their glasses.

"To all the presidents from whom we stole!" shouted Professor Szabo.

"To Lyndon through Donald!" shouted Professor Szabo.

They clinked glasses then took a sip, whereupon the naked one said, "Slide in. We must get a photograph to commemorate this moment."

"A photograph that will be commemorated in every history and science textbook till the end of time," the clothed one said as he shuffled his lawn chair closer.

"Well stated, Aldous."

"Thank you, Aldous."

They were having so much fun. They leaned toward each other so that their heads were almost touching, raised their glasses in toast, and smiled. The naked one raised his left arm, then snapped the selfie on his Apple Watch.

I didn't think Apple Watches had cameras, but I suppose if one can master time and space, programming a camera into a watch isn't that big a deal.

"Interesting," said the clothed Professor. "The face of your watch looks different from mine."

"Yes," replied the naked one with an all-knowing smile, as if he had had this conversation before. "And what is the difference, Professor?"

"Well, Professor," began the clothed one as he rolled up his sleeve to reveal that he too was wearing a shiny dark Apple Watch. "The maximum forward temporal destination settings don't match. Mine stops at this moment, while yours goes six minutes beyond, and ticking down. Five-fifty-nine, five-fifty-eight, et cetera."

"And why is that?"

"I suppose that mine stops at this moment because one cannot travel into the future because the future has yet to happen."

"Correctomundo. And yet I can. Why is that? Why can I when you cannot?"

"Hmmm."

"You can get this. I know you can because I did."

"Oh! Because six minutes from now is not *your* future. You would merely be returning from whence you came. Yet for me, it is the unknown and the as-yet-to-be."

"Five stars, my friend. Go to the head of the class."

They clinked glasses again and sipped some more, when the naked

Professor noticed me peeking through the crack in the door. "M'boy, m'boy! Come join us!"

"Take a drink with us and join the celebration!" added the clothed one.

I walked onto the roof with the biggest smile my face had ever worn. "You did it, you crazy son-of-a-bitch—sons-of-bitches. You really, really did it!"

"Yes, we really, really did!" said the naked one as he stood up to get a third glass from the crate, his ancient shriveled schlong flapping in the warm September breeze. He poured the Pappy into the glass and handed it to me, then replenished his own.

"Maybe you should take it easy," the clothed one cautioned. "You just had a pretty severe jolt to the heart."

"I'm fine, Aldous. Besides, the Pappy helps ease the tightness," he said as he replenished the glass of his counterpart. "You'll see when you're me. Stop worrying, and let's toast."

I took it upon myself to do the honors, and I must admit I was pretty choked up. "To the most amazing man—men—I have ever met. I salute you, sir—sirs."

I don't know if you've noticed but I've played pretty fast and loose with the word "sir" throughout my life, bestowing it mainly upon police officers, prison guards, and abusive foster fathers—but I never meant it. Professor Szabo was the only man I ever knew who deserved such a title, and I could not have meant it more.

"That's very kind, T.J.," said the naked one then turned to his counterpart. "Now, it's time for you to get going."

"Aw, is it? I was so enjoying talking with you."

"You are about to, again, my friend, but on the other side of the conversation."

"Of course," said the clothed Professor as he moved a few steps away. "The pain is quite severe, yes?" he asked his other self.

"Worse than we anticipated, but it eases up in due time. It's not nearly as bad as when I first arrived."

The clothed one shot back the last of his Pappy, set his glass on the table, and took a deep breath. "See ya around campus."

"Give my best to me."

"Will do."

He tapped on the watch, and he was gone. A sudden gush of wind pushed me and all the dust on the rooftop toward where he had been standing, except the wind was somehow in front of me, pulling not pushing, and I heard a simultaneous sound best described as *"crunch"*—as if the Professor's sudden removal from existence had created a vacuum that Mother Nature insisted on filling with a vengeance, and all that remained was the Professor's suit, footwear and underpants, all nestled innocently upon the floor, as if nothing had happened at all.

I looked to the naked Professor in shock. He began to put on the clothes that had been left behind for him, smiling from ear to ear, and then he turned to me. "In the parlance of your generation . . . how cool is that?"

"Pretty darn cool, sir."

"And right on the button, too," he went on as he showed me the face of his watch. "Look at that. Maximum forward, zero. I am now in my present."

"I don't know what I'm looking at."

"Oh, it's really quite simple. We—I designed it to be not only functional but elegant as well. Notice the wristband. Each strand alternates between graphene, which conducts the necessary electro-magnetism, and silicon, which makes this the smartest little computer in the world. But it's also rather chic, don't you think?

"Waterproof, windproof, dustproof. It's powered by its own movement because the last thing you want is getting stuck in ancient Rome in need of a battery.

"And the usability is a marvel, if I say so myself. Scroll here to set your temporal destination. Use GPS to store your spatial coordinates into memory—or you can just eyeball it if your destination is in plain sight—click 'Apply,' tap 'Send,' and off you go. Simple as texting, easy as pie. Returning home is even easier for every trip remains automatically saved. Tap 'present' to return to the present. Tap 'spatial destination: current,' and you'll arrive at the very spot from which you left. And again, 'Send.'"

"What are these icons over here?"

"Camera. Calculator. Instagram. Netflix. Of course, the Internet won't do much good in an era before it existed, and the dial-up connectivity in the nineties was horrid, but all the same." He took another sip of his Pappy, reached out his arms as if wrapping them around an imaginary woman, and then he began to dance. *"Moon river,"* he sang. *"Wider than a mile, I'm crossing you in style, somedaaaaaay."*

He was so happy, so deservedly proud.

Of course, the thought of stealing the thing crossed my mind—old habits die hard, and what a fantastic breaking-and-entering tool a watch like that would make. Just pop into a bank vault, stuff a bag with cash, and then pop back out. You wouldn't trip any alarm because banks don't wire the *inside* of a vault.

"Dream maker, you heart breaker, wherever you're going, I'm going your waaaaaaay."

But I would no more steal from this kind, old man than I would from Wendy. When he began to reiterate the benefits his creation could bring to humanity, I even felt a little ashamed for having had the thought in the first place.

"The mysteries that will be solved... *la de da de da*... the questions that will be answered . . . *de dum dum de dum* . . . the disasters that will be diverted . . . *da de la la la* . . . the lives that may be saved . . . *my huckleberry friend—*"

Then he stopped. He gasped, and clutched at his chest.

"Are you all right, sir?" I asked.

He tried to answer but he couldn't speak, couldn't breathe. He stumbled a few steps backward, then off the edge of the roof.

He fell off the goddamn roof!

I could hear his body crash onto the concrete below. I burst into the stairwell and shot to the ground level, leaping down four steps at a time. I bolted out the front door, raced to where he lay, and dropped to my knees beside him. I put my hand to his neck, his wrist, and felt nothing. I put my ear to his chest, nothing. He was dead.

He was goddamn dead!

But then I looked at what he wore on his wrist. He didn't have to be dead. I could bring him back to life.

Or could I?

CHAPTER TEN

I QUICKLY REMOVED THE APPLE Watch from the Professor's wrist and placed it on my own. The interface was user friendly enough so that setting the temporal destination was a mere matter of typing in some numbers, but the spatial seemed a little more confusing. Despite the fact that there was no actual need for me to rush, in the heat of the moment I felt that time was of the essence. I set the spatial destination to "current", tapped Send, and I was in the exact same spot only it was five minutes earlier, I was buck naked, and there was no dead Professor before me. Despite a very slight tightness in my chest, I charged back into the Annex and up the stairs, bursting onto the rooftop to see another me stupidly watching the Professor sing and dance just feet from the roof's ledge.

"There's such a lot of world to see..."

"Get away from there!" I shouted.

"M'boy, what are you doing here?"

The other me, the clothed me, was shocked, but I had no time to deal with me. I made a beeline for the old man, put my arm around his shoulder, and gently led him out of harm's way. "You really shouldn't dance so close to the ledge, sir."

And that was that. He was safe. I had saved him. I felt so Marty McFly.

"What are you doing with my watch?" he slurred in a friendly, drunken tone.

"I'm from a few minutes from now where you, um, well, you fell off the roof, sir, and you, um, died."

"Yeah? Wow. Weird."

"What is going on, please?!" the clothed me demanded.

"T.J.," began the Professor with his all-knowing smile. "Meet T.J.—T.J., T.J."

"How ya doin'?" I said to myself, then turned back to the Professor. "So I guess one *can* change the past, huh?"

"It certainly appears so, which is both good and bad."

"Why bad?" asked the other me. "He just saved your life."

It was a good question for I was wondering the very same thing.

"No, the saving my life part was good," the Professor chuckled. "And given that he only travelled back a few minutes, the only change he could have caused would be to the as-yet-to-be future, so we're safe. But if one were to go further back, years or decades or centuries back, even the smallest alteration could produce the largest of ripple effects—possibly wonderful, possibly apocalyptic. The fact that it is now conclusive that the past can indeed be changed makes this watch even more dangerous than I had suspected, more dangerous than a nuclear warhead—and I must take measures to treat it as such."

"I'm sure you will, sir," I and me said in unison.

"I appreciate the confidence, m'boys," the Professor replied, then unclasped his watch and turned to the other me. "And now, it is time for you to go back to do what your doppelganger just did. Unless, of course, you don't want to save my life."

"Of course I do, sir, but how? I didn't see you fall off a roof."

"How do you know that *he* did?" the Professor responded with a smile as he clasped the watch onto the other me. "Fortunately, he only *said* it happened, not whether he saw it with his own eyes." Then he quickly turned to me. "And don't you dare solve this mystery for us, m'boy, you'll mess up everything." Then back to the other me. "We have entered an endless, infinite time loop to save my life. This T.J. could be the first geometric point on that loop or the billionth—there's no way to know. All you have to do is appear on this roof a few minutes ago, yell at me to move away from the ledge, then walk me away as he did. The rest will come naturally."

"How can an infinite loop have a first point?" asked the other me. Again, I was about to ask the same thing.

"Why don't you be on your way," the Professor told him. "I'll explain it once you've gone, so you'll get your answer on the flip side. All right?"

"Of course," he-me said, then turned to me-me. "It hurts, huh?"

"Not too bad," I told me. "Like when you drink a glass of water too quickly and it gets clogged in your chest, but it passes after a few seconds."

"Really?" the Professor interjected. "For me, the pain was quite acute. I suppose it's because I have an old, decrepit heart filled with alcohol, cigar smoke, and sorrow."

"You have a very kind heart, sir," I and me said in unison again, then looked at each other and laughed a little laugh.

"Well, off you go," said the Professor. "Happy trails."

"See you in a few minutes ago," he-me said. He tapped "Send" and he was gone with a *crunch*, the vacuum once again lightly pulling the dust, the Professor, and me toward where he had been, leaving behind his-my janitor's uniform that fell gently to the ground.

Professor Szabo turned to me and said, "Thank you."

"It was a privilege, sir."

"Now get dressed. Who knows what sick, depraved things someone will think if they happen to walk by—a drunken old man and a naked young buck alone on a rooftop in the dead of night. And give me back my dang watch."

I laughed—he really was such a character—but that didn't mean I had forgotten my question. "So how could there be a first point on an infinite loop, sir? Doesn't that mean it's not infinite to begin with?" I asked as I began to get dressed.

"If you set out to draw a perfectly closed circle, you'd have to put your pencil to the paper somewhere, wouldn't you?"

"But that doesn't make sense. It's got to be infinite in both directions or it's not infinite, right? What am I missing?"

"Maybe my analogy was too simplistic. It's like this."

Then he gasped. He clutched at his chest, unable to breathe. He stumbled back a few steps, and then fell to the ground. No, he didn't fall off the roof—I had saved him from that dismal end—but it seemed that his kind heart had been a ticking time bomb all along, and no temporal travel could save him from that fate.

I immediately phoned campus security and told them what had happened. My trousers were on by then but my shirt wasn't, so I rolled it up and placed it under the Professor's head like a pillow, then knelt on the ground by his side.

"It was the jump," he whispered. "It was too much for my heart after all."

"Shhh."

The paramedics arrived a few minutes later, but it felt like hours. I rode along in the ambulance, and we arrived at Huntington Memorial Hospital minutes after that. The Professor was wheeled into the operating room, and I took a seat in the waiting room.

The television was set to CNN, so I tried to pay attention to the news in order to distract myself from my worries about the Professor, but it didn't quite work. Some Alabama Congressman, a John Ellis or something, was gleefully boasting of how he had blocked a certain child healthcare bill from passing in the House, deeming the bill to be further evidence of liberals' tax and spend policies. Jerk.

I decided I may as well worry.

Less than thirty minutes later, a doctor came to tell me that Professor Szabo was dead, and that there wasn't anything that anyone could have done to save him.

But I knew that there was still something I could do.

* * *

I WENT INTO THE bathroom stall so no one would see me vanish. I set the Apple Watch's temporal destination to the afternoon of three days prior, during which the Professor would be in his office—the time he kept available to consult with his students, and a time I knew he would be fully sober. He needed to be sober to hear what I had to tell him. I gave myself the time to learn the proper way to set spatial destinations—which actually only took a couple of minutes because, again, the interface was so user friendly—then I used the GPS in combination with my astute knowledge of the Caltech campus to set my destination for inside the maintenance room closet so I would have immediate access to clothing. Send.

And there I was—this watch was amazing! I was once again buck naked with the same slight tightness in my chest that quickly passed, although not quite as quickly as the one before. I grabbed a uniform off the hanger, got dressed, then headed back to the Sloan Annex where the Professor would be waiting in his office.

His door was closed, which told me that he was in conference with one of his students, but my wait was short. When the student left, I entered gingerly. I had no idea how to explain what I needed to explain.

"Professor?"

"M'boy, m'boy. What are you doing here?"

"May I have a minute?"

"I'm sorry, T.J. This is my time for my students. We'll chat tonight, as always."

"It works," I blurted out as I rolled up my sleeve to show the watch.

His mouth dropped open. "You're from the—"

"Yes."

He smiled. He had always seemed a happy man who smiled often, but this smile was so enormous I thought it was going to fly off his face. "Close the door."

I did as instructed, sat down on the chair in front of his desk, then told him everything. I described his joyful conversation with his other self, and the old man giggled like a schoolgirl. I described the first reality in which he had a heart attack and fell off the roof to his death, and the other reality in which the heart attack itself had killed him.

"You cannot make the jump, sir," I said in conclusion. "And I would strongly suggest you get your butt to a doctor, pronto. Whatever is going on in that kind heart of yours is not good."

He exhaled deeply, took a long moment to process what I had told him, and then he answered. "I'm afraid I cannot comply, m'boy. I *am* going to make that jump."

"Didn't you hear me? That jump will kill you."

"I'm eighty-four years old, T.J. I first conceived of this project in my early twenties, younger than you are now. It cost me two marriages, as well as several children and even more grandchildren who won't speak to me because of my neglect of them. But the one thing that kept me going was the hope, the prayer that one day, just once, I could master time and space. That I could travel through it. That I could give my gift to the world. Now you tell me that I have, will succeed? Then you say in the same breath that I shouldn't because it will cost me my life? M'boy, it already has cost me my life. All it can take from me now is a few lonely years."

"But, sir—"

"My decision is made, m'boy. But I do have two favors to ask of you, if you'd be so kind to indulge me."

"Of course," I said softly through the growing lump in my throat.

"After I'm gone, I'd like you to break into my office and steal all files related to this project. You're a thief, so I don't suspect that you will mind—especially since I'm requesting it. Then I'd like you to FedEx it, watch and all, to a Doctor Jean-François Benit at NASA. For your own safety, don't include your name or address, but add an unsigned, anonymous letter explaining that it is my life's work, and that I've chosen him as the one to see it forward. He's a brilliant man, and a good man. He'll know what to do, and he'll accord me my place in history."

He gave me the combination to his wall safe, then showed me which papers, spiral notebooks and flash drives to send to the NASA guy, and which to destroy. He gave me his computer password and showed me which files to delete.

"I'm happy to do this for you, sir, but why not just do it yourself?"

"Ah. And that brings us to my next favor. I would like you to go back to the moment before you came to see me today, and stop yourself from doing so."

"I don't understand."

"I do not wish to live my few remaining days knowing they're my last. Even now, it is so difficult for me to not examine that watch on your wrist, to not uncover the answers I've been seeking all my life. But that would deny me the actual moment of discovery, that eureka moment I've craved for sixty years. No, I want to solve this puzzle myself, and I want to do so without knowing that I will. I want to take that first historic jump through time without knowing it will end me. I want that giddy conversation with my future self that you described, and then the same giddy conversation that I must inevitably repeat with my past self, and I want them both without knowing I am soon to die. I want, in short, the conversation we're having now to have never taken place. Will you promise to make this so for me, m'boy?"

"Of course, sir," I said, finding it increasingly difficult to hide my sniffles. "But isn't there anything I can do to talk you out of this?"

"No. But there's no need to cry. You have made an old man very happy."

* * *

I KEPT MY PROMISE, and popped back to the maintenance room closet just a minute before I got there the first time. Inputting the settings for that jump turned out to be ridiculously easy because the coordinates had remained stored in memory, like a phone number in a cell phone's "recent calls" page.

My other-me's arrival seemed to be the diametrical opposite of the earlier disappearances I had seen. The sound was *"crack"* not *"crunch,"* the burst of wind pushed me backward not forward, and all the gray uniforms fluttered on their hangers. Mother Nature wasn't filling a vacuum this time—she was benevolently making space for something that had never been there before.

The other me—the one who popped in from Huntington Memorial hell-bent on warning the Professor—didn't notice any of it, just as I hadn't noticed any of it on my previous time-jumps. I guess we were just too consumed with our mission to be looking for it, but he was nonetheless quite startled to find me waiting for him.

I told me about my conversation with the Professor, and how he wanted to live his few remaining days exactly as he had, fatal heart attack and all. My other self was reluctant to comply at first, so intent he was, as I had been, to save the great man. But when I reiterated that it was the Professor's final wish, pointed out the sad logic behind his decision, and described the joy he had shown before his passing, he-me, like me-me, realized that we had no choice but to honor the man's last request.

I passed on all the information about the Professor's documents, how to access them, and what to do with them. After that, it took us a while to figure out what to do next. We were both inclined to pop back to the hospital bathroom stall where we began, but how could that work? Would we bump into each other? Would we merge together as one, or cancel each other out? Professor Szabo would know what to do, but he was no longer around for us to ask, and he never would be again.

After much talking to ourselves, it occurred to us that the us at the hospital would *always* want to come back to warn the Professor, and therefore he-we would always have to be stopped. Since I had already done the stopping, it was now my counterpart's turn to remain back to stop the next "us" who came along.

If you think you're confused, imagine how I and me felt. It was crazy confusing.

We said goodbye to ourselves as we wondered if we'd ever see each other again. I set the spatial destination on the watch to the bathroom stall—a simple matter of clicking "apply" because it, too, had remained in the watch's memory—and the temporal destination to "present." Send.

I was in the hospital men's room stall, the very moment I had left the first time. The toilet paper was flapping on its roll, the dust in the air softly descending back to the floor—yes, this time I paid attention—and I could only be grateful that this was a sanitized hospital bathroom and not one in a grimy highway gas station.

I could see my janitor's uniform falling to the ground from the moment I had left the first time. I picked up my trousers to get dressed, then I dropped them again and buried my face in my hands.

The Professor was dead, and I couldn't save him. I had begun two infinite time loops that accomplished nothing. Was this evidence that the past could not be changed after all? Or was it evidence that it could be changed, but that it doesn't matter anyway? Or did the whole little escapade prove squat?

Oh, in case any of you are expecting the Professor to make some Gandalf/Obi Wan type of ghostly resurrection later in this book, nope, it's not going to happen. I tried to save him twice, I did everything I could, but in the end, a kind old man had made his decision, and I had no choice but to honor it.

Professor Aldous Szabo was gone for good, and that was that.

PART 2

FOR PROFIT

CHAPTER ELEVEN

W E WALK ALONG THE STREET, she and I. It's night, and we're holding hands. The dark paved roads glisten and sparkle with the reflection of the city lamps. We're walking on stars.

We stop at a vendor on the curb, a child selling flowers. I buy for my love a single white rose. She purrs and smiles at the gesture. She sniffs the fragrant petals. She puts the stem between her teeth like a Spanish dancer, and she titters playfully. I take her in my arms, we kiss with the stem between our lips, and we giggle.

We know in our hearts that we were once a single soul in Heaven, one entity separated into man and woman who came to Earth to live our lives together, and we will never be apart. We can't be. We are one.

We're in a park, sitting on a bench, and she's sad. She says that she's grown feelings for someone else. She doesn't know how it happened, she says, she never expected or wanted it to happen. Her affection for me remains true, she says, but she has fallen for this other man completely. She will marry him, and our wedding will never be.

I don't understand what she is saying. It makes no sense. It's not possible. I can't look at her.

I know this man who has taken her from me. I had considered him a friend. I'm filled with rage towards this Judas, this snake. I look back to her, my heart filled with pain and fury, and I see the tears rolling down her cheeks. She's crying because she knows she's hurting me, killing me, and all I want to do is wipe away her tears, hold her in my arms, and make her feel better.

I wake up. I'm alone in my apartment, and I let myself cry. I don't know if I'm crying over her, or if I'm grieving for the Professor. I think both. Either way, I cry.

* * *

THAT NIGHT, I KEPT my promise and stole everything the Professor had asked me to steal and deleted all the files he had asked me to delete. It was the easiest job I ever pulled. Not only was I allowed to be alone in his office in the middle of the night, I was supposed to be.

As for sending it all to the NASA guy, I had every intention of keeping that promise too, but I didn't quite see the rush. With this watch on my wrist, I could get all my tuition money in one fell swoop—plus a little more for good measure—then officially retire from my life of crime. If Jean-François had to wait a few extra days, what was the harm? Once he had the power of time travel in his hands, a few days, weeks, months —they would all be the same. I could even just pop back to the same night I stole the files and send it to him then. Plenty of time to work that out.

I briefly considered going back in time to save my mom—if that was even possible—or, in some other way, to make my bleak childhood a little less painful—if that, too, was even possible. I decided against it, though. Professor Szabo had made very clear the possible consequences of altering history, even if the intention was for the good. Besides, if my childhood had been better, I may not have become a thief, wouldn't have tried to steal the Jackson Pollock, wouldn't have been sentenced to San Quentin, hence would never have discovered my life's true calling.

They say that everything happens for a reason. I don't know if that's true, but I don't know that it's not.

I briefly considered retaking my SATs because I now had the ability to get a look at the test days before test day, thereby guaranteeing myself a perfect 1600 score—and that wouldn't change the past at all, only the as-yet-to-be future. I decided against that one, too. If I'm not actually smart enough to be admitted to Caltech or MIT, then I wouldn't be smart enough to keep up with the other students. It was important that the college I go to be the right fit for me.

Professor Szabo's funeral was that Saturday at Mountain View Cemetery in Altadena. It was a beautiful autumn day in Southern California, low seventies, clear blue sky, bright golden sun and warm breeze. Over a thousand people attended, including political figures and prominent businessmen I recognized from the news.

I felt a little uncomfortable amongst all those dignitaries and noblemen, I being nothing but a janitor, but I took solace in the fact that I knew something about the Professor that no one else did—and I was wearing it on my wrist. Forget about its power, it was the nicest watch I owned. I wondered which of these men was the NASA guy, and I delighted in the knowledge that I would soon change his life forever.

It was a lovely service with lots of speeches, lots of tears, and even a little laughter, as those who knew the Professor best recounted some of his more eccentric antics. He would clearly be missed, and not just by me.

When I got home, I went to work. I hopped online in search of the best bank to rob, and I laughed a little laugh as I realized that I was about to become an actual bank robber. Who's Butch and Sundance now?

I knew better than to hit any of the nearby Pasadena branches, and then it occurred to me that I didn't have to hit LA at all. Traveling a million miles is no more difficult than traveling down the block. Talk about the perfect alibi. It would be considered absolutely impossible for me to have robbed a bank in, say, Philadelphia, while so many people had seen me that same day in Pasadena. I chuckled at the thought of the bank managers walking into their perfectly secure vault Monday morning to find so much of their loot gone, and I laughed heartily at the thought of the baffled cops assigned to solve the caper.

I chose a Wells Fargo branch in downtown Atlanta because it had been used as the set for many of the bank's television commercials— smiling faces, no lines, wonderful customer service, you know the type. Through a combination of GPS and those very same ads readily available on YouTube, I was able to pinpoint the precise coordinates of the vault's interior and save it to the watch's memory. Apply. I set the temporal destination to the middle of the night prior, during which I was mopping up at Caltech. I picked up my gym bag that I would soon be stuffing with cash, tapped Send, and I officially became a bank robber . . . except not a very good one.

I was standing in the vault, all alone, sacks of bundled cash everywhere. I was buck naked with a mild tightness in my chest, but no gym bag in my hand. The gym bag hadn't come with me! Yes, obviously, I should have realized that in advance. You probably did, and you were probably laughing at me for missing that very salient point. I guess I had just so excited about being an invincible bank robber that I hadn't properly thought through my plan. I wouldn't make that mistake again.

This was very bad news. If the gym bag couldn't come with me to Atlanta, then the cash wouldn't come back with me to LA—and there was so much of it, all right there for the taking. I picked up a few stacks, then I got an idea.

I pressed the stacks of cash against my naked chest, my arms covering and absorbing them as if they were an actual part of me and could therefore travel along with me. Temporal destination, present. Spatial destination, home. Send.

It didn't work. I popped into my apartment with nothing in my arms at all.

Damn it.

There had to be a way to make this work, and I wasn't willing to give up. What good is being able to freely pop in and out of a locked bank vault if you can't swipe any of the money?

I decided to take an analytic approach. Only the watch and the person wearing it can travel through space-time, that much was clear. A watch and a body. The watch is the watch, something whose workings I would probably never understand, but what is a body? When you come right down to it, a body isn't one thing. It's many things. A body is blood and organs and tissue and muscle and fat and teeth and spit and poop and undigested food and—

Undigested food!

What if, what if...

I raced to the fridge and got out a single grape. I eyeballed the spatial destination for the other side of my apartment, set the temporal destination at present—meaning I wouldn't be traveling through time, only space. I popped the grape into my mouth and let it nestle gently upon my tongue. Send.

I was on the other side of the room, and I was choking to death. The grape had come with me, yes, but it had slid halfway down my throat. I tried to gulp it out but it was lodged in too deep.

I flailed wildly around my apartment, unable to breathe. Was this watch going to kill me, too? Does space-time simply refuse to be messed with?

I slammed myself down hard against the arm of my Ikea sofa in a desperate attempt to give myself the Heimlich. The heinous grape popped out of my mouth, bounced upon and off my Ikea coffee table, and rolled innocently along the floor.

I dropped to the floor as well and tried to catch my breath, but I still wasn't willing to quit. I was making progress. Despite the fact that the little grape had almost killed me, it *had* travelled with me. Clearly, the notion of putting something inside me was a good one. It just couldn't be inside my mouth.

But how can I put something inside me if not in my mouth? Where else?

The answer came to me the moment I asked the question. It was pretty disgusting, true, yet a common prisoner and drug-smuggler trick. I took a dollar bill out of my wallet, and slid it up between my butt cheeks. I eyeballed the spatial destination for across the room, temporal destination for present, and Send.

It didn't work.

I appeared on the other side of the room, and I could see the dollar bill floating gently to the floor in the exact spot in which I had been a moment ago. Was this no different than hugging the stacks of bills to my chest? What if the bill had to be all the way in me, all the way up inside? Ick, but worth a try.

I picked up the dollar, rolled it up like a joint, and then shoved it all the way in like a nasty doctor's finger during a prostate exam. Send.

It worked!

I was on the other side of the room, and I could feel the dollar inside me.

Yes, it hurt a little for it seemed to have quintupled in size. My rectum burned slightly, and my stomach cramped with what felt like mild constipation. But the money did travel. I pulled out the bill to see that it was actually the same size it had always been—the jump had only made it *feel* larger.

It was also really quite gross—brown and soppy, not something anyone would ever accept as legal tender—but it did travel. The next solution was obvious.

The following morning, I went to a nearby Rite Aid and bought myself a box of Ziplocs and a tube of KY Jelly, then headed back home to take another whack at bank robbery. I lubed myself thoroughly, slid one of the empty Ziplocs up inside me, set the temporal destination on the watch to the middle of the night before, and the spatial destination to that same Atlanta Wells Fargo vault. Send.

I was back in the vault, surrounded by sacks of cash. I put five one hundred dollar bills into the Ziploc, the Ziploc up my finely lubed rear end, and hopped back home to drop off the loot and start over with a fresh baggie. The chest and rectal pain were mild, and it seemed like it would all be so easy. Piece of cake, I thought.

In and out of that vault I popped, over and over, in and back and in and back, adding a few hundred dollar bills up my rear with each successive pop. I'll spare you the messy details, but it became quickly apparent that the more bills I shoved up there, the greater the rectal burning and feeling of constipation each jump rendered. Fifteen seemed to be the most I could bear. When I tried twenty, I returned home only to pass out, waking up an hour later with my face in my own vomit.

Okay, maybe I didn't spare you *all* the messy details.

Furthermore, the chest pains were becoming excruciating, and they seemed to grow more severe with each successive jump. I had to wonder what physical damage I was doing to myself, and whether it was all worth it. The answer was yes.

After my ninth trip home, I pulled out the cash-filled Ziploc to find drops of blood on it. By my twelfth, the new Ziploc was drenched in red and brown, and the baggie had actually torn. Six of the bills inside had been rendered completely worthless, and two others questionable. I was sweating, my heart was pounding, and I felt as if I hadn't gone to the bathroom in a month. I decided to call it quits for the night.

Not quite the one-fell-swoop strategy I originally had in mind, but eleven thousand dollars in little more than an hour was nothing to sneeze at.

On the other hand, at fifteen hundred dollars a jump, I would have to make over a hundred more of them to achieve my tuition goals, and I was pretty sure that my body couldn't handle that.

There had to be a better way.

CHAPTER TWELVE

I WOKE UP THE NEXT morning with a pretty ferocious case of constipation and diarrhea, both. I had to go and I couldn't go, all at the same time. What was even worse was that it just happened to be the day of my monthly visit with Seymour.

Phoning in sick always felt like a lame excuse to me, even when it's true, but I really had no choice. I was in no condition to be driving through LA's downtown traffic. For that matter, I was in no condition to be behind a wheel at all. I barely had the strength to walk over to the nearby Rite Aid to purchase a mild laxative—although on that point I forced myself.

Seymour was actually very understanding about it all, at least that's how he presented himself on the phone. I say that because three hours later he was knocking on my door. He claimed he was concerned because I sounded so weak when we had spoken, but it was pretty obvious he came by to check out the veracity of my illness. He said that I looked terrible and that I should sit down, and then he offered to make me a cup of tea, which was really just his excuse to open drawers and cupboards in search of something nefarious. While the water boiled, he took it upon himself to tidy up the place for me, but really just so that he could snoop around some more.

He had made a surprise visit like this once before on the pretext of welcoming me to my new apartment, even though I had moved in six weeks before he came. He had brought me a Yucca Plant that he named Cornelius. It was terrifying—his snooping around, that is, not the plant.

"I see Cornelius is doing well," he said as he opened additional cupboards on the pretense of finding a glass with which to water his gift.

This visit was even scarier than the first because I had the eleven grand from the prior night's score, plus almost that much from all the jobs I had pulled since my release, as well as a shiny watch of silicon and graphene. There would be no way for me to explain all that loot on a janitor's salary, and I'd be back to jail before I could say boo. I wouldn't even have the chance to keep my promise to Professor Szabo.

But as long as Seymour stayed away from my framed print of *The Freewheelin' Bob Dylan* cover that hung on my wall, I'd be okay.

Seymour offered his condolences for Professor Szabo and empathized over how hard it must be for me. I had never hidden my friendship with the old man because there was nothing wrong with it. In fact, it made me look good that a man as important as the Professor would be looking out for me, and it gave Seymour validation in his belief in me as one of his good cancer patients.

I confessed how small I had felt at the funeral, surrounded by so many important people, but Seymour was actually quite supportive, or so he pretended. "Keep up your good work and you'll be important too one day," he said with a smile as he opened my closet on the pretext of hanging up my jacket. "But you really must keep a more organized closet," he added as he pulled out other jackets and games. "Cleanliness is next to Godliness, I always say."

"Yes, sir."

"Stratego! I haven't seen this game in years," he said as he opened the box. It was actually kind of sad how obvious he was, and I could only think that he would have made a terrible criminal.

Just stay away from the *Dylan*, I thought. Just stay away from the *Dylan*.

I told him about the progress I was making on my college applications, which had actually turned out to be a lot more complicated than originally expected. I had thought it would be a simple matter of filling out a few forms, but I was expected to write essays on *why* I wanted to study at each particular institution, *why* I wanted to study physics, why this, why that, and worst of all, an essay about *me*. A couple even required me to describe an ethical dilemma I once faced, and how I dealt with it.

Personally, I think my practice of only stealing from those who can afford it is pretty darn ethical, but I was pretty sure that wasn't what they had in mind.

I knew I couldn't lie about my criminal past because it was public record, but I didn't know if it would make me seem unique and interesting or a threat. Should I downplay it or play it up? At the time of Seymour's visit, I was still struggling with that.

I told Seymour that I had narrowed down my final choices, and would be applying to Caltech and MIT, duh, Berkeley, UCLA, three other UC schools, and the University of Redlands. It was exactly the kind of stuff he liked to hear. He always creamed when he saw me making legitimate progress—you should have seen his face when I told him about my SAT scores—and that pretty much wrapped up our little meeting.

He paused to tell me one last thing, but I could barely focus on his words because that was the moment when he began to straighten out the *Dylan* print on the wall. He just stared at the thing as he said something about taking his wife to a Broadway show a few weeks later, or a few months later, or something like that. It was lucky he knew I was sick or my flop sweats would have surely given me away.

"Bob Dylan, eh?" he said disparagingly as he straightened the frame one final time. "Me, I like the Monkees. Wish you a speedy recovery, T.J."

And he left.

Jeez, right?

* * *

I PHONED IN SICK from work that night even though I was feeling a little bit better. The laxatives were working, but perhaps too well because now I was going every ten minutes—although that was still preferable to not being able to go at all.

I was channel surfing later that night, and just happened to land on CNBC when I felt the sudden urge to go again, and with no time to waste. I mean, sorry again to be gross, but these urges were coming without warning.

I could hear the finance pundits from my bathroom boasting about their great stock picks that had made their followers rich beyond Midas, and attacking each other over the wrong ones that had rendered their followers paupers. I remember thinking what a shame it was that the Professor's Apple Watch couldn't travel to the future. How simple would that be? Pop into some future year, find out what the hot stocks are, come back to the present and invest in them—one single journey, there and back, and I'd be done. No fuss, no muss, and the watch would be delivered to the NASA guy even earlier than expected.

Then it hit me. What about the past?

Duh!

It wouldn't be at all difficult to find out what stocks skyrocketed over the years. Pop back to some point during the Great Depression when everything was cheap, make one single investment—hence one single, solitary trip—then come home to collect a fortune. Technically, it wasn't even illegal.

Then I remembered Professor Szabo's warning about altering the past, how it could possibly lead to my never being born, and how it could even possibly lead to the destruction of the world. Hadn't he referred to it as a nuclear warhead?

But he had also said it may have no consequences at all. Weren't my attempts to save his life proof of that? I mean, I had changed *how* he died, but I couldn't stop him from actually dying.

Still, it was too big a risk to take. The Professor had entrusted me with his life's work. It was one thing to hang on to it for personal gain a little bit longer than I should, but it was quite another to use it to end life as we know it.

But my curiosity was piqued. How much money were we even talking about? What would be the nuts and bolts of such a venture?

I went online and taught myself everything from scratch—good thing I have a natural propensity for numbers. It was fun, actually. It seemed that 1932 would be the best year during which to invest, for that was when the stock market had hit bottom. IBM seemed to be the best company, for it was big enough in 1932 to make a sizable cash investment without raising any eyebrows, and it remained a major player through the decades. Merrill Lynch would be the choice for broker because it was respectable in 1932, hence probably honest, and is still in existence today.

I learned that thousand-dollar bills were quite common in the 1930s, and that there are plenty of antique currency dealers online today who would be willing to secure them for you for a fee. I figured that if I could find ten such bills, I could pull the whole job in one single time-trip, and at only two-thirds of my maximum butt allowance.

I factored in growth rate, stock splits, dividend reinvestment, compound interest, and inflation. I would only do one jump so that would be a ten-thousand-dollar buy-in, and no more. I calculated it all, and here's what I got:

Ten thousand dollars invested in IBM in 1932 would be, in 2017, just shy of one hundred and forty million dollars.

That couldn't be right, I told myself. That was way too high. I calculated it again and came up with the same answer. I calculated it a third time, same answer.

One hundred and forty million dollars!

I only needed a couple of hundred thousand for my tuition, after which I'd be receiving a fine salary. Even if I kept an additional million or two so I could be a physicist who drinks Pappy Van Winkle every night, I could give Wendy five million so she could retire in the lifestyle she deserves, then I could pour all the rest, over a hundred and thirty million dollars, into fixing the foster care system so no child would ever have to grow up the way I did.

I'd be a goddamn hero. Me, a hero, imagine that.

Or, I could destroy the world.

Damn it.

What if I was very careful? I wondered.

No, came my immediate response. I had had enough conversations with the Professor to know that there was no such thing as "careful." Something as simple as hailing a cab could have enormous repercussions. The person who was supposed to take that taxi would have to wait for the next one, and he'd arrive at his location later than he would have in the first reality. Perhaps in that first reality he had met the love of his life, married, and had a child who would grow up to be important, or that child would have a child who would grow up to be important—yet because of me, the couple would never meet.

Or, perhaps our taximan would be late for a job interview, and his tardiness would cost him. Someone else would get that job, affecting the lives of his, say, twenty other co-workers. How many lives would they affect in turn? Perhaps our taximan would get another job, one that would have gone to someone else in the first reality, affecting the lives of all of taximan's new co-workers, the man who was supposed to have had the job in the first place, and all the people in all of their lives.

What if I walked?

No, I knew that wasn't the point. My mere presence could have consequences beyond the imagination. There was no such thing as careful, and I simply couldn't risk it. No decent person could. It was more frustrating than being alone in a bank vault without the ability to snatch the loot.

Then I noticed something odd. Something startling and unnerving.

Before I had begun my calculations, my last bit of Internet research had been on Merrill Lynch. My laptop was still open to its page on which was a photograph of its swanky lobby in its swanky Wall Street head office. I enlarged my screen to confirm that what I thought I had seen was correct, and, oh my goodness, it was.

On one of the lobby walls hung an old black and white photograph taken in the original Merrill Lynch building, dated November 16, 1932. It was a picture of the original Charles Merrill and the original Edmund Lynch, along with a bunch of other stodgy white guys . . . and me!

I was in the back row, smiling and winking into the camera. I was there! Will be there! Am there! Whatever the correct tense of the verb, I didn't care! The me in that picture was clearly the second part of an infinite time loop that had already begun. I could go back to 1932 because I already had gone back to 1932 therefore I *must* go back to 1932! I wouldn't be changing history, I'd be fulfilling it!

Time itself had bequeathed me just shy of one hundred and forty million dollars!

Thank you, Time.

CHAPTER THIRTEEN

A VENTURE SUCH AS THIS had very little margin for error so I planned it out meticulously. A few little hiccups came to light along the way, but nothing that couldn't be solved with a little imagination.

First and most obvious, I would be arriving in 1932 naked so I would need immediate access to clothes. I used the Internet to scope out a rather posh men's clothing store in midtown Manhattan that I could pop into late one night. Small retail stores, then and now, typically lock their doors with a key from the outside, with no latch or button to press from within. In other words, although I wouldn't be breaking into the store, I would need to break out of it. That wouldn't pose much of a problem for a burglar of my caliber, especially back then, but it did mean that I would have to travel with one of my lock picks up my butt. The most versatile of my little picks, my half diamond, was only a few millimeters long and even less thick. I had had it since I was a kid, and it never let me down. Done. Next.

Unlike today where the stock market is electronic, back in the thirties, actual paper certificates were issued. Communications were conducted by snail mail so I wouldn't—won't? didn't?—receive the certificate until several weeks after the purchase. I'd need an address to which my brokers could mail it, and I'd need some form of legal identification before I could even open a brokerage account through which to make my investment. I knew how to take care of the ID problem—I had learned that in San Quentin—but that, too, would take time.

The upshot was that I would have to stay in 1932 for quite a while so I would require money to support myself. I'd need to bring eleven, not ten, thousand-dollar bills back with me—ten to invest, one on which to live. That would be the rough equivalent of twenty thousand dollars today, so plenty. I'd also need to start off with at least one smaller bill for any immediate expenses because I couldn't expect some corner store or cabbie to make change for something as big as a thousand, bringing my bill tally up to twelve. If I counted my little lock pick as three bills, that would make fifteen, and I was up to my carry limit once more. Ick, but problem solved.

I scoped out a section of old Greenwich Village in which I intended to rent a room. The Village seemed like a cool place to hang for a few months, not too expensive at three dollars a week, and not too far from Wall Street. Lodging, done.

A 1928 thousand-dollar bill would cost me two thousand dollars per bill, give or take depending on the seller, plus commissions, fees and taxes—that is, if I had any intention of paying for them. I found seven major antique currency dealers around the country that had old thousands and twenties in stock—and all in surprisingly pristine condition—but I didn't want to steal more than two or three bills from each because it seemed mean to hit any one of them too hard.

I still had to work my night job at Caltech so I did my robbing during the day, then time-jumped back to the night prior. I discovered that the pain was manageable as long as I gave myself a few days of rest between each pop, and as long as I didn't stuff myself to capacity. I also realized that the greater the distance I'd travel, be it temporal or spatial, the greater the pain. Needless to say, I wasn't looking forward to jumping eighty-five years across a continent with a literal butt load of cash.

The next problem to solve was how to get the stock certificate back with me to the present. If the Ziploc can tear once, it can tear again, and there was no point going through all this trouble only to come home with a hundred-and-forty-million-dollar document rendered worthless by blood and poop.

My first thought was to place it in a locker in Grand Central Station where it would await me for eighty-five years, except that Grand Central stopped providing lockers after 9/11. My next thought was to have it wait for me in a safety deposit box, except safety deposit boxes are tied to bank accounts, and bank accounts get shut down if they remain dormant for too long—they began that unfortunate practice way back in 1962. I had one other idea. Pretty low tech and a little risky, but I was pretty sure I could make it work.

It did, however, mean that I would have to make my return to modern day New York, so I wanted everything to be set, ready, and waiting for me. I went online in search of a hotel room—cheap and discreet being my primary criteria. Cheap because I didn't know how long I would need it, and discreet because if anyone paid attention to my comings and goings, it would appear as if I hadn't left the room for weeks at a time, raising the question of why I hadn't starved to death.

It only took me five calls to find the winner, an anonymous little hotel on the outskirts of Jersey City, just a forty-five-minute cab ride to Wall Street. I asked the man about their room rates, and he laughed as if he had never been asked such a question before, then asked if I wanted to rent by the night or by the hour. I knew in an instant the kind of place it was—some roach-infested rat hole where nobody asked questions. It was perfect. I booked a room for two days hence. The guy didn't even ask for a credit card.

And no, I had no intention of taking advantage of any women who may be there. My taste in working girls runs toward the elite. Besides, I'd be on a job.

I scoped out a remote abandoned spot in the 1932 boonies that remains untouched in the present day, about thirty miles from the Jersey hotel, stored its coordinates into the watch's memory, then FedExed two packages to myself at the hotel address so they would be waiting for me upon my arrival. In one I placed my driver's license, social security card, and other forms of legitimate ID that I knew I would need, and in the other I placed an untraceable cell phone and five thousand dollars in cash that had been hiding behind my *Freewheelin' Bob Dylan* poster. I sent them in separate packages because I didn't trust the hotel people not to steal my cash, and the ID was actually far more valuable for my purposes.

I waited a few days, performing my Caltech janitorial duties all the while. During that time, I went online to find a men's clothing store not too far from the Jersey hotel. The first four shops I looked at were too specialized, selling suits but no shoes, shoes but no pants . . . you get the idea. The next batch I found were fine clothing-wise, but they had alarm systems that were unnecessarily sophisticated for my needs. At last I stumbled upon the winner—or loser, depending on your point of view. It had everything I required—an alarm system I was quite familiar with, no motion detectors, and the apparel was even quite trendy.

I lubed myself thoroughly, put my trusty lock pick and a few hundred-dollar bills into a Ziploc—the cash needed in case the hotel people stole the money I had FedExed to myself. I slid the Ziploc up inside me, set the spatial destination on the watch to inside the shop, and the temporal destination to three o'clock of the prior morning. Send.

I was in the store, naked, in the dead of night. The chest pain was relatively minor because I had only travelled twelve hours, but the rectal pain was insane! Crazy insane! Oh my God! The tiny scrap of metal in my bowels felt like a freshly sharpened katana ripping me apart from the inside. The pain knocked me to my knees. I yanked the contemptible hardware out of my innards as fast as I could, yet the agony remained.

I knew right then that there was no way I could carry the lock pick inside me through an eighty-five-year time-jump as I had planned, for it would most certainly kill me. I'd have to come up with some other way to find clothing in the thirties.

Also, the Ziploc tore again, and my hundred-dollar bills were ruined —my fear confirmed—so I was glad I had come up with an alternate plan to get the stock certificate home. Still, I would have to give the Ziplocs' unreliability some serious consideration to protect the cash I would need to take with me to the thirties.

It was almost twenty minutes before I could stand again, and even then, I was moving pretty slowly. The tiny flashlight on the watch was perfect for burglary, for it was both bright and intensely unidirectional. The odds of someone passing by to see the moving light at three in the morning were slim to begin with, and I had developed a third eye over the years to look out for such things just in case.

I selected a nice pair of embroidered jeans, a plaid shirt, a black leather jacket perfect for a Northeast autumn, and a super cool pair of red high-tops. I hobbled toward the cash register and took five twenties from the till. I could have taken more, but the shop didn't seem very successful so I figured I was taking enough.

I wobbled to the back of the shop and disengaged the alarm system, then limped back toward the front door. It took me less than a minute to pick the lock, then even less than that to relock it from the outside—with luck, they wouldn't even know they'd been robbed.

If you wonder why I didn't take any other clothes, it was because I didn't want to be walking through the city in the dead of night with a shopping bag with the store's name on it. There would be plenty of cash waiting for me at the hotel—God willing—so I could buy a new wardrobe the old-fashioned way the next day.

I walked several blocks as briskly as my achy rectum would allow, tearing the price tags off my new clothes along the way. Fortunately, I was able to hail a taxi to take me the rest of the way to the sleazy hotel that was called, simply, "HOTEL." Three of the neon lights were burned out so from a distance it looked to be named "HO"—a fitting moniker for a place that rents by the hour.

I checked in without a hitch. Both my FedEx packages were waiting for me, and nothing had been taken from either. I was impressed. I told the clerk that I wanted to keep the room for the whole month, and we negotiated a rental price of nine hundred and ninety-five dollars, as long as I prepaid in cash. It was obvious that he thought he was getting the better of the deal, but it was far cheaper than anything I could ever find in Manhattan.

I slogged my way up the stairs to my third-story room—establishments such as these tend to lack elevators. The room itself was a rather typical hotel room, only smaller and dirtier. My stomach and behind still killing, I collapsed on the bed—not *in* the bed, for obvious reasons— where I would sleep till noon the next day. I barely noticed the screaming yelps of fake orgasms that blasted through the walls.

* * *

I woke up the next morning feeling only slightly better, meaning pretty awful. The flu symptoms I was experiencing were more severe than those I had experienced after that first night of bank robbing. I dragged myself out of bed and hobbled off to the nearest pharmacy chain where I bought a box of laxatives, a jug of orange Gatorade, a box of crackers because I knew I'd have to force myself to eat a little, a set of bed sheets because I didn't trust the ones the hotel provided, and the new John Grisham book because the TV in my room had no reception. After three days, I felt ready to get to work.

I had a light breakfast at a nearby Cuban diner, then set out to purchase a more extensive wardrobe, obviously avoiding the shop that I had robbed the morning I arrived. Next, I stopped at the closest FedEx depot to ship my half-diamond lock pick to myself in LA because I didn't want to travel with it up my butt ever again. I knew I could buy a new one back home, but the little guy had been with me since I was a kid so it just felt wrong to throw him away.

I went back to the room where I neatly put away my new clothes, then I scoped out various strategic spots where I could hide what remained of my five grand. There was a loose tile in the bathroom floor, so under that was good for a stack. The heating vent was easy to pry off the wall, so that was good for a few more. Like that. I hid two hundred dollars in my underwear drawer because it is the lamest hiding place in the world. If anyone were to steal my cash, that's where he or she would take it from, and it wouldn't occur to most people to keep looking for more. It was a way to test the hotel people, yet also an insurance policy. Yeah, I'll risk two hundred bucks to save over four thousand any day of the week.

You may want to consider doing the same if you ever travel with a lot of cash.

By the end of that first day, I had accomplished everything I needed. It had been four days since my last jump, my butt would be empty, and it was time to go home. I set the spatial destination to my Pasadena apartment, and the temporal destination for the very same moment I had left in the first place so I could perform my janitorial duties that night with no trace of ever having been gone. Send.

Chest pain minor, rectal pain nil.

I quickly set to work on a new entry plan—a.k.a., access to 1930s clothes without the need of a lock pick—and it didn't take me long to come up with an idea. The Internet is replete with photographs of Depression-era back alleys in which freshly washed laundry hangs on raggedy old clotheslines. It took only moderate effort to pinpoint the exact location of one not too far from a JCPenney where I could buy a pair of shoes, and I had my spatial destination stored in memory. Done.

Furthermore, since I would no longer be taking my lock pick with me, my butt would have room for three additional Ziplocs to safeguard against any tearing—no guarantee it would work, but I was hopeful. What choice did I have?

I got a haircut so I would blend in. I watched old movies to absorb the vernacular. I downloaded films, TV shows, books, and music into the watch so I'd have something to do while I was back there, as well as a road map of 1932 Manhattan to help me find my way around. Done, done, and done.

After five weeks of research and prep, I was ready.

* * *

IT WAS A MONDAY MORNING, D-day as I called it, and I was nervous as hell. Despite all my careful planning, I had no idea of what truly lay in store.

I put the twelve bills into a Ziploc, that one into another, that in another, and that in yet another. I lubed myself thoroughly, and then shoved my investment up inside me. I set the spatial destination for the back alley, and the temporal destination for six months prior to the date on the photograph of Mr. Merrill, Mr. Lynch, and myself.

I paused to run through my plan one last time to make sure I hadn't missed anything. This problem solved, check. That problem solved, check. I had my entry plan, my investment plan, and my exit plan. I had eleven thousand and twenty dollars in my intestine. My ID and over four thousand dollars in cash were waiting for me in my sleazy Jersey hotel room, and every spatial destination I would need was stored and labeled in the watch's address book, as well as a few I didn't expect to need at all, just in case. Best I could tell, I had covered everything.

I took a deep breath. Send.

I was there, June 1932, and my bowels felt like they were on fire. My chest felt as if a pair of elephants had danced a Conga upon it. My belly felt as if the alien from *Aliens* was going to burst out through me from the inside. My head was foggy, and my eyes felt as if they'd been stabbed with a blunt chisel. I was unable to stand, my knees buckled, and I fell to the ground.

Wet newspapers and garbage were flying all over the place. I lay on my back on the gravelly alley floor reeling in pain, and it was cold. I was freezing, and I was wet. I realized that it was raining, raining hard, pouring ice-cold cats and dogs upon me, and there was not a single item of clothing on the clotheslines.

The weather. I forgot to check the weather.

Idiot.

CHAPTER FOURTEEN

I WAS AWAKENED BY THE clucking sound of gossipy housewives, and I barely remembered crawling toward the alley wall to hide between the two garbage cans before losing consciousness. The sun was up but the sky was gray. My naked skin was dry but my hair was still a bit wet so I figured it had stopped raining sometime in the past twenty minutes. My watch told me I had been out for almost twenty hours.

The six or seven different women had their heads poking out through their various apartment windows, hanging the wet clothes that they couldn't the day before because of the rain, seeming to have organized laundry day into a social event like a modern era "let's-hang-out-at-Starbucks." Fortunately, they were all in the same building against which I was leaning, hence angled in such a way that they couldn't see me. I brought my knees in closer to my chest just in case, but I knew there would be no way for me to avoid being seen if anyone looked out a window in the building across the way.

The stomach flu symptoms I was experiencing were even more severe than they had been after my pop to Jersey City, and I had a mild head cold to boot because of the twenty hours I had spent naked in the cold rain. My throat was scratchy, my nose runny, and I had to time my coughs and sneezes to coincide with the housewives' laughter so as not to be heard. It was pretty bad.

Then, just as I feared, a window on the other side of the alley slid open and a new housewife joined the conversation. "Hi Millie, Hi Gladys," she began, interrupting herself the moment she saw a naked man leaning against her neighbors' wall. "What are you doing?!" she shouted at me, far more an accusation than a question.

My mind raced as I searched for a good lie, but there weren't any. The only thing I could think of saying was that I had been mugged and left for dead, but then why hadn't the robbers taken the fancy, shiny watch on my wrist?

"Harry!" the woman screamed out for her husband.

I had to run. I had to just grab the first batch of clothes I could get my hands on, then get the hell out of Dodge. But could I run in my condition? And would the first batch of clothes I could grab even fit me? Would they be adult clothes? Would they be men's? I wouldn't have time to get dressed before the husbands came after me, and I certainly couldn't run out onto the street in the buff. I had nowhere to go.

"What is it, Edna?" asked one of the other housewives.

Then it hit me. Much as I didn't want to, I set the watch for three hours later.

"There's a naked man sitting against—"

Send.

It was mid-afternoon, the warm June sun now felt nice upon my skin, and I was alone in the alley once more. The additional pain from the three-hour pop wasn't too harsh, but I had yet to recover from the eighty-five-year jump I had done the day before so I was still in pretty poor shape.

I felt a little bad for Edna who had seen a naked man across the alley simply vanish into thin air. How would she explain what she had seen to her friends, to her husband, to herself? Unfortunately, there wasn't anything I could do about that.

I was also a little worried that allowing Edna to see me disappear may have somehow changed the past. I knew I had been born—that part was certain because I wouldn't have been able to worry about it had I not been—but had I altered history? According to Professor Szabo, I wouldn't know it if I had because I would have grown up in a world in which the change I caused was the only reality I knew. ISIS, Al-Qaeda, crazy American gunmen gunning down schoolchildren? Was that my fault? How could I know what I can't know?

I made the assumption that the prior me, or "me's", who had come back to 1932 before me would have also forgotten to check the weather in advance, would have therefore ended up in the same predicament as I had, would have therefore also been spotted by Edna, and would have therefore also vanished before her eyes because it was our only option of escape. In other words, once again, I hadn't altered history, I had fulfilled it. This was only an assumption, of course, but I had nothing else to go on, and I would make myself crazy if I kept trying to understand that which could not be understood. Back to work.

The clotheslines were fully stocked, the clothes close to dry, so I could take my time picking out an appropriate outfit. The pain in my belly and bowels made it difficult for me to stand up, and I realized it was a good thing I hadn't tried to run. I staggered toward one of the clotheslines and picked out a nice white shirt from one, a pair of brown trousers from another, brown socks from a third, and a cloth handkerchief from a fourth. There didn't seem to be any men's underwear but it wouldn't be the first time I had to go commando. I got dressed, then took the giant wad out of my butt—thank God.

I could see that the outer Ziploc had indeed torn, brown and red and gross, but the bills inside looked fresh and clean, so at the very least the inner baggie had held firm. Good thinkin', Teej! I took out the bills and put them in one pocket, and the gross Ziplocs in another to be dealt with later. I removed the Apple Watch from my wrist and put it in the pocket with my cash so no one would see it and ask questions, then I wobbled out of the alley in search of a pair of shoes.

*　*　*

THE MANHATTAN OF 1932 didn't seem much different than it does today—bearing in mind that I say that as one who has never actually been there, and that all my prior knowledge of the town came from movies. The streets were crowded with cars, and the sidewalks were crowded with people, all of whom were in a hurry.

My biggest surprise was the colors. Everything I had ever seen from the Great Depression had been in black and white so I guess I subconsciously always assumed it to be a gray world—I mean, it was called the "Depression," right? But the grass was still green, the sky blue, the sun yellow, the billboards vibrant, and the few women who chose to dress flamboyantly sported the entire spectrum. Also, there were no fat people, everyone wore hats, and the big cars were really cool.

I walked into the JCPenney and immediately asked for a bathroom. I sat on the john for close to twenty minutes to try to make something happen, but I failed.

I headed over to the men's shoes department and picked out a pair of brown Penguin Waylons to match my trousers, and a new pair of socks because the one I was wearing was filthy from walking the streets. The socks cost ten cents, and the shoes four dollars—I guess the world had yet to come up with the whole $3.99 ruse.

I took a cab to the Village where I intended to rent a room, stopping at a pharmacy along the way. I didn't recognize any of the 1930s products so I had to ask the pharmacist for help. When I described all my symptoms, he suggested I see a doctor. I thanked him for his advice, purchased everything he had suggested, as well as a jar of Vaseline because it seemed the best time-travel lube they had in the era.

Renting the room was pretty straightforward. Nothing to sign and no ID required, just a simple matter of handing the super one week's rent in exchange for a key. He said the furnished rooms cost thirty percent more so I gave the man three dollars and ninety cents, then headed to my new quarters to collapse.

The room itself was nothing to speak of—pale blue walls, a single twin bed on an iron frame, a little wood table with two wood chairs, a small closet, a little kitchenette area I probably wouldn't use, and a small bathroom with a tub but no shower. It suited my needs just fine, and the bathroom was my first stop.

A little came out but not enough.

I filled the sink with warm water, and dropped in the Ziplocs to soak. To the naked eye, three of them had no tears, but I could see water seeping into one of those three, meaning that only two had remained intact. I would do an intensive, thorough cleaning once I felt better, when standing wasn't such a struggle.

I put the watch back on my wrist because there were only two places I could ever allow it to be—on my wrist when in the privacy of my room, and in my left front trouser pocket while out in public because I obviously couldn't let anyone in the thirties see such a thing. Either way, I absolutely always needed to know exactly where it was.

I took my mystery drugs, hoped that they would cure me and not kill me, and then got into bed. I was so exhausted that I didn't even notice the springs stabbing into my back through the ultra-thin mattress, and I wouldn't for another three days, at which time I started to feel better and could finally get to work.

CHAPTER FIFTEEN

D ESPITE A RATHER INAUSPICIOUS BEGINNING, my months in 1932 plodded along without a hitch. In fact, it was almost too easy. My biggest challenge was the boredom I had to endure between jumps. That's the problem with a perfectly laid-out plan—the execution of it lacks adventure.

During the bulk of my stay, I had most of my meals at the deli down the block from my room. The food was good, inexpensive, and most of the waitresses were quite cute. I knew better than to hit on any of them, or even engage them in any sort of meaningful conversation, for fear of altering the past. Another firm rule I had given myself was not to speak to anyone unless I absolutely had to, and even then, to make as little of an impression as possible. I couldn't even crack a joke. It was hard.

I had never been put in solitary confinement at San Quentin, but I imagined it not very different from my life in the thirties, except for the better food and sunlight. And the people all around you. And freedom. Okay, it probably wasn't similar at all.

I would order my meals then bury my head in that day's edition of the New York Times, which turned out to be a pretty interesting experience because so many of the stories had reporters guessing at things of which I already knew the outcome. The Democratic National Convention was soon to start, and Franklin Roosevelt, running as an outsider, was considered sure to lose. It would have been so much fun to tell everyone around me that he'd serve close to four terms as president, thereby becoming the greatest insider our country had ever known. That's the thing about outsiders—they lose their shiny outsider status the moment they win.

Also, Coke tasted much better back then. Also, they pronounced it Coca-Cola.

On my first morning of good health, I scrubbed the Ziplocs to pristine perfection, then carefully hid them along with my cash in various strategic spots in the room. I couldn't imagine what a 1930s person would make of such a thing, and I didn't want to risk having to answer any questions about it.

Next, I went to a nearby bank and got change for one of my thousand-dollar bills. As I had learned from my research, such bills were so common back then that no one batted an eye.

"How would you like it?" asked the clerk with the green bow tie and visor in a high-pitched, squeaky voice.

"Twenties, tens, fives and ones, please."

"What, no twos? What've you got against the twos?"

Twos? There were twos?

"I meant to say twos. Yes, twos also, please."

He counted them out at lightning speed, and that was that.

Next, I set out to purchase a full wardrobe, as well as a suitcase and a shovel—I'll tell you why later. The shovel was sturdy and solid, the suitcase, a heavy, clunky contraption made of leather and wood because man had yet to come up with the notion of attaching wheels.

I washed the clothes that I had taken from the clotheslines, then snuck back to the alley to return them because, again, I don't steal from people who can't afford to lose what I take. I even left a two dollar bill on Edna's windowsill to make up for her having to see a naked man vanish before her eyes, thereby making her think she was crazy—two bucks then being akin to about thirty-five today. I felt it was the least I could do, and also the most, and I was pretty confident that the me's who came before me would have felt the same way, hence done the same thing.

The next several days were spent at the New York City Public Library scouring the obituary sections of decades old newspapers. It wasn't until the start of my third week in the Great Depression that I found what I needed.

Clarence Roy Jameson had been born in Buffalo Mercy Hospital in February of 1901, then died of influenza three years later in Albany. I telephoned the Buffalo hospital, told them I was Clarence, and that my birth certificate had gotten lost during my recent move to New York City. They asked for my current address, then told me it would take four to six weeks for me to receive my new one in the mail.

By the way, this would not work in our post-9/11 world in which identity theft runs rampant. If you want to obtain a fake ID today, you'll just have to find a legitimate forger like everyone else. It was a more trusting time back then.

Through the duration of my search, I spent most of my nights in my room reading *To Kill a Mockingbird* for the first time, or binge-watching seasons one and two of *Game of Thrones* for the second. The series loses much of its epic majesty on a wristwatch-sized screen, but it's still a very compelling story. At bedtime, I would let Bob Dylan and Joni Mitchell lullaby me to sleep.

I went to see the original *Scarface* in a very majestic theater. It wasn't very good. The crowd oohed and aahed over the violent scenes that were barely violent at all. No blood, no guts spewing, come on. The Pacino remake was much better.

Needless to say, I was quite glad when I finally discovered Clarence. I knew I wouldn't have to wait around for the birth certificate to arrive in the mail because it had been weeks since my last time-jump, I felt fine, and I'd be jumping with an empty butt. I prepaid two months rent, set the temporal destination on the Apple Watch six weeks forward, and the spatial destination at "current." Send.

Rectal pain nil. The chest pain was notable, but nothing compared to the eighty-five-year jump I had made. I simply had to sit down for a few minutes, drink a little water, and I was fine. I checked my mail, and there lay my spanking new birth certificate.

I was ready to make my investment—except for the fact that I wasn't. I knew from the photograph of Merrill, Lynch, and me that I was to be in their building in mid-November, and it was only August. Everything had gone better and faster than anticipated, with no real problems to take up the additional time I had given myself just in case. I'd have to do another jump, but I had just done one that same day.

Three more days to kill. *Thrones, Mockingbird*, Dylan, Joni, added Pete Seeger.

The New York Yankees were in town—first time they'd been in town at the same time as me since I'd arrived—and I was very excited to get to see Babe Ruth and Lou Gehrig play live. The 1932 Yankees are considered to be one of the greatest teams in the history of the sport, with a win-loss record of 107-47, finishing the season thirteen wins over the second place Philadelphia Athletics to take the pennant, then beating the Chicago Cubs in four straight to win the World Series.

I dished out three dollars for the best available seat, got myself a dog and a Coke (no beer thanks to Prohibition), then I sat down to enjoy what no one born in 1989 could possibly witness firsthand.

Babe Ruth actually wasn't that fat by modern standards. Today we'd call him plump, a little overweight maybe, but certainly not fat. He went 0 for 3 with a walk, Gehrig went 1 for 4 with a fluky blooper base hit, and the Yankees lost to the Washington Senators by a score of 7-1. It could not have been more disappointing.

* * *

FOR AN ERA FAMOUS for its poverty, the Merrill, Lynch, Pierce, Fenner & Smith building sure was grand. It was tall and imposing with great stone columns and red brick walls adorned with ornate fasciae. It wasn't hard to imagine that this company would be worth billions some day.

The inside was even more impressive. Heavy oakwood walls enveloped an expansive marble floor, and it was loud, busy, and chaotic. I didn't see any offices for it was all one giant space in which two hundred stockbrokers sat at two hundred separate wooden desks on which lay multiple telephones. White men of all ages sat on pews gazing at a massive chalkboard, while teenage boys erased and wrote in new prices for each issue as the ticker tape instructed. IBM was selling for $31.05.

I told the receptionist of my intentions, and she told me to take a seat while she found me a broker. It was a very short wait before an affable young man in a gray pinstripe suit stepped out of the chaos with his hand stretched out to shake mine. He seemed to be only a few years older than me, an inch shorter, a pound or two skinnier, with a warm smile and a cheerful disposition.

"Mr. Jameson? I'm Gregory Dixon. I understand you'd like to make an investment. Let's see if we can help you out. Come with me, please."

He led me into the bowels of the chaos where we took our seats on opposite sides of his desk. He pleasantly asked what I was looking to do, and I told him I had ten thousand dollars I wanted to invest in IBM. His face went blank.

"Mr. Jameson, if I may make a suggestion. INS. Insull Utility Trust. Now, I have no doubt you have some kind of hunch about this IBM, maybe you heard some rumors, but a tabulating machine company will only take you so far. INS is electricity, and electricity is the future."

I let him go through his spiel because I couldn't exactly say I was actually *from* the future and therefore had a metaphorical crystal ball. His demeanor was so affable that I couldn't tell if he was truly trying to be helpful and was just plain wrong, or if he was trying to jack up the price of a stock he had gotten stuck with, or if he was simply peddling the garbage his higher-ups wanted him to peddle. He reminded me of Juan Gomez, my San Quentin, con artist cellie, who was also perpetually affable.

Before Gregory finished—just as he was describing the mansions and yachts I'd be able to afford if I took his advice—something in the distance caught my attention. "I'm sorry, Mr. Dixon, but would you excuse me for one moment please?"

He found my request odd but gave his consent anyway. "Of course, Mr. Jameson. I'm at your service."

On the far side of the giant space, Charles Merrill, Edmund Lynch, and a bunch of stodgy white guys—three of whom I assumed were Pierce, Fenner, and Smith—stood in three rows in front of a photographer and his assistant setting up for a shot. I had always assumed that I would be invited into the picture, and I was a little offended that I'd have to sneak my way into it. But we do what we've got to do.

I hung back till the last possible moment, then casually planted myself next to the white guy on the far right of the third row. He looked at me oddly so I flashed him my world-class, disengaging smile as if I belonged. He nodded and smiled back.

I imagined the future me, or prior me, accidentally discovering this very same photograph on his laptop in 2017, so I smiled and winked at him-me to give me-us the permission to come back here and acquire a fortune. That was the only reason I was smiling and winking in an era when people didn't smile in photographs at all.

Poof! The big camera erupted in a puff of smoke and a flash of light, then I casually strolled away before anyone had a chance to give me a second thought.

I returned to Gregory and thanked him for his advice, then explained that I only had ten thousand dollars to invest, that I knew a great deal about "tabulating machines," and that I had a very strong feeling about IBM. He accepted my decision graciously, and said that it was my money and that he was only there to help me.

"But mark my words, Mr. Jameson. INS. When you see the folly of investing in tabulating machines, come back to me. We can absorb your losses and turn them into profit by simply transferring it over. It's a simple sell and buy. I'm here for you."

After that, it was merely a matter of showing him Clarence's birth certificate and filling out a few forms, which were a lot shorter and less complicated than they would be today. There was a one-pager to open a brokerage account, another to show that I had indeed deposited ten thousand and eighty-eight dollars—the eighty-eight to cover the broker's commission—and a third authorizing all my future dividends to be immediately reinvested. He said that the trade would be called in and initiated the next day so he couldn't guarantee the exact price, although he didn't expect it to stray too far from its current $31.05 per share, and that I would receive my stock certificate in the mail in four to six weeks.

"Welcome to the world of finance," he said proudly as he shook my hand.

And that was that.

Three more days to kill.

* * *

I GAVE SOME THOUGHT as to why time travel hurts so much. My best guess was that it had something to do with the electromagnetic charge surrounding me, like sticking one's finger into a light socket except with

Einsteinian consequences (I made up that word, I think.) Or maybe it was because when I popped into a new reality, I had to shove the old air out of the way, and the air shoved me back. Truth is, I had no idea. I wished I were smarter. I missed the Professor.

One of the big hit movies of the year was *Tarzan the Ape Man.* It was dreadful, but the crowd loved it. Maybe the movie industry was just too young for its fans to have developed any actual taste.

I had once heard that *Tarzan* had been filmed in Tarzana, California, before it was built up—hence the name—and the jungles I saw would one day become the concrete suburb where I lived with cruel foster parents, and where I lived when Wendy first started taking me out for milkshakes. It had been so long since I had seen my beloved Fagin, and I missed her terribly. I reminded myself that I was going to make her rich, and that helped a little. (I would learn much later that Tarzana was actually the estate of Edgar Rice Burroughs, the author of the *Tarzan* books, and that the movie was filmed on the MGM lot. Still, I missed Wendy.)

More *Thrones*, more *Mockingbird.* Dylan, Joni, Pete, added Woody Guthrie.

Three days later I jumped six weeks forward, checked my mail slot, and there it was. My stock certificate!

I had done it!

Three hundred twenty-four shares of IBM, stamped, dated, and signed by an IBM vice president and a stock transfer agent. It was real. It was legal. It was mine. I could barely believe it. I thought about my months of planning, the physical pain I had endured, the constant agonizing fear that I was messing up history—and then I thought of all the people whose lives I would improve, and I burst into laughter.

I even got a better price than I expected at $30.85—leaving me $4.60 in change in my brokerage account because they didn't sell partial shares back then.

I turned my attention toward leaving. I knew how terribly painful the jump back to 2017 would be so I decided to give myself a full two weeks till the next one.

In other *New York Times* news, Adolph Hitler, who had lost the general election for German president back in March, had recently made a new foaming-at-the-mouth speech as he continued to drum up his populist following. The writer of the article clearly wasn't a fan, criticized and ridiculed the man, but he wrote about Hitler as a politician with whom he disagreed and not as the embodiment of all evil, the way one would write about him today. In fact, if the article had been written today, this writer wouldn't have even compared him to Hitler.

Polished off *Thrones* and *Mockingbird*. Dylan, Joni, Pete, Woody, added Joan Baez.

One day, I was passing by a grocery store when a hobo approached me—"hobo" being what they called the homeless in those days because it seemed to imply some kind of life choice, alleviating the guilt that the few haves must have felt toward the millions of have-nots, as if anyone would choose to be homeless.

"Brother, can you spare a dime?" the hobo asked me.

It was a situation with which I was all too familiar, and I went into autopilot. "Come with me," I smiled as I led the man into the store to teach him how to fish.

We were halfway to the dairy section when I realized that this could be a mistake because it may alter the past. But it had been so automatic for me that I had to assume that the me's who came before me had reacted the very same way.

When we got to the bin, I saw that the milk was in glass bottles, the small hole at the top maybe an inch in diameter. I sighed, and gave the man a dollar.

I was so bored, so lonesome, and the pretty deli waitresses I couldn't talk to were growing prettier by the day.

* * *

THE TWO WEEKS PLODDED by like a pregnant snail in a staring contest, but at last it was time to say goodbye to the Great Depression. I packed my 1932 clothes into the clunky suitcase, all but twenty dollars of my remaining cash, my meds, the jar of Vaseline, the Ziplocs, everything, and of course, my IBM stock certificate.

With shovel and clunky suitcase in tow, I said goodbye to the building super, who had always been quite nice and friendly, then hailed a cab to take me to the remote spot in the boonies that I had scoped out six weeks earlier, or six-and-a-half months earlier, or eighty-five years later, depending on your point of view.

I made sure the cabbie was out of eyeshot before I made my way into the woods, and then I began to dig. I was aware there was some risk that someone could stumble upon my buried treasure over the decades, find my stock certificate and keep it for himself, and that I could dig up the hole in 2017 to find nothing in it at all, but I also knew that I could take the proper time to recuperate, then travel back to that very moment in time and that very isolated spot in space—meaning, I wouldn't be risking altering the past because no one would be around to see me. I could then dig up my treasure and hide it in another, safer location . . . which would, of course, mean that I myself was the reason that it hadn't been there in 2017 in the first place.

These time loops were getting curiouser and curiouser.

Once I felt the hole adequately deep, I disrobed, placed my clothes and cash into the valise, placed the valise into the hole, then filled it back up with dirt. It was a rather brisk December morning but sunny so not too bad. No dick jokes, please.

I hid the shovel by a tree several trees away and covered it with brush in the hope that it would still be there eighty-five years later—it wouldn't be the end of the world if it wasn't, but it sure would be convenient if it was. I set the temporal destination on the watch to present—that same Monday morning on which I had left 2017 six weeks earlier, or six months earlier, or eighty-five years later—and the spatial destination to my sleazy Jersey hotel room.

I took a deep breath because I had no doubt about the chest pain that awaited me, yet I smiled proudly over all that I had accomplished. I would be rich, Wendy would be richer, and millions of foster children would be spared a life of hell.

I had done a good deed.

And I was utterly oblivious to the massive fatal flaw that had lain at the heart of my elaborate scheme all along.

Send.

CHAPTER SIXTEEN

I BELIEVE I'VE DESCRIBED THE intense pain of time travel often enough by now. Suffice it to say that the jump back to 2017 was as bad as any of them, and I was grateful to have had the foresight to acquire my lodging in advance. I went to the bathroom, took the medication I had purchased six-and-a-half months or six weeks or fifteen days prior, then spent the next three days recuperating.

The first morning I felt fine, I felt great! I was ready to claim my fortune! It had been hard, it had been difficult, it had been painful, it had been lonely, but it was all worth it. I put on the pair of work jeans and the plaid flannel shirt that I had purchased on my shopping spree for this very occasion. I grabbed a quick breakfast at the nearby Cuban diner, and then took a cab back out to the boonies, smiling all the way.

I made sure the cabbie was gone, then sauntered into the woods, finding the shovel which was exactly where I had left it eighty-five years or three days earlier. It was weather-stained and dirty, but seemed as sturdy as the day I bought it.

I was just about to ram it into the ground above the valise when I suddenly heard a voice. "What kind of moron are you? Don't you dare dig up that hole!"

I turned to the voice, and it was me.

He was wearing my embroidered jeans, my blue polo shirt, and my cool leather jacket, and there was no doubt that he was me.

"What—what are you doing here?" I asked confusedly.

"Saving you from yourself, nimrod," he-me replied. "You really haven't thought this through as well as you think you have."

It was a very strange experience. This was my first time being in a time-loop that I myself hadn't initiated, and I didn't know how to respond to my other self—especially since he was being kind of a dick to me.

"Take a breath," he-me calmly told me. "I know it's strange. This is the first time you've been in a time-loop that you yourself didn't initiate."

"Did you initiate it?"

"Yes."

"Wait. You're not supposed to tell me that."

"Why not?"

"Professor Szabo said it would mess up everything. Now when I go back to replicate what you're doing, it won't match."

"Sure it will. The next us will ask if you initiated this loop, and you'll have to say 'yes', just like I did. And because you'll be lying to him, you have no idea if I'm lying to you now. Turns out the Professor had been mistaken on that front."

"*Are* you lying to me?"

"No."

"But now I'm going to have to say 'no' when next-us asks, so I still don't know if you're lying."

"Finally. You're using your brain. It's about time."

"Why are you being such a jerk?"

"I'm just having fun with you. The last time we met we were sad and weepy because we couldn't save the Professor. Now the pressure's off."

"If you say so."

"Also, 'cause I just met a girl."

"What's that got to do with anything?"

"Nothing, I just thought you should know. She's really awesome. You'll like her. Anyway, feeling a little calmer now? Ready to get down to business?"

"Okay."

"You're an idiot!"

"You're being a jerk again."

"I'm very angry at us. You will be, too, in a second."

"Why?"

"Because here you are, having impeccably planned every iota of this caper down to the tiniest, most minute detail, and now what are you going to do? Walk into the Merrill Lynch building with your little stock certificate from 1932 in hand? What are you going to say when they ask how you got it? You're a goddamn felon. They'll just assume you stole it. You can't cooperate because you *didn't* steal it, so you have no credible story to give. And even if they don't assume you stole it, you're on parole. You're not allowed to leave LA, let alone the twenty-first century. No matter how you slice it, walking into Merrill Lynch is as good as walking right back into your San Quentin cage."

It took me a moment to process everything I heard, and all I could do was mumble softly to myself, "How could I have missed that? Stupid, stupid."

"See?" he-me said. "Told you."

"So what do I do? How do we-I claim it?"

"That one I can't help you with, kemosabe. I'm only a few hours older than you, meaning I haven't figured it out yet myself. But here's some advice I can give you. First, you absolutely do not dig up that hole."

"Why not?"

"Because we're going to have to come up with some new plan to claim the loot, and we don't know what that plan is yet. It may entail going back in time and changing what's buried down there. If the suitcase is still there, and the certificate still inside, we may not be allowed to change what we may need to change. Or we may create a paradox. Or not. We don't know how this thing works so the last thing we want is to give up our ability to improvise on the spot."

"Got it."

"Of course you do because I just explained it to you. But don't feel bad for being so dense, I was just as dense a few hours ago."

"Hey, come on."

"Okay, next. You hitch a ride back to the hotel—it'll only take a few minutes till a beat-up old pickup comes along to give you a ride. Go into our room, then pop back three hours. Past-you will still be asleep so just take some cash from his wallet. He won't notice. You didn't."

I checked my wallet to find that three hundred dollars was indeed missing.

"Then, about a block west of the hotel is this quaint little Starbucks. Go in, order your joe, hang out for a couple of hours, then take a cab back here to tell the next us what I just told you. After that, return to LA this past Monday so you can put in the time we missed at Caltech to keep Seymour off our back, and figure out how the hell we can claim our loot. At least, I think so. I haven't done that last part yet."

"Okay. Got it."

"You sure?"

"You tell me."

"Yeah, you're sure," he-me said as he began to tap on his watch. "Alrightee then, I'm off to LA. It was great to see you again, dude." Then he-me hugged me.

"Um, you too. Be well."

"Right back at you, man. And don't forget to pick up the clothes I leave behind and take them back to the room. Ciao."

He was about to tap Send when something odd about his plan occurred to me. "Wait!" I called out. "What's the point of the two hours in Starbucks? Why not just make it a shorter jump back and come right here?"

He looked at me and smiled. "Because Starbucks is where you meet the girl."

And then, with a *crunch* and a gush of reverse wind, he was gone, leaving only our clothes behind.

CHAPTER SEVENTEEN

A S FORETOLD, A BEAT-UP OLD pickup truck picked me up within minutes, and brought me to within blocks of the hotel. I went to my room, disrobed, neatly put my and future-me's clothes away, set the temporal destination on the watch for three hours prior, and the spatial destination for "current." Send.

I was back in my room three hours earlier—rectal pain nil, chest pain barely worth mentioning. I watched myself sleeping for a moment, which of course meant that future-me had watched me-me sleeping, and I found that pretty creepy so I stopped. I took three hundred dollars out of sleeping-me's wallet, and I wondered if that was technically stealing. I put on my embroidered jeans, blue polo shirt, and leather jacket because that's what future-me had been wearing. I set the timer on the Apple Watch for 11:30 because 12:15 was the time I had to stop myself from digging up the hole, and I knew I couldn't risk being late. I smiled as I realized this was the first time I had ever used the watch as an actual watch.

It occurred to me that future-me's approach to this was quite a squandered use of time travel. Why cab out to the boonies when I could just as easily return to the room and pop there? Had future-me, or whichever-me initiated this time loop, missed that? Or was there some piece of information he-they-me had neglected to give me-me? In the end, it felt prudent to simply trust myself and do as I was told.

The Starbucks was relatively quiet when I arrived. There was only one woman around my age, and she was quite the knockout. She was wearing a floral sundress that shaped her lovely thin frame, revealing just a hint of cleavage of her C-cup breasts—"C" having always been my favorite letter in the bra alphabet. A pink wool sweater wrapped around her shoulders, her long, straight blond hair fell effortlessly down to her lower back, and plastic, orange-tinted sunglasses shielded her eyes from sight. She grinned at the barista as she placed her order, and her smile was radiant.

Normally I would take some time to come up with a clever opening line, or I'd just be too shy to strike up any conversation at all, but I had already told me that she and I would hit it off so I knew that I didn't have to worry.

She was taking her wallet out of her purse to pay the barista when I moseyed over to her and said, "Let me get that for you."

"I can buy my own coffee, thank you," she testily snapped.

Oh-oh.

"I was just trying to be friendly," I answered.

She was about to comment when she at last actually looked at me, and stopped herself from speaking. It was a little strange because she wasn't so much looking at me as she was studying me. I flashed her my world-class, disengaging smile, and she smiled back. It usually works.

"What's your name?" she asked with a touch of suspicion in her voice.

"T.J.," I told her.

"Tell you what, T.J., I'll buy *you* a coffee."

"Okay, but I have to warn you. It'll take a lot more than a cup of coffee to get me to put out."

She laughed. Phew.

"Give him whatever he wants," she told the barista.

"Just a grande drip," I told the barista.

"Oh come on," the pretty girl said to me. "Don't be so boring. You have a hot chick buying you a drink. Show a little hubris."

"It's what I actually like."

"I don't care. I'm buying," she said then turned back to the barista. "Give him a Frappuccino."

"Thank you," I said to her, laughing.

"You're welcome," she said as she put out her hand. "I'm Cassandra."

"A pleasure to meet you, Cassandra," and we shook.

"Pleasure's all mine, T.J."

We got our drinks, then took a small table by the window. I was thoroughly getting a kick out of her. She had this wonderfully contagious laugh, and there was a toughness to her voice typically uncommon in women as pretty as she.

"So you live around here?" she asked. "You don't sound like a Jersey native."

"I'm from LA, actually. Just here on business."

"Uh-huh," she said as if she didn't believe me.

"What about you?" I asked. "From where do you hail?"

"I live in the city—New York, I mean. Soho, actually. I just came from a reading, and I have another one at noon so I figured it easiest to just hang till then."

"A reading? Are you an actress?"

"Not that kind of reading," she laughed. "I'm a spiritual advisor."

"Spiritual advisor?"

"A psychic."

"Get out of here."

"Seriously."

"Okay, what am I thinking?"

"It doesn't work that way," she laughed again. "Give me your hands."

"Why?"

"Just give them," she said as she took them anyway. She turned them palms up, then placed her own under mine. She sat up very straight, closed her eyes, and hummed softly.

"You had a very difficult childhood," she said softly through her trance.

"That pretty much applies to everyone."

"Shhh," she commanded, then hummed some more. "No one understood you. No one wanted to understand you. No one cared about you at all. You were shuffled from one family to the next. Were you an orphan?"

Okay, I thought, now it's getting weird.

"Yes, you were an orphan," she went on. "You were in the foster care system."

I tried to move my hands from hers, but she wouldn't let me, gripping my palms only tighter.

"But there was one family that was good to you. Yes. They loved you, and you loved them. They were going to adopt you, and for the first time, you were very happy. But then Jen found out that Jack was cheating on her, and it all went to hell."

"Whoa!" I shouted as I ripped my hands away from her, utterly freaked out. "How—how can you do that?"

"It's me, stupid," she said, chuckling with delight.

"Me?"

"I'm Myra."

She lifted her tinted glasses up to her forehead to show me the warm blue eyes I had never forgotten. I couldn't believe it. Myra! My long-lost almost-sister!

"Oh my God!" I chuckled along at my own expense. "How are you?"

Why hadn't future-me told me that the mystery girl was Myra of all people?

Probably because this was such a cool way to find out, and he didn't want to ruin the surprise. I'll do the same thing for next-me when it's my turn.

"I can't believe you didn't recognize me, you jerk," she laughed. "I knew it was you the moment I saw you."

Within seconds, we were talking like we had never been apart. We were ten years old again, but with the hard experiences of those in their late twenties. She still had the same annoying knack of knowing when I was lying so after a few failed attempts, I came clean about my life in crime.

No, not about time travel—no one must ever know about that until I get the watch to the NASA guy, and then *he* can decide who gets to know. It is far too powerful a device to fall into the wrong hands, and someone else may not be as responsible with it as I've tried to be. As much as I felt that I could trust my almost-sister, this one little secret I would take to my grave.

That said, it was fun and cathartic telling Myra the rest of my life story, and she was a terrific audience. She laughed at the funny parts, sympathized with the sad parts, was horrified by San Quentin, and was proud for me when I described my discovery of physics and my desire to go to college and to go straight.

"But if you're on parole in LA, how can you be in New York? There's something you're not telling me."

I knew that there was no point in lying to her so I smiled cryptically and simply said, "Yes, there is."

"That's all right," she replied understandingly, then smiled back. "For now."

"So what about you? What do you do for a living?"

"I told you. I'm a psychic."

"I thought that was just part of the joke you were playing on me."

"Both."

"A psychic, huh?" I laughed. "So you're a thief, just like me."

"I most certainly am not," she said with indignation.

"Excuse me. Confidence artist."

"I have a gift."

"Right."

"Okay, in all honesty, sometimes it's not there, and I have to rely on tricks, but for the most part, I have a gift. It's kind of like an athlete or a writer. Sometimes they're just in the zone. They're on fire. They can do anything. They don't know why, they just know they can. Other times, the basketball player can't sink a single shot, and the playwright can't drum up a single phrase. But a girl still has to make a living so I do the best I can and, you know, fake it a little. But even then, I only give my clients advice that will be helpful to them."

"You're serious. You really think you have a gift."

"I do. You should believe me."

"I do."

"No you don't."

"You're right," I said, and we both laughed.

Her life had been hard, I learned. Her time in the foster care system had been even harder than mine, and then still harder as she developed into a young woman. I think it's always that way with girls, especially the pretty ones. She never came out and point blank said that she had been raped, but it was clear that she had been on numerous occasions. Nor did she explicitly say that she had had to turn tricks to support herself for a little while after she ran out on her last abusive family at the age of sixteen, but that too was clear.

Who was I to judge? We all do what we must to survive. Judge her? I wanted to lean across the table and hold her, but I knew it would seem inappropriate in that particular moment.

Our time together flew by with much laughter, sorrow, pain, and then more laughter. Then, out of the blue, the alarm on my watch sounded, and I was pissed.

"I have to go," I said sadly.

"I know."

"Can I see you again?"

"You'd better. I don't want another eighteen years to fly by before I get to see my big brother."

"I've got to do this thing now, but after that I have all the time in the world—and I mean that more literally than you could possibly know. What are you doing for the rest of the day? I can hang out till after your noon thing."

Yes, my other self had said he was heading right back to LA, but that didn't mean it was true. For all I knew, he had simply popped back to the hotel to spend the rest of the day with long-lost almost-sister. Besides, I was in the present so I didn't need to worry about altering the future. We all alter the future, all of the time.

"Aw, gee, I'm booked through the afternoon," Myra answered. "And then I have a whole big séance thing tonight, lots of people, good money, and too hard to reschedule. How's tomorrow, Saturday night?"

"Saturday night it is."

We exchanged cell phone numbers, hugged and kissed each other on the cheek, and I headed out to hail a taxi back to the boonies.

I finally understood why future-me had been such a jerk. I wanted to hang with Myra, not waste my time telling my stupid doppelganger how he missed the most vital part of our whole plan. As the ride wore on, I grew increasingly angry at him. By the time I paid the cabbie and watched him drive off, I was furious.

I could see past-me sauntering through the woods with his ancient shovel in hand, obliviously smiling like a village idiot, so excited, so dumb. "What kind of moron are you?" I shouted. "Don't you dare dig up that hole!"

"What—what are you doing here?" he-me asked confusedly.

"Saving you from yourself, nimrod," I-me replied.

If I had thought it was strange having this conversation with me the first time, this was far stranger. It was my first time being future-me having the same conversation I had already had when I had been past-me. It wasn't exactly that I was repeating the words future-me had said during our first conversation by rote—no, I wasn't purposely trying to replicate anything. I was saying exactly what felt right to say in the moment, yet I would suddenly remember what I had heard the first time the instant after I said it this second time. It was like a perpetual déjà vu, an online video chat with a bad Internet connection, except the echo was all in my head.

Even when I told idiot-past-me that I was the one to initiate this time-loop, it wasn't because I was supposed to, I just wanted to mess with him. I was still angry at him-me-us for the giant flaw in our otherwise brilliant plot, so I decided to have a little fun at our expense.

"Wait. You're not supposed to tell me that," he-me said.

"Why not?" I smiled, feigning innocence. I knew his confusion, and he deserved it.

It did bring up the notion of free will, however. I was doing and saying exactly what past future-me had done and said, and all without trying. I considered throwing in some curse words or racial epithets like a Tourette's victim, just to exert my independence from fate—but what if that caused past-me to not trust me-me, thereby not showing up at Starbucks hours early, thereby not meeting Myra?

So even though I *felt* like I could change the past, I didn't. Did the prior future-me have these thoughts also? He must have. Does that prove that the past can't be changed after all, that I'm destined to do whatever I do because I had already done it? Or does it once again prove nothing?

If you think about it, it once again proved nothing.

It seems the only way to conclusively find out if the past can be changed is to purposely try to change it, yet the risk of doing so was far too great.

In the end, I affectionately hugged past-me goodbye because I knew I had been hard on him, and there was no reason to end things on a sour note. Who knew if we'd have to help each other out once more? Of course, the moment I hugged him, I remembered being hugged.

"It was great to see you again, dude," I told him.

"Um, you too. Be well."

"Right back at you, man," I said as I set my watch for my return to the Los Angeles of five days prior. "And don't forget to pick up the clothes I leave behind and bring them back to the room. Ciao."

"Wait!" he-me called out. "What's the point of the two hours in Starbucks? Why not just make it a shorter jump back and come right here?"

I looked at him and smiled enviously. "Because Starbucks is where you meet the girl."

Lucky bastard. Send.

I was back in my Pasadena apartment, chest pain minor, rectal pain nil. I turned my thoughts toward Myra, then turned them again to the great new challenge that lay ahead—how to claim my treasure. I had no ideas. I didn't even know where to start, or how to even approach such a puzzle.

But I'll tell you one thing. When I would finally come up with the solution, it would be a doozy.

CHAPTER EIGHTEEN

OPPING THE LONELY, HALLOWED HALLS of Caltech could not
have been more anticlimactic. I had been on a six-month or six-
week adventure, but as far as the world knew, it had been but a regular
old weekend. Professor Szabo's office had been cleaned out, and a new
instructor had just started moving in that day. It was the same desk but
with different tchotchkes upon it, and I found it sad. Sacrilege almost.

I wanted to phone Myra just to chat some more, but I couldn't. This
was Monday night, and we wouldn't meet for the first time until the
coming Friday morning. Even though we had arranged to see each other
the very next evening, I would have to wait out the entire week before I
could even speak to her. Talk about a time zone problem.

The next day, I drove to Watts to see Wendy. I still had no clue how
to claim my treasure, but if anyone would know how it would be her. I
just had to figure out a way to ask the question without mentioning the
watch.

I hadn't seen Wendy since the day before I left for the thirties,
which to her was only a few days ago. I hugged her the way one would
hug his mother after not seeing her for a month and a half, and all she
said was, "What's wrong with you?"

I had missed her so.

She put up a pot of tea, and we settled into our regular chitchat mode. We talked about movies and TV shows, sports, heists, and politics, our usual—yet all the while I was searching for a way to frame my question. Finally, I just said it.

"I may be able to get my hands on an old IBM stock certificate. Could you move something like that?"

"It's not really what I dabble in, sweet thing, but I may know a guy who knows a guy. How old?"

"From the thirties."

She almost did a spit take. "The *nineteen*-thirties?"

"Yep."

"Something like that'd be worth a hundred million dollars."

"More, actually."

"No, no, no, child. You don't want any part of that. I don't want any part of that. It's too big. The only way to cash out would be through an actual broker, and brokers keep records, and records lead to questions, and you got no answers.

"But you sure are moving up in the world. Damn, a thirty-million-dollar painting to a hundred-million-dollar stock certificate. You're a blue collar kid pulling white collar crimes now, and they're going to put you away for good."

"I'd sell it for fifty cents on the dollar."

"To who? The only people who could move something like that are the people who already have more than that."

"Okay. Let's get one of them."

"Look around, sweet thing. I run a pawnshop in Watts. I don't know those kinds of people, and the people I do know don't know those kinds of people. Just walk away from this. I'm still so sorry about putting you into that Jackson Pollock mess, but I'm telling you now for your own good. Walk away."

"I'll give you a chunk of it, Wendy. Honest to God, five mill. I had planned to give you that all along, even before I knew I'd need your help. You could retire, m'lady, and you could retire great!"

"There ain't no chunk to give me, sweet thing, and there won't never be. Get that through your thick skull. All that'll happen is that you'll get put away for the best part of your life. So walk away, Teej. Walk away now."

"Okay," I lied.

Back to the drawing board.

CHAPTER NINETEEN

I SPENT THE REST OF the week looking forward to my upcoming encounter with my almost-sister, and racking my brains for a risk-free way to lay claim to my legally-purchased stock certificate. Nothing came. My brain was as constipated as my bowels after an eighty-five-year time-jump.

I finished up the last of my college applications months ahead of schedule. I considered mailing them in early but decided to hang on to them for a while in case I wanted to change anything—most weren't due till January.

Yes, I was a little scared. No, I was super scared. I wanted this. I wanted to go to college. I wanted to be a scientist. I wanted to contribute to the world.

In case you're wondering, I played my criminal past right down the middle. I didn't hide it, but I didn't boast about it either. For the ethics essay, I relayed a modified version of my Jackson Pollock story. I told of how I had been seduced by the prospect of all that money—a fate not difficult for a boy of my humble beginnings. I admitted that I had failed a moral choice, but my years in prison had taught me the error of my ways, and that I was now a better, stronger person because of it, grateful for the experience because it had led me to physics, my life's true calling. Boring, I know, I just thought you might be curious.

Back to work. How do I legally claim my stock certificate?
Nothing.

* * *

WHEN I ARRIVED HOME from my shift Friday morning, I made myself
something to eat and watched some TV. I got into bed around 9:15,
which I realized was 12:15 on the East Coast, the very time that one of
me would be stopping another me from digging up my clunky suitcase. I
wondered if there were any other me's who had come to this particular
moment in time for reasons unknown. Just how many me's can there be
at once? How many angels can fit on the head of a pin?

Just sayin'.

Yet more importantly, how do I legally claim my stock certificate?
Nothing.

* * *

AT LONG LAST, IT was Saturday. Myra day!

We spoke on the phone that afternoon and arranged to meet at a
certain vegan restaurant in Soho not too far from her studio—of course
she's vegan, I laughed to myself. What else would she be? It wasn't a big
deal to me, though. True, I'm a devout carnivore, but that doesn't mean I
must eat a dead animal at every meal, and one can always find something yummy in a vegan joint.

I time-jumped to my sleazy Jersey hotel room that afternoon to
shower and change. Minor chest pain, barely worth mentioning. I put on
a pair of black jeans, a black and gray pullover, and of course, my leather
jacket, then went out to hail a cab.

It was during the ride to Manhattan that I began to wonder if this
was an actual date, or merely two long-lost siblings trying to reconnect.
Technically, we weren't siblings at all. We weren't related by blood, and
we had never been adopted so we weren't related by law either. But all
through the years, whenever I thought of Myra, it had always been as my
tough kid sister. Then again, I had also always thought of her as a ten-
year-old child, and she had grown up to be a damn hot woman.

I hadn't figured it out as the cab pulled up to the vegan joint where she was already waiting for me outside. She was wearing a tight, lavender blouse and a deep purple pencil skirt that she filled to perfection. "Hey," she said as we took each other's hands and kissed each other on the cheek like brothers and sisters are inclined to do. Nothing to read there.

The restaurant itself was nice and trendy, with laminated wood floors, servers in white, collared shirts and red bow ties, and a six-foot chalkboard on an easel spouting the day's specials. The place was about three-quarters full, but the acoustics were such that the joint never felt too loud. Myra gave the hostess her name, and we were seated at a table by a window through which we could see the Soho lights glistening in the air, and the crowds of people moving to and fro as they enjoyed their Saturday night on the town. It was really quite a romantic setting if I had wanted it to be, or not if I didn't. I still didn't know.

"So what's with all the black you got on?" she good-naturedly asked out of nowhere. "You don't believe in colors?"

"Black is a color," I said with a smile.

"Barely," she smiled back.

"Plus, I've got a little gray happening."

"I know. It's psychedelic. Hurts my eyes."

"Could've been worse. Just think how embarrassing it would've been if I showed up in the same skirt and blouse you're wearing."

She laughed. "I'm just giving you a hard time, Teej. It actually suits you. You got that whole 'I'm cute and charming so screw you' thing going on. You look good."

"Thanks. You look good, too."

"Oh. Um, thanks."

There was a sudden awkward pause, and it occurred to me that she too had been weighing out if this was a date or a catch-up. Fortunately, the waitress arrived to take our order before either of us could address it.

Myra ordered a cantina kale salad bowl and a micro-brewed lite beer. I got a garden burger with hummus, sweet potato fries, and the same beer. The waitress took our orders and moved off, taking our prior awkwardness away with her.

Despite Myra's stunning looks, I was thoroughly enjoying her company, and thoughts of sex with her gradually faded. I had never met anyone like her before, for she was quite the little kook. It was refreshing, and I realized how glad I was to have little sister back in my life.

"We always knew I had this crazy intuition about things," she said as she launched into the origins of her chosen profession. "I just never knew it was anything special until I was nineteen. No, twenty. No, nineteen. Whatever. I was dating this struggling playwright, an older guy, early forties, and he bought me a deck of tarot cards for my birthday. Yeah, it was twenty. I was nineteen turning twenty. So I started messing around with the cards just for fun, going online to learn what the various cards meant, buying books, but just playing really. I'd do readings for friends when they were over, or I was over, stuff like that. But then my friends would start coming back to me, like, weeks later, and they'd say, 'Remember what you told me last time? It happened just the way you said it would.' Or, 'Remember that advice you gave me? I did what you told me, and it all worked out perfectly.'

"And the more I read and learned about the spiritual world, the more I came to realize that this was my calling. This was my way to break the cycle."

"The cycle?" I asked.

"Whatever horrible thing or things I did in my past life, whatever bad karma I brought upon myself, this is my way to give back to the world. This is how I can atone for my sins so I can start my next life with a clean slate."

I told you she was a kook.

But a delightful little kook, right?

"What makes you think you did a horrible thing in a past life?" I asked.

"Look at my childhood. Look at my whole life before I learned how to turn it around. It sucked. You know it sucked. Yours sucked, too.

"But things happen for a reason, Teej, and the misery of this life is my punishment for whatever I had done before. So I can choose to wallow in a despair that will consume me and send me down a dark path, causing me to commit even graver sins, causing my next life to be even more horrific. Or, I can choose to use the gifts the universe has given me to help my fellow man. *That* is breaking the cycle."

"Okay," I said with a smile.

"You're laughing at me. You don't believe me."

"I believe you believe you, and your passion is compelling."

"Aw, Teej, that is the most back-handed compliment I've ever gotten."

"With most people I'd probably lie, but you always see through me. In fact, I've never known anyone who can see through me the way you do."

"Because I have a gift, duh."

We both laughed. "So what happened to the guy?" I asked.

"The guy?"

"The playwright who bought you the tarot cards."

"Oh, he was a jerk—and a terrible writer, too. He's long gone. But I still have the cards."

We laughed again as the waitress arrived to lay our plates before us. We did that thing people do when servers approach, which is to immediately stop talking, and Myra fired the conversation right back up the moment we were alone again.

"You should, too," she said.

"I should what?"

"Break your cycle. Give yourself a clean slate in your next life. Help others."

"I kind of am, actually."

"Ooh, this sounds interesting," she said as she squirmed excitedly. "Tell me."

"Um..."

"Oh. It's that thing you won't talk about."

"Yeah."

"How's that going?"

"I hit a bit of a snag, actually."

"Bummer."

"Yeah."

"But don't give up on it if it will help others."

"I don't plan to give up, and it *will* help others. Even you."

"Cool. But don't keep anything for yourself."

"There'll be a lot to go around. I can keep a little."

"Only take what you need to survive," she said with determination as she leaned forward and put her hands on mine. Sisterly advice, or was she making a move? "The universe rewards selflessness."

"But if you're only being selfless in order to be rewarded, aren't you therefore really being selfish?"

She looked directly into my eyes, then answered with certainty. "No."

In her nutty little way, she still had my back after all these years.

* * *

AFTER DINNER, WE WENT to a nearby British-style pub where we had a few more beers, then she asked me to walk her home so she could show me a real live psychic's parlor. We walked along the bustling weekend streets without holding hands, and with no sign of what our new relationship was destined to be.

I was coming to see the wisdom in keeping it platonic. As wonderful as I knew it would feel to have our sweaty naked bodies pressed against one another, I could always find sex. But lovers don't last, in my experience. A sister might last forever.

The outside of her storefront was pretty unoriginal, I'm sorry to say. It was on the ground level of an eight-story building, presumably an apartment building. It was small and nondescript, sandwiched between a Korean massage parlor and a store that sold live chickens. A sign on the door's glass window said merely: *Psychic Readings*, under which was a drawing of a big red hand, under which were the words *Tarot Cards*, *Palms*, and *Tea Leaves*. For someone as unique as Myra, I had really been expecting something with a little more panache.

The inside was quite nice, although just as cliché. Four plush velvet red chairs circled a stained mahogany table on which lay a small crystal ball. Yeah, a crystal ball, seriously. Crimson drapes hung from the wall as decoration only, as well as a framed poster of a man named Edgar Cayce. A doorless opening at the end of the room was shielded by strings of red and orange beads, and the smell of incense abounded. It was all very hippie-dippy, but still much nicer than my Pasadena dump.

"You live here, too?" I asked.

"Yeah, there's a little apartment area in the back. Bedroom, TV room, small kitchen. Like I said, I don't require much. You still into Dylan?" she asked as she opened a drawer to reveal a CD player.

"Absolutely. You?"

"Absolutely," she said with a smile as she put a disc into the machine and clicked Play. "Tangled Up in Blue" crooned softly through speakers that I couldn't see.

"*Blood on the Tracks*," I said fondly.

"The CD you tried to steal."

"Wow. You remember that."

"Like yesterday. I was on the far side of the store when I got this bad feeling our adoption wouldn't go through, and that I'd lose my brother forever. I went over to you just to hug you, and that's when I saw you lifting it. I was so mad at you."

"I remember."

"But I was also a little relieved—you probably didn't know that. I was sure your stealing was the cause of my bad feeling. You promised to never steal again—ha ha—so it seemed the problem was solved. I had no idea that, well, you know."

"Yeah."

There was another awkward silence that she soon filled. She was very good at filling silences.

"So, what are we?" she asked, and I knew exactly what she meant.

"The elephant in the room rears its ugly head at last."

"We've avoided it long enough, haven't we?"

"Indeed we have."

"We're not brother and sister," she began tentatively. "Not really. I mean, it's fun to call each other that and imagine the what if, what if, what if, but we're not blood, and we don't have the same last name. We're not anything."

"We're whatever we want to be, I guess."

We were somehow standing only inches apart at this point.

"Well, what do you want us to be?" she asked softly.

"I don't know. I've been going back and forth. What do *you* want us to be?"

Suddenly, out of nowhere and with no warning, she thrust her palm heels into my shoulders and pinned me against the wall. She grabbed my face, put her soft lips on mine, and her warm tongue into my mouth. My arms wrapped around her taut, lithe body as if of their own volition, and I slid my hands up behind her blouse to caress the soft, silky skin of her lower back. Our lips remained locked together as we began to frantically and furiously undress each other. With our tops off, our hands grappling with snaps and buttons and zippers, she suddenly stopped.

"Not here," she panted, dug her hand behind the waistband of my jeans, and dragged me willingly through the beaded doorframe and into her bedroom.

As you know, I normally describe a room into which I take you, but I had no concept of what the room actually looked like. The moment we entered, she once again shoved her palm heels into my shoulders. The back of my knees buckled against the foot of the bed so that I fell back upon it, and then she leapt—literally leapt—on top of me, her lips miraculously landing right upon mine, her hands grabbing my hands and holding them out to the extremes as if I were her prisoner. If I hadn't been so completely amenable, I would have thought I was being raped.

I don't remember precisely how or when the rest of our clothes came off, I only remember her riding me like a hobbyhorse, thrusting, pushing, releasing, thrusting again. Her body arched back as she moaned and groaned in delight. I sat up to bury my face in her perfectly succulent breasts. She wrapped her arms around my head and pressed me to her chest to the point that it was difficult for me to breathe, but there are more important things than breathing.

And at last, she screamed and tightened in ecstasy, and I exploded inside her.

She let herself drop down upon me, her face upon my chest, her luscious blonde hair flapping against her back like a ray of sunlight. The room was dark, but not so dark that I couldn't see her soft blue eyes and her warm, contented smile. She was happy. I was happy.

I kissed the top of her golden head, then closed my eyes, and the last thought I remember before drifting off to sleep was what a horrible mistake I had just made.

CHAPTER TWENTY

THE SMELL OF SMOKE WOKE me. I was alone in the bed. The room was dark for it was still night, but not so dark that I couldn't see Myra sitting on the dresser beyond the foot of the bed, wearing an oversized Bob Dylan *Like a Rolling Stone* T-shirt, and puffing away on a Virginia Slim. I didn't know she smoked.

When our eyes met, she exhaled hard and loudly, as if blowing out a heart full of guilt. "This was a mistake," she said sadly. "A terrible mistake. I am so sorry, Teej."

"Good morning to you, too," I flippantly answered because I didn't know how else to respond.

"Really, I am," she continued. "I'd been going back and forth on it all night. Well, not *all* night. Sometimes I was so engrossed in our conversation, like we were the brother and sister we were meant to be. I didn't even mind when you called me a kook or a nut because that's what brothers and sisters do, call each other out on stuff. But then other times, damn, you're so gorgeous. Especially when you smile. Don't get me wrong. The sex was great. This isn't about that. You were spectacular."

"Actually, you did most of the work."

"Yeah, I guess I did," she said with a smile that was somehow shy and proud at the same time. "The point is, I don't want to lose you again, and I know how these relationships work with me. Always. They start off all happy and giggly, and you find my flaws all endearing and cute, then they start to bug you. Then you want to change me, then rule me, then own me. But I don't want to be owned again. I made that decision when I was sixteen and I left those pricks—then I spent the next ten years walking right back into the same trap and letting myself get owned over and over again, but no more. I need a big brother, not a lover. I'm sorry."

"It's okay."

"Why's it okay? Wasn't I fantastic?"

I could only laugh. "You were incredible. But I've never had much success in the romance business either. I can't even think of a single relationship worth mentioning. Girls come and girls go, in my experience, and I want you to stay."

"Aww," she said as she stubbed out her cigarette, climbed back into bed with me, and laid her head upon my chest once more. "We sure are two peas in a pod."

"Seems so," I replied. "Should I go sleep on the couch?"

"In a little bit," she answered softly as she snuggled closer. There was a pause during which neither one of us spoke, then she added. "I just want you to know, if you ever introduce me to a girlfriend, it won't be weird. I'll be her bff, even if I hate her."

"I don't believe in girlfriends."

"I love that."

I smiled.

"You know what our problem is?" she asked.

"Many?"

"Yeah, but specifically. We're both messed up *and* self-aware. I really think a person should only have to be one of those things."

"Then I pick self-aware."

She laughed, then I did.

I never quite made it to the couch that night, nor did we make love again. We merely lay in each other's arms, talking and laughing until we drifted off to sleep.

I had never fallen asleep laughing before. You should try it. It's nice.

CHAPTER TWENTY-ONE

I T WAS CLOSE TO TEN when I was awoken by voices. I was alone and naked in Myra's bed, and she was nowhere to be found. I followed the voices, then peeked through the beaded doorway into the front parlor to find that my little sister had begun her workday.

The parlor was dark, almost as dark as it was when we had entered the night before, illuminated only by strategically placed red and orange candles. The smell of incense was stronger and fresher than it had been, and I could see several sticks burning in the corners of the room. Hippie-dippy sitar music droned softly from the speakers I still didn't see.

For the most part, Myra was dressed pretty normally in tight blue jeans and a yellow tank top. Other than the vibrant white scarf tied around her neck, the plethora of cheap jewelry on her wrists that clanged and rattled when she moved, and the fact that she chain-smoked, there was very little "gypsy" about her at all.

And yes, as it turned out, my little sister was, in fact, a flimflam man. I poured myself a cup of coffee from the pot she must have put up some time earlier, sat down in the kitchen, and listened to the show.

I didn't know all the ins and outs of what she was up to, but I did know my fair share. My San Quentin, con artist, cellie Juan Gomez and I had spent a great deal of time swapping stories of the jobs we had pulled because that's what we crooks do. In fact, prison is an excellent crime school if one is so inclined, and the tuition is free.

I hadn't always approved of Juan's scams because he had no misgivings about taking people who couldn't afford to be taken, but one does not bring up such moral judgments on the inside. Still, I had been fascinated by the calculated cleverness of his work, just as he had been mesmerized by the adrenaline-pumping tales of mine.

Juan himself never played a psychic but he often worked with a man who had, so he knew many of the tricks—hence I did, too. Myra was working them to the hilt.

First and easiest, men are typically more concerned about their careers, while women are typically more concerned about their love lives. This is not true in all cases, but it's a pretty safe starting point for a con when trying to get the mark's trust.

Second, talk fast. Fire off a lot of questions with authority, bam-bam-bam, as if they're one single question, even though most are polar opposites. If you just keep talking, you'll eventually stumble upon something that's true.

"You're-up-for-a-big-promotion," Myra told one man. "You-deserve-it-but-you're-worried-you-won't-get-it-you're-worried-your-boss-has-it-in-for-you-you're-afraid-of-losing-your-job-I-see-something-about-a-job-that's-plaguing-you-have-you-recently-lost-your-job?"

Did you catch that? Her first remark to her last? From a criminal perspective, it was kind of inspiring.

"I was laid off a few months ago," the astonished man replied shamefully. "I haven't been able to find anything since."

Third, always be right.

"Yes. Yes. That's what I see. That's right. And it hasn't been going well, has it?"

Fourth, logical guesses as spiritual insights.

"This card, the Knave of Cups, tells me you've been living on your savings, and you're worried that it won't last."

"How do you know all this?"

Fifth, don't be afraid to be specific, but never be wrong. Myra employed this to perfection on the next mark that came into the parlor, a woman.

"You've recently changed your hairstyle," Myra told the stranger with certainty.

"No, it's been this way for a long time," the woman said.

"I see a recent change in your life. Something has changed. Some big change you've made. Have you gotten a new job? Have you recently moved? Have you entered a new relationship? I see change."

"Well, my grandfather passed away about six months ago, and he left me a rather sizable inheritance."

"Yes, yes. That's what it is, that's right. And the money has changed your life considerably. Yet you're torn because although your inheritance is quite a blessing, you loved your grandfather very much and you miss him dearly."

Sixth, pay attention to body language and facial expressions—"tells", as they're called in poker.

"But he was an aloof man, yes? You always felt a distance from him, as if you barely knew him at all. Yes, I see a great distance between the two of you. Was it an emotional distance or a geographic one? I sense some kind of distance."

"I hadn't seen him since I was a kid," said the astonished woman as she began to well up. "He and my mother were estranged, so my parents kept me from him."

"Yes, that's right. Yes. And this inheritance was his way to make it up to you for being absent from your life. Did he leave some kind of letter or communication expressing this? He did, didn't he?"

"How do you know?" wept the woman.

You get the drill.

But to little sister's credit, she never bilked anyone, not the way Juan would have. She didn't try to sell anyone any magic potions, powders, or crystals at a zillion percent markup—the typical fraud's stock-in-trade. She didn't charge the unemployed guy at all, explaining that the spirits had instructed her so. She followed that up with a very inspiring pep talk to keep him hopeful, and to keep him trying.

But her goodness went far beyond pep talks and generosity, and she may have even saved the life of one of her marks. When a young couple entered the parlor around noon, it took Myra but an instant to know their story. Even with my obstructed view of the room, it didn't take me much longer.

The man was tall, buff, and slightly tattooed, the woman meek and frail, with a few bruises on her arms. When she took off her sunglasses upon entering the dim, candlelit space, the shiner on her left eye was evident. It had been a common sight in Myra's and my bleak childhood.

Myra played the couple just long enough to gain their trust, determining that the man was an assistant manager at an Arby's in Queens, the woman worked in telemarketing, and they planned to be married the following spring. Like everyone else who had visited the parlor that day, they were astonished at how Myra could know so much from merely holding their hands.

She had the man shuffle the deck of tarot cards, and then laid out certain ones on the table in a very specific pattern. She then feigned a startled surprise and offered the man a private reading.

"I'm sorry," she then said to the woman. "I don't usually do this with couples, but there are certain things I see in his future that are meant for his ears only. To be fair, I'll give you your own private reading right afterward, and then charge the two of you for one session. Sound fair?"

"Sure," said the man. "Seems like a good deal. Wait outside, baby."

The dutiful little woman did as instructed, and then Myra got to work.

"You're frustrated in your job," she began. "You watch others move up the ladder ahead of you, people without your abilities, and you're obliged to obey them. You find it humiliating. You know you deserve more than the universe is giving you, but something is holding you back. You don't know what it is, but you can feel some illusive force standing between you and your dreams. You can feel it, can't you?"

A pretty generic premise but the man was thoroughly impressed.

"Meanwhile, your relationship with your fiancée is quite rocky."

"I wouldn't say that," he said defensively "I mean, we argue more than I'd like, but we're working on it."

"*She* is what is holding you back, sir. Look at the cards. Love. Work. Death. As long as you remain together, the rewards you deserve will remain out of your reach. Nor will your relationship with her improve. It will only worsen as time passes because the bitterness of your failures will consume you. Deep within your heart, you know that it's her fault so you beat her. Don't you?"

"I—"

"You do. I see it here in the Queen of Swords. You don't mean to, the Nine of Wands tells me so, but you do it nonetheless."

The macho man began to weep. Gosh, li'l sis is good.

"You are out of harmony with the universe, sir. If you don't repair your imbalance, your life will only continue to spiral downward."

"What do I do?" he sobbed. "If I leave her, it will crush her. What do I say?"

"Be kind, but direct. Be sweet, sensitive, yet strong. The universe demands it."

"Thank you."

"I only cite what I see," Myra said. "Your gratitude should go to the universe itself, not to me." Then she charged the man quadruple her usual amount, reminding him that his fiancée's reading would be free, and that tips were appreciated.

The man paid her in cash—tipping quite generously—then went outside. A moment later, the woman returned and took her seat. Myra didn't even bother to draw the tarot cards back into a pile.

"Honey, you've got to leave that douchebag, and you've got to do it today."

"What? Do the cards say that? Aren't I supposed to shuffle them first?"

"The cards don't say that. Your arms and your eye say that."

"No, this isn't from him. This is from—"

"You fell down. You walked into a door. Honey, I've been where you are, been there more times than I can count. You've got to leave him."

Then the woman began to sob. "He won't let me," she uttered softly.

"I know, they get that way," Myra said, then sat on the arm of the woman's chair and put her arm around her. "The worst of them do get that way. But honey, if I did my job right—and I'm pretty sure I did—the son of a bitch will end it himself sometime today. Pretend to be crushed, but accept his decision without argument."

"How do you know this for sure?"

"I don't," Myra conceded, then took a business card out of a drawer in the table and handed it to the woman. "If he hasn't ended it by tomorrow, I want you to go to this shelter. They'll protect you from him, and give you legal counsel if you need it. Tell them Myra sent you. They'll take care of you. I promise."

"Thank you," the woman said through her tears. "Thank you."

I was so proud of my little sister—proud of her skills as a crook, yet even more proud of her impeccable sense of decency. I mean, wow, right?

On top of that, though, I could not have been more elated all through the morning because somewhere along the way I had a true moment of inspiration, a cartoon light bulb flashing atop my head. I finally knew how to legally claim my stock certificate.

The answer had actually been given to me by Myra's second client of the morning, the woman whose estranged grandfather had left her a sizable inheritance. The answer was so obvious I even felt a little dumb for not having come up with it on my own.

How do I legally claim my stock certificate?

Clarence Roy Jameson is going to bequeath it to me in his will.

CHAPTER TWENTY-TWO

W E ROLL IN THE SOFT, powdery snow, she and I. We're rolling on a cloud. We wear big, heavy jackets and itchy wool hats and fat leather gloves, and we giggle in each other's arms as we roll and roll and roll. There is snow in all directions as far as the eye can see, and its crystal white flakes fall gently upon us from the sunny winter sky above. Luscious green pines and giant naked oaks offer us protection from the elements if we want it, but we don't. We'd rather play.

We roll into the base of the snowman we had created together earlier that morning. Our first child, she had called it. The base holds firm but the head tips off, landing upon us like an explosion. It's cold, it's wet, and it shocks us. She screams, and then she laughs. She puts her sopping, freezing gloves upon my cheeks, pulls my face down to hers, and we kiss.

We know in our hearts that we were once a single soul in Heaven, one entity separated into man and woman who came to Earth to live our lives together, and we will never be apart. We can't be. We are one.

We're in a park, sitting on a bench, and she's sad. She says that she's grown feelings for someone else. She doesn't know how it happened, she says, she never expected or wanted it to happen.

"Teej," I hear a faint voice in the distance. What's a teej? I wonder.

Her affection for me remains true, she says, but she has fallen for this other man completely. She will marry him, and our wedding will never be.

"Hey," the faraway voice says louder.

I know this man with whom she will share her life. I had considered him a friend. I'm filled with rage towards this Judas, this—

"T.J.!"

I was shaken awake. It had been Myra shouting my name through my dream, saving me from the inevitable pain that I have and will experience over and over again. I was in my underwear, lying on a lumpy old couch in her TV room, covered by an itchy wool blanket, and the events of the night slowly came back to me.

Myra and I had gone out to dinner earlier that evening, where we talked and drank and talked some more. After dinner, we went to a crowded bar where we pointed out possible suitors for each other, purposely picking the worst possible candidates, then laughingly imagining the outcomes. It was so much fun.

It had been past three by the time I walked her back to her place, and it simply made sense to crash on her couch instead of grabbing a cab back to my sleazy Jersey hotel. But we kept the promise we had made to each other the night before, both of us knowing how stinky we were at relationships, both of us longing for our newfound siblinghood to be permanent. That's why I woke up on her couch.

"What?" I groggily asked her.

"You were having a bad dream," she said.

"I know."

"You still get those, huh?"

"I had them when we were kids?"

"You would occasionally cry in your sleep, but you never remembered why."

"That makes sense. I couldn't have understood this dream at ten."

"Do you understand it now?"

"Not really. But I remember it."

"Tell me," she said softly as she sat down on the edge of the couch, and as I sat up to make room for her.

I had spoken of my dream on numerous occasions to my prison shrinks, virtual strangers to me, so I saw no reason not to share it with my kid sister. I was already keeping one big secret from her, and one was enough.

I recounted all the wonderful beginnings that I remembered from the dream—my soul mate and I walking down sparkly streets, rowing in a boat, rolling in the snow, holding each other on beaches, all of them— and then, in slow, painful detail, I relayed the crushing, tragic end in which I always lose my one true love. Myra put her hand on my thigh to comfort me, and was even welling up on my behalf.

"It's a reincarnation dream," she said somberly.

"Oh please," I groaned.

"What else could it be?"

"A dream."

"No, it can't be. You know how in dreams everything moves so slooooowwww, like you're walking through molasses? You describe none of that. The colors you describe are too vibrant, and the details you describe are too specific for this to be an ordinary dream. No, big brother, this is a psychic memory."

"Okay. Another county heard from."

"Yeah, but the only county that counts," she smiled. "But if it makes you feel any better, it wasn't really true love, and the woman wasn't really your soul mate."

"It's a metaphor."

"It's not a metaphor. True love, soul mates, those are real things. It's rare, granted, maybe once in a hundred, a thousand years rare, but real nonetheless. Sure, people fall in love all the time. The lucky ones can even stomach each other after twenty years, but soul mates are something special. They can never be pulled apart, and they never ever weary of one another."

"Hey, it's my dream. I think I'm the one who gets to decide what we are."

"Tell me how you feel when you're with her."

"Madly in love."

"Specifically."

"That is specific, and it's general, and it's specific. The love I feel for her consumes me. It overrides everything else. I'm at peace, and I'm on fire. I'm whole and I'm complete, yet I know that I alone am only half of what she and I are together. My senses are heightened to the point that I can see, hear, smell, touch, and taste all of existence, all at once, yet all I can really see, hear, smell, touch, or taste is her. She is my life. She is my death. She is my everything."

"Wow," Myra softly conceded. "I've got to admit, that does sound like true love. But here's the thing," she said as she took my hands. "If she was truly your soul mate, how could she have ended it with you? What'd you say in the dream? 'A single soul in Heaven, one entity separated into man and woman.' So if you were one single soul, how could she dump you? It would be like cutting out half of her heart."

"It's just a dream, okay? My subconscious teasing me with happiness."

"I don't believe in psychology."

"Of course you don't," I smiled.

"Do you really believe that's all it is? Your subconscious preventing you from being happy?"

"I don't know what it is. I just know how much it hurts at the end, yet I'm still all right having it over and over because of all those wonderful beginnings."

"I can regress you if you want."

"What's that?"

"I hypnotize you and send you back, back, back to your childhood, then back further into your past lives. I've done it before. It usually produces answers."

"I so wish I hadn't told you about this."

"All right, fine. If you want to live in ignorance, that's your prerogative."

I couldn't help but burst out laughing. She smiled, clearly not sure if she should join in my laughter or be offended by it, and then she rested her head on my shoulder. She tilted sideways and my eyes met hers—so blue, so warm, so captivating—and then we both laughed together. I didn't even know why we were laughing at that point—I think we were just happy to have found each other.

It was just like when we were kids. Bickering and squabbling and pissing each other off like brothers and sisters are supposed to, and she still had my back whether I wanted her to or not. I was so glad to have the little nut back in my life.

* * *

DAMMIT! WE MADE LOVE again!

It was passionate and rough like the first time because that seemed to be her style, and it was wonderful and glorious and hot and steamy, and I knew that it could only lead to us losing each other. I knew she knew this as well as I did. Why couldn't she have grown up to be ugly? It would have been so much easier for me.

We lay on the couch, panting in each other's arms, until she finally broke the silence. "We broke our promise."

"I blame you," I replied with a smile.

"Why me?"

"You're the girl. It's the girl's responsibility to say no."

"Yeah, a lot of good that did me in the foster care system."

"Ewwww."

"Sorry."

"No, I'm sorry," I said as I kissed the top of her sunny, yellow head.

"Can we just promise that this was the last time, and mean it?"

"I think we have to."

"Shake on it," she said as she put out her hand, and so we shook on it. We lay in each other's arms in silence for well over a minute, until she spoke again. "You ever wonder what our lives would've been like had Jack not cheated? Or if Jen hadn't found out about it? Or if she had forgiven him?"

"Our last names would be Carpelli."

"Seriously."

"No, I never think about it. It'd only make me sad."

"I think about it constantly. I can't stop myself. Like, if you could go back in time and change one thing, what would it be?"

"Why did you ask me that?" I snapped, startled.

"Everyone asks that," she answered innocently.

"Oh. Okay. Well, the past cannot be changed."

"You're sounding like a physicist," she chuckled.

"Thank you."

"So, go on, Professor."

I sat up, actually excited for the chance to verbalize the thoughts I had been keeping to myself these many months, albeit veiled in a way that wouldn't reveal what I had actually been up to. "It's like this. Either you can't change the past because it's impossible. Or you shouldn't change it because it's immoral. So, either way, you can't change it."

"Why would it be immoral?" she asked as she, too, sat up, enjoying what to her was merely a fun, intellectual exercise. "What if you could go back to save someone's life?" she added.

"And what if by saving that person's life you create a ripple effect that causes hundreds or thousands or millions of others to die instead? What if your actions cause you yourself to be unborn?"

"You can't become unborn," she laughed.

"Let's say you do something that causes your parents to not meet."

"You'd still be born."

My turn to laugh. "How could you be born if your parents never met?"

"Because we're eternal souls," she said as if it was the most obvious thing in the world. "We are but a single drop in the great ocean of the everything in which all matter is connected, never to end, and never having begun. And if our incorporeal, eternal soul decides to come experience this meager, earthly, three-dimensional, time-space existence, there is no power in the universe that could stop us."

"Here we go again," I said in mock defeat as I lay back down.

"You may have different parents. You may be born in a different place, into a different class, different language, different everything, but you'd still be you."

"I quit."

"And you'd still come into contact with many of the same people. The tides and currents of the universe would make it so. Like attracts like, and we draw into our world the souls with whom we are truly connected."

"Enough."

She reached across me, grabbed a cigarette, and lit up. "You give up too easily, big brother."

"I thought we were going to be talking science."

"I was talking science."

Once again, I burst out laughing.

I would have to go back to LA the next day, and I was so going to miss her. On the other hand, I now knew how to claim my treasure, and my kooky little Myra would be well taken care of for the rest of her days. She would never have to suffer or struggle or scam again.

I kissed her on the cheek, then she headed back to her room because we both knew we would break our promise again if she stayed with me on the couch.

Break's over. Time to get to work.

CHAPTER TWENTY-THREE

IKE ALL FLASHES OF SUDDEN inspiration, nothing is as simple as it first seems, and the devil is always in the details.

The first issue was whether it was safe to take this approach at all. Before I had travelled to the thirties, I had seen myself in the Merrill Lynch photograph, and that had been my permission. This time, there were no signs. Was I unnecessarily risking changing the past, thereby risking my own birth, let alone all humanity? Or was I overthinking it? It came down to what prior me's had done, and I had no way to know.

Why can't a future me just come tell me? He-I can be such a jerk sometimes.

I felt it safe to assume that all prior me's had slept with Myra, as I had, so they too would have awoken the next morning to hear the woman whose grandfather had left her an inheritance. They would therefore have had the same inspiration I had, and would've therefore spent the following days searching for a rationalization to go through with it—as I was in that very moment. Why wouldn't they? They were me.

I was convinced there was no better way for me to claim my stock certificate, and I had come too far to give up. It therefore stood to reason that prior me's would have come to the same conclusion. In fact, it seemed that the mere act of me choosing to go through with my scheme would imply that they had done so as well. I decided to experiment. I made the decision. I was going to do it.

Yep, I was still born. Phew.

I had never received an inheritance so I could not leave one to myself until some future date, thereby preserving my own past. It would have to appear to be a complete shock to me in order to convince the authorities of its legitimacy because I had never told anyone that I had a rich grandfather. I would also have to remain as low key as possible as I travelled back through time once more.

To claim my inheritance, Clarence would first need to write a will, which would require a trip to the nineties, sometime after I was born, where I-Clarence, posing as my own grandfather, would hire a lawyer to draft the document. I also would need, in present day, a death certificate with Clarence's name on it. Given the size of the fortune, and hence the many suspicious legal eyes that would be upon me, it could not be a forgery. That meant that I'd have to get hold of a real dead body. I had never robbed a city morgue before, but I didn't think it would be too hard.

The problem was that Clarence would be a hundred and eighteen years old in 2017, and such ancient John Doe corpses are probably not so easy to find. Plus, wouldn't someone ask how such an old man had been living alone all that time?

Yes, they would. Doesn't work. Okay. Starting over.

I would have to do this in two steps. Clarence would be my *great*-grandfather. I'd go back to the thirties, create a new identity that would become his son, my grandfather, then Clarence would bequeath the stock to him. I would leave the will and stock certificate with the law firm, and therefore out of my hands entirely.

I'd then jump to some midway point where I'd fake Clarence's death so that Grandpa, meaning me, would legally inherit the stock. I would then jump to the late nineties to write another will in which I-Grandpa would bequeath the stock certificate to the real me under my proper legal name, along with a sad, sappy letter explaining why he had never been a part of my life. Then I'd once again leave the will and stock certificate in the hands of the law firm, and as far from mine as possible.

Remember when I thought all this would be easy?

For little T.J.'s address, I would use the home of the foster parents I had been living with at the time. Once the authorities discover I had been in the foster care system, it would lead them to my San Quentin record, which would lead them to Seymour, which would lead them all the way back to me in present day Pasadena.

I'd come back to the present, and steal another John Doe from the morgue. I'd have to figure out where to place Grandpa so his corpse could be found by anyone but me—a reasonable place for an old man to die, with the certainty that whoever found him would contact the authorities. In Grandpa's wallet would be his legal identification, and a note instructing the authorities to notify the law firm in the event of an emergency.

"Oh my God!" I'd shout when Seymour would tell me about my sudden fortune. "How-how is that possible?" I'd say with tears of joy, or maybe tears of bittersweet sadness. Maybe I'd faint. No, I'm not that good an actor.

I'd work on the specifics of the performance later.

I chose 1961 as the midway point. It would make Clarence sixty-two years old, a normal time for people to die back then, therefore probably not too difficult to find the appropriate John Doe. "Grandpa" would therefore have to be born sometime in the thirties so I could look the right age when I-Grandpa accept Clarence's inheritance. That would make Grandpa around sixty in the nineties when I would walk into a lawyer's office to leave everything to little T.J. I knew a couple of Hollywood makeup artists, and I was pretty sure one of them would help me out without asking too many questions.

But the main reason I specifically chose 1961 as the midway point was because April 11 of that year was when Bob Dylan had his first paid performance at Gerde's Folk City in Greenwich Village.

I'd get to see Dylan before he was Dylan. How cool is that?

* * *

It took me several weeks to get everything together. I didn't know how long the whole venture would take so I would need more old cash to support me while I was gone. I hit the same antique currency dealers I had before my trip to 1932, again never taking more than two or three bills from each because it seemed mean.

I hung out with Wendy as much as I could because I knew I would be gone a long time and that I would miss her. I rewatched the first three seasons of *Mad Men*, this time for educational purposes only.

I FedExed additional cash to myself at the sleazy Jersey hotel because I was spending every weekend in New York with Myra. Yes, sure, I had considered getting a nicer New York place to live in, but I thought better of it. The sleazy hotel was reasonably priced as long as I kept prepaying by the month, the sleazy people had proven to be quite honest, and I really didn't spend much time there anyway. It was really just a place I could pop into, indoors and unseen, where cash and clothes awaited.

My final weekend with Myra before heading back to the thirties was quite difficult for me, but I knew I had to keep my feelings to myself. I failed.

"What's wrong?" she asked.

"Um, I'm going to be mailing in my college applications this week, and I'm a little nervous."

"No, that's not it."

Why did I even try?

"No, it isn't," I told her with that same cryptic smile to which she had grown accustomed.

"It's that thing again, right? The thing you won't tell me?"

"Yes."

"Well, be careful. Okay? Please?"

"More so than you can know. See you Saturday night, little sister."

"You'd better believe it, big brother."

We hugged. I got into the cab, and I let out my sadness.

For Myra, we'd be seeing each other in five short days. For me, as far as I could tell, it could be a year or more.

CHAPTER TWENTY-FOUR

THE DIFFERENCE BETWEEN THE PAIN of an eighty-five year time-jump and a seventy-nine year time-jump is barely noticeable because both make you wish you were dead. I was again brought to my knees, this time in the abandoned spot in the boonies I had scoped out so long ago. Fortunately, it was a beautiful sunny day in 1938 with a nice warm breeze—yes, I remembered to check the weather this time.

I regained consciousness after roughly fifteen hours, and forced myself to get to work. The shovel was exactly where I had placed it when I left 1932, and so I began to dig, hoping with all hope that my clunky suitcase was there as well.

It was! Yay! Everything, including the IBM certificate, was exactly as I had packed it. The top layer of clothes was pretty grungy because I had dug that initial hole fully dressed, so I reached to the bottom to slide out the cleanest suit that remained. It wasn't exactly pristine but it would do.

I put the shovel back in its original hiding place, then lugged the clunky suitcase toward the road, and then toward town, hoping to once again find some kind stranger to pick up a raggedy-looking hitchhiker. I didn't. I walked the entire thirty miles, ruing all the days before the invention of suitcase wheels.

At the edge of Jersey City, I was able to get a taxi to take me to that same Greenwich Village apartment building, which luckily had a vacancy. Three days to recuperate, and I knew which meds to buy. I was definitely getting better at this.

I went to a nearby Bank of America branch, got change for one of my thousand-dollar bills, opened a savings account in Clarence's name, and deposited the remaining nine grand. If you wonder why I didn't add to my IBM investment, well, I sure had thought about it. But I had no evidence to show that prior me's had done so, therefore nothing to confirm it wouldn't alter the past. I felt it best to err on the side of caution—and once I had that thought, I had to assume that prior me's had thought so as well. Better safe than sorry. A hundred and forty million dollars is a lot of money, so no need to be greedy.

I headed to the New York Public Library to once again rummage through old obituaries. I needed two new identities this time—I'll explain why later.

I found my first alter ego on my very first day. Marvin Stanley O'Rourke was born in Queens in 1929, which would make him thirty-two in 1961, which was close enough, and he died in the South Bronx two years later in 1931. I phoned the hospital, and the birth certificate was on the way. Four to six weeks, as usual.

My second identity took a few weeks longer to find, and was certainly worth the wait. In fact, he was perfect. Theodore Alexander Jameson had been born in Wichita, Kansas, in 1933, which would make him twenty-eight in 1961, which was my age exactly, and he passed away in St. Louis four years later in 1937. But what made him perfect was that his last name was actually Jameson. Same as Clarence. I had expected to have to go through some complicated name-changing rigmarole, but no more. And as an added bonus, as Theodore Jameson, I could once again go by the name "T.J."

I called the hospital, jumped six weeks forward, and got both birth certificates out of the mail. Time to see the lawyer.

I had found the law firm of Pendleton, Smythe, Horrace, and Cheevers before coming to 1938. Like Merrill Lynch, they had a solid reputation in the thirties, and would be a prominent international firm in 2017.

I didn't shave for a few days, then rubbed talcum powder in my hair, both in an attempt to make myself look older because Clarence would be thirty-nine, and this in an era in which people didn't age well to begin with. It didn't really help much.

My choice of attorney was Eric Toms, a lanky young man who had graduated Yale Law School only three years earlier. I needed someone young because he would have to serve as the executor of my-Clarence's will because I didn't know anybody else, meaning that I needed an attorney who would still be with the firm, hence easy to find, twenty-three years later. It's not common for attorneys to serve as executors of their clients' wills, but Eric was one of those who had done so on occasion over the years, and he wouldn't retire until the mid-seventies as a senior partner.

God bless the Internet. How could anyone time-travel without it?

He seemed a pleasant enough fellow, and after some minor chitchat we got down to business. I told him I had been living in Europe for some time, but after the death of my wife, and with the continent on the brink of war, I decided to return to the States. I didn't have much, I said, but I wanted to leave it to my poor, grieving son. I gave him Clarence's birth certificate, my bank account number, and the IBM certificate which had risen in value somewhat but not close to the explosion that awaited it. I asked him to keep it in the file with the will that he would draft.

He offered his condolences for the loss of my wife, then suggested I create a trust so that "my son" could avoid a lengthy probate when the time came. I wasn't exactly sure what "probate" meant, but I did like the sound of legally avoiding it so I accepted his advice. I had a good feeling about this dude.

He jotted down some notes, then snapped a photograph of the birth certificate with a small Brownie camera, then looked back up at me, startled. "You're thirty-seven years old? Golly, you don't look it at all."

"Thank you," I said as I flashed him my world-class, disengaging smile. "That is so very kind of you to say."

"Truthfully. My wife would love to know your secret."

"Now you're just embarrassing me," I said modestly as I tried to blush.

"My apologies. So, who would you like to serve as executor of your estate?"

"I was sort of hoping, if you wouldn't mind, that you would agree to it?"

"Well, Mr. Jameson, that is not very common. Wouldn't you prefer choosing a trusted friend or family member?"

"The only friends I would trust with something like this are still living in Europe, poor souls. As for my family, we've been estranged for some time because they didn't approve of my marital choice. Now that my dear beloved is gone, I don't see how I could look at them without bursting into tears of hatred. Please?"

He took a moment, then said, "Of course, sir. I'd be honored."

He said it would take a week to draft the document. I jumped forward and returned to his office at the designated time. Two copies were signed, witnessed, and notarized—all the legal i's dotted and all the legal t's crossed. I was given a copy. The law firm would keep the original along with my IBM certificate. And that was that.

* * *

I ONCE AGAIN DECIDED TO GIVE MYSELF a full two weeks before my next jump to 1961. I had to stop reading the news because World War Two was so imminent. Hitler's invasion of Poland was less than a year away, Jews were already being stripped of all humanity, and it was even more depressing than the Depression.

We like to think our era is completely messed up, but I was starting to realize that there may have never been a time in history that wasn't completely messed up. Just sayin'.

Watched *The Sopranos, Deadwood, The Wire*, all those great HBO shows that I had been too young to watch when they first aired. Read *A Tale of Two Cities*. Dylan, Joni, Pete, Woody, and Joan lullabied me to sleep at night.

In movie theaters I saw *You Can't Take It With You, Bringing up Baby, Angels with Dirty Faces, Flash Gordon's Trip to Mars,* and *Laurel & Hardy's Blockheads*. Some were actually pretty good. *Boy's Town* remains the only movie that ever actually made me cry. Mickey Rooney plays an orphan like me who turns to a life of crime, then a benevolent Spencer Tracy takes him under his wing. It's touching.

I missed Wendy, I missed sushi and Mexican food, and I missed Myra.

After two weeks, I packed my wardrobe into the clunky suitcase, along with my copy of the will, Clarence's, Marvin's, and Theodore's birth certificates, my Bank of America Passbook, and all but twenty dollars of my cash. I took a cab back to that abandoned spot outside Jersey City, where the hole was already dug.

I waited for the cabbie to drive off, then made my way into the woods. I disrobed, packed my suit and remaining cash into the valise, the valise into the hole, filled it up, then hid the shovel once more.

I knew my work in 1961 could take months, and I wanted it done before I went to see Bob Dylan's debut performance in April so I could enjoy it without distraction. On the other hand, I sure didn't want to arrive naked in the middle of winter, so I set the temporal destination for the summer of 1960. I had scoped out the specific day before having left 2017 because, yes, I had checked the weather.

I set the spatial destination to current and took a deep breath as I anticipated the pain that awaited me, glad that my rectum was free and clear.

Sayonara, Great Depression.

Send.

CHAPTER TWENTY-FIVE

V ISUALLY SPEAKING, NEW YORK CITY in the summer of 1960 did not look very different from that of 1938, but that icky feeling of mass poverty and despair had vanished. Gone were the hobos and beggars, at least that's how it looked to me. The nation was enjoying a postwar economic boom because all the factories in Europe and Asia had been blown up fifteen years prior, so to a large extent, the U.S.A. was the only game in town.

The Manhattan streets were still crowded with people and traffic, the residents all in a constant hurry, and hardly any of them ever smiled. I guess they just didn't know how good they had it. Also, there were still hardly any fat people, everyone still wore hats, and the new big cars were even cooler than they had been in the thirties. I wanted one.

I'll dispense with the details of my arrival into the era because you could probably piece it together on your own by now, so my first order of business was finding two apartments.

For the first, I secured a lovely three-bedroom in midtown Manhattan and furnished it in style. One of the bedrooms was to serve—or appear to serve—as an office, while the other two were reserved for Theodore and Clarence. I hired a kindly, middle-aged African-American lady to tidy up on alternate Thursdays, and warned her that "my father" was a crusty old curmudgeon who should be avoided at all costs. I made sure that both beds seemed slept in on the mornings she came.

Sometimes I would plant myself in Clarence's room prior to her arrival, and I'd shout obscenities in a raspy voice for her to hear, pop back to my own bedroom from where I would loudly tell Clarence to knock it off, then I'd come out to greet our cleaning lady, apologizing profusely for my Daddy's crudeness.

Other times, I would apply eyeliner to create wrinkles on my face, put on my hat and overcoat, and pull the collar up so no one could get a good look at me. I'd enter or exit the building as old Clarence, mumbling obscenities in the elevator or hallway for the neighbors to hear. Other times, I would greet them as Theodore, and again apologize on my senile father's behalf.

It was important to create Clarence's presence so that there would be no odd questions asked after I reported his death to the authorities. That said, I did consider whether this was potentially messing with history, but in the end I came to realize that it was the smart play, so the me's who came before me most certainly would have done the same thing.

For Marvin, I rented a dumpy, cheaply furnished studio apartment in Queens, then got him-me a day job at the City Morgue. It was menial, boring work, but not terribly worse than my janitorial duties at Caltech, and I saw no other way to know when the right corpse would arrive.

The plan was simple, but the parameters very specific. The John Doe would have to be found with no identification on him. There could be no sign of anything nefarious that may cause the police to stay involved. In essence, he had to be some lonely old man who died alone on the street, and whose remains would not be missed by anyone. I had to do it this way both for my own protection from the law, and also because the thought of denying a friend or family member the ability to say goodbye just seemed rude. He had to appear to be around sixty years old, roughly my height, and look similar enough to me to support the myth that I was his son.

One of my duties at the morgue was to log the details of the arriving cadavers, so I simply wouldn't do the paperwork. I'd wheel old Clarence to the designated drawer, strap my Apple Watch upon his wrist, then pop him through space to my ritzy Manhattan pad, leaving no record of a missing body at all. I'd finish my shift, take a cab to the apartment, and exit Marvin.

How else does one steal a dead body?

I knew it would be quite unnerving for me to have the watch out of my physical possession, but I was reasonably confident it would be resting safely on the John Doe's wrist as he lay on Clarence's bed, awaiting my return. Just in case, I'd run a few tests on other corpses during my first week on the job, just popping them from one side of the room to the other when no one was around to see.

So the plan was simple, yes, but I knew it could take a very long time.

I amused myself by continuing to screen the downloaded HBO shows on my watch. In theaters, I saw *The Apartment, Psycho, The Hustler,* and *Tarzan the Magnificent.* Several were quite good. *Breakfast at Tiffany's* would've been great if it hadn't been so racist. The film also included the song "Moon River," which made me think of Professor Szabo, which made me sad.

But they had television! Yay! Black and white, sure, and most of it stank, but *The Twilight Zone* was creepily awesome, and *The Ed Sullivan Show,* which would introduce The Beatles to America years later, was really cool. It had all sorts of different acts—legendary singers and comedians just starting out, puppets, and people throwing plates in the air—although Ed himself was kind of stiff and weird.

The folk music scene was thriving, and it was glorious! I got to see Pete Seeger, Dave Von Ronk, Carolyn Hester, and Ramblin' Jack Elliot. Once January rolled around, I started checking out open mikes because that was the month that twenty-year-old Bob Dylan arrived in the Big Apple. I knew the exact date of his first paid gig, but I saw no reason not to try to catch him before then if I could. I never did.

I woke up one morning in March—still having yet to find my perfect dead Clarence—to realize that I had missed a couple of birthdays along the way, sort of. That is to say that I had never missed any actual birthdays—my real birthday is in January, which was still a few months away given the vantage point of my 2017 present—but I had lived through roughly four hundred actual days since I began this whole time travel thing. In other words, I was technically thirty even though I had never officially turned twenty-nine.

Curiouser and curiouser.

Screw it. I was twenty-eight, and I would continue to be so until my twenty-ninth birthday. Call it vanity. Just sayin'.

Not too far from my Manhattan apartment was a small coffee shop that I liked to frequent. Technically, it was a bakery that made its own bread, rolls, and pastries, with only two or three tables that hugged the wall across the counter—not unlike a small Starbucks outlet today but far less trendy. The smell of the place was always scintillating, the baked goods out of this world, and the lack of tables was perfect for one who wanted as little contact with the world as possible.

Late one Saturday afternoon in March, I was skimming through the paper, trying to decide which folk club to attend that night, when I just happened to look up and my eyes fell upon the most beautiful woman I have ever, ever seen.

She had twinkling green eyes, shimmering jet-black hair that flowed gently down below her shoulders, and an alluring, merry smile that exuded elegance, femininity, and genuine, genteel warmth. I was captivated. I was mesmerized. The feelings that blasted into my essence were ones I had never experienced before, feelings I had always ascribed to bedtime stories and bad movies. I was in love in an instant. Hopelessly, madly, head-over-heels in love, and yes, at first sight.

She was the woman from my dreams.

She was my soul mate.

I knew it in an instant. Myra had been right that such things were real. Little sister had been right all along. There was no doubt about it.

"Ruthie!" I heard a man's voice shout.

Yes, yes, that was my dream-girl's name. I knew it the moment I heard it. Ruth Anne Lee. Born April 1, 1937. Her older brothers used to tease her that she was an April Fool's Day prank, and she always resented it. It was March, 1961, which meant she'd be turning twenty-four in just a few weeks, which meant that she was in the final stretch of her first year as an elementary school teacher.

She happened to glance toward me, and our eyes locked in delight.

"Hiiiiiiiiii," she said with a giant smile as if she had known me forever, which she had.

"Hi!" I blurted, probably too fast and excited for the moment.

Then the man who had called her name approached.

"Where'd you go?" he asked her. "I thought you were right behind me." He put his arm around her, and she kissed him.

I recognized the man from my dreams, too. I had seen him every time I had looked in a mirror.

He was me, and I am his reincarnation.

PART 3

FOR LOVE

CHAPTER TWENTY-SIX

D*EAR DIARY,*
    Today was the strangest day of my life.

It began like every other third Saturday of the month, the day on which Edward and I pitch in at the West Street Soup Kitchen. After our shift was done, we headed over to Antonio's Bakery to pick up the cake for our pre-engagement-party party. That is to say, the small, intimate dinner with close friends and family that I had wanted from the start, as opposed to the big fancy one everyone else seems to think we should have.

Edward was at the counter paying the cashier when my eyes happened to fall upon this very handsome man who was sitting at one of the small tables along the wall. I had never seen him before, but I somehow felt that I had known him all my life. An inexplicable wave of joy swept over me, akin to accidentally running into a best friend from years gone by. No, that's not it. It was far stronger than that.

"Hiiiiiiiii," I exclaimed before I even had a chance to gather my thoughts.

"Hi!" the man immediately responded, as if delighted that I remembered him, even though we had never met before.

"Ruthie!" I heard Edward shout from the counter.

Despite the strange man's good looks, my feelings weren't dirty, at least I don't think they were. I love Edward more than life itself. He is my betrothed, my eternal soul mate, and I have loved him since the very first moment we met, the very first moment I laid my eyes upon him. It had been magical, and inexplicable.

It had also been not very dissimilar to the moment in which I found myself in the bakery, and I was finding it more uncomfortable with each passing second.

"Where'd you go?" Edward asked me as he approached with the cake. "I thought you were right behind me." He put his arm around me, and I immediately kissed him. Long and hard and passionately. I wanted the strange man to know that I was taken and unavailable.

Or was I just reminding myself of that?

"Well, I missed you, too," Edward quipped. "It's been almost three minutes since I last saw you." Then he noticed the man, and he seemed as startled by him as I was. "Hi," he said quizzically.

"Hello," the man said with a pleasant smile.

"Have we met before?"

"I don't see how. I'm kind of new to the city." Then he put out his hand. "T.J."

"Edward," my betrothed replied, and they shook. "This is my fiancée Ruth."

"A pleasure to meet you, Ruthie."

How did he know to call me Ruthie? Only Edward calls me that.

Of course. He had heard Edward shout it only a moment before.

"Likewise, T.J.," was all I gave him back.

"This is really odd," Edward went on. "You seem so familiar." Then he turned to me. "Does he seem familiar to you, too?"

"No," I lied. "He did at first, but I think he just resembles an old friend from summer camp. No offense, T.J."

"Not at all, Ruthie," he replied with a Cheshire grin, like he knew something that Edward and I didn't. I have to admit his smile was alluring, attractive, and I hated it.

I turned back to Edward. "Darling, we'd better get going if you want to make your handball match before the dinner."

"You play handball?" this T.J. asked, as if startled by the news.

"Ever since I was a little boy. Why, do you play?"

"I only picked it up four or five years ago, but I took to it right away. Now I know why."

"Why?"

"Oh, um, no reason," he answered with an almost embarrassed laugh, as if his own personal joke.

I liked his laugh, and I didn't like that I liked it. "Darling, we really should go," I told my one true love.

"One minute, kitten," Edward said then turned back to the man. "Maybe this is fortuitous. I have a court reserved for tomorrow morning as well, but my colleague had to cancel at the last minute. Would you like to step in?"

"Edward, you can't impose on a perfect stranger like that."

"No, no. No imposition at all. I'd love to."

"Terrific. Tomorrow morning, nine o'clock, Columbia University gymnasium. You know where that is?"

"I'll GPS it, er, I'll figure it out."

What on Earth is a GPS? The man was strange, this T.J., maybe even dangerous, and I did not want to know him. "Well, now that that's settled, we'd best be on our way. Pleasure to meet you, T.J."

"Pleasure's all mine, Ruthie."

I wished he'd stop calling me that.

* * *

Tuesday, March 21, 1961

DEAR DIARY,

Today I truly earned my stripes as a teacher.

Donny Jergens has always been a rather rambunctious little boy. Fidgety in class, overly energetic, prone to roughhousing with his buddies, always raising his hand to loudly answer questions whether he knows the answer or not.

He's also a very sweet child. One day, when I came to class wearing my red and yellow polka dot dress, he gave me the greatest compliment a first grader ever could. "You look so beautiful, Miss Lee," he said. "Just like a clown."

For the past week or so, however, Donny has seemed sullen. When I *call upon him in class, he merely looks to the floor and shrugs his shoulders with a muted, "I dunno." I've tried my best to draw him out, but in the end, I feel that such matters are best left to the parents.*

This morning, the mystery was solved. I was walking into the school when I noticed the other children in the yard teasing and laughing at little Donny. Donny, normally one who would immediately sling back, merely accepted the verbal onslaughts as he tried to keep his tears inside his eyes. As I listened closer, the reason for the ridicule became clear. Donny's mother and father were getting a divorce.

Scandalous for the parents, no doubt, but no child should have to pay the price.

"That's enough," I told them, knowing full well that such an admonition would be a very short-lived solution. "Come with me, Donny."

"Why? I didn't do nothin' wrong! They started it!"

"You're not in trouble, sweetie. I'd just like to talk with you."

I took him inside and tried to get him to open up, but he was too embarrassed to offer much. I told him that he would come to feel better in time—empty words that fell on deaf ears, but I had garnered enough information to hatch an idea.

After the second bell, and after the usual minute or so of the children's unruliness, I got the class to simmer down, then launched into action. "Who has a bedroom?" I asked them.

All the children raised their hands, of course. "Me!" "I do!" "I have a bedroom!"

"And who likes their bedroom?" I asked.

They all kept their hands up, except for Joey Palmer, who slowly let his fall back down to his desk.

"Why don't you like your bedroom, Joey?" I asked.

"Because I share it with my brother, and I hate my brother."

Nothing is more adorable than the unmitigated honesty of a child.

"Me too," said a few of the other boys who also dropped their hands. "So do I."

"I share mine with my older sister," said Suzie Jackson as she dropped her hand as well. "She's so mean."

With less than half the class still raising their hands, I continued. "All right, but what if you had the room all to yourself? Would you like it then?"

All hands shot right back up.

"I love my brother, but I'd like my room even more if he wasn't in it," said Petey.

"Well, guess what?" I continued. "Donny is going to have two bedrooms."

There was a sudden hushed silence as the new information was absorbed.

"Wow," said some. "Whoa," said others. Donny pursed his lips in an attempt not to smile as he felt the tide turn.

"Now, who likes Christmas?" I continued, and every hand shot right back up. "Donny is going to have two Christmases." Their mouths gaped open, and Donny was no longer able to contain his smile. "Who likes Easter?" I didn't even need to complete the thought because the children were already ahead of me, so I went in for the kill. "And who likes having a birthday party?"

"You're going to get two birthday parties?" Joey exclaimed incredulously.

"Uh-huh," Donny answered with the proudest grin I have ever seen on a little boy. "Two parties for every birthday. That's what they told me."

"You're so lucky!" shouted Petey.

"I wish my parents would get divorced," Suzie wistfully moaned, and all the boys and girls trumpeted their agreement.

Okay, so maybe I took it a tad too far.

* * *

Wednesday, March 22, 1961

Dear Diary,

Nothing much of interest happened today, yet I must force myself to remain in the habit of making my entries each night if I ever hope to be a real writer. All the great ones say that the best way to practice writing is by writing, and the best way to develop a keen, astute memory is by forcing oneself to jot down every pertinent detail that one can retain.

Difficult to do, however, when nothing of interest transpired.

I find myself thinking about that man Edward and I met at Antonio's

173

Bakery this past Saturday, and perhaps thinking about him more than I should.

No, that's all for today. Nothing of interest happened.

* * *

Friday, March 24, 1961

DEAR DIARY,

It seems that Edward has made a new friend. I never wanted to be one of those women who tells her boyfriend or husband with whom he may or may not be friends, but I just wish he would stop talking about him.

That said, perhaps some of the blame is my own because I do find myself asking many questions about the man despite myself.

The most peculiar part is Edward's insistence that he and this T.J. are similar when they could not be more different. Physically, there is no resemblance at all. Beyond that, Edward is an art history professor at Columbia, politically somewhat of a socialist, while T.J. is some kind of investor, which would imply that he's a pro-Nixon Republican like Father. Edward grew up in Long Island, one of the Montadels, a distinguished, reputable family that goes back generations. T.J. grew up poor in Southern California, and is rather secretive about his past. Edward is a devotee of classical music, and T.J. likes folk, a genre of which neither Edward nor I particularly fancy. Edward loves the theatre. T.J. is a movie fan, and he even likes television programs.

Where on earth is the similarity?

"We laugh at the same things," my love would explain. "We see the world in the same way. We make the same kind of pithy little comments. Half the time we finish each other's sentences. My gosh, we even play handball the same way. I can't explain it, but there's just something about the fellow that's, I don't know, endearing to me."

"But what can you boys possibly talk about if your tastes in everything are so vastly different? He doesn't even care for art, for goodness sake, and that's your greatest passion."

"You're my greatest passion, kitten," he said.

"Awww," I sighed. "And you're mine, my darling."

We kissed, and then, to my chagrin, he returned to the topic at hand.

"It's not exactly that he doesn't like art," my betrothed continued defensively on his newfound friend's behalf. "It's that he doesn't know it. He doesn't understand it. I sense that deep within him lies the soul of a poet."

"Are you getting sweet on him?" I teased.

He laughed along as he continued. "No, no, hear me out. The other day, after handball, we decided to go out for a beer. So we're walking along 57th Street, when we pass the Sydney Janis Gallery. Jackson Pollock's Number 4 is hanging in the window, and T.J. just stops cold. Do you know the piece?"

"I'm not sure, I don't think so. Not by name, anyway."

"It's actually quite a remarkable work. Stark contrasts, bold style. Instead of focusing on objects, Pollock gives us events and ideas, taking abstractions and making them concrete in a centrifugal style that draws you right in. Very interesting."

"And?"

"Like I said, T.J. noticed it, and he stopped dead in his tracks. He just stared at it, transfixed. His mouth gaped open. He was barely able to speak. And that was that."

"But you still asked him what he saw in it, didn't you?" I inquired with a smile because that's what my love always asks when trying to draw someone toward art. It was the first thing he had ever said to me.

"You know me too well, kitten," Edward laughingly replied. "I'm going to have to start being a little inconsistent, just to keep you on your toes."

Then it was my turn to laugh, but I returned to the topic. "So what did he say?"

"Well, his answer didn't quite make sense. The point of the story is how strongly the piece moved him."

"I'm just curious. What was his answer?"

"The thing you've got to understand about T.J. is that sometimes he says things that are just odd. Most of the time I can chalk it up to some quaint, California expression, but other times you just have to ignore it."

"What was his answer?" I playfully demanded.

"Well, without taking his eyes off the piece, still in his little trance, he said, 'If I broke through the glass of that window and tore that canvas to shreds, my life may have gone in a completely different direction.'"

I don't know why, but I could only laugh at the absurdity of this strange man's response.

Last night, Edward and I made love. I had to keep my eyes open the whole while because the few times I closed them, I felt T.J. inside me.

This is terrible.

I love Edward, and only Edward.

CHAPTER TWENTY-SEVEN

I HAVE TO SAY, IN all modesty, I was a pretty impressive guy in my past life. Right out of high school, I took a year off before college and went to Africa to help bring food and medicine to the impoverished. In essence, I joined the Peace Corps before there even *was* a Peace Corps. After that, I totally ticked off my parents when I walked away from my family's vast landholdings and real estate enterprises to study art. I knew I had no actual talent, but I felt that if I could inspire others toward greatness, or if I could help those less knowledgeable find the joy that art brought me, that would be my contribution to the world, and a legacy of which I could be proud.

To sum up, I liked Edward. Edward was awesome. So I felt a little bad as I set out to steal Ruthie from him, but I took comfort in the knowledge that he had had her up till now, and he would be with her again in his next life when he's me.

For I knew the moment I saw Ruthie that my destiny lay forever in 1961—time and karma had combined to make that crystal clear, and my own heart would never forgive me if I let her go. I began working on a new plan to get the rewards of my stock certificate to the appropriate beneficiaries—myself no longer included—and the Apple Watch to the NASA guy. I just had to figure out a way to make it work for all those I had set out to help in the first place.

My conversations with Edward were similar to the conversation I had had with my past self in that remote spot in the boonies where I had buried my clunky suitcase, but not identical. Memories would flood back as events unfolded, but only the big ones—more akin to memories of childhood. The details are hazy.

I could remember being Edward playing handball with T.J., but I couldn't remember the specifics of any one game. I could remember being Edward thinking that T.J. would love art, which I have to say is a little annoying now that I'm T.J., but I know Edward means well because I remember meaning well.

In terms of the few mistakes I made—mentioning GPS, wondering aloud what would've happened if I destroyed the Pollock, and a few other blunders that I've yet to mention—you have to understand that talking to Edward was like talking to myself, that internal dialogue we all have in the privacy of our own brain in which there's no need to self-edit. Yes, I knew I had to get a handle on that, but far too often I was just lulled into complacency because Edward and T.J. are one and the same.

But I had no concerns that my decision to remain in 1961 would alter the past because I knew with certainty that this had all happened before. I remembered some of it, dreamt some of it, and I could piece together the parts in between. I just needed to remain careful. I also needed a better understanding of this whole reincarnation-karma stuff, something I had always believed to be nonsense, and there was only one person I knew to ask.

One more thing before I move on. If any of you happen to have thought that Ruthie's "two bedrooms, two Christmases" spiel was unoriginal or cliché or something like that, remember, it was 1961, so shame on you, you modern-era snobs. There had been no research on the subject of divorce, no official advice to help parents or children navigate through it. Ruthie had come up with that notion all on her own, on the spur of the moment, just to help a sad little boy. As far as we know, she may have even been the originator of the idea.

If I seem to be a little defensive on her behalf, it's only because I am absolutely, madly in love with her. She has the most giving, generous spirit I have ever known, and the emptiness I have felt my entire life is magically gone whenever I'm in her presence. She is the part of me that has always been missing, and she makes me feel whole. This is true for

Edward, and it's true for me. She has been our soul mate from before time began and she will remain so long after it ends. So look down on me, thief that I am, but you'd better respect her.

Back to our story.

I set the temporal destination on the watch to present, spatial destination to my sleazy Jersey hotel room, and I took a deep breath. Send.

Three days to recuperate, then I took a cab to Myra's parlor.

Given the strangeness of our quasi-sexual-sibling relationship, I tried to come up with a sensitive way to tell her that I had found my true love. I didn't want to hurt her, yet I knew I couldn't lie to her because, well, she'd know. I tried to imagine how I would feel if the shoe were on the other foot, if she had been the one to fall in love with another. I realized I would be genuinely happy for her, and even somewhat relieved for it would cement our relationship as brother and sister once and for all. Of course, that didn't mean that's how *she* would feel. I needed to find a nice way to say it gently.

I had yet to come up with the right words when the cab pulled up to her curb, and I was surprised to see a line of clients in front of her parlor that stretched almost half a block. I started to walk inside since I wasn't a client, but the crowd turned on me as if I was cutting in. I won't repeat the Big Apple profanity that was loudly thrashed upon me, but it was pretty severe.

Before I had a chance to explain, Myra appeared, walking a woman out of the building. As usual, she looked good. "Myra!" I shouted over the mob's obscenities.

"T.J.?"

Bear in mind, despite the fact that I had spent over a year in the past, as far as Myra was concerned, we had said goodbye to each other only a few days prior. Also, our relationship till then had been confined to weekends only, so me showing up midweek naturally made her assume that something had gone astray. "What's wrong?" she asked.

"I've got to talk to you."

"Come in," she said without pause, whereupon the crowd turned on her. "No, no. He's not a client. He's my brother. I'll just be a few minutes, I promise."

We went inside. "What's going on?" I asked, referring to the crowd.

"I'm on. I am so on, man. I am on fire. So, I have this list of close

179

friends and regulars, so when I get like this, I text them and—" Then she cut herself off, and her tone shifted dramatically. "Oh my God! You met her!"

"What?"

"The woman from your dreams. You met her!"

"How can you know that?"

"I don't know. I told you, I'm on fire. Congratcha-freaking-lations!"

"Listen, I'm sorry it came out like this. I mean, if this is weird or callous or—"

"Oh, hush," she said as she gave me a warm sisterly hug. "I am so happy for you, big bro. I mean, the woman's going to crush you—we know that from your dreams—but at least you'll be happy till she does, and you'll be ready for it. And I'll be here for you to help pick up the pieces."

"She's not going to crush me."

"Your dreams say she will."

"I know, but she won't. That's why I have questions."

The rumblings and the hollers from outside grew louder.

"Listen," she told me. "I promise my people a first-come-first-served kind of deal, and if we talk too long, they'll think I'm reneging. Hang out in the kitchen, grab a beer, let me do my thing, then we'll hang and talk as long as you want. 'K?"

I agreed, she went to work, and she was most certainly "on". Be it tarot cards, palms, or tea leaves, gone were all the con-artist tricks I had seen that first morning I had watched her work. She spoke slowly and specifically, never once contradicting herself, and her advice was often surprising.

One male client had a difficult choice. He had been offered two jobs. One was a high-paying gig that he did not expect to enjoy, in an atmosphere of politics and deceit, the other comparatively low paying, but one that he was certain would fulfill him.

"Your reservations about the high-paying job will prove to be correct," she told him. "But your expectations of the other are idealistic, and wrong. In the end, neither job will fulfill you. If these are truly your only options, go for the money."

Some time later, she would discover that a close friend of the man took the low-paying job, and quit after three weeks when he discovered that the business was a scam. The man himself never found the job satisfaction he had sought, but he had an enjoyable life nonetheless by finding pleasure and fulfillment in his off hours.

A teenage girl who was several weeks late for her period had taken a home test to discover that she was pregnant. Her boyfriend was unwilling to help in any way. The girl was crying as she explained how afraid she was to tell her parents, and wanted to know how they would react. She wanted to know what life held in store for her if she carried the baby to term, or if she didn't. Myra placed the girl's hands palm up, then slid her own under them, as she had with me that first time we met.

It took my sister less than three seconds before she opened her eyes and said, "You're not pregnant."

"But the test said I am."

"You must have read it wrong, or done it wrong, or it was defective. I don't know. But you're not pregnant."

She gave the girl a small box, and sent her into the bathroom to try again. Minutes later, the girl came back, bawling. "You're wrong! I am! Look!"

Myra looked at the strip, and then told the girl to reread the instructions. The girl did as ordered, then burst into a new set of tears, these ones of joy.

"Thank you! Thank you!" she shouted as she hugged my little sister.

I could go on, but suffice it to say that it was all astounding, and all impossible. I could only wonder what Professor Szabo would make of this utterly unscientific display of truth.

By the time Myra walked her last client out the door, she looked drained. She came into the kitchen, plopped herself into a chair, kicked her feet up onto another chair, and let her arms dangle lifelessly by her side. "I'm done. I'm spent. I got nothing left. Sorry."

"It's okay," I laughed. "It was pretty amazing."

"I know."

"How did you do that?"

"I don't know."

"Because from a scientific perspective, it's—"

"I'm too wiped for that conversation, Teej. Sorry."

"It's okay."

"You hungry?"

"Yeah."

"Grub's on me. It's been a good day."

* * *

MYRA AND I DIDN'T discuss anything paranormal that night, which was fine because I had to give myself some time before jumping back to the sixties anyway. Word of her incredible day of being "on" had spread, and her bookings were off the charts. It wasn't until Friday that she finally had the time to meet me for a late night drink, a little after one.

She admitted that she wasn't "on" anymore, that she'd been faking it since Wednesday, but that she still had the knowledge and experience to answer any questions I may have. I told her how I had met Ruthie and Edward—leaving out the time travel part of it, of course—how I knew with certainty that Ruthie was my one true love, and how I knew with equal certainty that I was Edward's reincarnation.

"What?" she said as her eyes squinted and her nose rose up in a wrinkle. "I've never heard of such a thing. Are you sure?"

"He's what I look like in the dream. And I remember being him, and hating me for stealing her—and my face is what he-me thinks of at the time."

"Wow," was all she could say as she took a small sip of her micro-brewed beer. "I suppose that if time isn't linear, on a cosmic level, then there is no reason why a future life couldn't precede a past one, or vice versa, or why they couldn't completely overlap."

"Yes, that must be it."

She gazed at me, and I knew the look. I was ten years old the first time I saw it. "You're lying," she said.

"Yes."

"So you know what it is, you just won't tell me." I sighed, and she went on. "It's that thing again, right? Your big secret?" I nodded, somewhat ashamedly, but what else could I do? She went on, a little peeved. "In other words, you want me to help you, but you won't tell me the whole story. You want me to help you, but you won't tell me something I'm now truly dying to know and understand."

"Please?"

She laughed a little laugh, and shook her head. "I'm too good to you."

"You are."

"Okay, so first of all, if this is really true, if both you and this Edward are really her one true love, then, oh gee, the poor girl."

"Why poor girl?"

"Because it's not supposed to work that way, stupid. No one is supposed to have *two* one true loves. True love is like, it's like, like a giant supermagnet, the most powerful force of attraction in the universe, shifting world events to draw its lovers together without them even knowing it. So imagine two real, like sciencey-real, supermagnets with something in between them magnetically attracted to both. It could tear her apart."

"She does cry in the dream when she dumps me, er, Edward."

"No kiddin'," she said. "I can't imagine what the poor kid must be going through."

"You think I should bow out gracefully to spare her all this?"

"Could you?"

"No, probably not."

"Trust me, you couldn't. You have no choice in this matter anymore. You are as magnetically drawn to her as she is to you, as she and Edward are to each other. But your dream has ordained that she will choose you, and it just may destroy her. Man, this is the saddest love story I've ever heard."

"I never looked at it that way," I said. "So then she does choose me, huh?"

"Even without the dream telling us so, it would be obvious. You're the older soul. You'd be more attractive."

"I am more attractive."

"Not that kind of attractive. I'm speaking spiritually. You have the experience of Edward's life, plus your own life, plus however souls exist in between. You are the wiser soul, and in a head-to-head matchup, that is far more irresistible."

"He's smarter than me, actually."

"There's a difference between wisdom and knowledge. But at least she ends up with the nicer guy."

"No, on that you're definitely wrong. He's the nicer guy. He's the nicest, most giving guy I've ever met."

"He's a prick."

"You said you weren't on, and you never met the guy. You can't make that assertion."

"This isn't intuition, it's logic. From the moment of your birth, and through no possible fault of innocent little baby T.J., your life has been a living hell. One random tragic disaster after another—except there's no such thing as random. You brought it all upon yourself. And by 'you', I mean Edward."

"I'm telling you, this guy has never done a bad thing in his life."

"Then he will."

"Oh my God!"

"What? You remember something?"

I couldn't believe what I saw. Of all the gin joints in all the world, into our little saloon walked Mr. and Mrs. Seymour Lancing, my parole officer and his wife.

His eyes met mine instantly. "T.J.?"

"Just play along," I whispered urgently to Myra. "Please."

"What on earth are you doing in New York?" Seymour boomed as he approached.

I vaguely remembered him saying something about a trip to New York back when he was staring at my *Freewheelin' Bob Dylan* poster, back when I was recuperating from my first set of time-jumps. For me, that had been well over a year ago. For everyone else, barely a few months.

What do I do? What do I do? What do I do?

"Excuse me, sir," I said calmly. "Do we know each other?"

"Really?" he said. "That's how you're going to play this? Really?"

I knew it was a stupid way to go, of course I did. I just couldn't think of anything better in the terror of the moment—all I could see was my San Quentin cage.

He took out his cell phone and started to dial, then turned to Myra. "I'm sorry, ma'am, but you should know that this man is a wanted felon. First for armed robbery, now for parole violation. He's heading back to prison."

I wanted to point out that I had not been convicted of *armed* robbery, but that sure wouldn't have helped my cause. It may have even been a trap he was setting for me.

"Police?" He said into his phone. "I want to—yes, I'll hold." He turned to me with disgust. "If you're going to run, punk, now's the time."

"I know not to what you are referring, sir."

"Just stop it. You're supposed to be mopping floors at Caltech right now, T.J., and you're not going to charm your way out of this one. Honestly, I had such high hopes for you, son. You little punk."

Think, T.J.! Think!

I got an idea, but I had to absolutely commit to it. Absolutely commit. So I did. I just hoped committing was enough.

"Sir, I honestly don't know who you think I am, but I propose this. Why don't you telephone this—B.J., was it?"

"Nice," Seymour replied.

"Phone him. Please. If he is not where you believe he is supposed to be, I will walk with you to the nearest police precinct of my own volition."

I could see Myra trying to hide the shock in her eyes.

"Of your own volition, eh?" Seymour said. "Okay. I'm curious to see where this is going." He set his phone to speaker, and speed-dialed me.

"Hello," we heard me answer. We all did.

"T.J.?" Seymour replied in disbelief.

"Hey, Seymour, what's up?"

Myra was terrible at hiding her shock.

"Where are you?" Seymour asked telephone-me while continuing to stare at bar-me in shock.

"Same place I've been every night this week after ten. Caltech. Where else would I be?"

"Who's with you?"

"No one's with me. No one's ever with me. I'm just mopping."

"You have your mop and bucket with you right now?"

"Of course."

"Let me hear it."

"Why?"

"Just do it!"

Then we heard the sound of sloshing water and mopping. "Did I do something wrong, Seymour?" telephone-me asked innocently.

"No, T.J., you didn't," he replied, defeated. "Get back to work, son. I'll see you when I get home." He hung up the phone, and looked at me with the most apologetic face I've ever seen on an employee of the Department of Corrections. "I am so sorry, sir. But I swear to God, you have a perfect double living in Southern California."

"Well you should be sorry," I barked. "This has been very embarrassing for me. I have been trying to impress this young lady, and I think you have ruined my chances. My goodness, what she must think of me now."

"I don't blame you, baby," Myra said as she took my hand. "There are crackpots all over this town."

"Thanks, kitten," I said, and then turned back to Seymour. "Just be grateful I don't take this up with your superiors. Now please, at least have the decency to consume your beverages elsewhere so I don't have to look at your face a moment longer."

"Of course. Again, I am so sorry."

"Just go. Just go."

The moment he was out of eyeshot, I couldn't stop smiling. It was terrifying when I thought I was on my way back to prison, but in the end, it was so worth it.

"How the hell did you do that?" Myra asked, astonished.

"Um," I began.

"It's that thing you won't tell me again, isn't it?"

"Yeah," I said apologetically.

"One day you're going to have to tell me."

"I can't. I'm sorry. I won't."

"Bastard," she laughed.

Of course, the downside of all this was that the following morning I would have to pop back five days to Pasadena to spend the entire week performing my janitorial duties at Caltech so I could punch in my punch card each night and be at work on Friday to take Seymour's call—that was the promise I had made to the universe, and the only reason my dumb little plan had worked.

Yet all I wanted to do was head back to the sixties to woo the love of my lives.

CHAPTER TWENTY-EIGHT

D EAR DIARY,
      Last evening was spent celebrating my birthday at a small dinner at Father's and Mother's, with Willie, Tom, and Gene Jr. still spouting their juvenile wisecracks about how my existence was but an April Fool's Day prank. It's funny how after all these years my big brothers' dumb comments still grate on me, but letting them see that would only encourage them further so I merely rolled my eyes as if in good fun.

    After dinner, Edward and I went back to his apartment where he popped open a bottle of Burgundy and gave me my present. It was a delicate, white gold necklace from which dangled a diamond heart. "The white gold represents your purity, my love," he said softly. "The heart is mine, which you own completely."

    My true love is so romantic, and I cherish him so.

    We made love not long after that. I forced myself to keep my eyes open.

    We slept much of the morning, waking around eleven. I took the first shower, he the second, and I could just hear the water turning off when there was a knock at the door. I opened it to find T.J., grinning proudly, even though he was as surprised to see me as I was him.

"Oh, hi, Ruthie. I didn't know you'd be here."

"Why would you?" I replied, mustering all my defenses because he looked good and his smile was almost hypnotic.

"Go get your fellow. You guys have got to come check this out."

It was clear by context that he meant he wanted to show us something, but why didn't he just say so?

Edward got dressed, and we followed T.J. down to the curb to see the new red convertible he had just bought.

"A 1961 Thunderbird," he boasted, as if buying a car was some miraculous achievement. "A brand new '61 T-bird. I mean brand spankin' new. How cool is that?"

First, "cool"? Why was he speaking like a beatnik when there was nothing beatnik about him at all? Moreover, why was he so proud of buying an automobile that was new? Why wouldn't it be new? From what I'd been told, he was a well-to-do man.

"Let me take you guys for a spin."

Before I could come up with a valid excuse to decline his invitation, Edward piped in. "Sounds like fun," he said, and then opened the back door for me.

"You're making her sit in the back?" T.J. asked, as if my love was offending me.

"It's how things are done," I defensively insisted on my betrothed's behalf, although I did begin to wonder why it's how things are done. "Would you have Edward sit in the back? How would that look?"

"Hmmm," T.J. humphed judgmentally, although what he could possibly have been judgmental about, I had no idea.

He drove onto the turnpike, and then, boy oh boy, did he let that car fly.

"Slow down, old sport," Edward said with an amused smile. "You'll get a ticket."

"Maybe not," T.J. replied. "And if I do, it'll be worth it. Consider it the cost of driving fast."

Edward laughed, and I have to admit that I was enjoying myself. I had never been in a convertible before because Father had always been a Cadillac man, Edward owned a sensible Chrysler, and I still had the same little Dodge that Father had bought me as my Vassar graduation present.

But the warm spring breeze that massaged my face and tousled my hair in all directions felt quite liberating.

The problem was that I had taken my seat behind Edward, feeling it the proper thing to do, but making it impossible to see him. My eyes kept falling upon T.J.'s profile and his joyful, alluring smile, and I found myself drawn to him even more.

Stop it, I told myself. Stop it.

I closed my eyes, and I let myself get lost in the timeless, blowing wind.

After what felt like only minutes later, even though my wristwatch indicated otherwise, Edward told T.J. to take the next exit, then directed him toward a diner a few blocks away—one that my betrothed and I knew quite well.

"Let's get some pie," he said.

It had been our regular stop upon our return to the city after many of our romantic road trips, our secret private place, and I felt a little betrayed that Edward was willing to share it with anyone, especially this peculiar man.

"Wow," T.J. said upon entry, which was also quite strange. The food at this diner is quite good, but the décor is by no means impressive. "I remember this place," he muttered to himself.

"You've been to this greasy spoon before?" Edward asked, surprised.

"Sort of. Not really. Hard to explain."

What a peculiar fellow he was, but I realized that might be a good thing. The more peculiar I find him, the less drawn to him I will be.

We were seated at a booth by the window, and he continued to be odd. When the waitress came to take our orders, T.J. asked for the boysenberry pie, Edward requested apple pie with ice cream for the two of us, and T.J. quickly turned to him.

"Do you always order for her?" he asked.

"Of course. It's the gentlemanly thing to do."

Then he turned to me. "And you're okay with that?"

"Why wouldn't I be? It's gallant."

"Did he get it right?"

"What do you mean?"

"Is apple pie and ice cream your first choice?"

"Well, no," I had to admit. "It's my second choice, but I like apple as well."

"I'm sorry, kitten," Edward immediately responded. "Of course you should get what you want. What's your first choice?"

The truth is that my first choice was boysenberry without the ice cream, T.J.'s choice. "Peach," I answered. "Peach pie, with ice cream."

After all that, I ended up with my third choice, and still with the ice cream.

The boys fell into a conversation about T.J.'s new vehicle while I began to ponder the genesis of men ordering for women. It's chivalrous and proper, no doubt, but it really doesn't make any sense if you think about it.

"We're being rude," T.J. finally said. "We should talk about something Ruthie can participate in."

He was right once again. I just wished that Edward had been the one to say so.

"So, what would you like to talk about?" T.J. asked me.

"Art," I replied without hesitation because I knew it was a topic about which he knew little, a topic with which he was uncomfortable. I had no idea what a terrible path I had chosen.

"Oh God," he groaned good-naturedly. "I wish I hadn't asked."

Good. Now let him be the one to feel perpetually challenged.

"What's wrong with art?" Edward replied. "You would utterly appreciate it if you merely kept an open mind. Look how you loved that Jackson Pollock piece."

"I wouldn't quite call it 'love.'"

"You were transfixed."

"I think 'stunned' would be a better word."

"All right, stunned. The point is that it affected you. You connected with it. It made you feel something, think something."

"True, but it didn't make me think the kind of thing you think it made me think."

"That doesn't matter. All that matters is that it touched you. So, I propose this. Next Saturday afternoon, allow me to take you to the Met, the Metropolitan Museum of Art, and let me introduce you to a world I know you'll cherish."

"Why?" he asked with another good-natured groan.

"Because it will change your life," Edward told him. "Kitten, now that you know him a little bit, don't you think he'd find it a worthwhile experience?"

Only because I could tell for a fact that he would find it absolutely tortuous, I answered, "Yes, I do, darling. I would love to see T.J. spend an afternoon at the Met." Then I sat back to watch him worm his way out of it.

"Okay, on one condition," he began tentatively.

Oh-oh.

"Not Saturday, a week from Tuesday, the eleventh. There's this new, young folk singer I'd really like you guys to check out—to see. You accompany me to Gerde's, and I'll accompany you to the Met."

"Folk music?" Edward groaned with the identical, good-natured reluctance that T.J. had shown only moments before.

As you know, Dear Diary, I don't have any particularly strong feelings toward the genre one way or the other, but I did not want to spend a full afternoon and evening with this man. "We're not folk music fans. It doesn't seem like a sensible bargain for any of us."

"Keep an open mind," T.J. said as he smilingly mocked my one true love. "It will change your life."

"Cleverly done, old sport," Edward retorted. "All right, it's a date. Next Tuesday. We'll introduce you to the art world, and you can introduce us to the world you cherish."

I could not have been looking forward to it less.

* * *

Tuesday, April 4, 1961

DEAR DIARY,

T.J.'s father passed away this morning.

The moment Edward told me, an overwhelming sensation of sadness swept over me. It was strange because I barely know T.J. and I have never met his father, yet the sadness that consumed me went far beyond mere empathy. It was as if I imagined the pain he must have been feeling, and *brought it into my heart as if my own. I cried for him, for this boy I barely know, for this man who frightens me.*

"We should attend the funeral as a show of support," I found myself telling Edward. "I think it would be meaningful to him."

"You have such a kind soul," my true love said as he took me in his arms and kissed me on the forehead.

That was early this afternoon, and as I sit here writing this entry many hours later, I try to make sense of the feelings that came over me, and I can't.

Yet I still imagine T.J.'s pain, and I continue to feel it on his behalf.

What is happening to me?

* * *

Friday, April 7, 1961

DEAR DIARY,

It was a cremation, not a funeral.

Edward and I assumed we would blend into the back of the crowd to give T.J. the opportunity to be with family and friends, offering our own condolences when the time was right, so we were both quite startled to discover that we were the only ones who came. There wasn't even a minister or priest in sight.

T.J. was speaking to the crematorium manager when he first saw us. True to form, his reaction was peculiar. He seemed almost angry to see us. No, it wasn't anger. It was more like panic. Then it seemed that he got an idea, and he approached us sadly.

"Thanks so much for coming, guys," he said to Edward only. "You really didn't have to."

"Of course we'd come, old sport," Edward replied as he shook T.J.'s hand and patted him on the shoulder.

"I am so sorry for your loss, T.J.," I said as I gave him a consoling hug, but it didn't remain consoling for long.

A sudden surge of warm electricity shot through my system the moment our arms wrapped around each other. It reminded me of the very first time I held Edward in my arms. Images of all the romantic places I had ever been with my betrothed flashed in my mind's eye, only I was in all those places with T.J. instead.

He must have felt something similar for he suddenly took in a big gasp of air and held his breath, and his muscular body quivered.

"Are you all right?" Edward asked.

"Yes," he said as he pulled away from me, refusing to look at me. "It's just, it's been quite an ordeal."

"Of course it has," I said. "Poor thing."

"And sorry if we arrived too early," Edward added. "I could have sworn you mentioned that the service was at ten."

"You're not early. It's about to start."

"Then where is everyone else, if I may ask?"

"My father was a very difficult man," T.J. answered ashamedly, looking at the floor. "He burned a lot of bridges in his day, then spent most of his life living abroad. The truth is, I barely knew him myself, so I didn't know who to contact."

"I thought he was living with you all this time."

"Only since the summer, but yeah, and it's been hard."

"We're ready to begin, Mr. Jameson," said the crematorium manager. "Would you like to say something first?"

"No, thank you," T.J. answered. "Let's just get it over with."

"T.J., I think you're making a mistake," my betrothed said sympathetically. "I mean, I can only imagine what you're going through right now, but not saying at least a few words will be something you'll regret one day, and then for the rest of your life. You're not thinking straight, my friend, so let me think for you."

"I'm just not very good at public speaking."

"We're the only ones here," I chimed in because I knew Edward was right, and I did want to help the boy. "Just go up there, look at us, only us, and talk."

"I don't want to look at you and lie," he said into my eyes. "I will not, won't, look at you and lie."

It was again odd because it was said just for me, as if he would have no qualms about lying to Edward.

"Then don't lie," I simply told him.

He took a deep breath as he nodded his consent. He told the manager *he would speak after all, and then moved to the front of the room, next to the casket. He took yet another deep breath, and then he began.*

"Oh, Clarence," he said slowly. "I barely know you, yet it seems I've been masquerading as you for so long. It seems we've spent no time together at all, but you gave me your name, and for that I shall always be grateful. We've had our names on the same lease since last summer, and yet it's as if I've been searching for you all the while, and only upon your death have I found you. Goodbye, Clarence."

He kissed his fingers, gently touched them to the casket, then took his seat beside me.

"That was beautiful," Edward said softly as the door to the oven slid open, and the casket was rolled inside.

I looked at T.J., so stoic, so brave, so reticent to cry or show any emotion at all. Without realizing it, I took his hand in support. He looked at me and smiled as he squeezed my hand in a loving "thank you," and I felt that electrical charge once more.

It felt wonderful and sinful, both at the same time. Before I could gather my thoughts, Edward leaned over and whispered in my ear, "You are the kindest woman I have ever known."

He should trust me less. He should yell at me and scream at me.

But T.J. appeared to be consoled, and I believe he was glad we came.

In the end, I think Edward and I did a good thing today.

* * *

Tuesday, April 11, 1961

DEAR DIARY,

I'm starting to see why Edward believes he and T.J. to be similar despite their obvious, superficial differences—and the similarities revealed themselves throughout our afternoon at the Metropolitan Museum of Art. They both walk with the same confident swagger; they both clasp the fingers of their opposing hands when pensive; they both look straight into you with warm eyes when speaking, except when they feel the need to meticulously choose their words, in which case their eyes drift up and to the left; they both have this habit of exhaling through their closed mouths when frustrated, causing their lips to flutter, creating a brrr-brrr-brrr sound; they have similar opinions on most topics, and often finish each other's sentences; they enjoy the same jokes, my goodness, they even have the same laugh. And mostly, I feel a tremendous affection toward them both, one of which makes sense to me, the other of which does not.

I followed along quietly as Edward took T.J. through the same art appreciation exercise he had given me when we first met. He began with a certain untitled Picasso print because of T.J.'s fondness for the Jackson Pollock.

"It's stupid," T.J. said with a grin. "Why doesn't the guy just draw the thing to look like what it's supposed to look like?"

"But you enjoyed the Pollock?" I asked quite surprised, Picasso being somewhat of a "missing link" between the early realist painters and modern abstract impressionists like Pollock.

"It's okay, kitten," Edward said. "It doesn't have to make sense. Let's just mill about."

And so we did. Edward stopped pointing out particular pieces as we moved through the giant halls, allowing T.J. to take the lead most of the time. When he at last stopped at The Seine at Vétheuil by Claude Monet, Edward waited only a moment or so before saying, "Yes. I always liked that one, too. What do you like about it?"

"I don't know. It's, you know, pretty."

"It is. But why is it pretty to you? What draws your eye and fixes your gaze?"

"I don't know."

"Come on. Best guess."

T.J. was clearly embarrassed over his inability to speak intelligently on the matter, and it was adorable. Clearly, this is a man accustomed to knowing what he's talking about, or one who doesn't speak at all. Edward has the same trait, and I love him for it, too. (Did I write "too"? How strange.)

"This was a bad idea," T.J. whispered to Edward, shooting quick, intermittent glances toward me, as if hoping that I hadn't been listening. "I don't want to do this. Let's go. You're off the hook for tonight."

It suddenly occurred to me that I was the cause of his embarrassment, and that he was worried that he was somehow letting me down, me of all people. My heart went out to him, as if he were a lonely puppy dog wandering the streets, and one that only I could protect.

"It's okay," I told him in a soothing tone. "There are no wrong answers. It's all subjective. The way it affects you may not be the way it affects me. What does it make you think, how does it make you feel? You stopped at it for a reason. Is it the colors? A particular color? The setting as a whole?"

"I don't know," he repeated defensively. "It just seems like a nice place to hang out. Like, I could picture myself in it. It's like, I don't know, calm."

"That was my reaction the first time I saw it, too," Edward said. "I wanted to be inside it, just lying on the grass, letting the worries of the world fade away."

"Yeah," T.J. said dreamily, then quickly snapped himself out of it. "Okay. I get it now. I get art. We can go."

"Don't be silly. You're just getting started, old sport. Let me show you another Monet that I think you'll like even more. Oh, and I know a couple of Degas you will adore."

"You're a fan of the impressionists," I told T.J. with a smile, as I flung my arm around his neck to nudge him along in pursuit of Edward. "Who knew?"

He smiled back at me, a radiant smile that was far too big for the moment, a smile that told me he was proud that I was happy for him, a smile that would have said, if I didn't know any better, that he loved me.

I quickly removed my arm, and called ahead to Edward. "Darling, we should also show him some Renoirs."

"Absolutely," my true love said back.

And on the day went, T.J. relaxing enough to allow so many of the brilliant paintings to wash over him. "She clearly loves her baby," he would say about one piece. Or, "It's sad, so many innocent people being slaughtered." Or, "It's nothing. It's just colors and patterns, but it's trippy."

And regardless of his initial response, Edward would probe him to go deeper. "Why do you think she loves her baby?" "Why do you think the dying are the innocents?" "Trippy in what way?"

And no matter what T.J. said next, Edward would follow up with another question, then another, forcing T.J. to probe deeper into his very soul. By the time Edward began to speak of the piece's historical context, the life of the artist, or the religious symbolism, T.J. merely wanted to know more. Edward's lectures, which so easily could have seemed droning and pontificating, felt instead like an enlightening missing piece to a beautiful, mysterious puzzle. Even I was swept away, and I had heard several of the stories before. By the end of the afternoon, T.J. was hooked.

The favor was only partly reciprocated.

We grabbed a quick dinner at a wondrous steakhouse to kill time before the evening's entertainment was to begin. T.J., true to form, reacted oddly. He burst into laughter, and said, as if to himself, "Steakhouse? Holy hell, this is Myra's vegan joint."

"Who's Myra?" I asked.

"What's 'vegan'?" Edward asked.

"Don't worry about it," T.J. responded. "Sorry for mentioning it."

I looked to Edward, who merely smiled fondly and shook his head, silently telling me that this was one of T.J.'s odd comments that had to be ignored.

Once again, T.J. seemed judgmental over Edward pulling out my chair for me, and ordering my dinner for me. He never said anything, and Edward never noticed it, but I could somehow tell, and it once again made me wonder why men order for women, why we let them, and why we like it.

Edward actually guessed my dinner order right this time, but that didn't stop me from wondering. And when he changed the topic to politics, asking T.J. if he had been pro-Kennedy or pro-Nixon in the past election, T.J. merely shifted it to me.

"Who'd you vote for?" he asked me.

"T.J.!" Edward said firmly. "You don't ask a lady about her political beliefs."

"Why not?" he answered calmly. "I'd like to know."

"Because it's just not done," I told him.

Although, again, why isn't it? I agree with my betrothed on a great majority of the issues plaguing our country, but not all. Brilliant as my soul mate is, I sometimes see a better way. Why is it unladylike to voice my opinions? I know it is, but why?

On the dinner went, Edward challenging T.J., and T.J. challenging me, and Edward and I both admonishing him for engaging a lady on lofty topics. The problem was that Edward was chivalrous, polite, and gallant, yet T.J. was inspiring, and right.

And when he began to talk about the singer we were to see later that evening, his "Edward-ness" was in full bloom, or "on steroids" as he himself would say, an odd expression that made no sense but I came to figure out that it meant "very very." The passion and joy that T.J. exuded could easily have been Edward when discussing the first time he saw a Rembrandt or Van Gogh. Only the words were different, but the body movements, the flailing of the arms, the leaning forward or back, the moments when his voice went high or low . . . honest to goodness, it could have been Edward speaking.

"It's really the opening act we want to see. John Lee Hooker is good, I checked him out online—er, a club called The Line—and he's good. But the opening act, he's going to blow your mind. I'm talking huge. Bigger than Elvis, as big as the Beatles."

"The what?"

"The Crickets. Buddy Holly and the Crickets. But way bigger. More important than his music itself, which is amazing enough, this kid is going to change the world."

How can a singer change the world? I wondered. How could he be more important than the songs he sings? But T.J. was so excited that it didn't seem proper to ask.

"I envy you guys, hearing him for the first time. Man, that is so cool. I was so young the first time I heard him."

"How could you have been young when you first heard him? I thought you said he is young, and this is his first performance."

"Um, um, um," he muttered, then turned to Edward to answer the question that I had asked. "I meant, he made me feel young the first time I heard him, which was at an open mike night, um, not too long ago." Then he turned back to me to complete his thought, "Tonight is his first scheduled, paid gig."

Gerde's Folk City in Greenwich Village was a dark, dingy nightclub, which somewhat surprised me. I had heard of it, of course, and knew it to be one of the more prominent clubs of its musical genre, so I could only wonder about the griminess of the less successful joints. The showroom was less than half full, which made sense for a Tuesday night, and it was apparent that the rest of the folk music crowd did not share T.J.'s enthusiasm for this new opening act.

We took our table two rows back from the stage on the left side of the room, and I don't think I ever saw a man as excited as T.J. in that moment. He couldn't stop talking about how "awesome" this night was for him, and even Edward was smiling at this twenty-eight-year-old child who seemed to be eating his first cone of ice cream.

"Ladies and gentlemen, Bob Dylan," said a man on the stage as this scrawny-looking kid walked up to take his place. He had an angelic little face and a head of uncombed hair under a dark corduroy cap, creating a bizarre mix of bohemian and altar boy. He had no stage presence whatsoever, and merely sat down on a stool in front of a microphone, strapped a harmonica to his face and placed a guitar on his lap, as if he didn't need to impress anyone because his music would speak for itself. The applause from the crowd was polite at best, and very underwhelming. It was apparent that everyone else in the room had come to see John Lee Hooker.

T.J. was on the edge of his seat, elbowing Edward in his side with a "get-a-load-of-this" smile.

The boy strummed a few chords on his guitar, blew a few notes on his harmonica, and then he began to sing . . . and he was terrible. His voice was nasal, froggy. Yes, that was it. If a frog with a runny nose could sing words, this Bob Dylan is what he would sound like. Sometimes he wasn't even singing at all, just talking to music, like a froggy Rex Harrison. After only a few bars, Edward turned to T.J. and asked incredulously, "Is this the right guy?"

T.J. didn't take his eyes off the stage as he nodded and bounced up and down in his chair to the rhythms, wearing that ridiculous (yet still alluring) grin all the while. When Edward tried to speak another word, T.J. merely shushed him.

"He was a good sport at the museum," Edward whispered in my ear. "We have to keep our end of the bargain and wait it out."

But then something strange happened. By the third song, the young singer's voice stopped seeming bad. Different, to be sure. Unique, most definitely. But not bad at all. Brilliant, in fact. I began to feel its resonance, its searing intensity that drew me right into his world. He would close his eyes as if in a wondrous daydream, as if searching for his next word, pulling you forward in anticipation, and then belt out the next phrase like a magic trick. I looked at T.J., swaying to the rhythms with that same giant smile on his face and a single tear on his cheek. I looked around the room to see that Mr. Dylan had won over the entire crowd in the same way that he had won me over. He had gone from "who is this kid?" to "what an awful voice" to "my goodness!"

That is to say, he won over the entire crowd, except Edward. Yes, my darling was smiling pleasantly, lightly tapping his hand upon his thigh, but I knew the smile to be his polite, phony one, forced upon his face, only to be supportive of his friend.

By the time the boy left the stage, the round of applause was overwhelming, especially in comparison to the lukewarm response he had initially received. I myself could not remember ever having been so moved in a nightclub.

Just as the applause was starting to die down, T.J. suddenly jumped to his feet, as if unable to contain himself. "Be right back," he told us, then he raced to the stage to catch the singer before he was gone for good. "Mr. Dylan, I cannot tell you what an honor it is for me to be here tonight," I could hear him say. He grabbed the man's hand and vigorously shook it as he went on. "You've been my comfort when things were bad in my life, and an inspiration to the world. Thank you. Thank you so much."

The young boy just looked at T.J. for a moment before responding, "That's pretty weird, man." And then he left.

John Lee Hooker was very good, too, but how does one follow what we had just witnessed? By the time his set was done, Edward merely patted T.J. on the back, and pleasantly smiled. "Sorry, old sport. Just not quite our cup of tea."

T.J. then turned to me, as if silently asking me for my opinion, so I shrugged and nodded in agreement. What else would I do? I was certainly not about to take sides against my betrothed, and especially not in public.

"Uh-huh," he replied with that Cheshire grin of his, and I could tell that he saw right through me.

And I hate to admit it, but I liked that he saw through me.

No, this is terrible.

I love Edward, and only Edward.

* * *

Monday, April 24, 1961

DEAR DIARY,

The young singer's music has been haunting me for two weeks. I can see why T.J. believes he will one day become important, although how a singer can ever become more important than the songs he sings still eludes me.

I yearned to hear him again, but the boy had yet to produce a record, so attending another performance was my only means.

I knew there was no point in asking Edward to take me. He'd likely concede if I begged hard enough, but then I would have to see his polite, phony smile, and hear his barely audible sighs of boredom, which would defeat the purpose of going in the first place.

I considered asking Dottie or Trudy to come along, but there was no telling if they would love this utterly unique artist as I had come to, or be bored by him as Edward had been, and the thought of them leaning toward Edward's taste would also ruin the evening.

No, I had to go myself or not at all. I had never gone to a nightclub unaccompanied before, and the notion of being a single woman alone at a table in a dark, dingy space was somewhat intimidating. Mother would say that I was asking for trouble, Father would flat out forbid it, and Edward would insist on tagging along only to keep me safe. But I'm twenty-four years old and it's time to grow up. I can order my own beverages, and I can open my own doors.

Would I have thought this a month or so ago, or has T.J. gotten under my skin?

I took a taxi to avoid having to search for parking, and I arrived at Gerde's a few minutes early in order to get a good table, one close enough to the stage to get a good look at the boy, but not so close that I would be noticed. Although not filled to capacity, the place was significantly more crowded than the last time I was there with Edward and T.J. It appeared that word of the boy singer had been spreading.

Before I could even choose a table, I heard my name called out. "Ruthie!"

It was T.J., sitting exactly where we had sat the last time. He smiled at me, and waved me over.

Shucks. Now Edward will know, with Mother and Father soon to follow.

I walked over to him with a pleasant smile, knowing that I would soon have to ask him to keep my presence tonight our little secret.

"Are you following me?" I asked, as a joke.

"I was here first," he joked back. "You must be following me."

"No, I'm not," I said with the smallest of laughs.

"Pull up a seat," he said, never rising for me, and making no gesture to pull the chair out for me.

Yet I joined him nonetheless. Nothing wrong with that. True, I was a soon-to-be-married woman sitting in a nightclub with a man I barely knew, but he was the new best friend of my fiancé. To say no to him would be rude, and to sit by myself would draw stares. The truth is, I didn't think about it that much. He asked me to sit, so I sat.

"I thought you said he wasn't your cup of tea," he said playfully.

"Well," I began, caught red-handed. "I think he's spectacular."

"So why'd you imply otherwise?"

"What was I supposed to do? It's not ladylike to publicly take sides against your beau. Everyone knows that."

"That must suck, er, stink, er, be hard."

"Not at all. It's simply good manners."

"Shhh," T.J. said as young Dylan came out and took the stage with little fanfare and even less applause. But roughly thirty minutes and one cheap white wine later, he once again left the stage to a thunderous roar of applause, whistles, and cheers. Those who had heard the rumors were clearly not disappointed.

T.J. didn't well up this time, he merely smiled the whole way through, softly singing along to many of the songs. As for me, I knew it would not be the last time I'd watch Bob Dylan perform. The only thing that made the performance less than perfect was the gnawing inevitability that I would have to ask T.J. for a favor once it was over.

"This is a little embarrassing," I began after the applause died down. "But would you mind not mentioning to Edward that you saw me here tonight?"

"Have a drink with me, and mum's the word."

I was shocked that that was his answer.

"You mean, if I don't have a drink with you, you'll tell him?"

"Nah, mum's the word either way. But have a drink with me anyway."

I couldn't help but laugh. Against all I knew to be appropriate, I tossed aside the mores of my parents and ancestors and continued on my quest for individuality.

"All right," I demurely conceded.

"Great," he said, then added, "Just wait here one sec, okay?" Then he moved quickly toward the stage where the singer was still packing up. "Bob! Sorry, man, I got to take a raincheck on tonight."

"Aw, man," Bob Dylan replied. "I was counting on it, Teej. What's up?"

Apparently, T.J. had been coming to see the singer every night since we all saw him that first time, taking the boy out for drinks right after. The headliners weren't particularly pleased about losing part of his audience to his opening act, but T.J. considered drinking with Dylan too great an honor to pass up. Yes, "honor" was the word he used.

"Is that her?" Bob Dylan asked, referring to me. "Is that the girl?"

"Shhh," T.J. said quickly. "But, listen, I feel bad for flaking on you—"

"'Flaking.' Good word."

"So go have a night out on me," T.J. continued as he put a twenty-dollar bill in the breast pocket of the singer's jean jacket.

"No, man. Thanks, but I can't take that."

"Please. It'd be an honor for me. And quite the story to tell once you're huge."

"You are so weird," Bob Dylan said laughingly. "But okay, thanks. G'luck."

The bar in the Merton Hotel was only a few blocks from Gerde's, and we were seated at our new table before I knew it. T.J. seemed utterly fascinated by every little detail about me, no matter how dull, as if the facts were irrelevant and he merely enjoyed the sound of my voice, like a beautiful song in which one can't make out the lyrics. Incidentally, I didn't have this insight at the time, and it would have made me quite uncomfortable if I did. It also would have made me quite uncomfortable if I had been aware of how completely comfortable I felt, babbling on and on about myself to this man I barely knew, this man I felt I knew so well.

I was telling him about the year I took off after high school to travel through Europe—explaining that that was why I had finished college at twenty-three instead of the usual twenty-two, and describing my family's villa in the south of Italy—when it occurred to me that I had not let him get a word in edgewise. The fact that he didn't seem to mind is of no consequence. For a lady to monopolize a conversation like that is simply rude.

"What about you?" I asked.

"What about me what?"

"Did you go to college right out of high school, or did you also do something else in between?"

"Um, I didn't go to college," he said slowly and thoughtfully.

"Oh," I answered. "That's all right. You seem to have done quite well without it. Tell me about your high school life. Where did you go to high school?"

He took a deep breath, as if contemplating the severity of my question, as if it wasn't among the most mundane of small talk openings. Finally, he decided to answer.

"San Quentin Prison."

"I don't understand."

"I got my high school degree in prison," he said shamefully.

"Seriously?" was all I could think to say, and he nodded. "For what?"

"I tried to steal a painting, a very expensive painting," he answered. "That was the crime I got caught for. There were many smaller ones before for which I didn't."

"Look, if this is making you uncomfortable—"

"No, no," he said somberly. "You can ask me anything."

"I'm sorry. It's just that I had no idea. Edward never mentioned any of this."

"Edward doesn't know."

"You never told him?"

He shook his head. "So you keep my secret, and I'll keep yours."

"Why'd you tell me if not him?"

"I dunno," he said softly, like one of my first-graders when they don't know the answer. "I just don't want to keep anything from you, Ruthie, unless I absolutely have to. I mean, everyone lies, I guess, but with you, I just don't want to. Does that make any sense? It probably doesn't to you, but it's true."

He seemed so vulnerable at that moment, so sad, all his cockiness and crazy expressions having evaporated into thin air. My hand slid across the *table to take his, but then I came to my senses and reached for my wine glass instead.*

I love Edward, I reminded myself. It's Edward that I love. Edward.

"So what do you lie about?" I asked with a smile to lighten the mood.

"If I told you, it wouldn't be a very good lie, would it? What do you lie about?"

"Everything."

"Wow. That's honest."

"Don't take it personally. I lie to everyone because I lie to myself first."

"About what?"

"How would I know?" He laughed, which was an enormous relief.

"Can I guess?"

"Absolutely not."

"Okay."

"All right. Guess."

"Okay, here goes. Your life has been so good, so easy and wonderful, that it just made sense to do what you're told. You followed the rules, even when you didn't want to, and it all worked out for you. So why not keep following the rules? Live according to other people's standards, and everything is peachy-keen. Only now you're starting to realize that by living according to everyone else's rules, you don't know who you are."

"Shut up."

"Okay."

"How'd you know that? Did Edward tell you that?"

"No, I promise. It really was a guess, based on movies and books of the era, I mean, of your class. Even as I said it, I was afraid you might punch me or something."

"Ladies don't punch."

"Whose rule is that?" he said with a smile, so I punched him in the arm. "Ow!" he exclaimed as he laughed.

"Tell me about one of your crimes," I asked.

"Not a chance. Then I'd have to lie to you."

"Isn't withholding information a form of lying?"

"No, it's a form of withholding information," he answered. "For I can tell you with absolute honesty that I will not give you the specifics of any job I've ever pulled."

"Then don't be specific. I've been reading about adventures all my life, imagining I'm the hero or heroine, saving the day against insurmountable odds and great peril, but I've never actually had any, nor met anyone who has. I've been all over the world, but I've never done anything that bears any risk at all. So spill. What's it like?"

"Okay, but only in generalities," he said, then took a moment to compose his thoughts. "It's terrifying. Truly terrifying. But at the same time, it's thrilling. And it's the terror that breeds the thrill. You know that if anything goes wrong, you'll get busted, hurt, killed even, so you do your best to put all that out of your mind, and focus only on the task at hand. Your chest is pounding. Adrenaline blasts through your veins. Your brain is flying in a million directions at once. Every possible outcome, good or bad, plays out in your mind's eye in the same split second like a thousand parallel universes. And when it's all finally over, and you've gotten away with it, and you've taken that triumphant exhalation, that giant 'phew' of pride, you realize just how stupid you were to have risked so much for so little."

I was mesmerized. What this man had gone through to get where he is. I couldn't speak. This wasn't a fairy tale story or a dime novel, this was a real man's real life. A deep man, filled with pain and remorse, about whom I yearned to know more. And only when I began to search for words to fill the silence did I realize that my hands were upon his.

I withdrew them slowly, so our hands would not become the new topic of conversation, taking a sip of my chardonnay as the casual excuse.

Edward. I love Edward. It's Edward that I love. Edward I will marry.

It began to dawn on me how often I had been telling myself that since we arrived at the Merton, so I felt it best to call it a night, just in case I neglected to remind myself of it once more.

When the bill came, he looked at me and, with all sincerity, asked, "Split it?"

"What?"

"Okay, I'll get this one. You can get the next one, but the next one will include food so it'll be more expensive."

"Why do you insist on challenging me every step of the way?"

He looked deep into my eyes, beyond my eyes and into my soul, "Because you need me to."

My heart stopped. I was dead for a moment. "You pay. There won't be another."

"Okay," he said with that nonchalant confidence I despised and adored. He threw some cash on the table, and then offered to drive me home.

Here's the conversation that took place in my mind:

"No, no, thank you, T.J. I'll just take a cab."

"That's silly, you're on my way anyway."

"I don't want to be alone in a car with you. I don't want you walking me up to my door, with you expecting to be invited in. No, a taxi is just fine."

But what I said was, "All right, thank you."

The top of his convertible was down, and he drove like a lunatic once again, weaving in and out of traffic, rocketing through all the yellow lights. The warm spring air caressed my face and messed up my hair, and I loved it. I felt free.

He pulled up to the curb of my building and parked, but left the engine on. "I hope next time Edward and I go out, you're willing to come along."

"You're not walking me to my door?"

"Oh, right, right. People do that here. Sorry. Okay."

He turned off the ignition, got out of the car, and then he stood on the sidewalk with no intention of opening my door for me. It's strange to say it, but at this point it was somehow starting to feel like a compliment.

He really did see me as an equal. Neither Father nor Edward nor my brothers nor any boyfriend ever has.

We walked up to my door talking about, oh, I don't even remember what, as I wondered if he was going to try to kiss me, and how I would slap him if he did.

We arrived at my doorway, and he told me how much he enjoyed our evening together. He wasn't leaning in toward me, but he wasn't leaning back and away either. Was he waiting for me to make the first move?

"Our engagement party is this Saturday," I mentioned for reasons that I still can't fathom. "I'd love it if you could attend."

"I thought you had your engagement party that day we all first met."

"That was the pre-party dinner, the one I wanted. This is the fancy, expensive one that I didn't. Would you like to come?"

"Won't Edward find it odd, given that you weren't supposed to be out tonight?"

"Yes, he will," I sighed as I realized it. "I'll suggest to him that he invite you."

"Then I'm there, Ruthie. I'm wherever you want me to be."

"Awesome," I said.

Awesome? Really? What is happening to me?

He never tried to kiss me, and I never got to slap him.

CHAPTER TWENTY-NINE

A LITTLE BIT OF HOUSEKEEPING before we move on.

First off, my time alone with Ruthie ignites no old memories. Remember, my so-called *déjà vu's* emanate directly from Edward's recollections, the recollections of my own past life. Outside of Edward's presence, I was flying blind.

In terms of winning her over, it was a strange endeavor, one I had never experienced before. It wasn't about the pursuit of sex, absolutely not, yet that had pretty much been my entire m.o. when it came to women. This was a whole new ball game.

I knew from my dreams that we would be together in the end, and forever, but Myra had made me quite sensitive to the insane inner conflict my poor beloved was going through. I'd be an utter heel if I made it any harder on her—a heel that would then be unworthy of her. I couldn't know what events would transpire to bring us to one another, the final straw that would turn her away from Edward and toward me, I just knew that she had to come to me of her own volition with no manipulation on my part. It's why I didn't kiss her that first night I drove her home. In fact, if she had tried to kiss me, I'm not sure I would have let her, much as I wanted to.

As far as I-Edward not responding to Dylan, that may be the strangest memory so far. I wasn't being a snob, I just authentically didn't get him. I wanted to get him because I knew it meant so much to my dear friend T.J., I just honestly found his music boring. So I now hold in my head a devout passion for the music and a simultaneous aversion to it, and both feelings are real.

Also to that point, much as I liked Edward and proud as I was to have been him, I really wasn't too crazy about how I treated Ruthie when I was. I didn't like that I called her "kitten" because it's so condescending. I didn't like that I ordered her meals for her because it was patronizing and also stupid. I didn't like that I expected her to give up her career once we were married. Oh, sure, I would allow her to continue if she truly desired it, I just expected she wouldn't because she'd want to stay home to raise our children. And did you catch that I actually used the word "allow"? That's Edward-think.

Hey, I meant well. I had been raised to believe that a man is supposed to protect and take care of his woman. It was the proper, respectful, chivalrous thing for us men to do back then, the way parents today are supposed to protect and take care of their children. No difference at all.

Except that Ruthie wasn't a child. She was a grown woman with a college degree and a worthwhile profession at which she excelled. She was self-sufficient, despite what her imposing father or I-Edward happened to think. That's why I-T.J. challenged her so often. I wanted her to find the strength I knew she kept buried deep within her heart.

I would be her knight in shining armor, not by slaying the dragon for her, but by helping her see that she has the power to slay the dragon herself, as much as any dude.

Yes, Myra was right again. I was the better choice for Ruthie, the wiser soul. But that was all right. My dear friend Edward, whom I so admired and was so proud to have been, would be the better choice for her in his next life when he's me.

* * *

I HAD A REALIZATION regarding time travel and the preservation of history, and how I would have to deal with it moving forward, and it kind of sucks.

Simple logic dictated that it was okay for me to go out drinking with young Bob because there was no way that any past me would have turned down such a super-cool opportunity. I knew it was okay for me to stay in 1961 because my dreams told me that the "other guy" (me, T.J.) remained with Ruthie forever after, and I knew from the Merrill Lynch photo that I was destined to travel to 1932. In other words, I was meant to do all those things because I already had. No worries there.

But what about all the *little* things I might do as I remained permanently in the sixties? I had no signposts or landmarks beyond my dream. Had my occasional accidental use of the word "awesome," as one example, been the decree of fate, or was it just a dumb mistake? Was I the one who planted the seed that would cause the word to slowly grow into common usage decades later, or had I introduced it too soon, thereby creating some kind of ever-growing ripple effect that had somehow harmed future history without my even knowing it? Or was it just a word, and whether I used it or not really didn't matter?

There was so little I could know for sure, and all else was a crap-shoot. I'd have to spend the rest of my life parsing every little decision, asking myself time and again what past me's may or may not have done. I could only assume that such a practice would eventually become a habit, or render me a basket case. I hoped for the former.

So I gave myself three basic rules. First, I had to stay clear of all historical events. If my small actions could alter future history, there's no telling what a connection to a big event could do. Second, I had to choose my words carefully. This, by the way, is not as easy as it sounds. Don't believe me? Randomly pick a word you often use—not a swear word—and then vow to not say it for a week. Let's see how well you do.

Third, I could no longer pursue a career in physics.

Sucks, right? My career over before it even began. But my fear was that I may have learned something in my twenty-first century prison high school that remained unknown in the sixties or seventies, subsequently mention it to someone, and inadvertently become the guy who made the discovery. I considered that it could possibly be my destiny, one of those things that time or fate had already decreed, but a thorough online search found no significant physicist by the name of Theodore Alexander Jameson.

But don't feel too bad. Giving up physics for Ruthie was hardly a sacrifice.

* * *

MAKING A PERMANENT MOVE across decades is a pretty arduous task. Imagine moving from one city to another, then multiply the effort by infinity. I came up with a pretty good plan, but it still had one giant hole in it.

Shortly after Clarence's cremation, I made an appointment at the law offices of Pendleton, Smythe, Horrace, and Cheevers. I told the secretary of my father's passing so that they would have time to retrieve Clarence's file from their archives, then I went to see Eric Toms—official, legal death certificate in hand. He was in his mid-fifties by then, a partner of the firm, and sharp as a whip.

"My God," he said, miraculously remembering our two short meetings after what was to him twenty-three years. "You are the spitting image of your father."

"Well, not anymore," I said sadly in an attempt to change the subject.

"Yes, of course," he replied sympathetically. "I'm so sorry for your loss."

I told him that my father had been living in Algeria since the war, having only returned the past summer, and that I knew he didn't own anything of particular value, but he had instructed me to contact Mr. Toms nonetheless.

That's when Eric gave me the "startling" news. He told me that my father had purchased shares of IBM in 1932, the value of which was currently estimated at two hundred and seventy thousand dollars, roughly two million dollars today. I feigned surprise, shock, delight, and sadness.

"Why didn't he ever say so?" I said with moist eyes. "Why did he live as such a pauper if he had such wealth?"

Eric tried his best to console me, and I let him.

Legalese, legalese, fees paid, more legalese, and the certificate was mine.

I immediately asked Eric to draft a new trust for me, that is to say, Theodore. I said that I was in no dire need of money, and felt it best to let the security continue to grow. On the other hand, I didn't want such a fortune to dissolve into the ether if I were to be hit by a car or something. I said that I had no spouse or children, and that I wanted to leave the certificate to my dear friend Marvin Stanley O'Rourke. I gave him Marvin's address, Marvin's rent having been paid through the end of the following month, even though he hadn't shown up for his job at the city morgue for over a week. Legalese, legalese, fees paid, days passed, more legalese, and the new trust was signed, witnessed, notarized, and dated. Done.

The certificate would never go to Marvin, of course, I just wanted it kept in the firm's vault for the next several decades to maintain the legal trail of ownership.

I packed my clunky suitcase from the 1930s with some of my clothes and cash from the 1960s, took a cab to that same remote, abandoned spot in the boonies, then dug. Spatial destination, current. Temporal destination, the summer of 1999.

Send.

Rectal pain nil because I had travelled empty, chest pain significant but I got through it. I somehow made my way into town, got a cheap hotel room where I recuperated for three days, then rented an inexpensive apartment in Brooklyn. I only needed it for a few days, but I had to pay first and last month anyway.

Oh, the times they'd been a-changin'.

I once again phoned the law offices of Pendleton, Smythe, Horrace, and Cheevers, said I was Theodore and that I'd like to come in to amend my trust, then asked how long it would take them to access the old one from their archives. Eric Toms was long gone by then, as were Pendleton, Smythe, Horrace, and Cheevers. I made an appointment for four days hence.

I bought a nice suit, one becoming of a sixty-six-year-old man, and went to an off-Broadway store that sold theatrical makeup. I knew exactly what to purchase because my dear friend Adriana had taught me before I left for 1938 over a year ago, or eighteen years later, depending on your point of view.

Adriana, by the way, was one of my first prostitutes back when I was a teenager living on my own in North Hollywood, and we had remained close friends ever since. She is now one of the entertainment industry's primo makeup artists, garnering two Emmys and an Oscar nomination. So don't judge. People do what they've got to do. Just sayin'.

Also, Adriana was her whore name. No way I'm giving you her real one.

Back to our story.

I chose an elderly lawyer this time because I didn't want him around eighteen years later. I'll tell you why in a bit. Ryan Pinkett was pushing seventy, all business, a protégé of Eric Toms as it turned out, who seemed to possess all of Mr. Tom's legal skills yet none of his charm. There was no small talk whatsoever, and he got right down to it. I was just glad my makeup skills passed muster.

I appointed Wendy as executor, then bequeathed to her and Myra each three point five percent of the stock, an amount that would be just shy of five million dollars in 2017, and the remaining ninety-three percent to The North American Council on Adoptable Children, an almost one-hundred-and-thirty-million-dollar donation.

Wendy's pawnshop was already well established by 1999, so I had all her necessary information, address, birthday, et cetera. Myra was a little trickier. I knew her birthday, of course, and I knew she was living with Jack, Jen, and myself in 1999—the reason I chose that specific year in the first place—so I gave the Carpellis' address in the hope that the authorities would use the foster care angle to track her down, as had been my plan when I was leaving the fortune to myself. However, in my case, there had been clear records, hence a direct line, from foster care to San Quentin to Seymour to me, and I had no idea to what extent Myra was currently off the grid. Based on my research, the agencies selected for such tasks were pretty good at finding those that needed to be found, but "pretty good" didn't feel good enough. I would have to come up with something to ensure that the loot found its way to little sister, and I had an idea. Two, actually.

That, by the way, wasn't the hole in the plan that I referred to earlier.

I had also come to the law firm prepared with logical explanations as to why a sixty-six-year-old white man such as I was leaving a fortune to an old black woman in Watts and a ten-year-old girl in Torrance, but Mr. Pinkett never bothered to ask.

Legalese, legalese, fees paid, time passed, more legalese. Signed, witnessed, notarized, and dated. Done.

Wendy and Myra would never know the money came from me, but that didn't matter. Well, maybe it did a little, but not a lot.

Oh, if you're wondering why I didn't amend the trust today, in 2017, thereby allowing me to easily list Myra's current address, there were three very good reasons. First, it may have seemed a little suspicious for a man to change his will then die shortly thereafter, and given the humungous value of the holding, I wanted as little suspicion surrounding it as possible. Second, makeup. It was one thing to make myself appear as a robust man in his sixties, but I simply didn't have the confidence in my makeup chops to pull off eighty-four. Third, and most importantly, there was far too great a risk that a 2017 attorney would get a look at whatever corpse I'd happen to steal, and would know in an instant that it was not the same Theodore Jameson he had met with days or months prior. That was also why I wanted an attorney who would be long retired when Theodore's dead body was found.

I jumped home to my present day Pasadena apartment and went to work on the final part of my plan—that is to say, the final part that I had figured out. Remember, I had no intention of touching any part of the IBM certificate—that was for Wendy, Myra, and the foster kids—but once I committed to my permanent life in the sixties, and once I sent the Apple Watch to the NASA guy, I would no longer have the ability to pop through time, yet I needed a solid income to support my true love in the lifestyle she deserved.

I went online to scope out every great stock from 1961 to present— Kodak and McDonald's in the sixties, Coke and Gillette in the seventies, Disney and Hasbro in the eighties, Microsoft and Harley Davidson in the nineties, Nike and Google in the aughts, Netflix and Facebook in the teens.

But it wasn't as simple as merely recording all the gems because I would have to appear to have a well-rounded portfolio or else I could raise suspicion for being too perfect and maybe get busted for insider trading or something—or even worse, become famous, thereby altering time. No, I would make a good living as a savvy investor, but not so savvy that anyone would notice me. I would have to purposely buy some misses, dogs as they're called in the biz, as well as some steady, safe, slow-growth stocks. It took weeks to find all the information I needed, then I snapped one screenshot after another onto the watch, which I would later copy into a notebook in 1961. I would obviously need to keep such a notebook very well hidden but, as you know by now, I'm pretty good at hiding things.

The annoying part was that by being back home in the present for such a length of time, I had to punch in at Caltech every night, mopping and picking up people's garbage—all the while knowing that my beloved soul mate and young Bob Dylan were a mere time-pop away.

On the other hand, I got to see Wendy a lot. It had been so long for me since I had last seen her, and I knew how much I would miss her once I left the twenty-first century for good.

Seymour made one of his surprise visits during that period. He told me how he had met my perfect double while he was in New York, and how he had so embarrassed himself with this complete stranger. I chuckled along as if I didn't know the story already, and he had no idea why I was really laughing as hard as I was.

One night, while mopping up at work, it occurred to me that old me, the one who had remained in 1961 and then aged normally over the years, could be around somewhere. He-me would be in his mid-eighties today, and I wondered if I'd recognize him-me if we met. I wondered if old me would seek me out, then wondered if he-me already had.

One afternoon, I was doing my stock research at a local Starbucks when an elderly man asked me for the time. I wondered if he was me, and if his question was a pun, the exact kind of pun I may have made. He didn't particularly look like me, but who knows what I'll look like in fifty-six years. As he walked away, I shouted, "T.J.!" He didn't turn around.

After I completed my stock analysis, I did one final Google search for Jack and Jen Carpelli. Jen had never remarried. Jack had twice, and divorced both times. I felt bad for them both because, despite it all, I still remembered them as fine, decent parents.

That Saturday, I popped to my Jersey hotel room to spend time with Myra.

As with Wendy, but in a very different way, I had missed her so much, and I couldn't imagine how difficult it would be to never see her again. We spent a lazy afternoon hanging out at her place, drinking coffee and watching college basketball.

"You know, I've never met anyone who actually has a soul mate," she said enviously during one of the commercials. "Do you know how rare that is?"

"Only because you told me."

"Once in a hundred, a thousand years rare. It's why we love the fairy tales so much—because we can never find true love in our lives but we know deep in our souls that it's real nonetheless. I guess the rest of us can all give up because it's not going to happen *twice* in a hundred years," she added with a sardonic laugh.

"Don't give up," I told her. "I have a hunch you're going to meet the perfect guy some day."

"Honey, I gave up long before we reconnected."

"So had I."

"Good point," she said, muted the TV and turned to me wistfully, dreamily, like a little girl desperate for a bedtime story. "What's it like? Is it really as the fairy tales say?"

"Well, yeah," I answered guiltily, like a piggish man telling a starving person about the great feast he just had.

"Don't be embarrassed," she said as she slapped my thigh. "It's awesome. I'm happy for you. I really, really am. Just tell me. What's it like?"

"It's, like, all the pain I ever felt is gone when I'm with her. No, not gone like a memory you forgot, more like gone because it just doesn't matter. It's like half of me had been missing my entire life, only I didn't know it till the emptiness got filled."

"Wow. Is it filled when you're not with her, like now?"

"Yes and no. All I have to do is think of her and, whoosh, I'm whole again. And, by the way, if I had ever heard anyone say this, especially a dude, I would've laughed in his sappy little face. Yet it's real. It's the most real thing I've ever known."

"More," she demanded. "This is amazing. Tell me more."

"She makes me a better person. No, that's not it either. She makes me *want* to be a better person. I want to be my best with her, for her—better than my best.

"And I can't lie to her. Not the way I can't lie to you because I wouldn't get away with it. I don't want to get away with it. It would be ugly to get away with it."

"Have you told her about that thing, your big secret?"

217

"No, that I can't tell anyone, not even her."

"What if she asks?"

"She won't."

"What if she does?"

"I guess I'll do the same thing I've been doing up till now when cornered. I'll turn to someone else and lie to them instead."

Myra burst out laughing. "You're such a dope."

"I know," I laughed along.

That night at our vegan dinner, I finally got around to asking the question I had wanted to ask all day.

"You ever think about trying to contact Jack or Jen?"

"Yeah, sure, I've thought about it, but no."

"We should try. What do you say? Let's try."

"No way, José. What if they don't care? What if they turn us away again? Or worse, what if they don't even remember us at all?"

"Then at least we'd know."

"I couldn't handle that. Just drop it."

"But—"

"Please?"

"Okay."

That night, I returned to my Jersey hotel and drafted a letter to Jack and Jen, claiming to be a girlfriend of Myra's. I said that Myra wanted to get in touch with them but was afraid they wouldn't take her call. I suggested they reach out to her, gave them Myra's address and cell phone number, and begged them not to mention this letter so as not to embarrass her, and to act as if reaching out was their own idea. I mailed them each a copy.

Whether either of them would actually contact Myra was irrelevant. Once the authorities tracked them down—and they were remarkably easy to track down—they'd have Myra's 2017 contact information, ensuring that my sister would receive the five million dollars that Theodore Alexander Jameson had bequeathed to her.

I traveled back to 1961, arriving four days before Ruthie and Edward's fancy engagement party, giving myself the necessary three days to recuperate from the jump. I had no idea who Ruthie and Edward's friends and family were, but I knew that I would remember them all the moment I saw their faces, the memories from being Edward blasting into my brain—those I liked, those I loved, those I couldn't stand, the boring and the vulgar all included—it was just how this seemed to work.

I felt good about all that I had accomplished, for Myra, for Wendy, and for all those unknown children, and my thoughts returned to the sole remaining hole in my plan.

If I send the watch to the NASA guy in 2017, how do I travel back to 1961 to live my life with Ruthie? And if I use the watch to make my one final time-trip to 1961, how do I get it to the NASA guy in 2017?

True, there was nothing stopping me from simply keeping the watch for the rest of eternity, and nothing stopping me from holding onto it till the present day when I'd be eighty-four and could ship it to him on the day of Professor Szabo's funeral, except that I couldn't know for certain if I'd make it to the age of eighty-four. I had no way of knowing if that old man in the Starbucks was me.

But I had made a promise to Professor Szabo, a virtual deathbed promise, and breaking such a solemn vow would be reprehensible. It would make me a man unworthy of my one true love, so then what's the point of any of it?

I would just have to come up with something.

CHAPTER THIRTY

DEAR DIARY,
    The party was as opulent and grotesque as any party Mother had ever thrown. The round tables with their fine linen napery littered the grounds and gardens, each one adorned with its own unique sterling silver centerpiece. Buffet tents on the tennis court overflowed with feasts personally catered by René Langlois. A twelve-piece orchestra backed up the singer Bobby Vinton, who exchanged sets with the comedian Joey Bishop, and crates of fresh oranges and lemons abounded like something out of The Great Gatsby, *which was, of course, by design.*

If this was the engagement party, I thought, I almost dreaded the wedding. So many worthy causes on which this money could have been better spent.

Still, I played the dutiful bride-to-be, smiling graciously for all, answering the same three questions throughout the night as if each guest was the first to ask. "No, we have yet to set a date." "Yes, a spring wedding would be lovely." "Yes, Hawaii (Mexico, Gibraltar, Venice, fill in the blank) would be an enchanting place to honeymoon."

If I hadn't had Edward by my side I might have just killed myself.

"Let's sneak out and elope," he jokingly whispered in my ear. "Right

now. Then we can come back, spring the news, and we'll only have to go through this once."

"But darling, then we won't get the presents," I joked back.

"Hmm," he feigned considering it. "We do need a good fondue set. All right, we'll stay."

I love him so.

Father was on the far side of the grounds, a large group of tuxedoed men huddled around him and hanging on his every word because he had made them all rich, and they wanted him to make them even richer. He was having the time of his life. I honestly don't know which Father enjoys more, the wealth that comes from his skills or the admiration he receives because of it.

Mother was playing the social butterfly, making a determined effort to speak to every guest for at least twenty seconds to ensure that he or she was having an enjoyable evening because that's what a good hostess does, and also so they could compliment her on the spectacular do she had put together, and on what a wonderful mother she must be to have raised someone as wonderful as me.

Ugh.

This was the setting into which T.J. entered.

I have to admit he looked quite dapper in his brand new tuxedo. It wasn't long before all the teenage girl cousins began to ogle him like he was Rock Hudson. I hate to say it, but I didn't like that.

Mother was closest to the French doors to the grounds when he appeared from inside the house, but her back was turned to him. Just sensing his presence, she began to speak to him before actually seeing him. "Oh, Edward, could you please—" Then she saw him, and apologized. "I'm sorry. I thought you were Edward."

"No, I'm T.J. And you must be Ruthie's mom."

"Why, yes. Have we met before?"

"No, ma'am, but Ruthie speaks very highly of you."

"Oh, posh," Mother said with false modesty.

Edward and I saw him from a distance, and we felt it prudent to make our way over before he started saying things like "awesome" or "no worries" or any of his other peculiar words and phrases.

"So glad you could make it, old sport."

"Wouldn't miss it for the world."

"Mother, this is my dear friend T.J.," Edward formally cited.

"Yes, we just met," Mother replied. "I thought he was you. You don't look at all alike, but I thought he was you."

"We seem to have many of the same mannerisms."

"Well, please do enjoy the party," Mother said, and then moved off to the next guest.

"This is quite the affair," T.J. said as he looked around in awe.

"I take it you haven't been to one of these things before," I said amicably.

"Nope. But I think I could get used to it."

"It comes with its dark side," Edward answered with a smile, then made a rather humorous segue when he noticed his father passing. "Speaking of dark sides—Papa! I'd like you to meet a friend of mine."

My darling was about to make the formal introduction when T.J. got his first look at Edward's father, and his tanned California skin went white.

"Papa?" he asked meekly.

"Excuse me?"

"Oh, I'm sorry. I mean, I'm just, um, um, I don't know what I mean. I'd like to just, um, excuse me." Then he headed off to one of the bars.

"This is your friend?" Papa Montadel asked judgmentally.

"He's a tad eccentric, yes, but he is also the most interesting fellow I've ever met."

"One of your arty pals, I suppose."

I sighed. I knew where this was going.

"Papa, not now," Edward pleaded. "Not here."

"I believe this is between you men," I said. "If you'll excuse me." And off I went.

I had no desire to see my father-in-law-to-be once again chastise my true love for following his passion, and I certainly had no desire to once again hear the origins of the Montadel fortune, the three brothers who came to the New World, two who disappeared from history, and one who forged an empire. As I headed away, I could see T.J. sitting alone at the bar by the pool. It was clear he needed company, for he seemed to be, to use his own vernacular, "freaked out." I pulled up the stool next to him and asked if he was all right.

"Don't let me meet Edward's mother," he begged. "Please?"

"Edward's mother passed away two years ago."

"That's right," he replied as he breathed a sigh of relief, and then his eyes grew a little watery. "Yes, she did."

It was the most peculiar that the peculiar man had been to date.

"What's going on with you tonight?" I asked.

"Hey, let me meet your dad," he said quickly and all chipper, clearly trying to change the subject, so I let him.

As Edward had told me early on, sometimes you just have to ignore the things T.J. says or does. I led him to Father to introduce them, and there once again seemed to be an immediate recognition on T.J.'s part before I even got to say a word.

"Father, I'd like you to meet my friend, T.J. T.J., this is my father, Eugene Lee."

"A pleasure to meet you, son."

"Right back at you, Gene," T.J. said with an inappropriate measure of familiarity. "So I hear you're in the investment racket."

Father sighed, knowing full well what was coming next. "You're looking for some free advice?"

"Nope, I have some for you. American Hospital Supply. AHS."

Father burst out laughing. "You're giving me a stock tip?" Then he turned to me. "Snuggles, this boy's got gumption."

"Father boasts one of the top track records on all of Wall Street," I warned T.J. "It's how he grew his firm so large in such a short time."

T.J. looked straight into Father's eyes with no acknowledgement that he was the butt of a joke. "It's selling at about thirty right now. Get as much as you can, hang on to it for a few months, then dump it at forty-eight. You may be leaving a little on the table, but better safe than sorry, I always say."

"All right," Father said, his curiosity piqued. "I'll have my people look into it."

"Don't let them look too long," T.J. replied cockily. "It could explode any day."

They delved into a conversation about the merits of the particular security, which led to them discussing another, then another. T.J. seemed so ignorant about so many, yet so knowledgeable and cocksure with respect to an isolated few.

Father was intrigued by the young man's approach. In fact, I have *never seen anyone win him over so quickly. Maybe it was because of T.J.'s similarity to Edward, who had gained Father's respect for being the only man in our circles with the courage to stand up to him, which is largely due to the fact that Edward is the only one who authentically wants nothing from him. But it took Edward months to gain that respect, while it took T.J. a matter of minutes.*

Truth be told, I have never seen anyone so comfortable so quickly with so many complete strangers. It was as if T.J. had known our families and friends for years. He even came to be comfortable with Papa Montadel, admonishing him to be more accepting and respectful of his only son. For a time, Papa even heeded the advice.

As the evening drew to a close—the guests starting to leave and the men untying their bow ties to leave them draped over their shoulders— Father actually invited T.J. to remain back to join us for the party-after-the-party, a little family tradition where our inner circle shares a cocktail or two to laugh and lament over the events of the evening. Someone as new as T.J. being brought in was unheard of. Even Papa Montadel has yet to be included.

"Now's when the real fun begins," Father said as he put his arm around the boy and led him into the parlor. "Edward here is going to regale us with his left-wing, socialist gobbledygook. It'll be nice to have another real Republican on our side."

"Oh, I'm not very political."

"Of course you are," Father pleasantly countered. "You make good money, and the government takes it away from you. It would be an unholy sin for you to not try to stop them, and that's politics."

"I don't mind paying my fair share. I wouldn't want to be a rich man living in a poor country."

"Well stated, ole sport!" shouted Edward as he refreshed T.J.'s drink.

"It's not mine. I heard some German guy say it on CNBC once."

"What's CNBC?" Willie asked.

"Oh. It's, um, it's a radio station."

"Never heard of it."

"CNBC. It's rock 'n' roll. You wouldn't like it."

"A socialist investor," Father quipped. "Now I've seen everything."

"That's because T.J. is a compassionate and reasonable man," Edward retorted. "In your world, Gene, the rich will continue to get richer

while the poor will continue to get poorer, and before you know it, we'll all be living in medieval times."

"In our world, people get off their behinds and fend for themselves," Gene Jr. shot back. *"We did it, and there's no reason why anyone else can't."*

"You didn't do any of it," Edward countered. *"Your father did it all for you, and he gave you everything. That's my whole point."*

On and on they went, Edward taking on my father and brothers like a true champion, from taxes to President Kennedy to the plight of the Negro, all yelling on the outside even though everyone could tell they were enjoying the battle on the inside. T.J. said little, speaking only when specifically drawn in, both Father and Edward trying to get him to take their side as if he were the final arbiter, while Mother, Aunt Franny, and I remained proper ladies and said nothing at all.

But when the conversation shifted to the brouhaha in the south, things truly began to spiral out of control.

"These coloreds are just making trouble," said Father. *"Just making things worse for themselves."*

"I couldn't disagree more," Edward countered. *"If not for these brave souls, we wouldn't even know what was going on down there."*

To paraphrase the issue, not too long ago the Supreme Court deemed segregation unconstitutional, but Southern states continue to practice it nonetheless. A group of very brave Negro activists, along with many caring young white people, have bonded together to bring the issue to light. They travel on southern buses where the Negroes purposely sit in the front, the whites in the back, and white and Negro couples sit together holding hands, purposely violating all the unconstitutional laws. They drink from the wrong water fountains, they use the wrong public bathrooms, and they sit together in the whites-only sections of restaurants. When arrested, they refuse to pay bail so they can force the issue into the courts, and hence, into the news.

Their goal is to bring the social injustices that Negroes continue to endure to the forefront of the American consciousness, and their cause has been growing in awareness since their first sit-in in a Greensboro, North Carolina diner, as flocks of white and Negro volunteers continue to join them.

They call themselves the Freedom Riders.

"*Truman desegregated the military,*" *Father explained.* "*Branch Rickey got the coloreds into baseball. But these things take time, and these coloreds are just making all the good people uncomfortable. Come on, T.J., you've got to be with us on this one.*"

"*I don't really know much about this issue. I'd like to know what she thinks,*" *T.J. answered, referring to me.*

"*Me?*"

"*So would I, come to think of it,*" *said Father, smiling in delight.* "*Come on, Snuggles, tell your fiancé what a horse's ass he's being.*"

"*Darling!*" *Mother exclaimed, speaking for the very first time.* "*Language.*"

"*Well, kitten?*" *Edward asked.* "*I know which side you're on. Go ahead. Tell them.*"

It was uncomfortable to have all eyes upon me, but especially T.J.'s. It was as if his gaze was challenging me to tell the truth, to be true to myself. It was a challenge I decided to meet. I took a deep breath, and jumped. "*I think we should go join them.*"

A sudden silence swept the room, but was soon broken by Gene Jr.'s laughter, then Willie's and Tom's, Father's, Mother's, Aunt Franny's, and finally Edward's.

T.J. didn't even crack a smile.

"*That's what I love about my kitten,*" *Edward laughingly said as he put his arm around me.* "*She's even more idealistic than I am.*" *Then he kissed the top of my head.*

"*I'm serious,*" *I insisted, possibly more forcefully than I should have but I was deeply offended by the laughter.* "*You're always saying how important their cause is. You're the one who made me realize how important it is. This isn't a Negro problem, it's an American problem. Don't you remember saying that?*"

"*Of course, but I never meant to imply that we should go down there ourselves.*"

"*Why not?*"

"*For one, we'd be arrested. That's the whole strategy. You just began your career. You don't want a blemish like that on your record.*"

"*I don't know,*" *T.J. said as he jumped into the fray.* "*Something like that on a rap sheet could look pretty impressive in years to come.*"

"You're disappointing me, T.J.," said Father. "How on earth could being thrown in jail be impressive?"

"Well, she'd be getting in early on the right side of history."

"What are you doing?" Edward shot at him. "It's as if you're encouraging her."

"I'm just sayin'. I mean, do any of you guys even know any black people?"

"T.J.," I helpfully whispered to him. "They're called 'Negroes'. Calling them 'black' is prejudiced."

"Sorry," he responded with that Cheshire grin of his.

"And being arrested would be the least of our worries," Edward continued. "Policemen are beating Riders and protesters with clubs, and spraying them into walls with powerful hoses. The Ku Klux Klan is coming out in droves. It's too dangerous. No."

"She doesn't mean any of it," said Willie, shaking his head with a patronizing smirk. "This is just more of her silly little girl talk."

I hated that.

"You take me," I told T.J.

"Me?" he stumbled. "Oh, um, me, no, I can't."

"Why not?"

He thought for a moment, then turned to Edward to give his answer, a habit of his that I had always found particularly rude. "The thing is—"

"Don't look at him," I demanded. "I asked the question. Look into my face and answer me. Why not?"

"It's, um, it's a time thing."

"What, you're too busy? The stock market won't be here when we get back? You're supposed to be the adventurous one. What's wrong with you boys?"

Even as I write this, I don't know what had gotten into me, only that T.J. had somehow put it there. I was speaking my mind in a way that I had never done before. This was an important cause, and participating in it was the right thing to do.

It was as if I was a different person . . . and I liked this girl.

But T.J.'s response startled me, and his words crushed me.

"Hey, don't put this on me," he shot back angrily. "What do you need me for anyway? What do you need Edward for? What do you need anyone for? You're a grown woman, and this isn't a night at the prom. If you want to go, go. If you think it's important, do it. If not, then don't. But stop begging for a date."

"T.J.! That's enough!" Edward bellowed on behalf of my honor. "I will not have you talking to her like that!"

"No," I said softly. "He's right. I should go. By myself if need be, but I'm going."

"Over my dead body," shouted Father.

"Over no one's dead body, Father," I said timidly, standing up to him for the very first time in my life. "But I am going."

"Kitten, you mustn't," Edward said softly, apologetically. "It's too dangerous."

"Darling, I would love for you to join me," I said, it being also the first time I had ever denied my betrothed's wishes. "I would love it if either of you fellows would join me. But in the end, none of you men can stop me."

"Ruth Anne—" Mother began.

"Nor you, Mother. I'm going to do this, and that's all there is to it."

I meant every word I said. This is an important cause. I will go, and I will not let my family prevent it. I know in my heart that I must do this, and I feel good about my decision. I feel strong.

For the first time in my life, I feel strong.

And I'm terrified.

CHAPTER THIRTY-ONE

I WAS SO PROUD OF HER.

She had never stood up to her father or to me-Edward before, certainly not with that level of determination. I was watching her grow into the strong young woman she had always been but was afraid to accept.

I felt a little bad that I had lashed out at her the way I had, but she had to hear it from someone, and she knew I was right. I was so proud of her.

I had no worries that anything bad would happen to her on her Freedom Rides because she had yet to dump me-Edward for me-T.J., and I knew from my dreams that that event, in which she was whole and healthy, was destined to happen. I just didn't know when.

But my lack of apprehension changed a few days later when Edward came to my Manhattan apartment. He looked bad, as if he hadn't slept, shaved, or showered for several days. He chastised me for egging her on the way I had, but before I could explain my reasoning, he stopped me.

"Something terrible could happen to her," he said, welling up. "It's so dangerous. A single white girl, all alone down there. Arrests, beatings, the Klan."

"Then why don't you go with her to protect her?"

He looked down to the ground, and softly, shamefully answered, "I'm afraid."

Don't judge him. You'd only be judging me because I remembered feeling the very same fear and shame the moment the words left my mouth. I-Edward wasn't being a hypocrite—my political convictions were pure—it's just that the fear of danger was so excruciatingly overwhelming, and it made me feel like less than a man.

Would you have gone?

It occurred to me-T.J. that despite all the beatings I had taken in my early life, the fear of being beaten is far more horrifying for those who have never been beaten before. I-Edward had simply led too good a life to handle danger, just as I-T.J. had led too crappy a life to possess the good sense to avoid it.

"We have to stop her," Edward went on. "*You* have to stop her. You're the only one she'll listen to on this matter anymore."

"Let me look into it," I told him sympathetically.

"Look into it?" he asked. "What does that mean?"

"I don't know much about this Freedom Rider business. Maybe it's as bad as you say, in which case I'll have the facts to dissuade her. Or maybe it's actually safer than the news makes it out to be, in which case I could put your fears to rest."

"How?" he asked shakily. "How can you find out more than the news?"

"I'm very good at research," I told him. "It's what I do."

That night, I jumped home to my Pasadena apartment. It wasn't a jump I had ever factored into my plans so I was a little pissed. Three days to recuperate, two weeks of waiting to go back to 1961, all the while mopping up at Caltech every night.

Once I felt up to it, I hopped online and went to work. My first instinct was to find some facts to calm Edward down, but as I read on I discovered that his fears were justified. It occurred to me that I may have been too proud of Ruthie too quickly. Yes, she looks beautiful and whole when she dumps me-Edward in the dream, but I had no idea when that would actually happen. What if she had been seriously hurt, and the breakup only took place after a year or two of a slow, painful recovery? What if the damage to her had been internal, therefore not showing in the dream, leading to complications later on, or even an early death?

What if she had been arrested and forced to spend time on a Southern chain gang—many of those brave Riders had—causing psychological damage that would last her whole life?

I knew I would feel foolish if I had to do a one-eighty and convince her not to go on the Ride after all, but I would feel far worse than foolish if she were to come to any harm because of me. For days, I scoured everything I could find to see if anything bad had happened to her, but there was no evidence of her presence at all. Not a single mention. Maybe she hadn't gone in the end, which would imply that I was to talk her out of it. Still, I plodded through old police reports and historical essays and newspaper clippings, until I finally found something that blew me away.

It was a grainy, black and white video clip taken in a church in Montgomery, Alabama, in May of 1961. A predominantly black congregation was singing some hymn. The camera then panned to the pulpit where the Reverend Martin Luther King Jr. cautioned everyone to stay calm and to remain nonviolent despite the anger they were feeling, as help was on the way. But what totally threw me for a loop was that among the few white congregants were Ruthie and me.

It appeared that I was going to Montgomery, Alabama, with my one true love because I already have gone to Montgomery, Alabama, with my one true love therefore I must go to Montgomery, Alabama, with my one true love.

I could protect her.

But I felt it best not to mention it to Edward till we got back.

CHAPTER THIRTY-TWO

WEDNESDAY, MAY 10, 1961

D EAR DIARY,
    Today I finally mustered the courage to phone the CORE office, that is, the Congress of Racial Equality, the Negro civil rights group behind the Freedom Rides. The man on the phone was very gracious when I told him that I wanted to volunteer, and particularly grateful when I happened to mention that I was Caucasian.

I told him that a week from Friday was to be my last day of school, and that I could join them any time after that. He said the Riders would be leaving Birmingham for Montgomery early that Saturday morning. If I could book a flight to Montgomery for Sunday, I could catch up with them there. There was to be a mass meeting at the First Baptist Church to honor the Riders that night, during which many CORE leaders would be speaking, and I could get the rest of my instructions then.

I booked my flight and hotel before telling Edward that I was officially going, and I wish I hadn't told him at all. He forbade me immediately. Yes, he actually used the word "forbid". Ironically, only a month or two ago, I most likely would have acquiesced, but his attempt at dominance merely served to strengthen my resolve.

Voices were raised, words were spoken . . . words I regret. He called

235

me a child. I called him a hypocrite. He called me naive and pampered. I called him a coward.

Then he said nothing at all, and I knew that I had gone too far.

In fact, I don't want to describe the rest of it.

Suffice it to say that I feel terrible, and I will have to apologize to him when I return home. It is the first real fight we have ever had, but I know in my heart that the depth of our love will enable us to overcome it.

* * *

Sunday, May 21, 1961

DEAR DIARY,

I don't know how to begin, for I am still terribly shaken by all that transpired.

I was quite proud of myself as I boarded the airplane early this afternoon, albeit still quite frightened of what lay in store. I tried to read, but my excitement was such that I couldn't concentrate. I tried to sleep because my fright had kept me up all of last night, but sleep wouldn't take. So I simply looked through my window and watched the world get smaller as we ascended to the sky.

No sooner than the Seat Belt and No Smoking signs blinked off, and people began to light up around me, that a man appeared next to the man sitting beside me. It was T.J.

"Hey, you mind switching seats?" he asked. "I'm kind of friends with her."

"I'm all settled in."

"I'm in first class so it's a pretty cool upgrade for you."

"All right."

The man left, and T.J. took his seat. "Hey," he said with his captivating smile that I disliked so much. "Crazy that people are allowed to smoke, isn't it?"

"What are you doing here?"

"I'm going to Montgomery. You invited me to come along, remember?"

"And you said no."

"I changed my mind."

"So you actually called CORE and volunteered?"

"Nah, I figured you took care of all that. I'll just tag along and get on whatever bus they tell me to get on."

The truth is that despite the strange, conflicted feelings that T.J. always ignites in me, I was glad that he showed up, glad to have some company, glad there would be at least one familiar face as I dove into the frightening unknown.

We chatted aimlessly for a while, and it was nice to be able to let my mind wander away from my anxieties. And as my apprehension faded, my sleepiness grew stronger. The next thing I knew, I was awoken by the *"bing"* of the Fasten Your Seatbelt sign that signified our descent into Montgomery.

My head was resting on T.J.'s shoulder, and I was quite embarrassed to realize that I had nodded off while he was speaking, but before I could apologize, he spoke:

"Hey, you finally slept with me."

"That's rude," I snapped as I quickly sat up straight.

"I thought it was funny. Sorry."

The plane landed smoothly. We got our bags from the carousel, and then shared a taxi to the hotel. He had not yet booked a room of his own, and requested one on the same floor as mine. We adjourned to our separate quarters, agreeing to meet in the coffee shop for dinner in three hours' time, after which we would head to the church.

It was at dinner that we learned the horrific news. Yesterday's Freedom Ride from Birmingham had been given an Alabama State Police escort due to warnings of a Ku Klux Klan ambush, but when the bus reached the Montgomery city limits, the Highway Patrol disappeared. The local police that had been guarding the Greyhound terminal also disappeared moments before the bus' arrival. When the Riders disembarked, hundreds of Klansmen attacked with baseball bats, broken bottles, and lead pipes. News reporters were beaten and their cameras smashed so there would be no photographs or evidence.

Men and women riders, white and Negro alike, were assaulted to bloody unconsciousness. Teeth were bashed out of jaws. After allowing the Klan to run rampant for quite some time, the police finally showed up; but the mob, having grown to over a thousand by then, moved off from the terminal to attack Negroes on the streets, even setting one teenage boy on fire. The police didn't arrest any of them, but instead served the Freedom Riders with injunctions to blame them for the violence.

I was shaking. T.J. put his hand on mine to comfort me, and I appreciated it.

"It'll be okay," he said.

"I know," I lied.

"You still want to do this?"

"Now more than ever," I lied again. "Do you?"

"If you do, I do. If you don't, I don't. You're in charge here."

Wonderful, I thought, now I'm in charge. I almost wished he forbade me, or that Edward or Father had been around to forbid me. If someone had forbidden me in that moment, I just may have relented.

"If we back out now," I said truthfully, "the bad guys win. We have to do this."

"Okay," he said with a comforting smile. "You'll be all right."

"I know," I lied again.

When the waitress put the bill in front of T.J., he slid it across the table toward me. "I told you the next one would include food." I couldn't help but laugh.

There seemed to be over a thousand people at the church when we arrived—mostly Negro, but a fair share of whites—as well as a handful of federal marshals. I didn't notice any city or state police.

I found my CORE contact in little time. He thanked us for volunteering, then said he wasn't sure when the next ride would be, adding that there may not be any, given yesterday's events. We exchanged information, and he promised to stay in touch.

"My God," T.J. suddenly exclaimed as he noticed a mustached Negro man by the front church door. "It's him. It's really him."

Our CORE contact seemed impressed that T.J. knew of the man, and offered to introduce them after the service. T.J. was beside himself, responding with his characteristic "awesome" and "amazing." Who was he? I could only wonder.

We took our seats inside. The church was filled to capacity, and the speeches were moving and powerful. Reverend King, the one with whom T.J. had been so enamored, was particularly inspiring. Yet as the meeting unfolded, we began to hear voices emanating from outside. The voices *grew increasingly louder, eventually drowning out the speakers them-selves with blistering racial epithets.*

Over three thousand heckling white protesters had surrounded the church, and the few federal marshals were far too outnumbered to do anything about it.

Suddenly we heard an explosion as the mob outside overturned a car and set it on fire. Inside, we sang hymns in defiance. Rocks then shattered through windows, and tear gas bombs were flung inside. Some of the Negro men removed guns from their pockets in case the segregationist protesters entered the church.

Reverend King moved back to the pulpit, and instructed everyone to remain calm. The Alabama National Guard was on its way, he said, and he urged everyone to stay inside. He then made a special plea for all to continue to adhere to nonviolence despite the anger that they justifiably felt. It was our testing point, he said. We had won the moral victory, and we must continue to win it.

I was amazed at how calm most everyone remained. Many of us left our seats, true, but only to mingle and stretch our legs. It occurred to me that as terrifying as this was for all concerned, it was not something wholly unique for my new Negro comrades-in-arms. I had led a blessed life, and I felt a little ashamed because of it.

My CORE contact found us, and said that Reverend King had a moment to meet us.

"Now?" T.J. asked. "I mean, I don't want to bug the man."

"He's made his phone calls, he's done what he has to do. All we can do is wait."

"Awesome," T.J. said as he let our CORE contact lead him to the good Reverend. I followed behind, until I was stopped by a slender Negro lady and her little daughter. The girl seemed to be about the same age as my first-graders. She struck me as stoically brave and cute as a button, even though her mother was a mess and in tears.

"Miss? Miss? My name's Alicia Washington, would you please help me? Would you take my baby girl to my sister's house for me? Please?"

"The Reverend said we should all stay inside."

"It won't be dangerous for you, not for a nice white lady like you. Here, look." She hid the little girl's hair underneath a faded blue baseball cap. "Now her hair don't seem so nappy, see? And we'll do this." She took

some white soot from the fireplace and rubbed it on the little girl's face, which did not produce the desired effect at all. The girl scrunched her face in an adorably cute way, but didn't protest aloud. "They'll all think you're just a nice white mama with her little white baby girl out on an evenin' stroll."

"I really think we should listen to the Reverend."

"Please," she pleaded as she began to weep. "I already lost my husband from these Rides, my li'l girl's daddy, but not her, too. If the good Lord sees fit that I perish, so be it. But not her."

I sighed. How could I say no? Yet before I could give my consent, T.J. returned. "What's going on?"

"She wants me to take her daughter to her sister's house."

"We're supposed to stay inside."

"That's what I said," I told him, and then whispered. "She already lost her husband."

"Ruthie, come on. I mean, I've never been one to follow rules but this is Martin Luther King. I'm pretty sure his rules are pretty okay. We shouldn't do this."

"I don't recall anyone inviting you," I snapped at him. I then dropped down to my knees and took the little girl's hands. "What's your name, sweetie?"

"Wendy, ma'am," she answered. "Wendy Washington."

"Hi Wendy. I'm Ruth. Would you like to go for a walk with me?"

"Whoa, wait," said T.J., startled. "Wendy Washington?"

"Yes sir."

"Wendy Washington. Montgomery, Alabama. Really? Wow. Okay, I'm in."

"T.J., I am perfectly capable of walking a little girl home on my own."

"And I have a lot more experience running away from bad guys than you do." He turned to the mother. "Does she know where to go?"

"You betcha," little Wendy boasted before her mother could answer. "Aunt Greta's house. By the woods. Easy as pie. Don't worry 'bout nothin', mister."

"Then let's go. No, not the front door."

"There's a back exit," said Mrs. Washington. "I'll show you."

"Not that, either," T.J. said pensively. "That opens to a road, and there'll be protesters there, too. I noticed a restaurant next to the church when we first came."

"Jo-Jo's Barbecue," Wendy piped in fast. "Best ribs in all Montgomery. Spicy. Mama don't like spicy much as I do. I like spicy more than anyone. I'm the spicy queen."

I could see T.J. suppress a laugh, then return to formulate his plan. "Does the church have some side door that faces the restaurant?"

"In the basement," Mrs. Washington answered. "Leads to a stairway that takes you back up to ground level. But Jo-Jo's be closed now on 'count of everyone's here."

T.J. had her take us to the basement exit nonetheless, and then told us to wait. He quietly snuck outside, only to return seconds later with a confident grin. "It's perfect. The rib joint has a side door looking right at us. Anyone have a paper clip? A hair pin?"

"I got me one," said the woman who removed it and gave it to him.

"Okay, here's the drill. We go out, crawl up the stairs, and then lie still below the top one. When I give the signal, fast as we can, we sprint across the lawn to the rib joint. We stay low, and quiet. As soon as we get to the other side, you two hit the ground."

Mrs. Washington hugged her little daughter goodbye, thanked T.J. and me profusely, and then T.J. went outside. Wendy and I followed, crawling quietly up the brick steps. We lay still near the top for what seemed an eternity, T.J. intermittently poking his head out beyond the rail and back. He slowly raised his arm to tell us to be ready, and then flung it down fast. The three of us dashed across the lawn, dropping to the ground upon arrival. T.J. jiggled the hairpin in the lock for but a moment before he had the door opened, and we all went inside.

"It's so dark," said Wendy.

"Shhhh," I whispered.

"Oh, still?" the little girl whispered back. "Sorry."

We moved across the large space to the glass wall on the other side, when T.J. stopped. "Damn it," he said softly. "I was hoping there'd be another side door."

He pressed his face against the glass to see the roads, and then he went into the kitchen. He returned with an iron skillet that he held like a baseball bat in front of the glass.

"Okay, the moment we get out," he whispered quickly, "we head toward the back road. We get there, we turn our backs to the church, fast and hard, and keep walking as if we'd been there all along. We move quickly, but we don't run. Wendy, you'll be in the middle. We hold hands, and we stay tight. Ready?"

"Ready, willing, and able," Wendy answered with an excited smile.

Rocks had been flying sporadically through the church windows for more than an hour, and T.J. held the iron skillet to time the impending crash accordingly. At the precisely correct moment, he swung his base-ball-bat-skillet into the glass, the sound of the crash being utterly camouflaged.

We took Wendy's hand and briskly walked toward the back road. I could see the protesters and Klansmen not too far off, but all their atten-tion was on the church. As instructed, we made a fast, right-angle turn away from the mob, and the plan worked to perfection. In short order, we were blocks from the church and on our way.

I have to admit, T.J. was very impressive.

The night sky could not have been darker. Many of the streets were deserted, creating a spooky, eerie feeling, while others were filled with Ku Klux Klan members in search of trouble, some on foot, some on horses. Given the choice, I preferred spooky and eerie.

My heart was pounding. Sweat dripped from my pores. I could feel my teeth.

T.J. took nothing for granted and made Wendy and me remain back each time we had to turn a corner. "Okay," he'd say as he motioned us forward, or "Nope, we got to loop around," as he returned back to us. He had us walk through backyards and gardens to stay off the streets when-ever possible, doubling back on numerous occasions.

"We can take this street the rest of the way," Wendy finally said. "Their house is just on the other side of the woods."

"Then let's cut through the woods," T.J. said. "Safer."

It was nice to be hidden. We had a clear vision of the roads but no one could see us. At any sign of trouble, we could drop to the ground and wait for the threat to pass.

With the high tension dissipated, T.J. began to converse with the girl. He seemed to have a true paternal instinct toward her. It was a quality I would not have expected from him. "So what grade are you in, sweet thing?" he asked with that Cheshire grin of his.

"Sweet thing!" she exclaimed. "That's what Mama calls me. How'd you know?"

"Lucky guess."

How did he know? I wondered.

But Wendy was far more interested in us than answering any questions about herself, labeling us "the bestest, kindest white folk she had ever done met". And her mouth dropped open in awe when she learned that T.J. was from Los Angeles.

"Like Hollywood?" the little girl asked. "Where the movie stars live?"

"Something like that," he said with a smile.

"Do you know any of them? Like Dorothy Dandridge or Pearl Bailey?"

"Can't say I do. Know a couple of stuntmen and makeup artists though."

"Why don't you know no movie stars?"

"Movie stars are just people like anyone else. They're really not that special."

"You mean, I could be a movie star?"

"Um—"

"Of course you can," I insisted. "Don't discourage her, T.J." Then back to Wendy. "You can be whatever you want to be. That's what the Freedom Rides are all about."

"I can't run for president. A girl can't run for president, and a colored can't for sure."

"Oh, you'd be surprised," T.J. said, smiling.

"So I can be a movie star? Yippee!"

"No, um—"

"There it is," she shouted as she pointed to her aunt's little cabin and led us out of the woods and up the hilly road.

Greta's husband, Wendy's Uncle Dale, opened the door. Before I had a chance to explain our presence, Wendy jumped in to describe the journey, wildly exaggerating our heroism to no end. By the time she was done, Aunt Greta had also come to the door.

They thanked us repeatedly, and offered to repay the debt in any way they could.

"If you have a car or something," T.J. humbly began, "would you mind giving us a ride back to the hotel? I'd rather not be walking the streets any more than necessary."

"I don't know if it be a good idea for you white folk to be seen out with us colored folk, not on a night like this, not good for no one. But fair is fair. I could loan you the truck for the night if you promise to bring it back in the morning."

"Thank you, sir. That's very kind."

Before Uncle Dale could lead us away, Wendy wrapped her arms around my waist to thank me, and then the same for T.J. He hugged her back, and I honestly thought he was going to cry. Aunt Greta finally took her hand and led her into the house, and we could hear the little girl boast, "You know what he say? He say I could be a movie star 'cause they ain't all that special. And he'd know, 'cause he's from Hollywood."

T.J. seemed to be in some kind of bittersweet trance. "You all right?" I asked.

"Um, yeah, let's go."

Uncle Dale led us to his beat-up old pickup truck on the side of the house as he launched into all the vehicle's particular peccadilloes. "You gotta give the ignition a couple of jiggles before she'll turn over," he said, and then leaned in to start the engine as a demonstration. "And it's got quite a lurch when you first put her into gear, like it jumps to fifteen or twenty mph right off the bat, so don't let that startle you. The wife says I oughta get that fixed, but me, well, I kinda like it this way."

Suddenly we heard the sound of horse hooves on pavement. Six hooded men on horses in full Ku Klux Klan regalia trotted toward us. "Well, lookie what we got here," said the leader. "Coupl'a goddamn nigger-lovers."

Uncle Dale leapt to our defense. "No, sir, they's just—"

"Get in the house, Dale," the leader said firmly. Dale gave us a helpless, victimy, apologetic look, and then did as he was told. The leader went on. "Goddamn nigger-lovers."

"Many," T.J. answered with a smile. "That is to say, I love many of them. But I've got to admit, there's also a whole bunch I'm not particularly crazy about. Guess you could say I judge a person by the content of their character."

"What the hell's he talking about?" said one of the hooded villains.

"I don't know who I hate more," the leader continued. "The goddamn *trouble-makin' coons, or you goddamn nigger-lovin' rabble-rousers come down from New York City to stir 'em up in our good town."*

"Actually, I'm originally from California."

"T.J.!" I whispered frantically. What was he doing?

"Well, I never done had me a California woman before," the Klan leader went on, suddenly eyeing me in a way that made my heart plummet down into my tummy. "Any you boys ever have yourself a California woman? This goddamn nigger-lover just offered us up his California beach bunny. Well, thank you, nigger-lover."

"No, she's from New York," T.J. replied, that cocky smile plastered on his face. I could only assume he had an idea, and I could only hope it was a good one. "But I have something you may like more," he went on, and then he leaned into the pickup and put it into gear. The truck lurched forward and rolled fast down the hilly road toward them.

"Run!" T.J. shouted as he grabbed my hand and whisked me off. I could hear the horses bolting, and the Klansmen shouting and cursing, but it was still two minutes or more before I heard the horses after us, but gaining on us.

We turned a corner, and saw a whole new group of Klansmen, these on foot, less than a block away. They could tell we were being chased so they decided to join in the fun, and we were stuck in between.

The woods were not too far to our right, and a dark alley was a half a block ahead to our left. "We have a better chance of losing them in the woods," I said quickly.

"But they'd know their own woods better than we would. This way." He yanked my arm and ran us into the alley. And he was wrong!

For on the other side of the alley, there was nothing but a brick wall.

"We're stuck," I screamed in mortal terror. "We're trapped. There's no way out."

"There is for one of us," he said as he removed a strange-looking wristwatch from his pocket and proceeded to tap on its face.

"What are you talking about? What are you doing?"

He strapped the watch onto my wrist as he stared into my eyes while the sound of hoofsteps grew ever louder. "Promise me that if I don't get out of this alive, you'll take a hammer and smash this watch to bits, then take the broken pieces and throw them into a river. And if I do get out alive, please take very good care of it."

"What are you talking about?" I cried, tears now dripping down my cheeks.

"Just promise!"

"All right. I promise. But—"

He put his hands to my face and kissed me. It was hard and passionate, but also soft and tender. I don't know if it was the fear of being raped, or the intensity of the whole night, but I knew in that one long, magical kiss that the powerful feelings I've had for this man from that first moment I saw him could no longer be denied.

"I love you," he said. "I've always loved you."

Before I could reciprocate, he tapped on the watch and I was, well, I was somewhere else. I don't know any other way to explain it.

I was standing alone in the woods, and I was completely naked. I could barely make out T.J. in the alley in the distance, and the Klansmen were approaching him. Although I was alone, I felt very vulnerable, so I lay down on the brush to try to conceal my naked body as best I could, even throwing leaves up upon my behind.

T.J. opened his arms in a friendly gesture as he approached the Klansmen in an obvious attempt to talk his way out of it, but to no avail. Two of the Klansmen grabbed him, while three more took turns punching him in the head and belly. When he fell to the ground, the hooded villains took turns kicking him all over his body.

Then I heard gunfire. Bullets exploded into the alley walls, and the Klan halted its onslaught. I turned to the source of the shooting, and there was T.J., lying in the brush six or so yards from me, naked as I, blasting the rifle that was pressed against his shoulder. I looked back to the alley, and there was T.J., lying on the ground bleeding.

One of the Klansmen took a bullet to his calf, and fell to the pavement.

I looked back to the naked T.J. near me. "I meant to miss," he said. "Honest. I'm just not much of a gun guy."

With the shooting momentarily halted, the T.J. in the alley forced himself to sit up. I could see him speaking, presumably saying something to scare off the villains. Then there was one final rifle blast, and the Klansmen ran away. I looked back to the T.J. near me to ask what was happening, but he was gone. Only the rifle remained.

The T.J. in the alley rose slowly, and I could see the pain in his move-

ments. He picked something up off the concrete, and I realized that it was my clothes, having remained on the ground exactly where I had been standing when we kissed.

He limped and hobbled toward me. His face was cut up, his eyes swollen and purple, and he was bleeding badly. "Here," he panted, and then dropped my clothes beside me. "Now give me my watch," he panted again as he let himself drop to the ground.

"Turn away," I said modestly.

"Give me the watch first."

I did, and he breathed a tremendous sigh of relief. He even kissed it before putting it back into his pocket. "Okay, you can get dressed now," he said as he turned away.

I had no idea what was happening, no understanding at all of the impossible events of the evening, but clearly that watch was somehow at the center of it.

Once dressed, I helped him get up, and let him lean on me as we began to walk the eerily abandoned streets. "Wait a minute," he said. He thought for a moment, and then came to a decision. "There's a car around that corner. Key's in the ignition."

"How do you know that?"

"You have to drive, though. Get us back to the hotel."

"No, I have to get you to a doctor," I said as we moved toward the supposed car.

"No. No doctors."

"You're hurt."

"I'll be fine by morning."

"You don't know that."

"Just get us to the hotel. Please?"

"Fine. But if you're not perfectly okay by morning, I'm taking you to a doctor."

We turned the corner and, as magically predicted, there was a brown Chrysler sedan parked on the side of the road. The doors were unlocked, and the key was in the ignition. I helped T.J. into his seat, and then took my own behind the wheel.

"All right. What is going on?"

"What do you mean?"

"You know exactly what I mean. How is any of what happened possible?"

He sighed. *"It's kind of hard to explain."*

"I don't care."

"Can I tell you tomorrow?" he begged. *"I did have a, you know, a bit of a night."*

How could I say no? The man had almost been beaten to death. *"I don't know how I'm going to describe any of this in my diary,"* I mumbled to myself.

He suddenly perked up. *"You keep a diary?"*

"Yes. Why?"

"Um, no reason."

I got him into his room, into his bed, and I shut my eyes as I helped him out of his clothes. I turned off his lights as I left, assuring him that I would absolutely be taking him to a doctor in the morning if he was not completely better by then, and that he would have to explain everything to me on the way. He promised that he would.

I also told him that I loved him.

CHAPTER THIRTY-THREE

I DON'T TRUST DOCTORS FROM olden times. Would you? I mean, seriously? Did they even have MRIs or X-rays back then? I was pretty sure they were past using leeches, but I had no idea what other barbaric procedures they practiced. I would have to research all that before making my permanent move to the sixties.

Still, Ruthie had been absolutely correct when she said I was in desperate need of medical attention, but it had to be a twenty-first-century doctor. It also had to be one of those doctors who doesn't ask questions because I had no plausible answers.

I waited a few minutes after Ruthie left, in case she came back, then I set the temporal destination for "present-minus-two"—meaning the Friday night before the Monday of my last trip back—and the spatial destination for the couch in the home in which I had sought refuge ever since I was a little boy, one of the backup destinations I had stored in memory before my very first trip to the thirties. Send.

Rectal pain nil, yet it was one of the most painful jumps I had ever done. Not only did my chest feel like it was about to explode, but every bruise and cut on my body was magnified by a factor of ten. My black eyes filled with pus and I could barely see. The bones I was sure the Klan had broken felt like they had shattered into a million pieces. It was actually more painful than the beating itself.

"Wen . . . dy . . ." I softly moaned, for even talking hurt. "Wen . . . dy . . ."

The light in her bedroom went on. She came out in a terrycloth bathrobe, and I can't imagine what she must've thought when she saw me so beaten and naked.

"What the hell?" she gasped. "Sweet thing, what happened?"

"Doc . . . tor . . ."

"Of course. I'll be right back."

She moved off, returned to cover me with a blanket, then moved off again. I heard her make two phone calls. The first was obviously to a doctor, but I couldn't figure out the second. She came back and sat down beside me.

"Help's on the way, sweet thing," she said.

"Thank . . . you . . ."

"Shhhh," she said as she stroked my hair. "Poor sweet thing, shhhh."

She was the best. I would so miss my wonderful, lovely Fagin.

I must have fallen asleep because the next thing I knew I was being tapped on the shoulder by a very large black kid—I'm talking football-line-backer large, gang-member-muscle large. He held out his hand to help me sit up, slid a pair of jeans onto my legs and an LA Rams sweatshirt over my torso. He held out his hand to help me stand, but my knees buckled, and I fell back to the couch. He gently dug his massive arms under me, and easily lifted me off the couch as if I wasn't five-eleven and exercised regularly. He carried me down the stairs and out to the curb, then laid me in the back seat of his decked-out knight rider—yep, gang, not football.

He got into the driver's seat, Wendy into the passenger's, and we drove for an hour to a condemned hospital in an abandoned part of town. The kid flashed his headlights three times. A moment later, the front door opened from the inside.

Although the pain from the Klan's beating persisted, the pain from the time-jump had eased somewhat so I didn't need to be carried. I was a little wobbly as I leaned on the giant boy for support, but not much worse than I had been with Ruthie a few hours earlier or fifty-six years earlier, depending on your point of view.

A rotund, little bald man in his forties greeted us at the door with a warm, pleasant smile. "So we got a little banged-up, did we?"

He led us through the creepily empty giant space into an examining room that was surprisingly filled with the most modern medical equipment. A very attractive, young black woman in a nurse's uniform was setting up for my examination. If I hadn't been madly in love, I may have even made a move on her.

The plumpish man told Wendy and the kid to wait outside, then proceeded with a full, extensive examination—X-rays, blood tests, CT scans, EKGs, does-this-hurt, does-that-hurt, did I lose consciousness, on and on, all the while cracking an endless barrage of bad jokes and puns in an attempt to be fun and friendly.

After several hours, the upshot was that nothing was actually broken and there was no internal damage, but my ribs were severely bruised. He gave me a vial of pills for the pain, instructing me to take one up to four times a day as needed.

The cute nurse was bandaging me up when the smile on the roly-poly man's face turned grim, and he proceeded to give me the bad news. According to my EKG, I had had several myocardial infarctions over the past year or so—which is a fancy way of saying heart attack. He said that they were mostly mild, but added that a man my age shouldn't be having any at all. He then proceeded to ask me a plethora of new questions in an effort to determine the cause.

Of course I knew the cause—you know the cause, too—but I sure couldn't tell *him* the cause so I bluffed, answering "yes" to all of his guesses. "Yes, I have chest pains." "Yes, they're brought on by exertion." "Yes, I have trouble walking up flights of stairs." He insisted I see a specialist as soon as my ribs healed—roughly six weeks hence—and I lied that I absolutely would because I, too, wanted to get to the bottom of it. The truth was, I was just glad my days as a time traveller would soon be coming to an end. He gave me a vial of nitroglycerin pills to take whenever I felt a chest pain coming on, explaining that I was to put one pill under my tongue and let it dissolve in my mouth.

Chest pain pills! Duh! Why hadn't I thought of that before?

Seems there was some silver lining to being almost beaten to death after all.

The bill came to three grand plus a hundred-dollar tip for the cute nurse, which Wendy paid on my behalf with an overstuffed envelope—

making it very clear that I would be paying her back in full, with interest, the juice starting Thursday.

Oh, Mom.

* * *

THE KID DROVE WENDY and me back to her apartment, Wendy having insisted that I spend the rest of the weekend at her place and under her care. They hugged, she thanked him, and he left. She had me lie on the couch, covered me with a blanket, put up a pot of tea, and then took the seat beside me once again.

"I'll sit with you till you fall asleep, sweet thing," she said lovingly.

It was just like old times.

"So what happened to you tonight?" she asked.

"I don't want to tell you."

"You can tell me anything, you know that."

"It's embarrassing."

"Yeah, I guess it must be," she sighed.

We remained in silence for a few minutes when I finally got the nerve to ask the question I'd been wondering about for hours, the question I'm pretty sure you've been wondering about yourself.

"Wendy, why'd you come to LA?"

"To be an actor. I told you that a bunch of times."

"I know. I mean, why'd you want to be an actor?"

"All little girls dream of being movie stars or princesses, same way all little boys dream of being rock stars and athletes. Seeing how princess wasn't particularly open to little colored girls, movie star seemed the way to go."

"Yeah, but most only dream of it, most don't try."

"I was one who did. Shoot, it was fun. I got me all the leads in the school plays, then dropped out to do small pay stuff back in Montgomery. And I was good. And I was hot. You seen pictures of me back in the day. Wasn't I hot?"

"You were very hot."

"So it just made sense to come out here and try my luck. I was going to be the next Dorothy Dandridge."

"But what made you decide to do it in the first place? Was there one specific moment that inspired young little Wendy? A specific person who encouraged you?"

"No, no one comes to mind. Why?"

"Oh, I was just wondering what makes people make the choices they make."

The kettle whistled, and Wendy went off to make us tea.

"None for me," I said. "I think I'm going to sleep now."

I guess I'll never know if I was the one who had inspired Wendy toward her failed attempt at a career in acting, which led to her dropping out of school, which led to her coming to LA, which led to her life as a fence and criminal. I'll never know if by trying to help the little girl, I had only succeeded in ruining her life.

What would have happened if I had simply refused to take her out of that church so many years ago?

Ruthie would have taken her anyway, is what would have happened. Ruthie would have likely gotten raped or worse, and Wendy very likely killed. It seems that even with the power of time travel and the Internet, no one can know everything.

On the other hand, I was glad that Wendy didn't remember me from that scary, dark night of her childhood. I was glad to learn that she hadn't been so good to me all these years simply out of some sort of temporal gratitude, glad that she and I weren't stuck in an endless time loop of payback.

No, she really was that nice and kind. She really was.

I fell asleep smiling, feeling all warm and fuzzy.

Of course, that could have been the pain medication.

* * *

THE WEEKS PLODDED ON with excruciating slowness. I knew it would be foolish to time-travel until my ribs were fully healed. The pain of the jump alone could do me in, not to mention the fact that it had become apparent that I needed to be at my physical best while bopping through the past, especially if I were to continue to join Ruthie on the Freedom Rides, which I had every intention of doing.

It had only been a few days since she had told me that she loved me, and I would have to wait six long weeks before I could hold her in my arms. This was so going to suck.

To add insult to injury—literally—I still had to show up at Caltech every night to perform my janitorial duties. To call in sick would inspire another visit from Seymour and a laundry list of questions I couldn't answer. Even if I told him I had been robbed and beaten in some dark alley without getting a look at the culprits, he'd ask why I hadn't gone to the police—not reporting a crime is a crime, and a particularly spotty one for those on parole. If I told him I had been in a car accident, again, why hadn't I reported it? And how did I know my ribs were bruised if I hadn't gone to a doctor? And why hadn't I gone to a doctor? And if I had, which one?

No, I just had to tough it out, and that too sucked.

Work hurt. A lot. I was able to get through it, but the pain pills I would take when I got home just knocked me out. All I could do was wait it out in my dumpy apartment and watch TV or Netflix. It was like living in the thirties all over again.

Friends would drop by from time to time, but even then I couldn't do much.

Even traveling through space without time to go see Myra could slow down or even reverse my recovery. Still, I FedExed half my nitro-glycerin pills to myself at my sleazy Jersey hotel so they would be there the next time I needed them.

I phoned Myra and told her about the beating I received—obviously leaving out 1961 and the KKK—and explained that I couldn't come see her for awhile. She asked who did it, and I said that it was dark and they were wearing hoods. All true.

She offered to come out to the west coast to see me, and I couldn't wait. But she kept getting big-paying gigs to mess up her plans so her trip never came to fruition. Our time difference plus my night job made it difficult to talk during the week, but we Skyped quite a lot on weekends.

I found myself growing a little too reliant on the pills, so after a few weeks I felt it best to just tough out the remaining pain. I went online to find a book about the Freedom Rides, figuring that if Ruthie and I would be continuing on them, I should learn as much as possible. The book that seemed most recommended was dry and academic and hard to get through, yet chock-full of information. It described the events leading up to the Rides, as well as the Rides themselves, and it was clear that there was a lot more peril in store for my true love and me. It gave dates, and mentioned most of the Riders by name, but not a word about either of us. I recalled that I hadn't found any evidence of our presence on the actual Rides that first night I researched it either. Had our confrontation with the Klan scared her into quitting? I didn't think so, based on everything she had said, but it was the only guess that made sense.

So I returned to the work at hand—the sole missing piece that was preventing me from living in the past with my one true love forever.

If I send the watch to the NASA guy in 2017, how do I travel back to 1961 to live my life with Ruthie? And if I use the watch to make my one final time-trip to 1961, how do I get it to the NASA guy in 2017?

I racked my brain, but it was constipated again. Nothing came.

CHAPTER THIRTY-FOUR

W ITH MY CUTS AND BRUISES healed, and my ribs feeling fine, I
was at long last ready to return to the sixties, although I knew I
still had quite a bit of work to do before I could be with my Ruthie. I had
made promises to time, commitments to the universe. Who knew what
would happen to the world if I didn't honor them?

I was initially thrilled when the beefy doctor had given me the nitroglycerin pills, yet it only occurred to me moments before my jump what
a quandary they posed. Assuming the pills could in fact alleviate my
chest pains, the only way to bring them with me would be up my butt, in
which case I'd get the constipation and diarrhea, which was even worse.

On a hunch, I decided to jump with an empty butt, and take a pill
beforehand. Maybe it would help, maybe it wouldn't, but what did I
have to lose? Spatial destination, my Montgomery hotel room, temporal
destination, May 21st, 3:15 p.m., during which time past-me was taking
a long, hot shower. Send.

The pill helped some, not fully, but enough. Cut the pain by nearly
half. Yay!

I could hear the shower running, and I could hear other-me singing
Me and Julio Down by the Schoolyard by Paul Simon. Yes, I love Bob
Dylan, he's my favorite, but I like other songs and singers, too. I mean,
come on.

I knew which outfit other-me would wear to the church, so I chose another, then took my driver's license and a few hundred bucks out of his-our wallet. It was the second time I had stolen from me, and I realized I should start checking my wallet more often. Not that I would ever prevent any future me from stealing from me, but I think it's generally a good rule to know how much cash one has on hand.

I walked over to Hertz to rent a brown Chrysler sedan, and I knew exactly which one because I had memorized the license plate six weeks earlier, or eight hours later, depending on your point of view.

I drove to a gun shop to buy a rifle. I didn't know which one to buy because I never saw other-me with it, and I know nothing about guns. I asked a lot of questions, told the shopkeeper the range I required, confessed my total lack of experience, and then I let him choose for me. I paid for gun and bullets in cash, and that was that.

Man, if we think it's too easy to buy a gun now, back then it was just stupid.

I got back into my car, drove to the woods near the alley where the KKK had beaten me to a pulp, and parked the sedan where I had deemed it to be. I walked into the woods, placed the rifle where I thought the gunfire had come from—my best guess—then covered the gun with brush just the same. I committed the spatial destination to the watch's memory, and then walked back to the hotel. It was dark by the time I got there, and I knew Ruthie and past-me were already at the church.

I told the desk clerk that I had lost my key, and that I required another. He gave me a new one, saying that I would be charged an additional fifty cents.

I went back to my room. From there, I popped into Ruthie's room to search for her diary. I set the watch to camera, and then I snapped pictures of all the relevant pages because it seemed it would make a super interesting way to tell my tale, knowing full well that it would be my first such infraction of many.

Hey, don't judge me. I did it for you.

Once completed, I jumped to the dark woods in the dead of night to the place where the rifle lay. I could see the Klan beating me to a pulp.

Why hadn't I arrived before the first punch was even thrown, you may ask? Because the other me's hadn't. Why not? I have no idea, but they didn't. My guess is that they-me arrived the moment the me-being-beaten-up had the thought to do so.

The one thing I did decide to change, however, was not to shoot that one Klan guy in the calf. I don't know why past me's had felt the need to do so. These were just supposed to be warning shots to scare them away, and I knew for a fact that it would work. It was a minor injury to the man, wouldn't even cause him a limp, so missing him this time couldn't possibly alter history. I focused all my attention on missing his calf, focused so much on his calf that that was exactly where I nailed him. I sighed, turned away for a moment, when I saw naked Ruthie looking at me.

"I meant to miss," I told her. "Honest. I'm just not much of a gun guy."

Down in the alley, I could see other-me telling the hooded goons that if they made one more move toward me, my sniper friend would blow them all away.

"Your nigger-lovin' sniper-buddy seems all out of bullets, nigger-lover," I could see the Klan leader saying. So I fired one more blast into the back wall. The red bricks crumbled into debris, and the bad guys ran away.

I set the spatial destination on the watch for my Montgomery hotel room, and the temporal destination for later that night, arriving shortly after past-me had jumped to Wendy's couch in search of medical assistance. I put on a pair of underwear and a T-shirt, and then got into bed. I knew I'd have to tell Ruthie about time travel in the morning—I knew it the moment I strapped the watch on her wrist and teleported her into the woods to save her from the bad guys.

I just had no idea what I could possibly say.

CHAPTER THIRTY-FIVE

D EAR DIARY,
    I can't stop crying.

I woke up this morning, a bundle of conflicted emotions. I wanted to kick myself for telling T.J. that I loved him, but another part of me was so very glad that I had. I would visibly shake when I thought about how close I had come to being raped by the Klansmen, yet I was proud that I had been brave enough to take the little girl to her aunt's house in the first place. I was desperate for T.J. to explain the impossible events of last night, yet I was afraid of what those answers could be. Mostly, I wanted to kick myself for telling T.J. that I loved him. What was I thinking?

I phoned my parents to tell them that I was all right, and asked them to pass the information on to Edward because I didn't feel ready to speak to him just yet. I showered, got dressed, and headed to T.J.'s room. I was certain I would have to take him to a hospital, and I expected some resistance. His irrational fear of doctors was such that . . . that doesn't matter.

I had left his door unlocked last night so he wouldn't have to get up to let me in, but I still felt it only proper to knock. "T.J. It's Ruthie. Are you decent?"

"I guess that's a matter of opinion," I heard him quip as he opened the door.

There wasn't a scratch on him. The swelling and purple of his eyes were gone, and he stood in the doorway smiling, fit as a fiddle.

"How, how can that be?" I stammered.

He put his two hands over mine, and softly said. "I'm going to tell you." He led me into the room, kicked the door closed behind him, and had us sit next to each other on the poorly-made bed.

"I'm about to tell you something no one in the world knows but me," he sighed, as if he was the one having difficulty with all this. "Given the bad shape I was in last night, how long do you think it would take for me to fully heal?"

"I don't know. At least a month."

"It took me about six weeks, actually."

"What?"

He sighed again. "I'm from the future."

"What?" I repeated. It was the only word I could think to say.

"I'm from the year 2017. I won't even be born for another twenty-eight years."

All I could wonder was why he was telling me such a cockamamie fish tale, and it was making me angry. "How did you heal so fast?" I demanded.

"I didn't heal any faster than anyone. This watch on my wrist is a time machine. I can teleport myself through time and space. After you left my room last night, well, your last night, I jumped back to the present, well, my present, your future, where I received the medical care you wanted me to get, and I took the time to fully heal. From my vantage point, I haven't seen you for six weeks."

"Last night, you promised me that you'd explain everything, and you're reneging," I snapped. "How was I in one place, then all of a sudden in another? How were you in two places at the same time? How did you heal so quickly?"

"Do you want to try it?"

"Try what?"

"Time travel. I can put you into a brief time loop to see for yourself."

"Fine," I seethed. I didn't know what he was up to, but I was absolutely going to call his bluff.

He tapped on his watch a few times, then removed it from his wrist and strapped it on mine. "I only set it for a few minutes back, that way it won't hurt."

"It hurts?"

"Not if it's just a couple of minutes. Besides, you'll be so freaked out, you wouldn't even notice if it did. Hang on a sec." He quickly jogged to the bathroom then returned with a towel.

"What's that for?"

"You'll see."

We sat in silence for a moment, as if he was waiting for something to happen.

"Now what?" I asked.

"Just decide that you'll do it."

"I have. I already told you."

"No, you have to make a real, firm commitment to the universe that you'll do it. Not that you want to, but that you will. And you have to mean it—you can't just say it."

"I mean it."

"No, you don't."

"You don't know what I'm thinking."

"I know what will happen once you make your decision."

"I have made it."

"You haven't."

"I have! I will do this!"

I heard a "crack" sound as a burst of air pushed into my face, forcing me to close my eyes. I could hear the papers on the hotel pads and the edges of the pillowcases flutter, and when I opened my eyes, standing right before me was my identical twin, except I don't have an identical twin. She was wearing the exact same watch that T.J. had placed on my wrist moments earlier, and nothing else. I screamed. She screamed. T.J. covered her with the towel, and she began to laugh.

"This is real?" she asked through her giggles. "This is really real?" She moved toward me with an enormous yet mesmerized smile, studying me all the way. She reached her hand out toward my hair, then turned back to T.J. "Can I touch her?"

"I don't see why not."

"No," I insisted as I slapped her hand away. "You may not."

"I'm sorry," she said, chuckling all the while, then turned back to T.J. "I remember her saying that, that she's sorry, the other me, I mean. And I remember her turning to you and saying that. And that. And that."

"It's like a perpetual déjà vu, isn't it?" T.J. told her.

"That's exactly what it's like."

"How are you doing this?" I demanded of T.J. It had to be some kind of trick, and I didn't want either of them to think I was so gullible that I'd fall for such nonsense.

The woman sat on the bed next to me, and took my hands in hers. "Sweetie, this is real," she said soothingly. "He wasn't lying. I'm you. You're me. We're each other."

"It's not possible."

"I know. Just a moment ago I was sitting where you're sitting, thinking this is all one big trick, just like you are now. And a minute from now, you'll be sitting where I am, saying exactly what I'm saying." Then she turned back to T.J. "This is so strange."

"You get used to it."

"I'm not sure I want to," she said with a nervous laugh.

"So I'm supposed to memorize everything you're saying?" I asked the woman.

"You don't have to memorize anything," she answered. "It just comes out."

"I've got to say," T.J. interrupted, "I'm glad you ladies are getting along so well. Me and my other me's sometimes have our issues."

"T.J., knock it off. This was hard for me when I was her. It's not funny."

"Then why are you smiling?"

"Well, because it's funny."

"No, it's absurd," I insisted, then turned to T.J. "How are you doing this?"

But the woman answered for him, the supposed other me. "Ruth, we have to start opening our eyes to what's in front of us. We have to stop denying what we know to be true. We've done it for far too long. You know what I'm talking about, don't you?"

On the surface, she seemed to be talking about accepting time travel as a reality, but I somehow knew that she was really talking about my feelings for T.J.

"Yes," I answered softly.

"And now, it's time for you to go," she replied warmly.

"How?"

"Just tap on the little Send square on the watch," T.J. said. "I already set it."

"Okay, but after I do and nothing happens," I told both of them, "and after you guys get your great big laugh at my expense, you're going to explain how you did this."

"You'll be the one laughing, sweetie, I promise," said the woman who seemed to be me. "Would I lie to you?"

"We lie to ourself all the time."

"Good point. And we really must stop that. Now, off you go."

I didn't believe anything would happen, but I sort of did. I took a deep breath, tapped on the Send square, and I was suddenly standing in the center of the room, completely naked, looking at myself sitting on the bed next to T.J. The other me screamed. I screamed. T.J. covered me with a towel, and I began to laugh. It wasn't that I found it funny per se, rather more akin to the laughter that's provoked after jumping in your seat after a startling moment in a scary movie. "This is real? This is really real?"

It was so hard to believe, yet it was undeniable. I could only wonder if I was dreaming. I walked to the girl on the bed to touch her, to feel something to prove to myself that I was awake. "Can I touch her?" I asked T.J.

"I don't see why not."

Then the other me slapped my hand away, and I remembered how spooked I had been when I was her. I sat down next to her and took her hands to calm her, to explain it all, and I could remember hearing everything I was saying.

I felt for her, poor Ruth Anne. She simply could not accept what she was seeing even while seeing it. How long had I, we, been living like that? Last night, in that one glorious kiss, I finally came to terms with the fact that I had fallen for T.J. that first moment I had met him, yet this morning I went right back to trying to deny it.

"Ruth, we have to start opening our eyes to what's in front of us. We have to stop denying what we know to be true. We've done it for far too long. You know what I'm talking about, don't you?"

"Yes," she answered softly. I knew she knew what I meant because I remembered knowing it.

"And now, it's time for you to go," I replied warmly.

After just a few more exchanges, she tapped on the watch, and she was gone. This time the sound was "crunch" not "crack", and a gust of wind thrust me forward toward where she had been, and only her clothes, my clothes, remained behind.

I sighed. I laughed. I sighed again. I laughed again. And then I sighed. I felt drunk.

"You okay?" T.J. asked as he brought me a glass of water, then sat down on the bed next to me.

"Yes," I answered. "I suppose."

"Any questions?"

"Too many questions."

"Take your time."

"How can this be?"

"You mean, like, how does it work?"

"Yes, all right, sure. Start there."

"I don't know."

"You don't know how it works?"

"I mean, I know how to use it, I just don't know why it works. I didn't invent it. It's the design of a very great and brilliant man."

"And he just gave it to you?"

"That's a very long story, and one not completely relevant to anything you're probably wondering about right now, so let's save that one for another day. I don't want your head to explode or anything."

"My head can explode?" I shouted. "Is that one of the side effects? What have you done to me?"

"No, no, chill," he said with a laugh. "It's just an expression. Your head won't explode."

I sighed, relieved. I rested my head upon his shoulder. I took his arm and wrapped it around me. I was still very confused, but I felt safe.

"So is that why I felt about you the way I did right from the start? Is this some kind of futuristic, super-duper, aphrodisiac love potion?"

"No," he said with complete certainty. "It really was love at first sight."

"Why?"

"You know, I didn't think I'd have to go into that particular part today, too."

"*Tell me.*"

"*You're not going to believe me, and this one I can't prove.*"

"*Tell me.*"

"*Okay,*" he sighed. "*How do I explain it? Ever since I was a boy, I've dreamt about you.*" I smiled. I liked that he dreamt about me. "*The beginnings were always different, but always wonderful and magical and perfect. We were madly in love, soul mates, and we were engaged to be married. But the dreams always ended the same. You tell me that you've met someone else, that you love him more than you love me, and that you're going to marry him instead.*"

"*Awww, that's a terrible dream.*"

"*The thing is, it wasn't me you were dumping. It was Edward. I mean, it was me because I am Edward. I'm Edward's reincarnation.*"

I could only look at him.

"*I know, I know, it's even more unbelievable than time travel, I know. But you and I are eternal soul mates, each other's one true love, and we have been since before time began. The problem is that Edward is also your one true love, and no one is supposed to have two one true loves. That's why you've been feeling so torn apart since we met.*

"*But in the end, you're going to choose me. It's been somehow ordained. I'm to move permanently back to 1961, to age and grow old from here so that we can spend the rest of our lives in each other's arms. And I can't prove any of this.*"

What he was saying was crazy, yet what was even more crazy was that I knew it to be true the moment he said it. Not merely because his words made sense, not only because all my questions had suddenly been answered and all my confusions suddenly explained, but because I just simply knew. I knew it to the depths of my heart, and to the deepest recesses of my soul.

I loved this man, and I always had.

"*Honest, if I could prove—*"

"*Stop talking,*" I told him, and then I put my hands to his face, and kissed him. Our arms wrapped around each other, and our tongues circled inside each other's mouths. The towel slipped off my body, and I let myself fall back onto the bed, bringing his powerful frame right along with me.

We made love three times today, each one more magical than the one before. T.J. and Edward share a similar style in terms of passion and tenderness, they even kiss the same, but T.J. knows things that Edward doesn't. Wonderful, dirty things that are not proper for a lady to discuss, not even in the privacy of her own diary.

Yet they are glorious.

I knew I had to choose T.J. I think I knew it all along. T.J. is all the things that Edward is, yet more. He's braver, more adventurous, more exciting. He's from the future, for goodness sake. And he's willing to give up his entire world, the only world he has ever known and everyone he has ever loved, just to be with me.

I don't think I ever really had a choice. It was as he said. It had somehow been ordained.

I love him, I've always loved him, and I have never been happier.

Yet I know that I have to end it with Edward, and that's why I can't stop crying.

CHAPTER THIRTY-SIX

"WHAT'S THE FUTURE LIKE?" RUTHIE moaned in that lovely, half-sleepy tone that women often adopt post-coital.

I was lying on my back, her head resting on my bare chest. It had been a short while since we finished making love for the first of what would be three times that day, and our eternal bond was cemented forever. I could feel it. We both could.

"It has its good points and its bad points," I answered.

"Start with the good."

"The technology is amazing."

"Like flying cars, jetpacks, and robots?"

"No on flying cars and jetpacks. Robots sort of, but not how you think. They're mainly for factories, and they don't look like people. But the Internet is amazing."

"What's the Internet?"

"How do I explain the Internet? It's like you hook up your computer, wait, let me start over. Everyone has a computer."

"Their own?"

"Yeah."

"Where do they keep it?"

"Anywhere, they're small. So you hook up your computer to a modem, which is the thing that enables you to access the Internet."

"What's the Internet?"

"I'm getting to it. So now that you're hooked up, you can go online—"

"What's 'online?'"

"It means you're on the Internet."

"What's the Internet?" she laughed, then I did, too, and we pretty much laughed our way through the rest of the conversation.

"This is turning out to be a lot harder than I thought. Okay, so now that you're online, meaning on the Internet, you can go anywhere."

"Can't people in the twenty-first century go places without the Internet?"

"No, I don't mean physically. You can go anywhere online."

"Which means that you can go anywhere on the Internet?"

"Exactly."

"What's the Internet?" she laughed again, then so did I again.

"Okay, let's say you want to know something—say, Leonardo da Vinci's birthday. You just type in 'Leonardo da Vinci birthday,' and it tells you."

"What if you can't type?"

"Everyone can type where I come from."

"Why?"

"So they can use the Internet."

"I still don't get it. So you type 'Leonardo da Vinci's birthday', and the little computer announces the date?"

"Well, most computers don't actually speak the answer. They can if you have the right app but—"

"What's an app?"

"Doesn't matter. So you type in your question, and a list of webpages pop onto your screen that can show you the answer. Then you click on one of the links, and you can read all about him—and not just about his birthday. There's text about his whole life, pictures of him, images of his paintings, everything."

"What's a webpage? What's a link? What does 'click on them' mean?"

"Let's try this. Imagine the biggest library in the world, in the privacy of your own home, through which you can access all knowledge ever known to man."

"Good. Because it seemed like a lot of trouble just to find an artist's birthday."

"You can pay your bills, watch movies, listen to music. You can access something called social media and become friends with people on the far other side of the globe—well, not *real* friends, they're called 'Facebook friends,' which is—"

"I don't care anymore," she laughed. "What's the bad part of the future?"

"Well, for some reason, there's a lot of people killing other people."

"Like World War Three?"

"No, that never happened. Communism fell in the eighties. Russia is our friend now. Well, not so much our friend, but—"

"Our Facebook friend?"

"No. We still don't like them, we just don't hate them as much as you guys do. But there's terrorism all over the world—organizations bombing nightclubs, flying airplanes into buildings. Or people going into schools and just shooting everyone." Then I felt a sudden pang. "You know what? Maybe I shouldn't be telling you this."

"Why not?"

"I may have made a mistake telling you anything at all. I don't think I have because nothing I've said so far is anything you can act upon, but if I keep talking, who knows what I may spill. Just to be safe, it's better you don't know anything."

"Tell me one more bad thing, and one more good thing."

"Climate change and cell phones."

She rolled onto her side and gazed into my soul with her sultry green eyes. "Your world sounds very complicated."

"It's an acquired taste."

Then she kissed me, and I kissed her back.

Round two.

* * *

"I want to see it," she said as she zipped up her skirt. "The future, I mean."

We were getting dressed for dinner after having spent the afternoon in bed. I sighed at her request. I didn't want to deny this girl anything, but physics is physics.

"You can't. No one can go into the future because it hasn't happened yet."

"You do all the time," she said as she clasped her bra. "You're from 2017."

"That's not my future, it's my present. It's your future."

"But 2017 is the watch's present, too, right? I mean, if someone is in the passenger seat of a car, she ends up wherever the car goes, doesn't she?"

"I never thought of it that way."

"Let me try."

"It's just not a good idea for you to know too much of what's to come."

"You do."

"And it's very challenging."

"Let's just take a minute to first see if it's even possible. What do you say? One minute into the future. What's the worst that can happen?"

"My guess is that nothing will happen at all."

"Then we'll know, and we won't have to debate it further," she said, wrapping her arms around me, moving her ruby red lips a hair's breadth from mine. "Please?"

"All right," I said, receiving a wondrous kiss for the effort.

For the record, I would have conceded even without her sexual ploy. Like I said, I don't want to deny this woman anything. Besides, I was pretty curious myself.

Spatial destination, current, temporal destination, sixty seconds forward.

I strapped it on her wrist, and had her tap Send.

At first glance, it appeared that my initial hunch was right. There was a barely audible *crunch*, and Ruthie stood right where she had been all along. But upon further scrutiny, I realized that the watch was gone.

The watch had travelled without her!

But had it gone a mere minute into the future where it awaited us, or had I sent it into oblivion? I couldn't know. This was only the third time I'd been without it since it came into my possession, the first being when I had sent dead Clarence off to his bedroom, during which I sweated it out despite my confidence; the second, while being beaten up by the Klan, at which point my mind was understandably preoccupied. This time, I had no idea where it was, and I just freaked.

What if it was gone for good? Everyone I wanted to help would get nothing. I'd never get to say goodbye to Wendy or Myra. What would they think? I couldn't imagine what they would think. And I would have completely betrayed the trust that Professor Szabo had placed in me.

Ruthie could see my panic and tried her best to console me. "It'll come back."

"You don't know that," I snapped. "I know way more than you do, and I don't know anything!"

"Even if it is gone, my darling," she said as she rubbed my shoulders. "You were planning on staying here with me anyway, weren't you?"

"There were things I had to do first," I bellowed as I moved away from her, having no desire to let her make me feel good. "Promises I made. I am such a screw-up! Stupid, stupid, stup—"

Before I could finish my third "stupid," the watch reappeared exactly where it had been before vanishing from Ruthie's wrist. Ruthie was no longer standing in the exact same spot, so the watch merely hovered in the air beside her for a split second, then fell gently to the carpeted hotel room floor. She picked it up as I collapsed on the chair by the little desk.

"There," she said as she crossed toward me. "I told you it would all work out." She knelt by the chair as she strapped it back onto my wrist. "Good as new."

"Sorry I freaked out on you like that," I said, a little embarrassed.

"No worries," she said with a smile, and her use of the surfer-dude expression only made me laugh.

Ruthie could not have known it, but she had given me the final missing piece to my puzzle. The way to remain in 1961 with my true love while still getting the watch to the NASA guy was clear at last.

The watch can travel by itself.

CHAPTER THIRTY-SEVEN

D EAR DIARY,
Our CORE contact phoned this morning to inform us that the next Freedom Ride was heading out tomorrow to Jackson, Mississippi. I knew I couldn't join them.

Edward and I had left things on bad terms, and it would be cruel to keep him in ignorance now that I knew I'd be calling off our engagement. I still love him. How could I not? He's my soul mate; that hasn't changed. He's T.J., or at least he'll become, has become T.J. I owed it to Edward to give him the sad news as quickly as I could.

I knew that T.J. was only doing the Rides because I was—he had made that very clear on Sunday—so I told our CORE contact that we would have to miss this next Ride due to personal reasons but fully intended to catch up with them for the next one. He was very understanding, although a little presumptuous.

"Ruth, listen," he said, "I know how frightening Sunday night must have been for you folks. If you and T.J. want to back out, no one will think less of you. This is dangerous business, and you don't have to give any excuse beyond that. The mere fact that you've been willing to come this far for our cause shows what good people you are."

"Not at all," I said in all earnestness. "I have every intention of being a part of this, and I assure you this is not an excuse. We are on the right side of history."

He thanked me, and we promised to stay in touch so that T.J. and I could catch up with them in a few days time.

"That explains part of it," T.J. mumbled to himself when I told him.

"What does that mean?"

"Nothing."

"You knew I was going to make this decision even before I made it, didn't you?"

He took my hands and sat me down once more. "Listen. I love you, and I never want to lie to you, so I need you to understand why I can't tell you certain things.

"I have to live every moment back here so carefully for fear that I may alter the past, and thereby harm the future, my present. I could destroy the lives of the people I love, I could render myself unborn, and it's only going to be more difficult now that I've chosen to stay here with you permanently.

"Don't get me wrong, you're worth it. But if I tell you the things I know, you will have to live the same way I do, and it really messes with your head. Every tiny decision is weighed down with constant, exhausting calculation. Can I do this? Can I not do this? Have I already done it, meaning that I must do it? Do I have free will, or is every action I take some divine decree of time or fate? Have I already changed things and I just don't know it? I don't want to put any of that on you."

I had never seen him so intense. "Thanks," I said with a smile.

I booked our flights home, then telephoned Edward to arrange to meet upon my return. Before I could say much of anything, he told me how sorry he was for our spat, putting all the blame on himself. He had read about Sunday night's events, was glad Mother had called to tell him I was safe, but mostly, he said, he was proud of me.

"You were right all along, Ruthie. This is an important cause, and you've shamed me into seeing so. I was a coward, but you've inspired me back to bravery."

Then he offered to come join me for the next Ride.

He was being so wonderful. I felt terrible.

I told him that I was flying home later that day, and he was elated. He said that he had a university function that evening that he couldn't get out of on short notice, so he suggested we meet in Central Park the next morning. We've always had such wonderful moments in Central Park— walking, talking, feeding birds, holding hands, and simply being in love— so it was an obvious choice for a reconciliation.

Poor Edward.

I got off the phone, and I refused to cry. I had cried enough. I needed to be strong.

It was as if T.J. could see the tears behind my eyes. "I'm sorry," he said.

I knew exactly what he meant. He was sorry for being the one to put me through this, sorry for having shown up in my life and forcing me to choose between two one true loves. But it was no more his fault than Edward's or my own.

Love defies logic. Love defies morality. Love is wonderful, and it is mean.

I hugged him. I love him so. I always have.

He said we had to run a few errands before heading to the airport. "We should have done them all yesterday but we were too busy being happy," he smiled.

The obvious one was returning his rental car, which we did last, but I couldn't figure out what the others were. How could he have errands to run in Montgomery?

We checked out of the hotel, threw our bags in the car, and he drove us back to the alley where I was almost raped. "Why do we have to come here?" I demanded. It was not a memory I wished to relive.

"You'll see," he said. We walked into the woods near where I had been lying naked only two nights earlier. He picked up the rifle and sighed, "I really don't like guns." He clutched it like a baseball bat and smashed it against one of the trees with all his might, and then he smashed it again, and again and again, grunting his exertion aloud all the while. Wooden chips and little gun pieces splintered into the air all around him. The wood handle cracked in two with half of it falling to the ground.

"If anyone found that thing and did damage with it, I couldn't live with myself," he panted as he looked at the dented barrel, making sure he had rendered the weapon useless. Then we buried its various parts in strategic spots throughout the forest.

We got back into the car and drove to Aunt Greta's and Uncle Dale's cabin. When Uncle Dale came to the door, T.J. apologized for the damage he had done to the man's truck, and offered to pay for the necessary repairs. Dale was beside himself as he complimented and thanked us.

"The estimate I got is pretty dear," he said. "Thirty-two dollars and ten cents."

T.J. couldn't make exact change so he gave the man a hundred-dollar bill. Dale's eyes widened as if he had never seen such a thing before. "I can't make change for that."

"Keep it," T.J. said.

"No, sir. I could not do that."

"That truck saved our lives, sir, meaning you saved our lives. It's the least we could do. Buy something nice for Wendy. Only don't tell her it was from me."

It's pretty obvious that T.J. somehow knows Wendy from before, that is to say, from the future. I'd ask him, but he's made it clear that he won't tell me anything about his world. I'm glad. Having to live your life second-guessing every little choice, even wondering if you have free will, seems a terrible burden. I don't know how he does it.

Among his many remarkable qualities, T.J. has a wonderful way of helping people take their mind off their worries. We talked and laughed the whole flight home, through dinner, and much of the night because he spent it at my apartment, where he displayed several more of his remarkable qualities.

I wonder if all twenty-first-century men are as sexually adept as he, or if this is particular to him. I'd ask him, but he wouldn't tell me.

Only now, as I make this entry, does my mind return to Edward and the painful task I must accomplish tomorrow.

I watch T.J. in bed. The soft lines of his face, the contours of his muscles, the deep sighs of his breath. My heart pounds for him, and my soul yearns for him.

Even asleep, he gives me strength.

CHAPTER THIRTY-EIGHT

I KNEW EXACTLY HOW HORRIBLE they would both feel because I had dreamt it. I had personally felt the agony and despair that Edward was about to undergo, the sense of betrayal and his new hatred toward me. I'm the Judas. I'm the snake.

I knew the difficulty with which Ruthie would perform the task, the tears that would flow despite her best efforts to keep them inside, and how I-Edward would only want to wipe them away and hold her to make her feel better.

Time or fate or the universe had ordained it all, even this bad part. I could only assume things would get better. What else would be the point of this giant, crazy circle?

I asked her if she wanted me to wait with her until it was time to go see him, but she said that she wanted to be alone, before and after. Then she asked me to come by later that evening. I wished her luck—empty words that fell on deaf ears, as she once wrote—but I didn't know how else to console her.

I got back to my place a little past ten and turned my attention to work, to test the feasibility of the final part of my exit strategy. Can the watch travel safely through time and space by itself with pinpoint accuracy? (Pinpoint accuracy being crucial to what I had in mind, and something with which I had never particularly concerned myself up till then).

I divided my experiment into three parts. First, space without time, then time without space, then both together. I set the temporal destination for current, and the spatial destination for my living room coffee table. Send.

I found myself standing on the table. Right, I had to take the watch off first. Idiot.

Temporal destination for current, spatial destination, the far left side of the coffee table. I placed the watch on the far right side of the same table. Send.

The watch just popped from one side to the other. This looked promising.

Temporal destination current, spatial destination, the kitchen table. Send.

I raced to the kitchen, and there was the watch waiting for me.

I drew teeny x's all over my apartment—on the coffee table, kitchen table and cupboards, my bedroom pillow, Clarence's dresser, bathroom counter—then spent the next half hour popping the thing from one location to the next.

Each experiment proved successful, the face of the watch landing dead center on the little x's, the straps flapping beside it like a beautiful falcon's wings.

Now the scary part. Time.

I had already seen the watch travel safely by itself through time so there was no logical reason that it wouldn't again, but my fears had nothing to do with logic. What if there was a limit to how far in time it could go without a body? What if there's a limit to how often you can try before it vanishes into nothingness? Or breaks? I so wished the Professor was there to help me.

I had already seen the watch travel one minute forward in time, so I sent it a mere five minutes forward. It was the longest five minutes of my life.

I was palpably sweating. My hands were shaking. I wondered if I had become addicted to the watch, the way Bilbo and Frodo became addicted to their ring of power. Would I be able to give up the thing when the time came? I knew that I had to, but could I?

And what if it didn't reappear?

What if both? What if I had become addicted *and* it didn't reappear? What if, what if, what if.

Then it came back.

This was very promising.

I set it for half an hour hence. If you think five minutes was hard, multiply it by, no, not by six, but by a zillion. I was pacing my apartment. I did pushups and jumping jacks to distract myself. I slapped myself in the face for being stupid. Then it came back, right on the button. Then I tried it for an hour, even harder. Then two hours, I thought I was going to kill myself. The watch always came back.

It was time to combine time and space. From the kitchen to the living room coffee table, five seconds only. Right on target.

From the living room to the bathroom counter, one minute. Worked.

From the bathroom to Clarence's bedroom pillow, half-hour. Worked.

From the living room to the kitchen table, full hour.

Works, works, works.

In fact, it was working so well that it was almost boring. Neither the spatial nor temporal distance caused any deviation of success whatsoever. Each landing was one-hundred-percent perfect. Professor Szabo was a genius.

Final test, four hours. If that turned out just as perfect as five seconds, I would have to assume that fifty-six years would be no different. There was no way to experiment with that one. Send.

Part of me was completely confident that this test would yield the very same results as the others, but four hours is a very long time to be naked—that's how I felt: naked, vulnerable. I phoned Bob to chat, to take my mind off my worries, but even that didn't help. Yes, that's right, chatting idly on the telephone with Bob Dylan just didn't seem all that important under the circumstances. Imagine that. When he said I seemed jittery, I told him that I'd had too much coffee, and that we'd talk later.

By the fourth of the four hours, I was banging my head into the wall, and I knew Ruthie would ask me why I had so many bleeding cuts on my forehead.

I showered and shaved around seven forty-five, and I knew I would most likely have to again because I'd continue to sweat until the watch returned.

Yet then, right on temporal time, and right on the spatial button, the watch appeared like a dart in a bullseye.

So here's the plan I came up with, and I had no doubt that it would work.

I'd jump back to modern-day Pasadena. A hacker friend of mine would show me how to hack into the New York City Morgue computer system so I could find the next appropriate corpse without having to actually work there. Once found, I'd pop to New York, steal the body as I had in the sixties, dress it up in a nice suit, put Theodore Alexander Jameson's identification in the corpse's pockets along with a card stating that the law firm of Pendleton, Smythe, Horrace, and Cheevers be notified in case of emergency, then I'd dump the body in front of the New York Presbyterian Hospital in lower Manhattan.

I could only hope it wouldn't take as long to find the appropriate body as it had in the sixties because I would have to be fulfilling my Caltech janitorial duties all the while, so that part would suck. On the other hand, there are a lot more John Does today, so I figured I could find the right one in a matter of weeks.

I'd spend my last day in New York with little sister, and say goodbye forever. She'd ask me why, and I'd tell her that, well, I didn't quite know what I would tell her at that early point in the planning phase. So, yeah, I still had a little work to do on that front, but I knew I could come up with something.

I'd jump back to my Pasadena apartment, where I'd put the Professor's documents, notebooks, and flash drives into a large box—a much larger box than necessary in order to provide me with a margin of error. I'd write the anonymous letter the Professor had asked me to write, address the box to the NASA guy, provide a bogus return address, then affix the necessary FedEx postage upon it. I'd place the box on my kitchen table, and log the coordinates into the watch's memory.

I'd go see Wendy to say goodbye, telling her that I'd decided to jump parole. She'd try to talk me out of it, I'd insist I needed to, she'd say I was wrong, but in the end she'd back me up because she's wonderful.

Then I'd ask the big favor. "There's a box on my kitchen table. The paperwork is filled out, the postage paid and affixed. Tomorrow, I need you to pick it up and bring it to FedEx and send it off for me. You already have a key to my place."

She'd ask me why I couldn't do it myself, why it's necessary, why, why, why. But in the end, I'd have no good answer, and she'd do it for me anyway because she's wonderful.

Then I'd come back to the sixties, delete from the watch's memory all data regarding my own temporal travels, leaving only the record of the Professor's first ten-minute jump, mankind's very first voyage through time. I'd kiss the watch goodbye forever, jump it smack-dab into the middle of the large box on my Pasadena kitchen table in 2017, and then spend the rest of my life with my one true love.

But first, I had to go console my Ruthie because it was time.

As I left my building to hail a cab, I saw a little girl selling flowers on the street. I figured Ruthie would probably appreciate some nice flowers under the circumstances.

"What do you get for someone you're crazy about, who has just gone through a great ordeal?"

"I dunno, mister. I'm just selling flowers."

"I'll take those."

"Buck-fifty."

"Here's five. Keep it."

"Wow, thanks, mister."

During the cab ride, my mind wandered back to my experiments. Maybe four hours wasn't conclusive enough. I decided that when I got home, I would send the watch forward a full day. If that worked, a full week. If a week worked with the same degree of accuracy as five seconds, I would have to accept that my plan was safe.

Besides, it would be a smart weaning process just in case I actually had become addicted. I seemed a little too happy to have it back in my pocket. I was actually caressing it.

I forced myself to turn my attention back to Ruthie. I knew she'd be a mess, I knew it from my dreams, and I had to be there for her. I had to be focused.

It occurred to me that my dreams always ended with me wishing I could console her, hold her, wipe away her tears, and make her feel better. It turned out that I would be able to do just that. That particular wish had indeed come true, yet still, I wished it wasn't necessary.

When I got to her place, her door was already open. I knocked a few times anyway. "Ruthie?"

I could hear sobbing from within, yet they weren't *her* sobs, so I walked inside.

Edward was sitting on the floor, crying and virtually comatose. Ruthie was lying limply over his lap, her arms dangling lifelessly by her side, and blood was oozing from her head.

"What happened?" I demanded.

"I'm sorry!" Edward wept.

I dropped to my knees, and put my hand to her wrist, to her neck.

"Edward!" I shouted. "What have you done? What have you done?"

"I'm sorry!" he wailed once more.

Ruthie was dead.

PART 4

SCREW TIME

CHAPTER THIRTY-NINE

"**E**DWARD!" I YELLED AS I shook him. "Talk to me!"

"I'm sorry!" he wailed.

I should have been able to remember what had happened. Ever since I had met the man, I remembered his memories the moment he had them, but not this time.

"Edward! Edward!"

Then I heard the sirens.

"You called the police?"

"I'm sorry!"

I had to think. I had to figure this out. I had to stay calm, but my heart was pounding and my brain was spinning. Thief head took over.

Get out! Thief head told me. *Figure it out! But not here! Go!*

There was only one person who could help me understand this, only one person who could help me remember what had happened. Send.

I was in my sleazy Jersey hotel room, and the chest pain was brutal. It took everything I had to drape a bath towel around me and race barefoot down to the front desk to retrieve the FedEx package in which lay my nitroglycerin pills. The desk clerk was talking to me but his words were but an echo of white noise. I ripped open the cardboard envelope and shoved a pill under my tongue. Within a matter of minutes, the chest pain was mild and easily tolerable. Damn, this stuff was good.

I turned back to the clerk and asked him what he had said.

"Your rent was prepaid for three months," he said. "That ends tomorrow."

"Yeah, okay. Let me go get some cash."

I sped back to my room and quickly got dressed as I tried to calm myself down. I realized that I probably should have time-jumped from another room when I left the sixties so that Edward wouldn't have seen me disappear, but the guy was so whacked out it would be easy to convince him that he hadn't seen what he thought he had seen.

I also realized that I wasn't really in any hurry at all. If it took me a whole year to come up with a plan, I could still pop back to that very same day in 1961 to fix everything. Of course, that was logic speaking. In my racing heart, it felt like I had no time to spare.

The only thing I knew for sure was that Ruthie was not going to die that day. I would not allow it.

I sprinted back down to the lobby, prepaid an additional three months' rent, then hailed a cab to Myra's. There was no line outside, and the main parlor was empty when I burst inside.

"Myra!" I shouted. "Myra! Are you here?"

She came in through her beaded doorway in a pink satin bathrobe. Her hair was wet, and she was drying it with a towel.

"Teej," Myra said. "What are you doing here?"

"I think I killed her," I wailed. "Ruthie's dead, and I think I killed her." Then I sobbed uncontrollably upon her shoulder.

She had us sit on her couch, and I told her the events of the morning and everything I had seen that evening—leaving out the 1961 part, obviously.

"But I can't remember what happened," I concluded. "I always remember Edward's memories, but I can't this time."

"You're in denial. Probably because Edward went into denial."

"You once told me there's a way you can hypnotize someone to remember his past lives. I forget what it's called."

"Past-life regression."

"Will you past-life regress me? I need to know what happened so I can fix it."

"You said she's dead. How can you possibly fix that?"

"I don't know yet!" I shouted. "Please?"

"Of course. But not like this. I need you to calm down first. Let me go make us some herbal tea."

"I don't want any damn tea."

"Too bad. You'll drink it, and you'll like it."

Isn't my sister the best?

* * *

"I want you to feel your toes," she said softly. My eyes were closed and my palms were placed before me on the stained mahogany table as she had instructed. I knew that by allowing her to hypnotize me there was some risk of her learning about the time travel, but I saw no other option. If that was the price I had to pay to save Ruthie, so be it. I'd deal with the fallout later if need be.

"I want you to wiggle your toes for me," she softly went on. "Now I want you to relax them. I want you to feel them melt into your shoes . . . I want you to feel your feet, and let them melt away as well . . . . Your calves, your knees, they're gone, gone . . . You are melting away, and all you can hear is the sound of my voice . . . . Your thighs, your hips, relaxed, relaxed, relaxed . . . There's only the sound of my voice . . . Your tummy, your chest, have melted away . . . All you know is my voice, my words . . . Your shoulders, your neck . . . Only my voice . . . Your ears, your head . . . What's left?"

"Your voice."

"What else?"

"Your voice."

"Good, T.J. That's very good. Now I want you to go back in time, just a few months, to that day we reunited in Starbucks. You see a blond lady at the counter, and you offer to buy her latte. I don't want you to remember. I want you to be there."

"She's very pretty," I found myself saying dreamily. "I want to bang her."

"Yes, yes, you do."

"She says she's Myra. After all these years. I'm so happy to see her. But she's had it rough."

"That's very good, T.J. Now I want you to go back to the year before that." I felt myself squirm in my seat. I began to sweat. "Where are you?"

"In my cell. With Juan. I don't like it here. Must get out. Must work hard."

"Then let's leave there, T.J. Let's go back further. You're ten years old."

"I'm happy now."

"Why are you happy, T.J.?"

"Mom and Dad are going to adopt us! They love us and they'll take care of us forever and ever.

"But Myra's mad at me. She's yelling at me in the mall. But I didn't take it for me. It was for their anniversary. They'll like it. I'm being good. No, I won't steal anymore. Ever. I promise. I don't want to be sent away again."

"Good, that's very good. You're doing very well, T.J. Now go back further in time, still further. I want you to go back."

"Okie-dokie."

"Where are you?"

"On Mommy's bed. We're playing Candy Land. I'm better at it. I win all the time. Do you let me win on purpose, Mommy? I didn't think you did. She's very happy. I like when she's happy because she's very sick a lot."

"And now go back further."

"There isn't further."

"Further. Gently, gently, further back, Edward. Gently further back."

"Ummmm..."

"Where are you now?"

"In my room."

"What does it look like?"

"It's white. There's just a bed. There's a little window on the door with bars on it so they can look inside to check on me."

"Are you in prison?"

"No. Not prison. Some people think it's prison, but I belong here. I'm not well so they take care of me. They take good care of me."

"What's wrong with you?"

"I'm not well in the head."

"What's your name?"

"Edward Montadel."

"Are you in a hospital, Edward?"

"Hospital for people who aren't well in the head."

"How long have you been there, Edward?"

"I don't know. Long time. Decades, I think. Don't know."

"Now, I want you to go back to the day you became not well in the head."

"No."

"I want you to go back to the day you became not well in the head, Edward."

"I don't want to. They always try to make me go there but I won't do it."

"Why won't you do it?"

"Hurts too much."

"Then go back to before it hurt, Edward. Go back to when you were happy."

"I love her so much. She is my everything. I am her everything. We've been together for a million eternities."

"Where is she now?"

"Why did she have to do that to me?"

"What did she do, Edward?"

"It doesn't make sense. We're soul mates. She knows we are. How could she do this?"

"I want you to go back to the moment when she did it."

"No."

"I want you to go back to the moment when she did it, Edward."

"No, no, no."

"I want you to go back to the moment when she did it, Edward."

"But it's supposed to be a happy day. I brought her flowers to make up."

"Where are you?"

"In a park. Ruthie's crying."

"Why is Ruthie crying?"

"She doesn't want to marry me anymore. She wants to marry T.J. I hate him. I hate him so much. It doesn't make sense. Ruthie loves me. I know she does. I love her. I want to help her stop crying because I love her. I try to hug her to make her feel better because I love her. She pushes me away. She runs away."

"What do you do?"

"It hurts so bad. So bad."

"Let's go later into the day."

"Hurts so bad. So bad."

"It's later in the day, Edward. Where are you now?"

"The bartender won't give me anymore."

"Have you been drinking?"

"He says I've had too much. I didn't. It still hurts. Must make hurt go away."

"What do you do?"

"Next bar won't serve me either. Says I'm too drunk. I go to a store."

"And you buy your own bottle?"

"Yes."

"Then what do you do?"

"Drink it."

"What do you do after that, Edward?"

"Doesn't make sense. She's making a mistake. I have to make her see. If we can make love once more, she'll feel her mistake. She'll remember she loves me. She'll remember we're soul mates."

"So you go to her apartment?"

"Yes."

"Then what hap—"

"'Edward, you're drunk.' 'I love you, Ruthie. You love me, Ruthie.' 'Let's talk about it tomorrow when you're sober.' 'Make love to me. You'll see.' 'Take your hands off of me!' 'You'll see. I know you'll see.' 'Edward! Stop!' 'Just make love with me one time more and you'll see.' 'Get off of me! Let me go!' Crash."

"What's 'crash'?"

"I ease her to the floor to make love. She'll see. She'll remember she loves me. She fights me. Pushes me away. She makes me let go of her. She falls from my arms. Her head hits the coffee table. Glass table. Pointy corner. Very pointy. Crash.

"Then blood. Lots of blood. Blood all over. Must get help. Phone police. Need ambulance. Sit on floor beside her. I bring her to me. Hold her in my arms. I love her so much. I'm sorry!"

"Is she dead?"

"I'm sorry! I'm sorry!"

"It's all right, Edward, it's all right. Now I want you to come back forward to me. Gently forward. You're in the mental hospital again. In the room with the white walls . . . Now forward still. You're a little boy playing Candy Land on Mommy's bed. What's your name?"

"T.J."

"Good, T.J. You're doing very well, T.J. You're with Jack and Jen and Myra now, and you're going to be adopted soon . . . Now you're in your prison cell with Juan . . . Now you're meeting Myra at Starbucks."

"She says she's Cassandra."

"Yes, she does. Now come all the way back to me. You're in Myra's parlor in Soho, and you've asked her to regress you. You're very relaxed now, T.J., very relaxed. I'm going to count to three, and you're going to open your eyes, and you're going to remember everything you just learned. Ready? One. Two. Three. Wake up."

I opened my eyes. I exhaled deeply. I didn't know how to feel. I was empty, drained, but I didn't know what else I felt. Experiencing your insanity then reflecting upon it moments later while sane is a very creepy sensation. The terrible thing I did so many decades ago didn't feel as if it were me, even though it did, nor did any of it correlate to what I had just seen in Ruthie's apartment only hours earlier. I felt ashamed and detached, both at the same time. Horribly guilty and strangely empathetic all at once. I didn't know how to feel.

Myra slid her chair next to mine, and patted my thigh. "How we doing?"

"I don't know," I told her, bewildered.

"Yeah, it's like that sometimes," she said warmly, softly. "At least now we know why karma gave Edward, meaning you, such a crappy next life."

"Karma's a prick."

"She sure is."

CHAPTER FORTY

LATER THAT NIGHT, MY SHAME and guilt, my detachment and empathy, all melded together into one giant ball of rage.

Screw Time!

I had been so careful to protect it, and it seemed that I was right every step of the way. Trump was still president, Putin still ran Russia, and Bob Dylan had still received the Nobel Prize. To the best that I could tell, my world was exactly as it had been before my very first jump.

I had done everything Time had instructed. I wouldn't have even started this crazy journey had it not shown me that photograph of myself in the Merrill Lynch building. One after another, photographs and video clips, recurring dreams and future me's had drawn me down this rat hole like a horse to a carrot, like I was Time's little bitch. When there were no definitive signs to follow, I applied logic as best I could. When there was no logic to be had, I always erred on the side of caution. Always. All so that Ruthie could die a young woman, I-Edward could live a sad, lonely life in a loony bin, leaving me to pay for our sin in which the cruel, evil circle would start all over again. What was the point of it all?

Screw Time.

What was I trying to protect anyway? What's so goddamn

wonderful about our world that is deserving of protection? Wars, terrorism, world hunger, school shootings. The goddamn foster care system. The richest country in the history of the world can't figure out a humane way to tend to its parentless children? Can't or won't?

Screw Time.

I'm going to save her. I am going to alter the past. And yes, on purpose.

I was well aware that I had tried this before when attempting to save Professor Szabo—failed at it twice, actually—but I was a novice back then. I had been traveling through time for almost two years from my vantage point, and I had learned a thing or two.

I knew I had to be careful, though. I knew many of Time's tricks, and I could only assume she had many more up her sleeve. I couldn't let her outfox me anymore.

The first obvious approach would be to simply jump back to a moment before Edward arrived at Ruthie's place and stop him. But that would not prevent him-me from committing our heinous act the next day or the next week, month, or year. I could not keep my eye on him every moment forward, and I could not be Ruthie's perpetual bodyguard, clinging to her at every second throughout the years. She had a job, she had friends, she had a life. I would make sure she had a life.

No, if I left anything to luck, if there was a single flaw in my plan, Time would win. It would be just like saving the Professor from falling off the roof, only to watch him die of a heart attack minutes later. I had to be careful, and I had to be clever.

My dreams always ended with me being horribly hurt, but I had always awoken before I snapped. I-Edward was not inherently crazy, there was no history of mental illness in my family, and I was certainly not a violent man. But this was not your typical breakup. Ruthie and I were soul mates, one entity in Heaven separated in two to be joined together on Earth. So when she told me that she was leaving me for T.J., it was as if half of me was suddenly gone. Half my heart, half my brain, half of all of me. This could only happen when karma and time travel sadistically collide, in other words, such a thing could never have happened to anyone before.

It was the first time in my life that I-T.J. had stolen something from someone who couldn't handle the loss. In my defense, I didn't know that

Edward wouldn't be able to handle it. I had assumed it was okay because he would have Ruthie in his next life when he was me, but I could suddenly see that that was a very meager defense. He-me snapped only because of what I-me had taken from him.

The solution became obvious. I had to stop Ruthie from breaking up with me-Edward. I wouldn't go crazy, I wouldn't get drunk, I wouldn't come up with the ludicrous, despicable notion that forcing myself upon her would win her back.

The sad bottom line was that I-T.J. had to let her go. She belonged with me-Edward, she always had. I don't know why Time intervened with this cruel, sick joke, but if I-T.J. pursue her, she will die. If I compete for her, I will win, and she will die. If I let her go, she and I-Edward will live a life of joy and happiness, growing together in accordance with our times, creating the kinds of glorious memories that have always filled the wonderful parts of my dream. If I keep her, she will die.

She would be safe with me-Edward ever after. I knew it with certainty because all I-Edward ever wanted to do was protect her—perhaps too much, and that had been my only crime till that snake T.J. appeared on the scene. I'd keep her safe, and we'd remain happy together as the heavens intended. I just had to get him-T.J. out of the picture, and it will crush me-T.J. to know that she's somewhere out there without me.

I bet that's what Time is counting on—that I simply wouldn't have the strength to let her go because I couldn't do it when I was Edward.

Screw you, Time, I do. That's how deep my love for her goes. I'll just have to remember her through Edward's memories, and pray to be with her again in some future life. That is, if I even get born at all. I hope I do.

Maybe *that's* what Time is counting on—that I'd chicken out from saving my true love because I'd be too afraid of not being born.

Screw you, Time. What's been so wonderful about the life you stuck me with that I wouldn't give it all up to save hers? Besides, if I can prevent Edward from committing that one atrocious act, he'll go on to live a good decent life because he's a good decent man, and then maybe he'll get reincarnated as someone else, meaning I'll sort of be alive anyway. Maybe I'll even have a happy childhood.

Either way, I don't give a damn. I'm going to save her. I'm going to save Ruthie. Time, you're going down, and you're going down hard.

Wait. Oh crap. If I'm not born, I'll never buy the IBM stock. Wendy, Myra, and the foster kids will get nothing. Yes, I was willing to risk my own existence, but how could I deny the others everything I had worked so hard to give them?

Oh, Time, you are a cunning little vixen.

But wait again. I've already existed—and that's not speaking of the future, but the past. There is a picture of me in 1932, which means that I had to have been born in order to be there. I had so consumed myself with whether my actions in the past could affect the future that I never bothered to wonder if actions in a present could alter what has already been. Can something I do in 1961 change what has already happened in 1932? Can drinking a Frappuccino in 2017 topple the Roman Empire a century before it toppled? Can destiny travel backwards?

Of course it can't. Wherever you are is the present, and anything you do may affect tomorrow, but there's nothing you can do to change yesterday. That should be on a goddamn refrigerator magnet.

I *was* in 1932, so any action I take in 1961 cannot possibly alter that. I can absolutely save Ruthie, and still absolutely be born, and Myra, Wendy, and the foster kids will absolutely receive what I bequeathed to them. They will get their money. Absolutely.

I think.

Pretty sure.

But one thing I've learned through all this is that "pretty sure" is as much as anyone gets, so it would have to do.

Screw you, Time.

The next obvious tactic to save Ruthie would be to stop past-me from meeting her at all. I could pop into our Manhattan apartment before he-me heads to the bakery that fateful afternoon I meet her, and tell him that Dylan is doing an open mike at blah-blah-blah, whether it's true or not. He'd believe me because I'd believe me, although I'd be a little ticked off at me if it turned out not to be true.

But as Myra once explained—and she'd been right about everything so far so there was no reason to doubt her—true love is like a powerful supermagnet that draws its lovers together without them even knowing it. Combining Myra's and Professor Szabo's conflicting wisdoms into one cohesive theory, if I didn't meet Ruthie at the bakery, my current memories would be washed away, yet the magnet that drew us together in the first place would cause us to meet somewhere and somewhen else. All the other events that led to her death would follow, and another me would be right back here trying to figure out how to change them.

For all I knew, I had been right here trying to figure this out a million times before. The wheels on the bus go round and round. Screw you, Time. I'm on to you.

I could stop past-me before he walks into that bakery, and honestly tell him the whole story, how the woman of his dreams is inside, and if he enters, she'll die.

He'd enter anyway. I know this because I would. "You had a whole relationship with her, and I can't even *see* her?" I'd say. I'd go inside just to get a look at her, and then the irresistible power of true love would consume me. Future-me would continue to warn me, but it would be of no use. Without actually seeing the blood spew from her head, without *feeling* the terrible thing I-Edward had done to her, I would think I could make it work, I could fix it, it would be different for me, thanks for the info, dude.

Yes, I can be an arrogant jerk sometimes, but at least I was finally aware of it. Time, you're going down.

I could go to Ruthie and tell her the whole story, explain how I-T.J. saw her death, how I-Edward had blasted a gasket, and how I had inadvertently killed her.

Maybe she'd have such faith in me-Edward that she wouldn't believe me-T.J. Maybe she'd risk death to remain with me, just as I was willing to abandon all my future happiness to save her. Or, maybe I'd succeed at convincing her, and she'd spend the rest of her life with a soul mate she deemed her second choice out of fear.

No, she must live her life with her one true love, and with no regrets.

I could see only one viable way to save her, and I hated it. I bet Time was counting on me to lack the balls to go through with it.

Screw Time.

* * *

IT WAS THE MORNING after Ruthie and I returned from Montgomery. I popped into my Manhattan three-bedroom around five, knowing that past-me was asleep in Ruthie's bed, to give myself time to recuperate from the jump. I had travelled with an empty butt, and the nitroglycerin pill I took before leaving helped a lot, but this was to be my first attempt at taking on Time as an enemy so I had to be at my best.

I got up at nine, showered and shaved. Past-me would be leaving Ruthie's place in one of my blue suits so I put on the other—hopefully she hadn't paid too close attention to my clothing. I took a cab to her place, and I could see past-me leaving her building. I waited in my cab until he got into one of his own and drove off.

I took the stairs to her unit as a zillion thoughts flashed through my brain. I knocked on her door, hoping I would have the strength to do what I had to do, hoping that I would still get born.

"T.J., did you forget something?" she asked.

"Listen," I said, good-naturedly laughing while forcing my way inside without an invitation. "I can't go through with this."

"What are you talking about?"

"Damn, you are so gullible. My friends would think I'm nuts if they knew I was giving up such a big score, but you were so easy it wasn't even fun."

"I—I don't understand."

"You were conned, darlin'. It was all about daddy's money. Marrying a rich bitch like you, I'd be on easy street. But waking up to your wide-eyed little face every morning, ick." I was dying inside. "And that Edward. What a rube. Letting me steal his girl right out from under him. Hell, he practically forced me on you."

"No, no," Ruthie said as she started to cry, and it took all I had to keep the deception going. "You and I are soul mates. You're his rein-carnation."

"Oh, please. Reincarnation? Really? I hung out with the guy for a few weeks to pick up some of his mannerisms before moving in on you, and you bought it hook, line and sinker. And oh my goodness. Time travel? How naive a sap can you be?"

"But I did it!" she shouted. "I was in one place, and then another—"

"It was a trick. You knew it was a trick. You even said it was a trick."

"How? How could that have been a trick?"

"I'm not telling you that, you naive little brat."

"No, you're lying," she sobbed as she moved to hug me, and then pounded on my chest instead. "You're lying. I know you're lying. Why are you lying?"

Tears flooded my heart, and I had to remind myself that I was saving her, saving her, saving her, saving her. It was for her own good. I was saving her.

"Get your spoiled little paws off me," I shouted as I slapped her beautiful arms away, then headed to the door. "Just consider yourself lucky I came clean before we got married."

"But I love you."

"No you don't. I'm just really good in the sack. That's when I had you for keeps, you inexperienced child."

"You're lying!"

"Grow up, Ruth. Go back to your one true love, and never doubt him again, no matter what handsome fellow happens to come down the pike. And stop being such a patsy, the both of you, because it's really very sad."

Then I walked out, slamming the door behind me.

I hated me.

I couldn't walk away at first. I could only stand there, listening to her crying through the door. Tears rolled down my cheeks. I yearned to return to her, desperate to take her in my arms and tell her the whole sordid truth so I could stop her weeping, to stop her from hating me, to feel her pressed against me once more and forever, but that would have been tantamount to killing her.

I took a deep breath.

Ruthie would be safe.

Edward would be whole, and Ruthie would be safe.

And that was

CHAPTER ONE

UNRAVELING THE MYSTERIES OF THE past through time travel is a lot more dangerous than some might think. One can possibly render oneself never-born if not particularly careful. I hope that doesn't happen to me. Sure, many of my people would say that the traveller's immortal soul would simply reincarnate into some new existence anyway—his selflessness rewarded with a wonderful life or his misdeeds punished with a miserable one—but I never believed in such hogwash.

I'm a criminal. I'm twenty-eight years old, 5'7", thin, and I never intended to be a criminal. In fact, prior to the age of twenty-five when I was midway through my postgraduate studies, I had never committed a single unlawful act.

My life began simple enough. My parents were kind, loving people —professors of physics at the Indian Institute of Technology in Bombay, as were their fathers, and one of their fathers before them. I guess you could call physics the family business, and there was never a doubt that my sisters and I would follow in their footsteps.

I wouldn't have had it any other way. I took to arithmetic long before I even began my schooling, finding the flash card games I'd play with Mother and Father far more enjoyable than most board games. By the time I completed the first grade, I had spent so much time at IITB that it felt like a second home, Ma and Pa's corner store, and it was a comforting feeling of security to know that my life had been laid out for me.

But all that changed when I was eight years old. My second-grade teacher, Mrs. Montadel, was an American. To the other boys and girls she was an old lady, but to me she was the most beautiful creature in the world. I wanted to marry her the moment I saw her. Remember, I was only eight. I had no idea what that meant, and I certainly had no sex drive, but little boy me was madly in love nonetheless.

She told us how she was traveling the world, immersing herself in every culture she explored. The year before she taught fifth-grade English in Naples, and the following year she planned to do so in Cairo. She'd titter with the loveliest laugh that ever touched my ears about how her parents had tried to quell her adventures when she was young, and how her children and grandchildren were attempting to do the same.

I would purposely misbehave in class so that I could be rewarded with a detention in order to spend more time with her. After not too long she saw through my little ploy, and sweetly told me—her voice was so sweet—that I didn't need to misbehave, and that if I acted properly in class she would allow me to stay after school to wipe down the chalkboard for her, pass out the next day's assignments, and the like. I was her little helper, and it only exacerbated my schoolboy crush.

She was the first truly happy old person I had ever met for she seemed to have lived a life with no regrets at all. Her husband of almost half a century had died of cancer a little more than eight years prior, not too long before I was born, and her eyes would light up whenever she spoke of him. She used words like "one true love" and "eternal soul mate," and explained how she fully expected to be with him again in their next lives—she believed that stuff. No wonder she came to India.

She described him as a man passionately devoted to things greater than himself, and spoke of how they had been political activists together in the 1960s and '70s, and anti-pollution activists after that. He seemed so brave. They eloped in an African-American church in the southern United States during something called the Freedom Rides. She had written a book about it. She had written many books about many things.

One day, she told me that I reminded her of her late husband. Little boy me took that to mean that she loved me because she so clearly loved him, and I couldn't sleep for a week because I was too happy.

Another time, she brought in her CD player and introduced the class to the music of her youth. A man called Pete Seeger, women named Joan Baez and Joni Mitchell, and of course, Bob Dylan. His songs were a thunderbolt of joy to my heart, and I knew my destiny lay in America. I wanted to go to their nightclubs, eat their foods, watch their movies, and I wanted to marry a woman just like Mrs. Montadel.

When the school year ended, I cried for I knew I would never see her again. She was off to Cairo, and I was to be stuck in the third grade. But she let me hug her goodbye, and through my tears I told her that I loved her. Yeah, seriously, I did.

I never forgot her, and her influence on me never waned. As my high school years whipped by, my desire to live in America only grew stronger. I kept my dream hidden from my parents because there was no need to create a controversy when unnecessary, but I secretly applied to several American universities nonetheless.

Lo and behold, I was accepted to each one, including the world famous California Institute of Technology, yet the biggest surprise of all was how supportive my parents turned out to be.

"We've all known of your secret desire to go to America," my father told me. "You couldn't hide it, hard as you tried. Are we disappointed you won't be joining us at the Institute? Of course. But we each must follow the path that lies within our heart."

Mother even flew with me to California to help me move into the dorm, buying me bed linens and such, which I must admit was pretty embarrassing.

I was a lucky man, and I knew it—but I wouldn't know how truly fortunate I was until my sophomore year when I would meet my future wife, the future mother of my child.

I first met Myra Carpelli at a frat party at UCLA. My buddies thought it would be a good idea to attend because, as my roommate Juan put it, that's where all the hot chicks go. I chose not to point out that those in our circle fail to attract the plain girls, let alone the pretty ones. Still, it seemed a fun thing to do so we made the long trek from Pasadena to Westwood.

At first, it seemed anything but fun. Being a straight A student and rather small all my life, I was accustomed to being picked on, but now in America, add the brown skin to the equation and it was a whole different kettle of fish. The rowdy jocks brazenly teased me about my accent, even though my English was a more proper one than theirs. They made cracks about my size, jokes about my nerdiness—they even started calling me a virgin, which at nineteen, I sadly was. I didn't feel under any physical threat, mind you, but it was loud and embarrassing and everyone was laughing at me.

Just as all seemed lost, this stunning blond girl appeared out of nowhere. She put her arm around my shoulders, and kissed me on the cheek.

"I'm bored, honey, and kind of frisky," she said to me. "Let's go home."

The bullies were stunned. "No way you guys are a thing," gaped one jock.

"Why not? 'Cause he's not very tall?" my savior replied. "Dudes, it ain't *height* a girl is lookin' for, and my man's got it where it counts. Let's see what you got."

And that was only where she started. Within minutes, the jocks were the butt of all jokes, the object of the crowd's laughter—and soon they were gone.

"Um, thank you," I said to the beautiful girl in awe.

"I love putting those kinds of jerks in their place," she said. "They pick on someone like you because you're not a football player, and they pick on someone like me because I look the way I look so I must be dumb."

"Are you?" I asked. Yes, it was a stupid thing to say, but I never knew how to talk to pretty girls. Fortunately, she took it as good-natured teasing.

"Grab me a beer, and I'll tell you," she laughed.

I got two Buds out of the vat, and we went off to the balcony. To my surprise and delight, talking to her was easy. She was smart, witty, and even loved folk music. I adored her laugh, and I had never felt so quickly connected to anyone in my life. I had no illusions that someone who looked like her would date someone who looked like me, but I did want to pursue what already felt like a wonderful, burgeoning friendship. We agreed to meet for dinner the following Saturday, whereupon I borrowed Juan's car and drove to Westwood. The Saturday after that, she came to Pasadena. The following Saturday, my turn, the following

Saturday hers, and on and on. She invited me to her parents' house in Torrance for American Thanksgiving.

Jack and Jen Carpelli had no qualms about my race or color, and remain among the kindest people I've ever known. They even turned out to be Bob Dylan fanatics. What are the odds, right?

After dinner, we went back to Myra's dorm, and I lost my virginity at last. We've been together ever since. I can't imagine loving anyone as much as I love her.

We were married midway through our postgraduate studies. I was making a little money as a teacher's assistant and researcher for my PhD thesis supervisor. Myra was pursuing a Master's in Psychology, the perfect career for her because she is the most intuitive person I've ever met. I'd often tease that she was a clairvoyant in a past life, and she would quip back, "Oh stop it with that Hindu malarkey."

It was a nice, small, secular ceremony in Jack and Jen's backyard—secular because my family is Hindu by birth but non-practicing, and the Carpellis felt pretty much the same way about their Catholicism. My parents, sisters, and a few old friends flew in, and everyone got along splendidly. Jack and Jen insisted I call them Mom and Dad, and my parents had Myra do the same with them.

We spent our honeymoon in Cabo San Lucas, Mexico, and then came home to begin our new lives together. We rented a nice little three-bedroom house in Pasadena, converted the first floor bedroom into an office where Myra could see patients, and one of the upstairs bedrooms into an office for me.

It was around that time that my thesis supervisor invited me up to the Sloan Annex rooftop to confess his big secret, which altered the course of my life forever.

Professor Aldous Szabo had been my favorite teacher as an undergrad—when he bothered to show up—and I was honored when I learned he was to be my advisor. He was eighty-four years old, and his list of accomplishments spanned several decades and many fields. One of his favorite pastimes was to sit atop the Sloan Annex rooftop at the end of his workday—which was often in the middle of the night—and soak in the institute that he so dearly loved, drinking mint iced tea or lemonade all the while. I was honored that he invited me to join him.

I had been working on several different projects for him up to then, specific tasks of which I often didn't know the ultimate purpose—but most physicists look at that as something for the engineers to figure out. He told me that my work had been exemplary, and that it had all been one singular project after all. I couldn't see how.

Then he confessed that for decades he had been illegally siphoning money from his grants in order to fund his secret, pet project.

Time travel.

All the separate tasks I had performed suddenly merged into one in my mind, and I knew in an instant that it was true. Time travel was possible!

It was the Professor's assertion that once his experiments were successful, and once he had the recorded data from the past to prove it, he would announce his findings to the world, publicly thanking all from whom he had stolen as benevolent donors who must share in the credit and profit. He was quite certain they would accept his praise and not press charges.

Until that glorious day, however, he was just a crook, and I was legally bound to report his crimes or I myself could be deemed guilty as an accessory and be sent to jail alongside him. Yet if I did so, he would be disgraced and ruined. Or, I could take him up on his offer to continue to assist him with full and complete knowledge of this miraculous discovery that would change the world forever.

And thus began my life as a criminal.

The next day, he showed me the extent of his decades-long work. I understood about eighty percent right off the bat, and the other twenty percent once he slowly and methodically explained it to me. My take-away was that he was close, very close. There were only a very few missing pieces of the puzzle that remained.

"So true, m'boy, so true," he agreed with a smile. "Then again, I've been telling myself that since the Mondale administration."

I worked tirelessly on it for the next several years. Even though the Professor had learned to pace himself over the decades, I was too young and excited to impose any such discipline. Then, late one glorious night in the spring of 2017, one month to the day after Myra told me she was pregnant, the phone rang. It was the Professor.

"M'boy, m'boy, come quick!" he shouted with glee. "Your work on the graphene wristband as an electromagnetic conductor may have done the trick. May have done the trick, m'boy. Be on the rooftop in ten minutes." He hung up before I could tell him that it would take me at least fifteen minutes to get there.

I tried my best not to wake Myra as I got dressed. I had never told her about time travel because that would have made her an accessory as well, but she knew there would be aspects of my work that would have to remain secret, just as I knew she couldn't discuss her patients with me. It was fortuitous because she always had this annoying knack of knowing whenever I was lying, which was hardly ever—I only hoped she wouldn't ask me if she looked fat once she hit her third trimester.

"Big breakthrough?" she asked groggily.

"Could be," I said as I leaned in to kiss her forehead. "Could be." She grabbed my face and kissed me passionately on the lips.

"Try not to blow up the world," she said, then rolled over to go back to sleep.

I sprinted to the parking lot. I arrived at my seventeen-year-old Sputnik convertible, which still ran good as new, as I wondered why Russia made all the best cars. I hopped into the driver's seat, revved the engine, and doubled the speed limit toward the Caltech campus.

I parked badly and raced up the stairwell. Just as I was about to open the door, I heard the Professor talking to someone. Not meaning to intrude, I opened the door just a crack.

Professor Szabo was sitting slumped back on a lawn chair, naked as the day he was born except for our shiny Altair Watch time machine strapped to his wrist. He was sweating and breathing hard, as if he had just run the London Marathon. Sitting next to him, fully clothed, was Professor Szabo. He had done it!

"To all the presidents from whom we stole!" shouted Professor Szabo as he raised his glass of lemonade in toast.

"To Johnson through Addison!" shouted Professor Szabo who clinked back.

The naked Professor snapped a smiling selfie on his watch to commemorate the historic event, then he noticed me in the doorway.

"M'boy, m'boy. Come join us."

I walked onto the roof smiling, so proud to have been just a tiny part of this miracle. I took it upon myself to make the next toast, and I was quite choked up. More chitchat, more laughter, more self-congratulatory pats on the back, and then it was time for the clothed Professor to travel back to meet his other self.

"The pain is quite severe, yes?" he asked his doppelganger.

"Worse than we anticipated, but it eases up in due time. It's not nearly as bad as when I first arrived."

The clothed one set his glass of lemonade on the table. "See ya around campus." He tapped the watch, and he was gone. The other Professor and I, along with the rooftop debris, were pulled slightly toward the vacuum as it snapped shut with a *crunch,* leaving behind nothing but the Professor's clothes, which lay innocently on the floor. I had always wondered what it would look like.

The naked Professor got dressed as he commended me on my contribution, then reached out his arms as if around an imaginary woman and began to dance.

"Moon river, wider than a mile, I'm crossing you in style, somedaaaaaay."

"Sir, maybe you should dance a little further away from the ledge."

"Dream maker, you heart breaker," he sang as he danced his way toward the center of the roof. *"Wherever you're going, I'm going your waaaaaaay. Moon river, la la de da da...* The mysteries that will be solved... *la de da de da...* the disasters diverted... *da de la de de...* the lives saved... *my huckleberry friend, and meee-ee-eee—"*

Yet before he could complete his big finale, he gasped and clutched his chest.

"Are you all right, sir?" I asked.

He tried to answer but he couldn't speak. He stumbled a few steps backward, and fell to the ground. I immediately phoned campus security and told them what had happened, then knelt on the ground by his side to comfort him.

"It was the jump," he whispered. "It was too much for my heart."

"Shhh."

The paramedics arrived only minutes later, but it felt like hours. I rode along in the ambulance, and we arrived at Huntington Memorial Hospital only minutes after that. The Professor was wheeled into the operating room upon arrival, and I took a seat in the waiting room. I phoned Mrs. Szabo to tell her what had happened.

The television was set to CNN, so I tried to pay attention to the news in order to distract myself from my worries about the Professor. A Congresswoman from Alabama, a Wendy Washington or something, was gleefully boasting of how she had just pushed through some child healthcare legislation that included a two-hundred-million-dollar earmark to improve the failing foster care system. Good for her.

Not too long after that, a rotund little doctor in his forties came to say the Professor was fine—it had been a mild heart attack, and he was ready for visitors.

He sure didn't look fine, though. He seemed tired. Even though I knew he was in his eighties, he had always seemed young and vibrant to me, but not on that night.

"I can't do it," he said weakly as I pulled up a chair next to him.

"You've already done it, sir. It works."

"No, I mean the traveling. This was not my first attack, m'boy, but one more jump through time may end me. I need you to be our guinea pig from here on."

I cannot express how honored I was over the place in history that had just been bestowed upon me. Columbus, Magellan, Neil Armstrong, and me.

About time an Indian was on the list, and on the top of the list to boot. I was to be the greatest explorer of them all.

"Aldous!" Mrs. Szabo shouted as she burst into the room. "Not again!"

The Professor hushed me, and that was that.

* * *

OVER THE MONTHS THAT FOLLOWED, the Professor and I experimented with every permutation of close-range time travel we could imagine as we prepared for my big jump back to 1963 where I would record the assassination of John F. Kennedy. I never travelled further back than a month, and never off continent, mainly bopping between our Caltech offices, our Pasadena homes, and the Professor's condos in Manhattan and Whistler Mountain, British Columbia.

We knew from the start that the watch's electromagnetic field would play havoc with the nerve impulses controlling the heart, brain, and digestive system, but only through trial and error could we truly examine it. My initial pains weren't as bad as the Professor's because I was younger and healthier, my discomfort being more akin to drinking a glass of water too quickly, but the pain increased with each successive jump if we didn't allot the adequate healing time. We also confirmed that as we increased the distance of the jump, whether temporal or spatial, the pain grew proportionately more severe due to the increased electromagnetic charge.

Fortunately, the Professor's doctors had given him nitroglycerin pills for his heart condition, which he shared with me. A pill before a jump would cut the pain by half, while one right after would cut it by almost ninety percent.

The one thing that still concerned me was the fact that I would be arriving in 1963 naked and penniless, and I couldn't see how I'd possibly manage, but the Professor had solved that problem decades earlier. The man was a genius.

"I came up with this notion in the mid-1950s, and the possibility of nakedness was apparent. I took to traveling, hiding large sums of money in my hotel room's underwear drawer. Many of those times, I would return to my room to find the money stolen, along with one single outfit of clothing. I had to assume that some future self had been the culprit. That, or I was the unluckiest victim in the world.

"As my wealth and position grew, I was able to make such trips frequently, and all over the world—two or three times annually, I still do them—but early on, I lacked the means to have a future me rob me more than once every few years.

"I kept detailed records in these spiral-bound notebooks. Of course, it was random. I had no crystal ball to know the historic events in advance. For example, I was in Atlanta in January of 1964, two months *after* the event we wish to record.

"But on March 18 of 1961, I was staying at the Bristol Hotel in New York City, room 709, for a symposium on quasi-stellar objects, quasars as they're called today. I left my room at 12:45 p.m. and returned at 3:15. Seventy-five hundred dollars—the rough equivalent of forty thousand dollars today—almost all the money I possessed at the time—had been taken from my drawer, along with my driver's license and my favorite brown suit. Shame on you for taking my favorite suit."

I could not stop smiling.

"You will jump to that moment. My suit will be a little baggy for you, but you will take the cash, rent an inexpensive room to recuperate from the jump, and then buy a full wardrobe. You'll take an airplane to Dallas, where you will rent another inexpensive room. With the money well hidden, you will jump forward two, three months at a time, as much as your chest can handle, until you arrive at November 22 to record President Kennedy's assassination, and discover once and for all who was behind it.

"Now what is with that incessant smile, m'boy?"

"Bob Dylan's first paid performance was on April 11 of that same year, less than a month after I'll be arriving in New York. I'll get to see Dylan before he was Dylan. How cool is that?"

The Professor laughed. "I've always been more of a Perry Como man myself, but bully for you, m'boy. Perhaps it's providence that it worked out this way, if such a thing as providence exists. Time will tell, I suppose. Providence indeed."

* * *

THE MORNING OF THE jump I was beside myself. Thoroughly excited to be sure, but also quite nervous because, with the sole exception of having left my home for the United States as a teenager, I had never been on any kind of adventure before.

"You okay?" Myra asked me at breakfast.

"Yes, it's just a big day in our experiment."

"Maybe you should call it off."

"I can't," I said, startled. She had never said anything like that before. "Why?"

"I just have a bad feeling about this one."

"I'll be fine," I assured her, even though she was scaring me a little— like I told you, her instincts have always been impeccable.

"Oooh!" she yelped as she clutched her expanded belly.

"What? What happened? Are you okay?"

"He kicked," she said with a smile. By the way, without the benefit of ultrasound or amniocentesis, Myra had known her exact moment of conception, and she had known with certainty that it was a boy. She took my hand and put it to her belly. I felt the kick, two kicks, three kicks, and they were strong. Very strong. A football player my boy will be—not your football, my football, what you call soccer.

It was time for me to go. Myra stood up as I did, then took my hand to walk me out, something she had stopped doing by her fifth month. "Just be careful," she said sadly, almost as if afraid she was going to lose me. When we arrived at the door, she took me in her arms and kissed me passionately. "I love you so much, Ravi."

"I love you so much, too," I told her from the depths of my heart, knowing I could never love anyone more than her, knowing how ridiculously lucky I was to have found her, desperately wanting to assuage her worries even while they were kind of freaking me out. "I'll be home tonight for supper. I promise. Yours forever."

She put her hands on my face, and peered deep into my soul. "I know you mean it, baby," she said softly. "I just don't know if you're right."

* * *

I MET THE PROFESSOR in his office, and he seemed as nervous as I was. He went over and over what we had gone over a million times before. I should attend the parade and film Kennedy's car, then jump back to the same morning to film the grassy knoll, back again to film the book depository from the street, back again to film Oswald inside the depository, back again to film Zapruder filming the whole thing, and on and on. It was like the scene in *The Godfather* where Marlon Brando gives Al Pacino the advice he had already given him a multitude of times.

"I know, sir," I told him. "I got it."

"Did I mention to go inside the book depository to film Oswald in the act?"

"Yes sir. Many times. I got it. I promise."

A bittersweet smile crept over his face. "I envy you, m'boy. I always wanted to be the one." Then he hugged me. Despite how close we had become over the years, he had never hugged me before. He took a seat at his desk, and prepared his cell phone to record my disappearance. "Remember, when your tasks are completed, you are to return to this very moment. From my perspective, it will seem as though you weren't even gone at all."

"Got it," I said as I popped the nitroglycerin pill under my tongue. Then I stalled. I had no intention of backing out, of course, but I just needed another moment, or twenty. "Sir, if your first recording of stuff stolen was 1959, doesn't that limit us? What's a time traveller to do for clothes and money if he or she travels to an era before that?"

"Once we go public with our discovery, there will be a worldwide sensation. Brilliant men and women everywhere will be contributing, analyzing, and expanding on our findings. Someone clever will come up with something.

"You'll do fine, m'boy," he added assuredly, obviously sensing my apprehension. "Now go make me proud."

"Yes sir," I said. I took a deep breath. "See you in a few months, or seconds."

I tapped Send, and I was in a mid-priced hotel room in 1961. The chest pain was more severe than any I had yet to experience, and it knocked me to the ground. All I wanted to do was rest, but I knew that if some chambermaid were to enter the room, I wouldn't be seen as a humble contributor in a grand scientific experiment, but merely as a common immigrant burglar.

I forced myself to my feet, put on the Professor's brown suit—which really wasn't all that impressive. I took his cash and ID from the drawer, and then peeked out to make sure no one was in the hallway. Once I was in the elevator, I felt safe.

I hailed a taxi to take me to the Greenwich Village apartment building that the Professor and I had chosen prior to my departure, every aspect of my journey having been meticulously planned in advance. My chest was feeling better, but still not tip-top, and I wanted to feel closer to normal before dealing with the paperwork and hassle associated with renting an apartment. In other words, I needed to rest.

About a block before the apartment building, we passed a quaint little bakery. We were at a red light, my window was open, and the aroma of freshly baked goods was tantalizing. I told the driver to let me off there, and headed into the bakery to complete my recuperation. I ordered a cup of hot tea and a raspberry muffin, then picked up a copy of that day's *New York Times*.

It turned out to have been a good idea because in little over an hour I was feeling like my old self, much of the pain gone. I folded up the newspaper and was preparing to leave when my eyes fell upon the most beautiful woman I have ever, ever seen.

She had twinkling, green eyes, shimmering jet-black hair that flowed gently below her shoulders, and an alluring, merry smile that exuded elegance, femininity, and genuine, genteel warmth. I was captivated. I was mesmerized. The feelings that exploded inside me were ones I had never experienced before, not even with my beloved Myra, feelings I had always ascribed to fairy tales and bad movies. I was in love in an instant. Hopelessly, madly, head-over-heels in love, and yes, at first sight.

This woman was my soul mate. My one true love. My eternal other half. I had always considered such notions preposterous, yet I knew in that instant that they had always been true.

"Ruthie!" I heard a man's voice shout.

The woman happened to glance toward me, and our eyes locked in delight.

"Hiiiiiiiiii," she said with a huge smile as if she had known me forever, which I knew in that second that she had.

"Hi!" I blurted, probably too fast and nerdy for the moment.

Every fiber of my essence wanted to be with her. I was willing to throw away everything I had, everything I had ever achieved or ever would achieve only to live my life with her, and I knew that she would do the same because we were meant to be together. It was providence, just as the Professor had said.

We were one, we always had been, and we were meant to be together.

But I was a married man with a child on the way. I loved my wife with all my heart, and I knew that I would soon love my new baby son, too.

"Nice to meet you," I told the beautiful woman, and I walked out of the bakery.

And that was that.

Indie books and authors rely on support from their readers. If you enjoyed this story, please take a minute to leave a review. Thank you!

AN EXCERPT FROM: THE GIRL WHO WOULDN'T DIE

BY JEFF ABUGOV

LONG ISLAND, NEW YORK
NOVEMBER 2016

LIKE SO MANY EPIC TALES, hers began with a death.

It was a beautiful day for a funeral, which was kind of weird. Funerals are almost always gray and rainy and cold—it's a statistical anomaly that it works out that way, but anyone who's been to a few knows it to be true. Yet on this particular day, the soft warmth that shone from the golden sun above, the cool breeze that tempered its heat, and the plush green grass and the luscious trees with their multicolored leaves that enveloped the Locust Valley Cemetery prevented the hundreds in attendance from grieving over Al's death, leaving them to only celebrate his life.

A World War II hero, then a distinguished Toledo, Ohio police detective, Alan Herbert Lang took early retirement from the force at the age of forty-four to study finance at New York University in New York City, New York. With his lovely wife and three of their four children in tow, he took one giant financial step backward in order to soar so many millions of dollars forward.

Al's remaining children, all in their sixties, had stood by their father's side as he battled the pancreatic cancer that destroyed him. They watched as he endured the excruciating pain far longer than most mere mortals ever could or would. It was a testament to the great man's inner strength, and yet they each had secretly hoped that he would give up the ghost to at last be at peace. They would miss him terribly, but they took solace in the fact that he was in a better place.

It was their mother who they now worried about.

Millie Lang was a kind, witty, often funny-as-heck, stubborn ole biddy. She had been a strict mom when they were children—always making sure their homework was done, their teeth brushed, and their TV limited—yet a genuine champion of their choices once adults, always fighting for their right to make any life decision they believed best for themselves, regardless of what she or Al had thought. She had spent almost every waking moment by Al's bed as he fought the fight he'd never win, watching her once big man wither away to nothing, distracting him from his pain with stories of their grandchildren or moments of their life together. She cried only when alone, and offered comfort to all others who shared her soul-crushing sadness.

But her memory was slipping, her kids knew. Her grasp on her surroundings went in and out. She wasn't able to get around like she had only a few years prior, even with her walker. The kids had hired round-the-clock nurses for Al during his final months, paying them a little extra on the side to keep an eye on Mom, and the reports were never good. She'd often forget to turn off the stovetop after making herself a cup of tea, or leave the front door wide open after spending an evening by herself sitting and musing on the rocking chair on the front porch.

It was obvious to everyone who knew her that she should no longer live alone, especially in a house as large as the Lang's, but she refused. "Strangers living in my home, muffing up my affairs, stealing my cutlery? No way, José." And the ninety-three-year-old lady wouldn't even entertain the idea of assisted living. "Sit around and wait to die? Just when I get to be a hot-to-trot single broad again?"

It had fallen on Michael, the middle of the three remaining Lang kids, to re-broach the topic with her, a task to which he wasn't looking forward. As the casket was lowered into the ground, he studied his mom from a distance. The little woman's shoulder-length gray hair was pulled back in a bun. Her conservative black dress was collared to the top of her neck and dropped down to just below her knees, purposely revealing that ugly old three-inch scar on the back of her right calve. No one ever understood why she so refused to cover it up. Michael, his siblings, and even Al sometimes, would try their best to convince her to, but she'd never listen.

"It's a part of me," she'd answer. "It's who I am. And I'm not going to hide who I am just because the likes of you think it's a tad unseemly."

As the casket hit bottom, Michael couldn't help notice that his mother seemed lost, as if she wasn't completely sure where she was or what was going on—she even flashed a smile at one point. At the gathering at his kid sister Caroline's house that followed, Millie was genteel and gracious, welcoming the handful of Al's old retired cop buddies with big warm hugs, thanking them for traveling all that way, and telling them how happy Al will be to see them after all this time.

No, Michael was not looking forward to the conversation at all.

* * *

Long Island's Gold Coast boasted some of the grandest homes in all America, and the Lang estate was, although by far not the largest, one of the most admired. The couple purchased the barren two-acre spread in 1982, shortly after Al was promoted to managing director of global bond trading at Salomon Brothers, whereupon the ex-cop hired the best architects he could find, personally scouring over every detail of construction, firing one architect or builder after another in order to get it perfect.

It had gravitas and style, yet remained utilitarian in nature, true to Al and Millie's humble beginnings. It had an exquisite master bedroom, nice-sized rooms for the kids and grandkids, a den for Al, a sewing room for Millie, and a two-bedroom guesthouse off into the woods. The downstairs was an elegant mix of modern technology and downhome charm with its handcrafted wicker furniture atop Persian rugs atop hickory wood floors, an oak bookshelf lining an entire wall, and a seventy-five-inch LCD television. There were rocking chairs and a swing set on the front porch to offset the grandeur of the opulent entranceway, and they had kept much of the original forest and swimming ponds intact to maintain that country feel, as well as for a serene setting in which to picnic and play with their grandchildren.

Michael's black Mercedes-Maybach cruised slowly along the majestic circular driveway toward the front of the small mansion, while Millie admonished him for driving too fast. He had tried several times during the ride to diplomatically broach the conversation that neither of them wanted, but Millie had consistently succeeded in finding ways to avoid it—talking about what a lovely service it had been or giggling at the awkwardness between Al's retired banker friends and his retired cop buddies. He pulled the car to a gentle stop by the front door and tried once more. "Mom, there's something I'd like to talk to you about."

Millie paused for a moment, then proceeded to open the passenger door as if oblivious to what he had just said—but the door was on auto-lock so the handle did nothing. "Your door's broken," she told him.

"It's not broken, Mom. It's locked."

She tried again to the same result. "You should have someone look at it."

Michael sighed, flipped the switch, and Millie opened her door.

"It's okay now, I fixed it," she told him.

He didn't know if he wanted to laugh or scream.

He got her walker out of the trunk and helped her into the house as he realized that gentle diplomacy would never work on his mother, not on this topic. He would just have to be blunt and firm and let the chips fall where they may.

"Mom, Chantal and I have been talking," he began.

"Would you like a martini?" she interrupted. "I'll make us a pitcher."

"No, Mom, thank you. Now listen. The kids are on their own now and doing fine. Why not come live with Chantal and me? You can have Allegra's old room."

"Live with you two? You're old fogies. You should go into assisted living."

"Mom, I'm serious," he said as he took her hands. "Everyone's worried about you. We have to talk about this."

She paused for a moment, sighed. "I know," she conceded. "But not today. It's been a long day today. Truthfully, I just want to be by myself for a little while, enjoy my martini, take a bath, a nap. Please?"

"Okay," he conceded back. What else could he say? "But tomorrow then."

"Yes, tomorrow."

"Promise?"

"Yes. I absolutely promise to disagree with you tomorrow."

He couldn't help but laugh. "Do you need a hand getting up the stairs?"

"No, the escalator-chair's working fine again. I fixed it."

"I'm sure you did, Mom," he smiled. "I love you."

"I love you too, Mikey," she said as she kissed his cheek. "Now, scat."

She patiently watched him off through the large stained-glass window as she leaned on her walker. Only once he and his fancy automobile were completely out of sight did she pull down the chenille drapes.

Time to get to it.

She dragged the walker behind her as she made her way to the grand oak staircase with a lively bounce to her step. She flipped the switch on the escalator-chair to send it chugging upward, then took the stairs two at a time to the second floor where another walker awaited, dragged that one toward the master bedroom, then into the bathroom. She turned on the shower's hot water and got undressed. Other than her face, hands, calves, and shins, there wasn't a single wrinkle on her.

She buried her face in the shower's wet heat in the hope that it would wash away her grief, but it didn't—only time would, she knew, and she'd have plenty of that. The gray dye dripped down from her hair and along her youthful body, yet it took soap and a brillo pad to scrub out the liver spots on her hands and the varicose veins on her calves. She peeled away the latex wrinkles on her face and legs, then let the soothing warmth bash against her sultry back for several minutes more while she wept for the loss of her true love.

The ninety-three-year-old woman stepped out of the shower, then towel dried her lush, soft blond hair as she stared at her reflection in the mirror—the epitome of a drop-dead gorgeous girl in her mid-to-late-twenties. She sighed nervously, and then forced a phony smile.

"Well," she told her reflection with a trace of dread, "it's show time."

* * *

You can read the rest of this story in *The Girl Who Wouldn't Die* by Jeff Abugov.

ACKNOWLEDGMENTS

From the earliest days of my desire to be a writer, I had been told that writers should write what they know. I have come to disagree. Write what you *don't* know, kids, and let your imagination soar. If I had stuck with writing only what I know, I would never have conjured up a tale that required me to reach out to so many brilliant, generous people so alien to the bubble in which I live.

Due to the fantastical nature of this tale, it was my goal from the outset to make anything that could be real as real as it could be. That said, if at any point in the process, accuracy or fact conflicted with a compelling narrative, I always chose the narrative. In other words, notwithstanding my heartfelt gratitude to my many expert consultants, I didn't always listen to them. So if you're their buddy or coworker and you catch a mistake they should have caught, don't give 'em a hard time. It was probably me.

Dr. Kevin Hickerson, nuclear physics Instructor at the California Institute of Technology, was my first science consultant on this project. He showed me around Caltech, informed me that it's "Caltech" and not "Cal Tech", an "Institute" and never a "University." I saw the joy in his eyes as he described the first time he came across Euler's Equation (which I had never heard of)—a joy not terribly different from what I myself exude when describing a book or movie that has inspired me. He offered his insights into the practical benefits of time travel, including a detailed explanation of the apocalyptic consequences of large asteroids crashing upon us. Unfortunately, Kevin had to bow out early in the process, yet his early help remains invaluable so, thank you, Kevin.

Fortunately, Dave Zobel, science writer and author of *The Science of TV's The Big Bang Theory*, stepped in. Dave started right from the beginning, correcting all my scientific blunders, informing me that graphene (which I had also never heard of) would make a far superior conductor of electromagnetism than my original titanium. We discussed countless theories regarding the time-space continuum, several of which found their way into the story and helped to make T.J.'s adventures far less pleasant (which is a good thing, fictionally speaking.) But Dave went way beyond the role of "expert consultant," and tirelessly delved into story and character, providing me with additional insights and provocative opinions. Thank you so much, Dave.

NJPD Detective Julia Torres kept me straight on all the criminal aspects of the story—the justice system, prison life, parole, even the proper way to smash apart a rifle. Here's how it worked: I'd make things up, and she'd tell me where I was wrong. And you know all those crimes with which T.J. was charged after failing to steal the Pollock? All Julia. In fact, her initial list of charges was much longer, but I felt seven was enough to make the point. Thank you, Julia.

Investment Counsel and UCLA Professor Steven Yamshon, along with financial analyst Robert Verdugo were . . . well, I bet you can figure out where they contributed. Before even beginning, before T.J. had a name or personality, I needed to know if such a caper would be worth his trouble. Steve and Robert's answer came quickly and definitively. Upwards of a hundred and thirty-seven million dollars! It sure would be. As the story and characters took shape, Steve and Robert were available to me every step of the way, answering one financial question after another, including a brief description of the original Merrill Lynch building. T.J.'s plan would absolutely work. All you need is a time machine, the Internet, and Steve and Robert. Thanks, guys.

I must additionally and absolutely thank Gay Courter, for educating me on the foster care system; Director of Caltech Admissions Jarrid Whitney, for running me through the Institute's application process, and providing me with the precise GPA and SAT scores that could allow T.J. to be hopeful without being confident; Clairvoyant spiritual advisor Mackenzie Barton, for keeping me honest about psychic readings and past-life regressions—my initial description of the regression turned out to be quite accurate except for the fact that it would take much longer to render the results I gave it, a literary license with which I felt comfortable; Estate attorney Arnold Kassoy, for explaining the legal process of wills and trusts; Artist Will Kleist and art expert Ilvi Dulack, for helping me make my art Professor sound like an art Professor; Emily Miscenik of the New York Metropolitan Museum of Art, for pinpointing the appropriate works that actually hung in the Met in 1961; Dr. Steven Herman, for (again) helping me make my doctor sound like a doctor, and ensuring that his diagnosis was valid; My copy editors, first Richard Crasta, and then Roz Perez-Abramovitz, thank you both for your diligence and commitment; and to civil rights activist and former President of the Dallas Negro Chamber of Commerce Edward Reid, for sharing his vast knowledge and experience regarding CORE and the Freedom Rides.

(Little point of trivia: What happened at Montgomery's First Baptist Church on that horrible night was all true, but I made up the rib joint next door. More literary license. Just sayin'.)

Last but absolutely not least, my greatest thanks must go to my dear friends who gave their time to read this story and provide their honest, sometimes brutal feedback. Some read it as a completed whole, others in the four different sections, others chapter by chapter—sometimes even versions of the same chapter over and over as I neurotically asked them to weigh in on changes I had made. Only because they would sometimes say the pages were confusing, or stupid, or dull, hurting my feelings terribly, was I able to believe them when they at last said that they loved it, giving me the inner confidence to move on. Without being able to quantify their invaluable help, I can only think to list them alphabetically. My heartfelt gratitude to Sandra Bettencourt, Kim Brumstad, Don Foster, Gary Loder, Jaye Portigal, and Shirley Vicich. You guys were amazing!

Lastly, I want to thank you, dear readers, for getting this far. I take that to mean that you enjoyed this tale, and I hope you will also enjoy whatever I happen to come up with next.

Thank you, all.

ABOUT THE AUTHOR

JEFF ABUGOV graduated from Concordia University Film School in Montreal where his two student films won national awards at the Canadian Student Film Festival. He began his professional career writing freelance for the NBC hit *Cheers* for which he eventually became a staff writer and then story editor. He served as executive story editor on *The Golden Girls*, then went on to write and produce such hit shows as *Roseanne* and *Two and a Half Men*. He served as executive producer of *Roc* and *Grace Under Fire*, and most recently of the animated series *Fugget About It*. He also wrote and directed the feature film *The Mating Habits of the Earthbound Human*, starring David Hyde Pierce and Carmen Electra. He has received a Golden Globe Award, a Peabody Award, and three People's Choice Awards, as well as being nominated for a Humanitas Prize, a Canadian Screen Award, and a second Golden Globe.

After having achieved success writing and producing within the

Hollywood system, doing as he's told and playing nice, Jeff has at long last decided to let his imagination run rampant and do it his own way . . . and he's having a blast!

He hopes you're having as much fun reading his stories as he's been having writing them.

Join Jeff Abugov on the internet at www.jeffabugov.com

You can sign up for Jeff's newsletter or email him at: www.jeffabugov.com/contact

ALSO BY JEFF ABUGOV

Novels

Zombies vs. Aliens vs. Vampires vs. Dinosaurs

Time Travel for Love and Profit

The Girl Who Wouldn't Die

Short Stories

The Autobiography of @

Visit Jeff at www.JEFFABUGOV.COM. He'd love to hear from you.

www.ingramcontent.com/pod-product-compliance
Lightning Source LLC
Chambersburg PA
CBHW010746250626
47155CB00010B/3516